EVERY NOW & THEN

Printed in the United States of America by IngramSpark
First Edition Printing, 2018

Published by Inkwell Book Co.
Graphic Design by Inkwell Book Co.

ISBN-13 978-0-9977644-5-1

www.InkwellBookCompany.com
www.MelissaPowellGay.com

EVERY NOW & THEN

A Mt Pleasant Novel

Melissa Powell Gay

To those who have gone before us
Allen, Jacob, and Paula.
Now we are five.

MELISSA POWELL GAY

CHAPTER 1 NOW

The City of Love was ignoring Iris Lee. She hated being ignored, especially when the neglect was deliberate. After a much-publicized meeting with the Louvre's president, Iris and Sotheby's agent Fred Kitter were getting the royal run-around. Each new contact seemed to be lower and lower in the pecking order of the bureaucratic line-up. The day before, this kid Julien Lambert told Fred and Iris that they may have to wait until the following week before the museum completed a review of their offer. Fred couldn't afford another week. His wife, Betty, was depleting the couple's nest egg buying décor accessories for their Connecticut B&B at a rate that was causing Fred's blood pressure to spike. Iris just wanted to finish and go home to Virginia.

Exactly what part of "we want to *give* the Bourbon artifact back to France" did these people find so complicated?

The authentic Louis XVI medallion, which had found its way into the pocket of the second-hand mink coat belonging to Iris' small-town socialite mother, wasn't going to the descendants of its original owner anytime soon. Someone had given the medallion to her grandfather and the albatross had brought Iris and her family nothing but aggravation ever since. She was eager to do the right thing, give it back. However, by her calculations, she and Fred were going back to the good ole U.S. of A. without closing the deal.

Not only was Iris being ignored for her generous philanthropic gesture but her mostly absentee boyfriend was failing to put in an appearance for their planned French rendezvous. Before her arrival, Iris contacted Manny via his sister Mary Margaret and suggested the couple hook up in Paris. On assignment as a State Department contractor somewhere in the Middle East, Manny seemed excited at the prospect of updating their bucket list of places to "date" and had agreed to meet her at one of Paris' finer hotels. But he never confirmed his arrival date. The two had not been in the same time zone in months. She missed him. But now, he, like Paris, was beginning to annoy her. His sporadic excuses delivered via text messages were just different versions of "maybe I can get away tomorrow."

Iris contemplated a one-woman pity party in the hotel's pastry shop while she waited for Fred. They were giving Julien one last chance before flying home the next day. If the tortoiseshell glasses-wearing beet-head didn't agree to take the medallion off her hands today, she'd put the thing up for auction and donate the money to her hometown's new library fund.

Her phone alerted her to Manny's latest lame excuse. "Stuck in meeting this a.m. ☹ When are you leaving?"

Disappointed, she decided not to reply. Let it go. Let him think her casual indifference matched his. She changed her mind. Fingers flying over her phone, she typed and sent, "Am hostage of Julien and his Gang of Procrastinators. It's your fault if I die of boredom."

She scanned the spacious lobby for the tardy art consultant. Midway through her search she spied a beautiful *jeune femme* standing with her large over-designed suitcase in front of the hotel's busy revolving doors. A man, his back to Iris, approached. With a

   MELISSA POWELL GAY

bit of envy, Iris watched the couple. The young woman, with yards of bare legs ending in platform pumps, reached for the man's arms and leaned in to kiss his left check then his right. Lingering on his right side, she tugged at his ear with her teeth.

Funny, Iris thought, from behind that guy looked like Manny. With her eyes locked onto the back of the guy's head, Iris side-stepped over to the concierge's desk. From the new vantage point, the guy didn't look like Manny. He *was* Manny, her David Emmanuel Scott. Why was that leggy babe gnawing on her man's ear like it was a warm beignet? And, why was he allowing her to do so? The couple's body language implied that their meeting wasn't a business affair. Iris' eyes dared Manny to turn around as she widened her stance and placed her hands on her hips. Instead of noticing her, the cheating slug signaled a bellhop for the woman's suitcase, and then offered her his arm. The two headed for the revolving doors.

"Sorry I'm late," came a voice from behind Iris.

She turned to Fred and said, "Wait here. I'll be back in a sec." She took off after Manny and his *amie*.

Outside, Iris spotted the bellhop, in front of a tour bus, cramming the ugly suitcase into the well of a taxi trunk. Trapped inside a swarm of sightseers she watched the couple get into the cab. As the vehicle pulled away from the curb and into the morning traffic, she stood beside the bell captain and swore out loud, "*Merde!*"

Iris loved this obscenity. Because most of her family, friends and business associates weren't familiar with its unladylike meaning, it allowed her to vent with flourish without treading on tender-hearted sensibilities. However, in her current fit of acrimony, she'd forgotten that this particular four-letter word was French.

The bell captain peered down his nose at her. His lip curled as if he'd caught a whiff of bad cheese.

"Where are they going?" she demanded.

Opening the door of the next taxi, he swept his long arm and said, "Would Madame care to leave for the airport?"

She hesitated. If she tracked the skunk down at the airport and confronted him about lying all over her text feed, what did that solve? A block away the couple's taxi stopped for a light and the man got out. Maybe it wasn't Manny. Everybody had a double in this world. Maybe that guy was Manny's.

"There you are," Fred said as he tugged at her sleeve. "What's wrong? You OK?"

"Fine as frog's hair," she grumbled. "Thought I saw somebody I know, but I was wrong," she added as she got into the taxi.

"Let's see what *M.* Lambert has to offer this morning," Fred said as he slid in beside her. "I sense they're eager to get this wrapped up."

"The truffle oil on last night's fries must be fogging your brain. You actually believe they're going to say 'yes' to our terms today?"

As Fred restated for the umpteenth time all the reasons their offer was a fair one, the taxi pulled up to the stoplight where Manny, or his double, had gotten out. Iris rolled down her window to get a better view of the side street. Nothing there but cobblestone and concrete.

"So what's our plan, then?" Fred interrupted her brooding.

"Be prepared to walk away," Iris said. She wasn't thinking about the failure of her half-baked idea of giving the medallion back to the French. Her fantasy of the whole of Paris waving those tiny tricolor flags as she rolled down the Champs-Élysées in the back seat of an open car vaporized when she'd met Julien and his entourage. Prepare to walk away? She was thinking about Manny. Was it really a relationship or just a convenience for the both of them?

"What? So we just leave Paris without an agreement? Not even a M.O.U.?"

    MELISSA POWELL GAY

"I put the odds of Julien keeping his appointment with us at fifty to one," Iris said. "If somebody shows up with his apologies, I'm walking."

Fred ran his hand through his graying mop top. "But, Iris. You can't just walk out on these people."

"Hey! It's not a nuclear arms negotiation. Either they want the thing or they don't."

"Maybe we should back off on some of the conditions," he suggested.

"No! So far we've made all the concessions. All we have left are your fees and expenses and the art education exchange program."

In preparation for the Paris visit, Iris and Jonnie Bailey, her friend and the family lawyer, contacted the local college in the next county over from Mt Pleasant. Together, they hammered out an arts and culture exchange proposal that would enable the college's art students to study at the Louvre. The college president was excited about the idea and had given Iris her full support. The museum's reaction was not as enthusiastic. As always, Jonnie was right. An institution as old and as respected as the Louvre wasn't wired like common commercial concerns.

"How 'bout this," Iris said. "We say we're interested in keeping the discussions open. Then we schedule a follow-up teleconference and go home," she said.

"What do I tell my boss?" Fred's face wrinkled with worry.

"That's your call. But I've got a feeling nothing's getting signed today," she said.

As she predicted, Julien was not available. His proxy, the interim assistant to the deputy of the associate director of *les objets d'art*, expressed *M*. Lambert's regrets and explained to the American guests that the museum was not prepared to accept their generous offer at this time. Having difficulty understanding the proxy's Frenglish, Iris heard a ragout of words like "authentication certificate," "incomplete" and "inconsistent."

In a sidebar snipe, Fred angrily assured Iris that the medallion had been authenticated by independent sources, including a Louis XVI academic at Paris-Sorbonne University. Iris recognized the situation as her cue to exit.

Saying their good-byes at JFK, Iris encouraged Fred to inform Sotheby's senior executives that the French had just blown a major raspberry all over their top guy's proposal. To challenge the authentication practices of one of the world's most prestigious auction houses should be of supreme concern to his firm, Iris warned Fred. For her cause and their image, Sotheby's might want to consider taking off the gloves and shooting off a rebuttal. Iris was goading Fred. But the only way her proposal would receive the serious attention it deserved was if Julien, Julien's boss, his boss's boss, et cetera, et cetera and et cetera, were ordered to do so. Iris could play the escalation game as well as anybody. She needed someone at the auction house, someone at a much higher pay grade than Fred's boss, to reach across the pond and get the Louvre's attention. Otherwise, as far as Iris was concerned, the medallion could go right back inside her mother's coat pocket and be forgotten for another 100 years or so. Donating the military medal to what Fred and his company advised as the appropriate collection wasn't worth the aggravation and the expense to Iris Lee.

At forty-seven Iris was an over-qualified, highly unemployable bank executive and on an involuntary job hiatus while she settled her father's estate and cared for her aging mother. Now, because of her desire for restoration and her impulsive drive to get things done in a hurry, next month's credit card bill was going to hurt.

In Roanoke, all the other arriving passengers had scurried from

     MELISSA POWELL GAY

the baggage claim area at the small regional airport. Where was Bert? Tired from the long day of travel, Iris rolled her luggage outside to look for her cousin. Blinded by the late afternoon sun, she shaded her eyes with her hand and gazed out at the flat valley and bordering Blue Ridge hills, a view she hadn't always appreciated.

Parked at the curb, the driver of a king cab truck waved at her.

"Hello? Miss Lee," someone said as the passenger side window slid down.

"Vinnie?" Iris asked.

Boundless curls and dreadlocks flopped about as the young man nodded his head in acknowledgment. Vincente Juan Ethan Quinn was hired by Iris to manage the day-to-day operations of her father's company, Lee Properties. Vinnie was the son of Ethan Quinn, Mt Pleasant's chief of police and an old friend of Iris.

"Where's Bert?" she asked. "And where did you get the redneck truck?"

He smiled. "Bought it off a classmate who needed some cash," he said as he loaded Iris' luggage behind her seat. At twenty-one, Vinnie was studying mechanical and civil engineering at Virginia Tech in Blacksburg, Virginia.

"I guess it beats the heap you were driving," Iris said as she buckled up. Oh, goody, her day was ending on a satisfying note. For the next forty-five minutes she'd sit next to the quiet, Hollywood-handsome hunk and imagine him shirtless and unmarried.

"Miss Bert asked me to pick you up," Vinnie said as he drove south toward Fallam County. "She'd forgotten about a church bake sale. She's making pies at Grove House."

"Lucky us," Iris said.

Roberta "Bert" Tyler Swanson, newly retired housekeeper for Iris' parents, Henry and Elizabeth Lee, still visited the Lee home on Grove Street most days. Neither Iris nor her mother inherited the knack for boiling water. As she was a Christian woman, Bert considered cooking for the pair as part of her ministering to the needy.

Traveling over the steep and curvy roads, the truck's passengers were transported away from the outside world and into a domain where interrupted Internet service was tolerated and "smart" phones seldom seen. Iris and Vinnie chatted about this and that concerning his efforts to get Lee Properties off life support and back among the profitable. The kid was a natural at restoration and managing building contractors. Iris was thankful that he had agreed to come and work for her after Mr. Henry's death. The Lee family owned most of the rusted out properties in the uptown district of Mt Pleasant, the sort of buildings situated in every post-industrial Southern town.

Vinnie's wife, Ludie, also worked for Iris as housekeeper. The nervous woman was everything Vinnie wasn't. Sharp-edged and skittish, Ludie was what Elizabeth Carter Lee's generation called a "handsome" woman, perhaps too raw-boned to represent the fairer sex. Her addiction to cigarettes was a common complaint of her predecessor. Bert had banned the spidery woman's puffing to the screened-in mudroom off the back of the kitchen.

Yes, while floating along in the stillness of the new truck's cab and taking in the views of the he-man hottie and the panorama of ancient and soulful mountains, Iris allowed her mind to forget about the troubles making her once shiny, coffee-colored hair fade to gray.

CHAPTER 2 NOW

WHERE'S HEYU?

The next morning, Iris stood barefoot in the backyard of her parent's Arts and Crafts-style home. Shivering in her summer cotton nightgown, she called out for Heyu. Not finding the beagle-schnauzer hound inside, she assumed he had yet to return from his sunrise inspection of the bordering boxwoods. Calling his name reminded Iris of Heyu's legal guardian, Manny. She'd agreed to look after Heyu while Manny spied on international bad guys. Becoming her condo roomie in Richmond, Virginia, Heyu's polite disposition had grown on her. Heyu had become her constant companion since Iris moved in with her parents in southwestern Virginia, an arrangement she assured him as definitely-definitely temporary.

Her two-day-old debate with herself over Manny's inattentiveness still bounced about in her head. Was the guy who allowed a frisky mademoiselle to gnaw on his ear in public Manny or a freaky body double? If it was Manny, the lunk wasn't getting Heyu back. No way was she giving up custody. Heyu was part of the Lee family now.

Aside from holding all of her confidences, Heyu made the

perfect grandchild. Iris sighed at the memory of a conversation she'd had with her father, gruffly telling him that Heyu was the closest experience to bonding with a grandson he'd ever have. In Mr. Henry's world, dogs stayed on the porch and never muddied the interior floors of one's house. Since her father's passing, Heyu enjoyed free reign of the house and the surrounding gardens.

The rumble of Mr. Henry's Reagan-era Oldsmobile amplified as its brakes squealed to a stop underneath the attached carport. Tiptoeing over the stepping stones to the raised annex, Iris watched Bert get out of the car. Bert looked younger these days. Or, was it the jeans she was wearing? While working at Grove House, Bert wore dresses covered by a twill bib apron. Come to think of it, the last time Iris actually saw Bert in a dress was the day of Mr. Henry's memorial service at Mt Pleasant Methodist Church three months ago. The day Iris learned the Lee's housekeeper was actually her blood kin. To be exact, her first cousin.

Leaving Mt Pleasant for college and only returning to her Southern patriarchal-dominated roots for life events such as Christmas and funerals, Iris had been kept out of the loop when it came to domestic secrets. Up until her forty-seventh year, Iris' parents, and the whole of Mt Pleasant it seemed, had managed to keep from her the fact that *her* "Miss Bert," her second mother, the one who smelled of vanilla extract and pancakes and still used her stare of shame upon Iris whenever she did something inappropriate, was also Uncle Benjamin "Ben" Robert Lee's daughter by a woman who had never been his wife.

Angry at being lied to about something as sacred as family, Iris sweated out her anguish in the town's municipal park with the help of a Marine veteran. Sometimes the resentment drove her to seek retribution by shooting at hay bales with Mr. Henry's Army issued Colt .45 at his farm.

     MELISSA POWELL GAY

With Mr. Henry gone and her mother enslaved by Alzheimer's, Iris, an only child, had little family left. Gaining an instant adult cousin, one whose idiosyncrasies she adored, soothed the sting that came with her discovery of the betrayal.

This morning Bert appeared upset. As she tugged at the hem of her bedazzled T-shirt, tears filled her dark eyes then spilled over her round, honey brown cheeks.

"What's the matter?" Iris asked.

Bert retrieved a tissue from her jeans pocket. As she honked into the crumpled wad, her short and tight, heather-gray curls fidgeted on top of her head. "I just got off the phone with Bennie's oldest, Sarah."

Iris' cousin Bennie Lee lived in California. His father, Benjamin Robert, died mysteriously when Iris was in junior high school. And since her parents never felt it necessary for her to know the details of his demise, she supposed she'd never get the whole story of the estrangement between Mr. Henry and her Uncle Ben. When the time was right, she'd ask Bert what she knew about the falling out. No way was she going to ask Bennie. She and Bennie only communicated through their lawyers these days. And, to a Lee, lawyer's time, ergo fees, needn't be wasted on inquiries as frivolous as familial anecdotes.

"Come in the house. What happened?" Iris asked. She latched onto Bert's elbow and guided the round woman through the mudroom and into the kitchen. "Sit down," Iris said. "What evil is your half-brother stirring up today?"

Bennie had been waving around frivolous lawsuits, claiming that he, not Iris, was the rightful heir to the anemic Lee Properties. Even though Iris' grandfather had left everything to the younger brother, Henry, Bennie had deluded himself into believing his position as the oldest male of the current generation of Fallam County

Lees qualified him as sole beneficiary.

Iris still blamed the excitement of his threats as the cause of her father's death. When Bennie discovered that Mr. Henry's will provided Bert a sizable chunk of his estate, presto-change-o, all of a sudden, the doting half-brother was inviting Bert out to California for a little family love-in. Having endured his disdain of all things Mt Pleasant, including herself, Iris had never known the bully to recognize Bert as anything other than the family help who fetched his meals and ironed his shorts during his parent-mandated, annual two-week visit to Mt Pleasant on summer breaks. When Bert talked about the newfound devotion of her half-brother's family, it made Iris ill. But the new familial bond made Bert happy, so she held her tongue.

"Don't talk ugly about your kin, sweet pea," Bert said. "He's been in an terr-'ble car wreck. I can't believe it. Some woman tried to kill him." Now, the tears were full-on streaming.

"Tried to kill him?" Iris asked. "What? Did she try to run over him with her car?"

"Naw," Bert replied. "He was behind her on the road. What do they call the roads out there?"

"You mean a freeway?" Iris asked. She filled Bert's Bank of the Brethren coffee cup and set it in front of her.

"That's right. Sarah said he was driving on the freeway and the woman just slammed on her brakes, got out and shot at him."

"Well, he was probably doing something to annoy her—."

Bert interrupted. "Iris, he's in critical care. I got to go be with him. He needs one of Jesus' disciples by his side. Sarah says he's in a terr-'ble way. He might not make it."

The overweening turd. This was probably a trick to get Bert out to L.A. so he could scam all her money, Iris thought. "When do you plan to go out there?" Rubbing her bare arms, she gazed out

    MELISSA POWELL GAY

the breakfast nook's bay window to see if Heyu had returned from his morning constitutional.

Instead of a direct answer, Bert began showing intense interest in the chip on the lip of her coffee cup. Iris knew that stall tactic, Bert used it often. Bert wanted something. "Sweet pea, I've never been on an airplane before. Let alone been to a place like Los Angle-eese. I'm scared to go by myself. Will you go with me?"

"Bert, I don't know," Iris hedged. If Bert had an incurable disease and the cure sat in a bottle propped against that lonely U.S. flag staked in a dusty crater, Iris would walk all the way to the moon and back to get it. But there was no way on God's green earth she was flying out to La-La land to visit Bennie Lee, even if he was in a coma and unaware of her presence. "I just got home." Yeah, good one, Iris.

"You know I wouldn't ask if it wasn't important," Bert said. She blew on her coffee to avoid eye contact.

"Why don't you get one of your cousin's kids to take you?" Iris asked. "They'd probably love a trip to the West Coast."

"They all in school or workin'," Bert said.

Waiting for a more substantial excuse to formulate, Iris stood and said, "Let me get dressed and check on Mom. Be right back." Iris pushed through the butler's door into the foyer and called up the empty staircase. "Mom? Coffee's on. You want some breakfast?"

"Where's Ludie?" Bert asked, following Iris. "Ain't today her day to clean?"

"I gave her the day off," Iris said as she ascended the broad front stairs to the second floor.

"You give that child more days off than Mr. Henry ever gave me," Bert protested as she labored with the banister. She stopped midway to catch her breath.

"What can I say," Iris mumbled to herself at the top of the

stairs. "I'm not like my father."

"What's that, sweet pea?"

In Elizabeth's bedroom, Iris found an empty bed. After checking the en suite bathroom, she stuck her head in the closet. "Hmm," Iris mused as she peered out the double window and down at the driveway and front yard. She called out, "Bert, I've lost my mother again."

"Dear Jesus, help those who wander from the flock," Bert said as she turned to go back down the stairs. "I'll search downstairs."

Calling out her mother's name, Iris roamed from room to room only to discover that Elizabeth was nowhere to be found in the stuffy upstairs. The place needed a major overhaul. She'd get to it, someday. In the hallway bathroom, she plucked her yoga pants and tunic off the floor and sniffed at the top's armpit. She shrugged, and quickly slipped into the outfit. She called for Elizabeth again as she descended the back stairs, which landed in the kitchen.

"Is she down here?" Iris asked Bert, who was coming through the butler's door that connected the kitchen to Mr. Henry's library.

"Naw, she's not in there. I checked her sunroom and she ain't there, either," Bert said with worry in her voice, dentures clacking.

"Can you check out back?" Iris asked as she slipped on her cross-trainers. "I'll check the front." Standing at the top of the wide slate steps of the broad front porch, Iris scanned over the blooming bushes and flower beds. No wandering Methodist out here, she thought. Circling the house, she waved to Bert, who was standing next to the carport.

Bert shook her head and locked her hands over her elbows, cradling her substantial bosom. "Want me to call Chief Quinn?" Bert called out.

"Not yet," Iris shouted back. Quickly, she walked down the wide driveway and picked up the newspaper. She looked to her right, north and toward the park. Then she looked to her left. A block away, a crowd gathered on Grove's sidewalk where Court Street dead-ended in front of Mt Pleasant's only bed and breakfast inn. Guests leaving for the day, her mind suggested. Distracted, she pulled the folded paper from its narrow plastic bag and glanced at the headlines. Then, tilting her head, she squinted. Were those Heyu's hairy paws in the middle of all those feet? What was he doing out of the yard? He knew he wasn't to leave without her. She shoved the paper and its wrapper into the mailbox and strolled toward the crowd.

The circle of B&B guests opened and there stood Heyu next to a very confused and barely dressed Elizabeth Lee. As Iris approached, she swallowed back her embarrassment of elder care incompetence. But somehow, she sensed, Heyu had her back and had rescued their charge from certain calamity.

"Mom," Iris said softly as she took her hand, "let's get Heyu some water. He looks thirsty." Stooping, she patted the wiry top of his head and whispered, "Well done, ole boy."

Bert appeared so relieved about Elizabeth's rescue, she hefted the cast iron skillet from its hook over the gas stove and volunteered to make pancakes for everyone, including Heyu. In the midst of cutlery clanking on crockery at the kitchen nook, Bert slyly came back to her appeal for an escort to Los Angeles.

"I can feel it in my bones," she said as she poured syrup over Elizabeth's second helping. "We need to be with him."

"Bert, I've been living out of a suitcase for the last three weeks," Iris complained. "I need to tend to things around here. What about Uncle Donnie?" Donnie Tyler was the younger brother of Bert's mother. He and Mr. Henry had been best friends since the two, as teenagers, shared a pack of pilfered Lucky Strikes.

Bert admitted, "Uncle Donnie said he wouldn't cross the street to go see Ben Lee's boy, let alone fly across the country to see him."

"And you think I would?" Iris asked indignantly.

The silence between them flooded the kitchen.

Locking eyes with Iris, Bert stated, "Uncle Donnie ain't Bennie's kin." She got up, slid her chair back under the table and pulled off her apron, the one she always hung in the mudroom. She took her time folding it, then wrapped the stringed sash around and around it. More deliberate silence on Bert's part caused Iris to put her fork down. Whoever spoke next lost the argument. Bert tossed the rolled apron on the table and walked out.

Iris called out after her, "I can't go. I don't have any clean underwear." She watched from the bay window as Bert's booty swayed toward the carport.

"Uncle Donnie *isn't*," Elizabeth corrected as she weighed in on the debate.

"What's that, Mom?" Iris asked.

"Uncle Donnie *isn't* Bennie's kin." She speared another square of pancake and stuffed it in her tiny mouth.

"You're right, Mom. He's not," Iris said.

Dang it all, Bert had won. Somehow Iris had gotten herself roped into flying to L.A. to comfort a misanthrope who had once referred to her as a "Miss Goody Two-Shoes twat."

CHAPTER 3 NOW
WHY THEY CALLED HIM MR. HENRY

Monday afternoon a phone call delivered good news. The bank approved a construction loan for the renovation of the first of the rundown rental houses Iris' grandfather built in the late 1920s. She and Vinnie Quinn planned to gut and restore two blocks of single-story cottages and shotgun shacks that had passed as Mt Pleasant's no income rental housing for far too long.

Judging from the receipt books, Mr. Henry had been personally subsidizing rent for a fair number of the town's poor and unemployed. Displacing long-term tenants, even if they were nonpaying, was going to be a tricky public relations move. She invited Donnie Tyler and Jonnie Bailey over to meet with her and Vinnie to talk about how to approach the squatters without violating rights, stomping on pride, or inciting a riot against a heartless landlord. The four sat around a table under the front windows in Mr. Henry's library. A distracted Jonnie fiddled with her phone as she fanned herself with the metro section of the morning's newspaper.

Dragging a box fan closer to the table, Iris opened the meeting. "I'm sorry about the heat. As you know Mr. Henry and Mom aren't big on central air. First up, Mr. Randal. His family moved him to

Elder Home last night. Vinnie's got a crew starting in the morning. But I'm worried about how we're going to vacate all the others."

"Iris," Uncle Donnie said, "You being too nice 'bout all this. If they owe money, go over and kick 'em out. Get Vinnie's crew to chain and bolt the front door."

Without looking away from her phone, Jonnie spoke up. "The boilerplate tenant agreements are month-to-month arrangements." Then she recited from memory. "The tenancy agreement specifies a thirty-day notice period for the tenant to vacate the property if the tenant remains in the property at the end of the notice period the landlord can apply to the courts for a possession order if the order is granted and the tenant does not comply the landlord can then apply for an eviction warrant from the county court." Drawing in a breath, she peered over her reading glasses at Donnie across the table. "The court, not the owner, will then arrange to send the bailiff to evict the truant tenant."

"They work the system. Jonnie, you know they do," Donnie warned as he offered the group one of his antacid tablets. "They get ninety, a hundred and twenty, most times two hundred days of rent for the price of thirty. Then, before the sheriff shows up, the rascals are up and gone over to another neighborhood and doing the same thing all over again. It ain't a way to live but I seen it. Seen it all my life."

"And, that," Iris said as she pointed to Donnie while looking at Jonnie, "is why Lee Properties needs to get out of the public housing business."

"I don't disagree," Jonnie said.

"What about Mr. Yopp?" Vinnie chimed in. "He doesn't have any place to go and he doesn't have family."

"There's the rub," Iris said. "How do we get everybody out without creating a massive PR nightmare? The fight with Bennie has already got me looking like a spoiled, money-grabbing brat. I don't want to add fuel to the flame."

"You have every right to evict a nonpaying tenant," the lawyer said.

"But Jonnie, some of these people have been living in these places since I was in diapers," Iris shot back. "I don't want to just kick them out on the street."

"It's your call." Jonnie shrugged.

"Uncle D, I was wondering if maybe you could be our goodwill ambassador," Iris said.

"Goodwill ambassador? What do you mean?"

"Go see these families and assess who's cheating the dole and who really needs help."

"Sweet pea, I can stand on the sidewalk and tell you that."

"Good deal," Iris said. "And since you rigged the short straw for me to take Bert to L.A., can you take care of this as soon as possible?"

The skinny little man rubbed the top of his bald head with an arthritic hand and grinned at Iris. "Will do, boss." Donnie Tyler didn't work for Iris. As the retired day janitor of Elder Home, he kept a cot in the broom closet, used the game room as his living room and helped out with the other residents on an as-needed basis. Bert told Iris that Uncle Donnie was having a tough time with Mr. Henry's passing.

Jonnie slipped her phone into her purse and said, "I need to get back to the office."

Iris followed her friend.

At the door, Jonnie turned and said, "Let's do lunch when you get back and you can catch me up on the Paris visit."

Iris nudged Jonnie out onto the porch. She said, "The trip was a bust. They're not interested in our idea."

"I'm sorry to hear that. You worked so hard on the proposal,"

Jonnie said.

"Don't be. I'm moving on. I'm putting the medallion on the auction block. Fred wants to feature it in their Christmas catalog."

"If you need my firm to review any agreements, call Claire and get on my calendar." Leaning into the opened car door, Jonnie asked, "How did things go with Manny?"

Iris looked down at her folded arms. "It didn't."

"What do you mean?" Jonnie asked. Her phone beeped. "Got to go. Conference call in ten minutes." Pulling her seatbelt over her chest, she said, "We'll catch up this weekend. You *are* coming out to the house on Saturday, right?"

"I'll try. But, as you heard, I've been drafted to escort Bert to L.A. Don't know how long we'll be there."

"Is that a good idea? I mean given the status of his lawsuit?" Jonnie asked as she started her car.

Iris shrugged. "Bert says he's in critical care and might not make it. If we *don't* go and the rat dies, Bert will disown me. We're flying out tomorrow morning."

"Iris, I'm so sorry. I had no idea it was that serious. Call me if you need me." As the car slowly rolled away, Jonnie called out, "I hope you can come on Saturday. Ethan and I are making an announcement."

"The winery?" Iris asked. Jonnie and Ethan Quinn were considering a business partnership in winemaking. Years earlier, when the Commonwealth of Virginia began paying him *not* to grow tobacco, Ethan's father planted acres of grapevines. A partnership between the two farms made sense.

Jonnie called out, "Just come," as she waved goodbye.

Striding up to Iris, Vinnie stood waiting to be dismissed.

"I appreciate you and Ludie staying with Mom while Bert and I are gone. We should be back in two days. Three at the most. Make

     MELISSA POWELL GAY

yourselves at home."

Pushing his curly hair away from his face with the heel of his hand, he said, "Ludie's anxious to get started on cleaning the sunroom. I'll see if I can figure out why the refrigerator keeps leaking."

"Thanks. Buy a round of doughnuts for everybody on demo day on the first house." She laughed and waved goodbye to Vinnie as he got in his truck.

Iris stood in the foyer and called out to her mom.

"In here," Donnie called.

Donnie and Elizabeth were sitting together at the table reminiscing over an old photo album.

"I'll be," Donnie laughed. "That's it. That's the one."

"What's 'the one?'" Iris asked as she sat next to Elizabeth.

"That's the '37 coupe the old man gave Hank for his birthday one year." He pointed at another picture of a young Henry and Donnie leaning against the front grill. "Gracious, will you look at those two? Partners in crime. Woo-wee."

Peering at the picture, Iris said, "Donnie, you're grinning like you just ate the canary. Mr. Henry looks sour about something."

"I believe Mrs. Lee, your grandma, took the picture," Donnie offered. "Hank was mad 'cause she'd just told him he couldn't drive outside of the county lines unless he was runnin' a delivery for his daddy or going to class over in Charlottesville." Gazing at the old photo, he grinned and added, "Ain't that somethin'."

"Why did you call him 'Hank?'" Iris asked.

"Your father always wanted people to call him 'Hank,'" Elizabeth said. She turned to Donnie and grinned. "But the name just never seemed to stick. I called him Henry because that's what his mother and father insisted he call himself."

"First time we met," Donnie said, "he told me to call him 'Hank.' 'Cept the first time I called him that in front of his mama

I got the stink eye. So I just started calling him 'Cap' for 'Captain,' you know. After he came back from being in the Army, he didn't like me callin' him that on account of he only made it to private first class and he didn't want people to think he was claiming to be something he wasn't. He said his sergeant and his buddies called him 'Hank'. But then Bert started calling him 'Mr. Henry.'"

"And it stuck," Elizabeth added.

"Bert was right, that name suits him better," Donnie said. His fingers tapped lightly on the photo of the best friends and old car. "That car seen a lot of fun times. First time I met your daddy, he was sitting in the back seat."

"What happened to the car? Is it still around?" Iris asked.

"Probably still in Hodge's junkyard. Mr. Henry give it to me when the engine blew up. Me and my cousin rebuilt the motor and drove it a year or two, then it died again. Mr. Hodge give me a set of tools for it." He grinned and added, "I'm gonna say I got the better end of that deal." Rubbing his temple, Donnie confessed, "I miss 'im. Sittin' here in his room, it feels like he's trotted up the stairs to get something and he'll be right back."

Iris freed the snapshot of Henry and Donnie from the black paper mounting corners and handed it to him. "Here," she said, "Take it. Get Bert to put it in a frame and hang it in your room."

Accepting the photo with reverence, Donnie slid it into his shirt pocket. "Did I ever—," he cleared his throat, "did I ever tell you about the time we snuck into a place called the Jazz Hall down at Richmond?"

CHAPTER 4 THEN
ROAD TO RICHMOND

Young Henry Lee held the grimy hubcap as his father tossed lug nuts into it. The family's '37 Olds sedan was jacked up on the side of one of the roads to Richmond. His tie tucked into his shirt, Allen Lee grunted and cursed at the last stubborn nut. Tom Tyler stood next to Mr. Lee, wiping his face then all sides of his neck with a wilting handkerchief. Even at this late hour of the day, the white-hot July sun had all four of the sedan's passengers wishing to be someplace other than on a lonely stretch of road among the chiggers and cicadas.

Henry freed one of his hands from gripping the hubcap to scratch at his neck. The starched shirt his mother made him wear for his first trip to the state's capital itched like the dickens. Why had she made him wear his church clothes on a Tuesday anyway? Why couldn't he dress like Mr. Tom's son, Donnie? He was going to Richmond, too, but he didn't have to wear a collared shirt.

Donnie Tyler climbed out of the backseat of the Olds and rubbed sleep from his eyes. Siding up against his daddy, he shifted his bare feet. "Daddy, I got to go."

The two men laughed at the disoriented twelve-year-old. Mr.

Lee said, "Tom, I'm ready for that spare if you'll lift it out of the trunk for me." Turning to Henry, he said, "Set that down, boy, and go with Donnie. We're not stopping until we get to the hotel."

With reluctance, Henry set the hubcap on the ground and motioned with his chin for the younger boy to follow him into the woods. Wading through the roadside wiregrass, he heard the men's soft and agreeable voices floating from the two-lane road.

Before the Olds blew a rear left, Henry's father and Mr. Tom were talking about VE day and whether or not Japan was going to surrender peacefully. The day before, Henry's older brother Ben, who was home from college, bragged to Henry about his intentions to enlist and go kick some ass in the Pacific. Henry didn't believe him. He was blowing smoke.

"Wait up," a lagging Donnie cried. "I ain't wearin' my shoes."

Henry stopped. "Hurry it up. Pokey."

"I ain't pokey. Punk." Donnie gave it back.

And with the exchange of those fighting words, a lifetime friendship began.

On the way back to the car, Donnie pulled from his pocket a greasy, folded flyer and bragged that he was going to the Jazz Hall to hear Walter and the Wailin' Sax Cats. Later, as Mr. Tom and Donnie got out of the car at Sixth and Broad streets, Donnie whispered encouragement for Henry to join him for the show.

The music of the Lee household ran the sound spectrum. Henry's sister M. Ellen practiced Methodist hymns on the family's piano every Saturday night after dinner. On holidays and special occasions, his parent's inclinations tilted toward classical symphonies, a little Gershwin and sometimes Caruso. When their parents weren't around, Ben and his friends played hillbilly music on the phonograph. Henry saw little purpose for the music his family favored.

After supper in the Earl Hotel's dining room, Henry's father

   MELISSA POWELL GAY

offered him the choice of listening to cigar smoking politicians or going up to their room. Henry took the key but made a left for the front desk. A skinny teenager with acne and a bellboy's cap cocked on his head led Henry out to the sidewalk and pointed north. "One block up, left and west to Second Street, then take a right. Can't miss it," the bellhop told Henry.

From a block away, Henry saw the illuminated Jazz Hall marquee and a crowd forming a line. He'd never seen so many colored people in one place before. He scanned the line for Donnie but it was filled with older kids, kids his brother's age.

"Whoa, whitey, you lost?" one kid shouted out to Henry.

Another called out, "This is the chitlin' circuit, kid. Tommy Dorsey's over at The Mosque." They all laughed.

Henry ducked into the side alley and pressed himself against the prickly brick. A commotion from the back of the alley caught his attention. Raised voices were followed by the pop of a slammed screen door. In the yellow haze of a bare bulb mounted on a leaning pole, he saw someone walking toward him. A barefooted kid in a striped T-shirt and dirty denims hopped over the graveled alleyway. Donnie Tyler's eyes brightened when he saw Henry.

"You came," he cried out.

Henry nodded shyly. "'Cause I'm white, am I not allowed to go in?" he asked.

Donnie laughed. "Naw, that only works one way, Cap."

"Call me Hank," Henry insisted.

Donnie shrugged and signaled for the older boy to follow him.

Henry followed the little guy back down the alley from the direction he'd come. The clang of pots and hurried voices seeped through the tears in the screen door. Beside it stood a wooden door with the word "Exit" painted over its frame. Donnie tried the knob, still locked.

"I'm waiting for H.B. to come unlock the door," Donnie said as he sat on one of the wooden boxes stacked against the opposite building.

"Who's H.B.?"

"My cousin. Ham Bone Harris. He does the sweeping-up here."

Henry realized Donnie meant to sneak into the show without paying. Reaching in his pocket, he offered, "I got money to pay. For the both of us."

Donnie slapped at his knee and laughed. "We can't go in the front door." He took up his laughing fit again but paused when he saw trouble on Henry's face. "We ain't old enough to go in the front door. That's why H.B.'s gonna let us slide in on the back side." Henry was glad for the darkness; it hid the flush of embarrassment on his face and his ample ears.

But all of the anxiety of waiting at the door, slipping by the backstage staff and slinking off to the balcony was worth every note. Walter's reedy melody swept out high, long and cool, then heated up with the speed of the master's fingers. The tune arced and twisted on itself. Repeated musical phrases jumped from instrument to instrument then fell away. The harmonies of the Wailin' Sax Cats propped up Walter's improvisation and carried it all the way down to New Orleans and back again.

Like the audience below, Donnie's body had become possessed by the probing drums. He toe-tapped, hopped, scooted, stomped, shuffled and twisted to the fusion of sounds. Henry felt the drum's cadence creep inside of him. He caught himself tapping his foot so he shifted his weight to stop. But the rhythm found his other foot and took over again.

He smelled beer, smoke, and hot, clean sweat. A couple embedded among the swinging dancers locked onto each other. The man's broad hand pressed against the woman's chest just below her

     MELISSA POWELL GAY

collar bone. Her eyes, half-closed, told the room that the couple was alone.

Giving into the swing, Henry closed his eyes, like Donnie, and let Walter's oboe rock his soul into another world. The living opera fused with his bones and mixed with his blood and ran its course throughout his body, altering his beliefs and his ideas of the kind of man he wanted to become. Six months away from his fourteenth birthday, Henry Lee heard the sound of color, the sound of life.

Three years later, the Olds' newest owner nailed the final roller skate wheel to a scrap of plywood. Turning it over, Henry pushed it back and forth with his foot on the carport's concrete. He lay on the board and pushed with his heels. The pocket flap on his Army surplus shirt caught on a bolt nut underneath the car, a tight fit but good enough. The Olds, a birthday present, came with responsibilities. He was required to keep it running and act as courier for his father's legal and property management businesses.

Mr. Lee paid his son fifty cents in town and a dollar for deliveries to the federal courthouse or law offices in Roanoke, thirty miles northeast of Mt Pleasant. Two bucks were slapped in Henry's hand for back rent collected on Eastend Street. Donnie rode with him whenever he visited the colored sections. Whatever he earned, Henry split fifty-fifty with Donnie.

Tonight, Henry and Donnie were riding over to Roanoke to a juke joint called the Lickin' Hole. A live Halloween lineup included a bebop jazz quartet from Washington, D.C. Donnie had asked Henry if his older sister, Violet, could swing a ride. She planned to attend Battina's School for Black Beauty while living at their aunt's boarding house in Roanoke.

Violet's beauty captivated Henry instantly. As a dazed Henry helped the young woman with her suitcase, Donnie interrupted his gawking by hurrying his sister into the back and folding the front seat back into place.

"Let's move on down the road, Slick," Donnie said. "By the time we drop Vee off, the first act'll be halfway through their set." The car vibrated with excitement as Donnie ticked off the opening act's jazz pedigree, the bassist had jammed with Bird Parker in Harlem.

"To save some time, why don't you join us?" Henry asked. He searched for Violet's almond-shaped eyes in the rearview mirror. When he found them, they both looked away.

"Aww, she ain't interested in jazz," Donnie complained.

"I've danced to the jukebox but I've never seen a live performance," Violet said. Sliding forward, she rested her slim hands on top of the front seat by Donnie's head.

Henry smelled summertime and ripe peaches. "Then it's settled."

The bouncer took one look at Violet and her curvy hips and waved the three through. They managed to find the last three seats against the wall just as the band stepped onto the raised stage of the low-ceilinged nightclub. Donnie wriggled out of his seat and disappeared. Watching the musicians set up, Henry sipped on his first beer.

"I'm twenty-one," Violet said. She sipped on her own. "How old are you?"

To avoid a lie, he replied, "I'm at the University in Charlottesville."

"I'm going to hair dressing school," she said. "When I get my license, I want to open my own shop. Be my own boss."

"I'm joining the Army to go fight communists." The comment came out cavalier and insincere.

She laughed.

But Henry was serious. His sister M. Ellen had married a missionary and they were somewhere in China. The family had not heard from her and were concerned. He opened his mouth to explain to Vee his plans to go find his sister but was interrupted by the blast of the first chord jumping off the stage. Amid the whoops and applause, the crowd rushed the platform. Some, in awe of the funky, off-beat sound, snapped and swayed with the horns' lead. Others grabbed their partners and found their swing beat. To see the band, Henry and Violet stood. She rose on her tip-toes, her chin in the air. He tapped on her shoulder and pointed to the chair, offering his hand to help her stand on its seat. Her soft hand was damp from the sweating beer bottle. Not counting his sister M. Ellen, this was the first time he'd ever touched a girl's hand.

"Want another beer?" he shouted.

She bobbed her head up and down.

Now the second band was kicking it and Henry's third beer lent him the courage to ask Violet to dance. Just as they found a spot on the dance floor, the song flowed to a slower beat. The swingers melted away, some to find a beer or a bathroom while others folded into their partner's arms. Uncertain as to what to do, Henry raised his hands and hunched his shoulders. If only he hadn't ditched Miss Anne's cotillion classes. Smiling, Violet waved him off as she swerved for the line to the ladies' room.

"Let me hold a fiver for ya, Cap," Donnie said as he found Henry holding up the wall.

"We just got paid this afternoon," Henry grumbled. He slid the bill into Donnie's palm.

"Where's Vee at?"

Henry nodded at the bathroom line. "Does your aunt have a curfew?"

"Yeah, we should go soon." Holding up his hand, he said, "Five minutes. That's all I need to win my money back."

An hour later the band announced its last number and picked up the beat. A girl shimmied her shoulders at her partner. Joining hands, they jitterbugged off to another spot. Henry tapped the side of his leg with his hand. Lickin' Hole was on fire.

Grabbing his hand as she sailed by, Violet led Henry to the edge of the dance floor. "My mama told me I should always dance with the boy that brung me," she yelled next to his ear. Tilting her head back, she laughed.

Tonight, if Venus wore rolled-down bobbysocks and jeans revealing smooth bronze colored calves, her name was Violet Tyler. Grinning, Henry stood in place exchanging her left hand for her right as Violet twirled around him. The drummer was running wild as the band leader sided up next to him with his saxophone. The place pounded and stomped along with the drummer's beat as the entire band wailed out one long, final chord. A snap from the sax closed the boys down. Violet naturally fell into Henry's arms. She placed her arms around his neck, all the body parts fit just right.

"One more! One more!" The crowd cheered.

Unsure where to put his hands, Henry's hovered around her waist. As the music softened, he tightened his hold on her. The lingering scent of coconut from her hair bid him to close his eyes. Her breasts and a rising knee stirred his head and other parts. She pulled away to search for his eyes. Hers, like the exotic Bedouin woman in his *National Geographic*, slanted up with the lashes curled at the corners. He'd never kissed a girl, never, not even on the cheek. The band slipped into the crooning sound of an ancient Benny Goodman tune as he lowered his head to kiss her on those luscious lips.

From the back of the club, Donnie was trying to do two things at once, walk and count his winnings. Stuffing all but the fiver he owed Henry into his front pocket, he glanced up just in time to see his sister swapping spit with his best friend right in front of everybody. If asked, everybody in the place would agree that Vee was the best looking thing around. So why did Henry, a white boy, have to go and ruin her reputation by ramming his tongue all over her tonsils in public? To gauge the damage, he browsed the room for witnesses. And, just his luck, not ten feet away, Wild Cat Mullins was staring a hole right through the back of Henry's head. Standing beside Wild Cat was Roanoke's newest bulldog shyster, Ben Lee. With all the nip joints on Old Lick Road, these two picked Lickin' Hole to walk into and see this. When Ben ran his mouth off to their parents, Henry's driving privileges were getting revoked and he, Donnie, wouldn't be able to sit for a month from the whupping he'd get for exposing his sister to the sins of drinking and the carrying on it caused.

Raising his arms to create a diversion, Donnie boogied toward the two former college defensive tackles and, with as much hip-cat bravado as his teenage voice could muster, he said, "Y'all lookin' for some hot dice? Fresh game just startin' out back."

"Get out of my way, puddin' head," Ben murmured.

Under the hum of the band's encore, the smart ones cleared out fast. The not-so-attentive, including Violet and Henry, continued to sway under the spell of the band's rendition of "Don't Be That Way."

With all his self-serving pretension, Ben crossed the dance floor like Moses strolling into the Pharaoh's palace. Quick like a cat, he grabbed Henry by the back of his jacket collar and lifted the boy clean up off the floor. A spew of uglies flew out of his mouth as he slammed Henry down, hard. "Whatdoyouthinkyou'redoingherebehavinglikeajackassGetyourselfbacktoyourmamawhere-youbelongrightnowboy."

Henry lost his balance and fell in the middle of the dance floor. Deciding the show was no longer on the stage but down on the dance floor, the band stopped playing. When Henry tried to stand, one of his brother's size twelves pressed down on his chest. Leaning over Henry, Ben's voice carried for everybody to hear, "Are you going to do what I tell you to do, little brother?"

Offering a hand, Ben pulled Henry to his feet. He cupped his little brother's face with those mitts of his, and whispered, "She's too much woman for a boy like you," then lightly smacked each cheek.

Out of nowhere, BAM! Henry, the skinniest hundred-forty pounder Donnie ever knew, gut punched Ben. With his arms pressing into his stomach, Ben stooped in pain, his face turning red as he struggled to breathe. Henry walked out the door, saying nothing to nobody. Before Donnie could stop her, Violet waltzed up to Ben and hauled off and smacked his face so loud the boys out back heard it.

CHAPTER 5 NOW

L.A. BOUND

Iris stood behind a husky plumber as he rammed his plunger into Elizabeth's toilet. On the back of Ed's T-shirt, a red parrot quoted, "Time flies when you're having rum — gin, vodka or whiskey." Even though she had managed to close the main valve to the commode, the water level on the bathroom floor had risen high enough for the spilled cotton swabs to float. Ed plunged away while complaining about missing the second half of an NBA playoff game.

"I've got Cleveland and ten points," he said as he reached for the sewer auger on his utility belt and threaded it down into the main pipe. The commode sucked and gurgled as he strained to recoil the rod. "OK, here's your problem, little lady," he said. Stepping back from the toilet, he turned and held up a soggy hand towel.

"How in the world?" Iris asked, mostly to herself. Then she recalled Elizabeth mumbling over dinner something about rinsing out baby diapers in the toilet before putting them in the diaper pail. She sighed. "Can you check to make sure that's all that's down there?"

"Yes, ma'am. If I was you, I'd get my main office to work up an order to get me out here during regular business hours. It's just a matter of time before this crapper craps out." He laughed at his own joke.

When Ed finished, she led him down the back stairs and out the mudroom door. Elizabeth, who was making herself a jelly sandwich on the kitchen's butcher block, asked Iris, "Why was that man upstairs? Was he in your bedroom?"

"Yeah, ma," Iris said. "Me and Ed were upstairs having sex." She glanced at the plumber's bill for one hour's work. "He used his plunger to ream me good."

"Iris!" Elizabeth hissed.

"Arr! I'm joking." Iris felt her blood overheating. Placing her hands on her hips, she scolded, "Somebody flushed a hand towel down your commode. Any idea who might've done that?"

Elizabeth gathered up her arms over her little pot belly and said, "No. No I don't."

"When you find out who did it, let me know so I can send them the bill." Playing back what she'd just said, Iris reminded herself that she was the mother now and a mother tried patience first. She picked up her legal pad of lists and read around the jelly smears at what was left to do before her head hit the pillow that night. The mounted Westclox read 10 p.m. and she was picking Bert up at 4 a.m. to catch the first flight out.

"Maybe Henry did it." Elizabeth offered.

"Ha! Yeah, I bet it was Mr. Henry," Iris said. On her list, below the word "laundry" she wrote "mopping up Mr. Henry's mess." Going to bed now and flying to L.A. commando-style was not an option.

Something sharp poked at her arm.
"Iris!"
"What!" Iris shouted.

"You was snoring loud enough for the folks in first class to hear," Bert said. "The captain said we're getting ready to land."

Iris had taken a couple of Aspirin PM in Atlanta once she got a reluctant Bert seated for the final leg of their journey. The flight from Roanoke to Atlanta had run into summer storm turbulence, their descent had Bert convinced the plane was going to crash. On the walk over to their connecting flight's gate, Bert protested that she was tempting the Lord's will by getting on another airplane.

Once seated for their flight to L.A., Iris shook the aspirin bottle and said, "Take a couple of these. It'll help you relax."

"You know I don't do drugs," Bert said, then reached into her grocery recycle tote, pulled out her worn Bible and hugged it. "Do they serve anything besides coffee? That coffee they gave us on the other plane tasted like last night's dish water."

Iris swallowed three aspirins, dry, and prayed to the friendly skies for fair weather for the rest of the trip.

With their luggage in the trunk of the rental and Bert belted in on the passenger side, Iris keyed the address of the Irvine medical center into the car's GPS. As they pulled into one of the center's parking decks, Iris turned to Bert and said, "Ready?"

"Wait a minute," Bert said. She placed her hand over Iris'. "I got something that needs to be said before we go in there. I know you and Bennie don't get along."

"Bert—."

"Don't interrupt me. Let me finish with what I have to say. Some people are just pure evil. It's like the devil owned them the day they came out of the womb. I don't think it's right what he did to you and your daddy. That lawsuit and everything. But Sarah says he wants to see you and tell you something important. Maybe he wants to ask you to forgive him. Try to be kind to his poor soul. Try and forgive him."

"Hardly. What are you getting at?"

"Just that his daddy … my daddy … did a lot of hurtful things. To his family. To my mother."

"So you want to have that conversation *now? Here?*" Iris asked. To avert eye contact with Bert, she pulled down the sun visor to check her lipstick. With mourning her father's death and the chaos around the medallion and Paris, Iris had pushed away thoughts of her family's deception. She was still numb from the shock of it. Bert was her first cousin. How could her entire family have kept this from her all these years? What had she done to make her parents, and Bert, feel the necessity to exclude such an endearing fact from her? *But, hey, Iris, it's not about you,* she thought. It was about the shame of denying the birthright of one of their own. But she was family. Why would they hide something like this from her? Maybe admitting their disgrace to her was like admitting it to themselves.

Bert folded her arms and grabbed her elbows with her strong hands, "What is it you want to know?"

Iris chewed on her lip then said, "Why wasn't I ever told that you were my cousin?" Her head nodded toward the parking deck's elevators, "His sister?"

"I don't know why your parents never told you," Bert said. "I'm sure they had their reasons."

"Why didn't you tell me?" This question hurt the most and she felt tears cuing up behind her eyeballs. She looked away.

"I wanted to when I first come to work for y'all. But your daddy asked me not to. As you got older, I felt really bad about it. Not telling you. Then time sort of erased the importance of me sayin' it. Like it didn't ever need to be said."

"He had no right, Bert," she eked out. She placed her head on the car's window and tried to calm her breathing. She felt heat rising from her chest.

Bert placed her hand on Iris shoulder to soothe her. "I know. I know. But he had his reasons."

"What about Bennie? When did he find out?" Iris fished a tissue out of the travel tote in her lap and blew her nose.

"I don't know."

"What do you mean you don't know?"

Bert shot Iris one of her "don't get on my last nerve" looks. "Just what I said. I don't know. It was so long ago. A time when things like this weren't talked about."

"You never said anything to him?"

Bert played with the zipper on her gold lame jacket. She said, "Wont my place to tell him."

"I see. So now that he might be dying, you're having, what? Some kind of moral crisis about never telling him or talking to him about it? Is that why you dragged me across the country?"

"No!" Bert struggled with unhooking the seatbelt. "Let's just go see him. Like I said, he's got things he wants to say to you." She opened the door and hauled herself out of the car.

Chasing after a fast walking Bert, Iris said, "Bennie wants to talk to me without his lawyer in the room? He's up to something."

Thirty minutes and a mile of walkways and stairs later, Iris and Bert found themselves in the main lobby of the hospital, an open three-story area of glass and steel. A single volunteer sat at a beech wood-veneered workstation, behind her water cascaded down a wall of rippled concrete. The waterfall reminded Iris that she needed to pee.

"No, dearies," the lady with fading freckles said. "I don't see a patient here by that name."

"Can you look again?" Bert insisted. "We came all the way from Virginia to see him." The last part echoed throughout the chamber.

"Bert, if he's not here—," Iris tried to save Bert from embarrassment. "Are you sure this is where Sarah said they took him?"

"Try Benjamin Robert Lee," Bert insisted. She added, "Junior."

"No, I'm afraid we don't have anyone by that name listed as a patient at this time."

Over the phone, Sarah confirmed to Iris that her father was fine, just fine. He'd been released from the hospital earlier that day. "Come on over to the house. I know he'd love to see you." She said this as if the travelers from Mt Pleasant just happened to be in the neighborhood.

Around three o'clock local time, Iris parked across the street from the suburban address. She noticed a "For Sale" sign planted in the square foot of grass in front of the airy Southern California house. Four vehicles were double parked in a short driveway. Bert was still wrapped up in her blanket of silence, imposed when Iris lost her temper in the hospital lobby after it was revealed that Bennie had rolled out of the hospital very much alive and that Bert's secondhand report of his pending death had been greatly exaggerated. However, in a way, Bennie's early release was fantastic news. After an hour of small talk, she and Bert would get a room at an airport hotel, change the date of their return flight and be home in time for a late supper tomorrow. Silver linings, Iris, she reminded herself.

Blonde and willowy, Sarah greeted them at the front door. Escorting them to the back of the house, she tweeted on about her dad's recovery. Iris realized the girl was in denial overload when she expressed how *wonderfully* excited her father became when he learned Iris was coming over for a visit. The back of the house opened up to a spacious outdoor of terra cotta tile and a sweeping view of brown hills and a far off mountain range. A homecoming was underway, and the guest of honor, Bennie, wasn't around.

     MELISSA POWELL GAY

"Everyone," Sarah called ahead. Iris heard nervousness and uncertainty in her voice and suspected Sarah, or Bert and Sarah, had cooked up this whole trip as a way to get her to reconcile with a man who, she was positive, would rather drink a gallon of blood with shards of glass than spend time with her.

Why did people do that? Try to fix relationships that could never be fixed?

"Look who's come to visit us," Sarah sang out.

Iris followed Bert, who was carrying her purse and her recycle grocery bag with her Bible, out onto the covered terrace. A brown hill hid the traffic hum on a nearby freeway. The other guests, a man and three boys, stared back at Bert as if she was a lioness on the hunt and they the wounded and helpless impala.

"Let me introduce everyone," Sarah said. Pointing, she said, "This is my husband Zach and our two: Justin, 10, and Brian, 8." Grabbing the arm of the third boy, she added, "And this young man is Damian." As she mussed his dark hair he jerked away, combing through it with his fingers. The boy looked older than the other two; Iris guessed fourteen or fifteen. Judging from his vibes, she was positive he didn't want to be there, either.

"Iris, Bert, can I get you anything?" Zach asked. He offered his hand.

"I'm good," Iris said. As an afterthought, she added, "Nice to meet you."

"I'll take a cup of coffee if you got some already brewed," Bert said.

"Justin, Brian, you guys help me out," Zach ordered. He ushered the two back into the house.

"Take a seat. I'll go check on Daddy," Sarah pushed Damian toward Iris. "Talk to your cousin, silly."

Bert extended her hand to Damian. "Hi, I'm Roberta. You must be Megan's boy?"

Iris almost missed Damian's slight nod. "Your mom and dad here?" she asked.

"No," the kid said. Showing no further interest in the guests, Damian sat on the wicker sofa and fired up his Android.

Holding her father's elbow, Sarah guided a shaky and fragile Bennie through the great room and onto the terrace. Dressed in pajamas and a robe, his head was covered with a gauze turban. Sarah helped him to the matching wicker chair and said, "Let me check on that coffee."

Alarms went off in Iris' head. Something wasn't right. Was she being set up? She looked at the kid. She searched Bert's face for clues but found none. Unable to delay it any longer, Iris stared at her cousin. Not counting the grainy video deposition calls they had made from each other's lawyer's offices, the last time she actually saw her cousin face-to-face was the summer he set off the cherry bombs in her parent's mailbox. Was it 1975 or '76? She noticed a lot of changes, even since the last deposition. His now gaunt face highlighted his cheekbones and his once brilliant white-blue eyes were bloodshot. He nodded up with his chin at her; not even a grunt for a greeting.

With that slight nod of his, she felt the condescension and disdain rolling back over her from all those years before; she felt her father's ghost. Those two were more alike than either cared to admit. His nonverbal greeting to her and his ignoring his sister completely put Iris in no mood for polite conversation. She'd wait him out, make him say the first words.

"Damian, this is your first cousin twice removed," he finally said. His words carried intended contempt.

She wanted to ask him out right, *what did I ever do to you to make you hate me so?* Instead she blurted out, "Bert said you were

     MELISSA POWELL GAY

on your deathbed," In the long silence that followed her unorthodox salutation, Iris felt Bert's and Damian's eyes boring through her. "Will someone tell me what's going on?" She pleaded.

"Damian, son, can you show me where the bathroom is?" Quickly, Bert motioned for the boy to follow her back into the house. Iris trailed behind. "Naw, sweet pea, you stay and talk to your cousin."

Iris turned to Bennie. "Is this some kind of legal maneuver? Summon me to your place for home field advantage? I'm getting sick and tired of your petty tricks. Tired of paying my lawyer for the time she spends keeping private squabbles off the front page of the newspaper."

"Sit down," Bennie said.

"And why should I do that?" she asked. She wanted to do the exact opposite. She wanted to walk out the front door, get on a plane and fly away to anywhere. She'd been ambushed, tricked into coming here.

"Telling you I was almost dead was Sarah's idea and your maid's."

"My maid? You mean your sister? Roberta?" Iris spat back.

"Sit down."

"What do you want, Bennie?"

"I *am* dying," he raised his voice. "They found cancer in my brain when they did an MRI for the concussion caused by that woman—."

Stunned, Iris slowly sat on the edge of the sofa across from him.

"I won't go into the details. Just use that pea-sized brain of yours to focus on the fact that it's nasty, the kind that grows fast, inoperable." He winced as he tried to make himself more comfortable in the chair.

Whenever her banking clients dumped fatal news all over her in front of a boardroom full of executives, Iris layered one hand over the other to calm herself and to clear her mind. She did this now and waited for him to continue.

"You know and I know that Lee Properties belongs to me. I'm the oldest male of our generation. It belongs to my grandsons, Justin and Brian. I'm willing to drop my suit against you and your lesbian lawyer if you concede and place the estate in a trust for the both of them. When they come of age, they can take over the business or sell it."

Out of respect for his condition, Iris bit hard on her lower lip to keep herself from saying anything. Clearly, the guy's mind had turned to scrambled eggs. Technically, using his twisted logic, Damian was the oldest male of the next generation.

As if he'd read her mind, he said, "Megan, my youngest, has a bastard child. Son of a cholo, her drug dealer. The boy's a street urchin, headed down the same path as his father. Gangs, guns, drugs. His mother's a whore and his father's a thug. Megan's living on the streets, prostituting herself for dope. But Sarah's got it in her head that if the little burrito eater was taken away from his environment, he'd have a chance to—."

A weary Iris rubbed her face as she listened to her cousin's racist crap. Surveying the room, her eyes landed on it. Leaning against the chair in which Damian sat earlier was an overstuffed backpack. Her brain clicked. No. No. She was not taking her cousin's problem grandchild home with her.

"Daddy?" Sarah interrupted. She held a service tray high in the air. "You need to calm down. You know what the doctor said about keeping your blood pressure in check. This is not helping it." Setting the service on the patio dining table, Sarah poured coffee in a mug and handed it to her father. Turning to Iris, she smiled, revealing a perfect set of American girl teeth, and chirped, "Coffee?"

Iris slowly shook her head.

"Sofia's making your favorite dinner, Daddy," and, facing Iris,

     MELISSA POWELL GAY

she continued, "We'd love it if you could stay and have dinner with us." She sat on the arm of her dad's chair and placed her hands on his shoulders.

What was this girl on? Iris was incredulous. Sarah acted like this was just an ordinary day, birds singing outside, as daddy called her sister a whore and her nephew a shiftless bastard. Iris thanked her lucky stars for the parents the heavenly lottery had thrown at her. She pledged to herself that never again would she talk bad about Mr. Henry or his faults. When she got back to Mt Pleasant, she'd take Elizabeth out for a scoop of rocky road ice cream over at the Valley Farm Creamery anytime she asked.

"You see, Damian has gotten himself into a bit of trouble." Pausing, Sarah wrapped her straw hair behind both ears. "And we were thinking … if he could spend some quality time, you know, away from his toxic environment, he'd be better off. And what daddy is trying to say—."

"Shut up, Sarah. I'm quite capable of making myself understood." To Iris, he said, "You're family, you need to take the brat back to Virginia. That'll get him away from the spicks."

Iris didn't know what to say. If she was inclined to paranoia, she'd believe they, Bert, Sarah *and* Bennie, were in this together, conspiring to determine the destiny of her future life by turning her into a full-time caregiver. She'd just met this kid, a kid who may or may not be skilled at all kinds of illegal mischief.

"What kind of trouble is he in?" Iris asked.

"Well, he's kinda been caught—." Sarah said.

"He's been charged with burglary, breaking and entering, and taking something that didn't belong to him. This is the third time," Bennie said, his face red with anger.

"As you've pointed out on a number of occasions, cousin, I'm no lawyer. Can't we get into trouble by helping him flee prosecution?"

"That's right. You aren't a lawyer," Bennie said.

Sarah chimed in, "His social worker convinced the juvenile courts' prosecutor to suspend charges if the family agreed to take over the custody."

"Sarah, I have all kinds of sympathy for you and everything your family is going through right now. But I don't see how I fit into this. I mean, I've got Mom to care for. I've got a business to run."

Sarah's eyes watered up as she squeaked, "I'm at the end of my wits. He and the boys aren't getting along and—."

"Damian was bullying Sarah's kids, so I let him stay here."

"But then Daddy's prognosis came," Sarah added. The waterworks were at full throttle as she dabbed at the corner of her mascaraed eye with the sleeve of her yoga jacket. "We're in crisis mode here. You've got to help us out."

"And Alexis?" Iris inquired about Bennie's ex-wife. "Can't she step in?"

"I've not talked to my ex-wife in over ten years," Bennie said.

"Believe me. I've tried to get Mom to help but she won't," Sarah whined.

"What about the father's family?" Iris interrupted. The second they left this house, she was going to chew off both of Bert Tyler Swanson's ears with what she thought of this plan to visit a sick relative.

"As usual," Bennie hissed, "you're missing the point. Believe me when I tell you, if there was any other way, I would have acted on it. Aside from Sarah and me, the boy has no one. And I'll not have the little cretin terrorizing Justin and Brian. And since I'm no longer able to provide a roof over the mongrel's head, I see it as your obligation to do so. You're his only hope."

"Well, that's not exactly true. Now is it?" Iris asked.

"What do you mean?"

     MELISSA POWELL GAY

Iris was going to regret what she was about to do. For a split second she wished Jonnie was sitting next to her to talk her out of it. "There is another family member. Or did you forget?" She watched with pleasure as Bennie's eyes caught on to her meaning. His lower lip and chin quivered with ire. Looking up at Sarah, Iris commanded, "Ask the others to come out here." Then she leaned in and said with as much calm as she could maintain, "I'll take Damian for the summer under the following, nonnegotiable, conditions. One, stop the frivolous lawsuits. If Jonnie doesn't get an email from Ulysses Marshall by close of business tomorrow, the deal's off. Two, anytime, and I mean anytime, Damian or his parents want him home, he's on the next flight out on your dime. Three, I'm going to sit back on this nice, comfortable sofa and listen as you say 'hello' to Bert, call her 'sister,' and introduce your child and grandchildren to their *Aunt* Roberta Tyler Swanson."

CHAPTER 6 NOW
FAMILY TIME

A balmy breeze blew up from the beach as Iris and Bert sipped morning coffee on their patio overlooking the ocean. Sarah drove over to the Laguna Beach hotel to spend a spa day with her Aunt Bert. She also arranged for Damian to come so he could spend time with his East Coast family, meaning Iris. Sarah's pitch for Damian to experience life in Mt Pleasant was hooey. Damian cramped her suburban California lifestyle and she was using daddy's dying wish to get him gone. This "helpful daddy's girl" routine was wearing thin on Iris.

In his shamelessness, Bennie was probably playing along with her to get in another twist of the family feud knife by saddling Iris with his problem child. She had lots of reasons to suspect Bennie of faking his fatal illness to jam up her own life. He'd done it before, many times. Once when they were kids he told her that her parents had a son but he died so they adopted her. When she finally screwed up enough courage to accuse her father of lying about his paternity, he shook a crooked finger at her and told her to go to her room. Later, her mother consoled her with a plate of Miss Bert's cornbread and black-eyed peas. Her mother assured her that she was the true daughter of Henry and Elizabeth Lee by pointing out all of her physical traits. "You've got your grandmother Lee's square shoulders." Air kissing, she added, "And my pretty face." Giggling, she added, "Thank goodness you didn't get your daddy's ears."

The night before, while Iris and Bert were in Bennie's guest bathroom freshening up for dinner, Bert confessed her part in the scheme. After Mr. Henry died, she contacted Bennie but he refused to have anything to do with her. She wrote a letter to Sarah and the two hit it off right away. They talked on the phone once a week.

"Then when the child called and said Bennie was dying, I had to come. But, Iris, I swear to you, Megan's boy coming to Mt Pleasant, I didn't know nothing about that."

After the family dinner, Damian sat out on the terrace alone with his game app while the other guys bonded over an NBA game in the great room. At the dining room table, Sarah laid out the unabridged version of the homeless boy's story. Bert fell for it, all the way down to the bottom of the old abandoned mine shaft. Iris noticed Sarah could turn on the waterworks on cue. Must be due to the close proximity to Hollywood, she mused.

Watching Sarah in action answered Iris' earlier question about those who try to help others. People tried to fix other people's relationships because they couldn't fix their own.

Now, Sarah and Bert were chattering away on the hotel bed like sorority sisters. Iris and Damian sat on the patio watching palm crowns sway. She wondered what she was going to do with a streetwise fourteen-year-old for the next four hours and for the next two months. Mt Pleasant wasn't exactly a hotbed of entertainment for millennials.

"Want to take a hike up into the hills?" she asked him.

She noticed a slight shrug. A half-hour later, she led the non-verbal Damian up a fire trail toward a view of the Pacific Ocean. What was it with Lee men? Why were they so sullen, so angry with the world? And Damian? What kind of name was that for a kid, anyway? Wasn't there a horror movie with a devil-possessed character with that name?

She stopped on the trail and glanced over her shoulder. The kid had disappeared. She backtracked all the way to the trailhead's car park at the foot of the hill. No Damian. Her phone pinged with a text from Sarah, *D txt me. Didn't have ur #. He's @ the beach.* Driving slowly along the beach road she spotted him sitting on an outcropping of rocks jutting over sand dunes. She parked the car and maneuvered over to his perch.

"Guess we need to exchange phone numbers so we can text while standing next to each other, huh?" she said as she sat. Her legs dangled over the rocks. Grains of sand sprinkled throughout his mop of curls. He was playing a video game on his phone.

She asked, "Want to add me to your contacts list?"

He slid his phone into the pocket of his oversized denim shorts and gazed out at the ocean.

"You're right. This feels more like a beach day."

No response. He pulled out his phone, resuming his game.

A minute rode off on an ocean breeze.

"Look, you were there last night. I had nothing to do with planning your summer vacation. Your grandfather wants this. You're welcome at my place anytime."

Another minute floated by.

"I don't see things like your Aunt Sarah does." Trilling her fingers in the air, she continued, "Sparkly unicorns spreading happy dust over everything. Making sure everybody gets a soccer trophy." She gazed out at the ocean. "Life's a shit sandwich, kid. The sooner you accept that fact, the better off you'll be."

Damian laid back on the rock and covered his eyes with his arm.

"Damian? Is that what your friends call you?"

Nothing.

The approaching clouds and the kid's detachment put her in a funk. "I'm going for a walk up the beach. You can come along, or hang out here or in the car 'til I get back." She tossed the key fob at Damian then jumped from the rocks and waded over the dunes to the berm. Not looking back, she headed north. Forty-five minutes later, Iris searched for the jutting rocks and for Damian. Spotting the rocks, she didn't see the kid. Picking up her pace, she covered the distance back in half the time. As she crested the road, she looked both ways but saw no white mid-sized sedan. Two hours later found Iris back at the hotel.

"He didn't steal your car," Sarah insisted. She had finally returned Iris' call. "And if he did take it, I'm sure he's just kidding around."

"You hear me laughing?"

"He'll turn up. He disappears like this all the time."

"So you can understand why I have reservations about being responsible for him."

"Please. Just give him a chance. He's obviously got trust issues," Sarah reasoned.

Iris laughed. "If anyone has a right to have trust issues, it's me. If the car isn't parked in the garage of this hotel within the next hour, I'm calling the police to report it stolen."

"Please don't do that," Sarah pleaded. "If you do, he goes to the detention center. You're his last chance."

"One hour." Iris disconnected the call.

The car was returned but Damian had not. At the airport the

following day, Bert and Sarah hugged, throwing air kisses and promises to visit each other again. Iris asked Sarah to share her phone number with Damian. "Tell him he's always welcome in Mt Pleasant. But it's his decision to come. I'll not chase after him or make him come."

By the time the plane soared over the Grand Canyon, Iris turned to Bert and asked, "Do you think Megan will ever be able to care for Damian?"

"That's hard to say," Bert said. "Not all mammas are like the one who raised you."

"Tell me about your mother. You never talk about her."

Bert stalled by looking out the plane's window, then said, "Everybody called her Vee. We lived in an apartment over her beauty salon. Next to the colored Laundromat. You got up there from stairs on the side of the building." Talking to the clouds below, she added, "She was real pretty and what they used to call a free spirit."

"If Uncle Ben's views on race relations were anything like Bennie's, how did the two of them end up together?"

Bert faced Iris and said, "Child, I don't know. All's I remember was Uncle Donnie saying your daddy and my daddy fought over her. Uncle D said Mr. Henry didn't like how Ben treated Vee."

"Meaning?" Iris asked.

"It was a long time ago, sweet pea, and I'd rather not talk about it. Uncle D told me my parents ran with a pretty shiftless lot and that they all congregated in our apartment. But I don't remember any of that. I was too little, I suppose. I went to live with my Grandma but when she died I went to live with my Uncle Tom and Aunt Melba." She busied herself with stuffing paper napkins in her empty coffee cup and raising it for the steward to retrieve. "Grandma Alice said after he came home from the Army, your daddy made sure the lights stayed on and the oilman's bill was paid

     MELISSA POWELL GAY

every October." Bert fell silent.

In all of its miserable existence, shame ruined too many lives, Iris thought. The flight attendant returned with juice and pretzels. The two traveled in silence the rest of the way back to Virginia.

CHAPTER 7 THEN
BETRAYED

In December 1949, the day he turned eighteen and two months from the day he first saw Violet Tyler, Henry Lee drove to the recruitment center and enlisted in the United States Army. At a simple turn of the clock's hand, Henry had officially become an adult and, most important to him, he could now live by his own convictions.

The first order of business was getting out from under his parent's roof and their lectures on what he should or shouldn't do with his life. The second was to drive to Battina's School of Black Beauty in Roanoke and ask Violet to leave Virginia with him, certain in the knowledge that she felt as trapped as he among people who saw things only in black and white. Sure of her affinity for his plan, he stopped at his mother's jewelers to search for a special Christmas gift for her on the way to the beauty school. With the help of a pudgy jeweler, Henry selected a promise pin — an enamel violet flower with three small seed pearls. Parked across the street from the beauty school, which was nothing more than a two-chair barber shop in need of a coat of paint, Henry sliced an apple with his penknife as he waited for Violet. The gift was safely tucked away in the glove box.

After abandoning Violet and Donnie at Lickin' Hole the night he gut-punched his brother, he had called on her at her Aunt Sketta's boarding house to apologize. The visit led to friendship, then romance. The two spent every Friday, Saturday and Sunday night together either in the boarding house's parlor or cruising the country roads looking for a quiet spot to park. Only Donnie, Aunt Sketta and Violet's best friend Naomi knew about the courtship. Once, while the aunt was away visiting, Violet smuggled Henry into her room. Lying in her bed tangled in moonlit sheets, he confessed to her it was his first time being with a woman. Years later, after all that had transpired, he recalled that she hadn't responded with her own declaration of first love. She had merely smiled down at him.

Popping an apple slice into his mouth, he watched her long, slow gait crossing the street. Her beauty was wasted on this place. She belonged in New York or Paris. Yet, at times, the tiny cracks in her near perfect glamour — her hard selfishness — caused him to question his devotion. But not today. They were going to plan a future together today. As she reached the car, he got out and went around to open the door for her. He tried to kiss her but she turned away.

"Someone will see us," she warned with unnecessary sternness.

"I don't care," he replied. "Get in. I've got something to tell you. Is your aunt at home?"

"Let's don't go there. I'm starving. Let's go to Junior's for a burger. We can sit in the car."

After spreading a burger wrapper over a paper napkin on her lap, she bit into the greasy sandwich.

Too excited to eat his own burger, Henry said, "I've enlisted."

She stopped chewing and gathered a questioned look on her face.

He wiped away a greasy spot from the corner of her mouth with his thumb. "I report to basic training at Fort Dix the fourth of January."

She placed the burger in her lap and held up her hands, not sure what to do with them.

"Remember? I told you about my sister. She's in China and we haven't heard from her in months. I'm hoping once I get over there I can try and look for her," he said.

She rewrapped the sandwich and stuffed it inside the white paper bag and handed it to him. "Take this. I'm not hungry anymore."

"Here's what I was thinking. The recruiter said enlistees bring their girls with them all the time. After basic training in Fort Brag, the recruiter said I'll most likely be sent to California. We can get an apartment off base and live together. That is, until I get shipped out."

She wiped her fingers with the napkin. "Recruiters lie. They say anything to get boys to join."

Henry shrugged.

"And even if it was the truth, who's gonna rent to an unmarried white man and a colored girl? Henry, for a smart boy, you can be thick sometimes. Take me home."

As the car maneuvered through the city, he stole glances at her. Looking straight ahead, she let the tears fall where they may, keeping her arms folded. He parked his car in front of the boarding house and she got out without saying a word. Henry wasn't sure what he'd done to upset her. "Violet. Wait." He followed her into the vestibule of the Victorian house. "In California people don't care who you live with," he said quietly. "We can leave here—."

She interrupted, "How could you be so selfish?"

"What?" He tried to take her hand but she stepped away from him.

"I got dreams, too, ya know. When I finish my training, I'm getting my own place, making my own money."

In a flash of inspiration, Henry said, "Why not get your own place in California? That's where I'll end up and you can get a shop there."

She placed her hands at her narrow waist and beaned him with her stare. "Who I know in California gonna give me a place to set up my shop? Huh?"

"I don't know. We'll work something out." Henry realized she was right. He hadn't thought his plan through but pressed on. "Don't you want to get out of the South? Be part of the bigger world? Live some place where you're appreciated?"

She laughed that high-pitched, witch's laugh she used when she and her friend Naomi made fun of one of their duller friends. "You think the South's the only place a person's singled out for being colored? You a bigger fool than I gave you credit for, Henry Lee." She hurried up the steps to her room without looking back.

Henry's parents were about as thrilled as Violet on hearing of his enlistment. His father called his action imbecilic. More specifically, if Henry wanted to get his head shot off, he needn't go halfway around the world. All he had to do was show up on Turkey Knob the first day of deer hunting season. His mother forbade him to leave Fallam County as he stormed out of the house without his coat and hat.

Outside, the sleeting snow pricked his neck and the back of his ears as he got into his car. He started the engine, turned up the heat, and blew into his hands for warmth. With nowhere to go, he hunched over the steering wheel smoking cigarettes and listening to the new FM radio station out of Roanoke until all the downstairs lights went out. He didn't care what they said, he was eighteen now and old enough to make his own decisions. He was going to Korea to fight the Communists then go find M. Ellen and bring her home. As for Violet, he imparted to the icy night, she'd come round to his idea of them leaving together once he gave her the pin.

Alice Tyler's skills as a seamstress were much sought-after by every Mt Pleasant woman who couldn't thread a needle. Mrs. Lee, however, felt the dressmaker's talents were wasted on hemming work dungarees and lining curtains. Twice a year Matilda Lee invited Mrs. Tyler to her kitchen for tea and the pair discussed the latest styles while thumbing through the pages of fashion magazines. Mrs. Tyler gave Matilda a list of items needed from DuPree's notions department to fill an order for the season's dresses, skirts, blouses and an occasional coat or jacket. And a few weeks later, Matilda Lee modeled her new couture at church or one of her many volunteer committee meetings.

The day before Christmas Eve, Henry drove round to Donnie's house to deliver the annual Christmas gift of country ham and a box of chocolates for Mrs. Tyler. Along with the gifts, Henry handed her an envelope stuffed with cash in payment for the dressmaking services. "Merry Christmas, Mrs. Tyler."

In return, as always, Mrs. Tyler presented Henry with a brick-sized fruitcake wrapped in tin foil for him to deliver to his parents. Henry never understood their fondness for the block of sticky goo. But his parents said Christmas wasn't Christmas without Alice Tyler's fruitcake. "Merry Christmas, Henry."

"Is Donnie around?" he asked, hefting the silver block in his palm.

"He's in his room."

"What's shakin', Slick?" Donnie asked as Henry entered his bedroom.

Henry pointed at him with his index fingers like two six-shooters.

    MELISSA POWELL GAY

Trampling through puberty at sixteen, Donnie's uneven voice didn't quite fit his attempts at bohemian panache. The hundred and ten pounder sprang up from his bed and reached for his worn corduroy jacket and said, "I got Christmas money from Uncle Bo Bo. Let's go throw some bones behind the Lickin' Hole."

"That money burning a hole in your pocket already?" Henry asked. He always asked Donnie that question when Donnie itched to gamble his hard-earned money. At times, the question was accompanied with a lecture on the merits of saving and compounded interest.

And Donnie always replied, "Hank, you so tight, when you walk, you squeak like the Tin Man." Tonight, he added, "Let's beat feet, brother. We got many a mile to go."

Henry chucked the fruitcake on the back seat of the Olds and the duo set out for the down and low side of Roanoke.

"You did what?" Donnie asked when Henry told him about his enlistment.

"I report to Fort Dix, New Jersey, after New Year's," Henry said as he passed a farm truck on the icy county road. "And don't feel compelled to call me a fool for doing it, because your sister and my parents have already done a respectable job of letting me know what an asinine idea it is."

"Why you want to go over there and get your fool head blowed off?" Donnie asked with true concern.

"I said don't call me a fool."

Donnie sucked on an incisor and said, "Looks like a duck."

"Dad wants you to continue collecting rent. If you still want the job." Henry had pitched the idea of Donnie collecting rent to his father. After some hesitation, his father agreed but only if Henry covered from his Army pay "any shortfall the young colored boy created." Angry at his father's mistrust of Donnie, Henry had pulled the rent ledgers from behind Bets Jones' desk. Pointing at the column headed "collector," his forefinger ran down the page as he counted out loud the number of collections "DT" had made. "He's been working for you for over a year. And rent collections are up because of him." Henry had tossed the book on old lady Jones' desk and stormed out.

As they rode across the county line, Donnie asked, "Will I have to work with Ben?"

"I suppose so. Why?"

"I'll have to think about it."

Turning left on Old Lick Road, Henry asked, "Will you talk to your sister for me? When I told her about enlisting, she 'bout burned a hole in my forehead with that look of hers. You know the one I'm talking about."

Donnie lifted a toothpick out of his coat pocket and held it between his teeth.

"She said I was selfish. How is serving your country selfish, Donnie?"

Donnie chewed on his toothpick and let the man talk.

"She won't talk to me. When I call your Aunt Skeeta's house, she won't come to the phone. I went by the beauty school and they ran me off. They said she doesn't want to talk to me anymore. I even wrote her a letter and it was returned, unopened. Say something to her. Ask her to talk to me."

"Did you forget? I'm her *younger* brother. She ain't gonna listen to me."

"Is she coming to Mt Pleasant for Christmas? Maybe I can come by on Christmas Day. I have a gift for her."

"Now you talkin' Vee's language," Donnie said. "Park right there."

"Why? We're two blocks away," Henry complained. "I know I

can find something closer."

"No, you won't. You do this every time. We ride around for an hour looking for a closer spot." Donnie laughed and said, "Damn, Hank, you ain't gonna last a day over there."

"Shut up," Henry said. He parked the car.

From a block away, Henry felt the levitating energy arcing from the joint. The holiday merited a live band and it was swinging loud. Ever since the new owner Ferrol Smiths installed a jukebox, live acts were infrequent. He argued to a complaining Henry and Donnie that it was cheaper than live bands because it didn't drink up all his beer profit. If they didn't like it, they could go someplace else.

The pair cut down the side alley before passing the bouncer at the front door. A fire in a rusted oil barrel projected gamblers' shadows onto the brick wall opposite the rear of the Lickin' Hole. Donnie greeted one of the dicers and the group opened up and allowed him into the circle. Henry found a spot next to the barrel to warm his hands, then he snuck in the back way to buy a beer and see who was steaming up the place inside.

The band was loaded with horns and reeds and some cat was blowing away Hal Singer's hit *Cornbread*. Henry tattooed the beat on the bar as he waited for his beer. With the beer to his lips, he turned to watch the swingers on the dance floor. He recognized a few then noticed someone a head taller than all the rest. His brother Ben was twirling someone around smack in the middle of the dance hall. And that someone couldn't be Ben's new bride because Sarah Duncan, the youngest child of a federal judge, wouldn't be caught dead in a low bottom dive the likes of the Lickin' Hole. Henry watched his brother's face change with the mood of the music. He'd never seen such heightened emotions permeate from his brother or, for that matter, from anyone else in his stoic family except, maybe, M. Ellen when she played the piano. At one point,

Ben smiled down at his partner and bent to say something in her ear. Henry stretched to see who she was.

The song ended on a squeal. The band leader announced a short break, encouraging everyone to order another round or two. Henry watched his brother as the crowd thinned. His dance partner was clinging onto Ben like he was the last life jacket on the Titanic.

As the floor cleared, he saw her. Her graceful bare arms stretched to reach around his brother's broad neck. Ben's enormous hands encircled her narrow waist. Her exotic hair was tied up and away from her tilted neck as she arched her back and pressed into him. He buried his face into her neck and she responded by raising a knee up his inseam.

Henry set his unfinished beer on the bar and left.

"Hank, why we leaving?" Donnie complained as Henry pulled him from his rowdy game of dice and bid his friend follow him out onto the sidewalk.

As they circled the block to return to Mt Pleasant, Henry spotted his brother's car. He slammed on the brakes in the middle of the street.

"I don't know why we had to leave. I was winning," Donnie said. "Why we stopping here?"

Leaving the car running, Henry got out and said, "Wait here."

Following Henry, Donnie said, "Boy, what are you up to?"

"Keep your voice down," Henry ordered.

Donnie watched as Henry squatted next to the front left tire and stuck his penknife in the tire's nozzle to deflate it. "You trying to get us thrown in jail?"

"Get the other side," Henry said as he glanced around for witnesses.

Donnie held up both hands and said, "I ain't got a dog in this fight. No, sir."

"Then get back in the car," Henry whispered. He popped the trunk on Ben's brand new Olds, a gift from their parents for passing the bar, then lifted the spare tire out and rolled it across the street.

Headlights flooded the lane as a police car slowed, then stopped.

"You boys need any help?" an officer asked.

Donnie's eyes grew as wide as teacup saucers. Henry propped the tire against his car then squatted to eye level with the policeman. "No, sir. Looks like some hooligans let all the air out of my left front and when I went to change it, I noticed the spare was flat, too." He pointed at Donnie and continued, "Bubba here is giving me a ride to the Esso so I can get some air in it." He patted the tire. "Ain't that right, Bubba?" Henry worked hard to keep from laughing.

"That's mighty white of 'im," the policeman said as he stink-eyed Donnie.

Henry pounded the top of the patrol car and said, "Thanks for stopping, officer."

The policeman sniffed around Henry's tale and the situation. After what seemed an eternal minute, the car slowly rolled forward. Henry watched and waited for it to turn the corner. Folding the driver's seat forward, he hefted Ben's spare into the back seat. The shimmer of the foil of Mrs. Tyler's Christmas fruitcake caught Henry's eye. "Hang on. Be right back." Unwrapping the sticky cake, he casually walked back to Ben's car. He placed the cake in the driver's seat and slammed the door shut. Under his breath, he said, "Explain that to Sarah."

"Where we going? You missed the turn to go to my house." Donnie said a half an hour later.

"We got one more stop to make and then we'll roll on home."

"Where we going?"

Henry didn't answer.

"I hate it when you get like this. What's eatin' at you, anyway? You been broodin' like an ole hen ever since we left the Hole."

Henry parked in front of a sagging Victorian on South Main Street two blocks down the hill from the Farmer's Market. The house was dark.

"Who lives here?" Donnie asked.

"Ben and his wife, Sarah." Henry's ire simmered as he thought about his just-married brother snogging on *his* girlfriend in a seedy juke joint.

"Why we here?"

"Be right back." Henry retrieved Ben's spare from the back seat and rolled it through the wrought iron fence gate. Halfway up the walk he stopped and scratched his chin as he surveyed the low roofline over the wrap-around porch. He unfolded his penknife and stuck it in the tire's nozzle.

"Is this gonna take all night?" Donnie asked.

Henry jumped.

"What are you up to?" Donnie asked.

"I'm trying to decide the best place to put the tire so Ben can see it."

"You crazy." Donnie rubbed his hands together to generate some heat. "Can we hurry this along, my man stuff's about to freeze off."

CHAPTER 8 THEN
PAST CHRISTMAS PRESENTS

On Christmas Day, Matilda set a dinner place for her daughter, M. Ellen, as she had every evening. Henry's parents had not received correspondence from her in months. They worried about her and her husband, who had been called to serve in a mission in China. Each time Henry tried to reason with his mother that his enlistment was a way to bring M. Ellen home, his mother's eyes filled with tears and she'd retire to her bedroom.

Christmas night, the Lee family went through the motions of celebrating the holiday. An eight-foot cedar that Henry had felled from the farm, sparkled in the grand front windows. In hopes of cheering his mother up, Henry lit a fire in the sandstone fireplace. As the family settled in for a cozy winter's evening, Sarah relayed to Matilda a story about a car tire discovered on the roof of her porch.

"Why? What's the reasoning behind doing such an absurd thing?" Sarah asked.

"It's called a prank, Sarah. Something your proper sensibilities wouldn't understand," Ben said. He said this as if he was tired of hearing her repeat the story.

Henry stoked the fire to hide his glee.

"I know what a prank is," Sarah said, "I just don't understand why someone put it on *our* roof."

"Has your father heard any controversial trials of late?" Mr. Lee asked. Sarah's father, Judge Duncan, and her mother lived next door to Ben and Sarah. "Maybe they got the wrong house?"

"I asked him about it last night and he said 'no'." Sarah pulled her cashmere wrap, a Christmas gift from Matilda, tighter around her shoulders.

"Ben? That impudent crowd you represent? What about them?" the old man asked.

"Mr. Young's a middle-aged businessman with better things to do than litter his attorney's yard, Pop."

Mr. Lee struck a match. Before he lit his pipe, he said, "Reuben Young and his brothers are bootleggers and scallywags. And you know how uncomfortable I am about our firm representing them."

"Well, there aren't a lot of innocent men walking around needing our services," Ben said. "Besides, he pays his bills on time, unlike your stuffy banker friends."

"A tire on the roof? That reminds me of something I read in a magazine," Henry said. He warmed his backside in front of the fire.

"What are you saying, boy?" Mr. Lee asked.

Henry looked at Ben and said, "I believe I read something in the *National Geographic* about a phenomenon called Appalachian Justice. And one of the tenets was called 'the wandering wagon wheel' law. Broken wagon wheels were heaped in front of the house of any man accused of infidelity."

Logs crackled in the fireplace.

Ben called Henry's bluff. "You're full of it." Deflecting the bit on infidelity, Ben said, "He's pulling our legs. There's no such article and no such thing as Appalachian Justice. You cut-up, you had me going there for a minute." He laughed, nervously.

"What an off-color thing to say, Henry," his mother said. She stood and said to Sarah, "Come help me fix a tray of coffee and sweets. For some reason, Alice Tyler didn't send us one of her fruit-cakes this year. We'll have to make do with store-bought cookies."

When Ben broke the seal on the season's first fifth of bourbon, Henry used the excuse of going for cigarettes to leave the house.

Across town he parked a block from the Tylers' home. Despite the frigid air and darkness, family and visitors crowded the porch and front yard. As he walked up the dirt path to the porch, firecrackers exploded at his feet. The shock propelled him into a holly bush and, as he pulled himself up, he heard Donnie's bray over everyone else's laugher. More chaos erupted as bottle rockets screamed into the air and kids squealed while running around with sparklers in each hand.

Donnie greeted him on the path. "That's for calling me 'Bub-ba.'"

Henry said, "Ask Violet to come outside. I've got something to give her."

On the porch, Henry coaxed Violet into taking a ride with him. Under a streetlight, amid the children's playful kissing sounds and the jump rope rhyme, "Henry and Violet, sittin' in a tree…," he opened the car door for her.

Before he started the car, he rubbed his palms over his wool trousers, preparing himself. Over the past week, he'd practiced in front of his shaving mirror what he was about to say to her. Seeing her with his brother hadn't changed how he felt about her. In fact, the incident only hardened his resolve to convince her that she loved him as much as he loved her. Pulling it from the glove box, he held out the small jeweler's box wrapped in lavish paper. Looking into her eyes, he shyly said, "Merry Christmas. I love you, Violet Tyler. I want us to be together always."

She placed her slender fingers at the base of her throat. "Henry, you shouldn't say things like that."

"Things like what?"

"Things that aren't allowed. Things you'll later regret and deny."

"The heart wants what the heart wants. Mine wants yours and nobody can say different," he said, surprising himself with such sentimental confidence.

She responded to his romantic affirmation with a burst of mocking laughter that cut through him.

Placing the gift in her lap, he said, "Go ahead, open it up. I hope you like it."

She ripped it open with a child's greedy impatience. Showing no gratitude, she clasped the delicate gold-trimmed enamel violet pin on the collar of her coat.

"When are you leaving?" she asked as she rolled down the car's window and tossed out the wrappings.

"January third," he said. Disappointed at her reaction to the promise pin, a gift the jeweler assured him was every girl's desire this Christmas, he added, "I have something else for you." He started the car and drove toward town.

Haunted with ghosts of Christmas present, downtown Mt Pleasant's shops were locked up, unlit, and their owners snug at home with loved ones for a single night of peace and quiet. Turning west on a graveled Iron Works Road, the car bumped over railroad tracks and into the colored retail district, a single block consisting of a general store and pharmacy, a Bank of the Brethren annex, a restaurant called Piggy's, a dress shop and a laundry service. And like its white counterpart, the entire block was closed for the Christmas holiday.

Violet asked restlessly, "Where are we going?"

"We're almost there."

The car stopped in front of a boarded-up building that in another lifetime had been the ticket office for the defunct Fallam and Roanoke Railroad Company. While researching a property deed at the courthouse, Henry had stumbled upon the plot. Acting on his father's behalf, he offered half what the owner was asking and to his and his father's astonishment, the owner accepted. Lee Properties now owned the place and was waiting for an "opportunity to present itself," as his father put it.

"What do you think?" Henry asked.

"What do you mean, what do I think?"

"This could be Violet's Hair and Beauty Salon," Henry said.

"Yeah, and pay rent to a dirty old man who pinches me on my titty. No thank you."

"What if you owned it? Wouldn't it be a great spot for a hairdo place?"

"You been nippin' at your daddy's egg nog. How am I supposed to pay for it?"

"Then go with me to California," he pleaded. "You could get a job in a shop in San Francisco."

"You got a thick head. I told you I don't want to go traipsing off after you while you play army and get yourself killed." Tears filled her chestnut eyes. "Why did you do it? Why did you sign up?" She struggled with the door handle, then managed to get it open. Frigid air spilled into the car. Wrapping her wool coat around her tightly, Violet strode down the middle of the road as the harsh headlights poured over her young body. He sat and watched as she crested the mound at the railroad crossing.

The car caught up to her. Henry called out, "Violet, get back in the car."

But she kept walking away from him.

"Damn it, Violet, it's freezing. Please, get in the car."

She ignored his plea and kept walking.

Henry stopped the car, got out and jerked her by the arm. "How long?"

She turned her head away from him to hide her regret.

"How long have you been stepping out with my brother?"

She tried to pull away from him but his grip on her arm was too firm.

"It's not what you think."

"How do you know what I think?" Pushing her away, he dropped his hands to his side. "Please, get in the car. I'll take you home."

Christmas carols crackled over the radio on the ride back to Violet's.

As soon as the car stopped in front of her house, Violet pulled at the door handle.

"Violet," Henry said. He placed his hand on her arm. Looking straight ahead, she relaxed against the seat. "What we did together, you know, in your room, did it mean *anything* to you? Or was I just a good time and a free beer?" He paused and said, "Look at me. Did you have any feelings for me at all?"

"You don't understand. You'll never understand." She busied herself with her gloves, then her headscarf.

His plan for them to run away to California was a fool's folly. In atonement for his misguided idea, he offered, "I'll pay the rent on the building and lend you money to start your business. Just promise me you'll stay away from my brother."

"I don't want your money and you can't tell me who I can or can't be with. You don't own me, Henry Lee." She was warming up for an argument.

"Of course, I don't. But if you fall in with my brother, it'll all be on his terms, never yours. He'll use you and throw you in the gutter when he's finished."

Pulling her arm away from his touch, she said, "Have you ever thought I might be using him?"

"Did you know him before we started, you know, going steady?"

She laughed to cover up her guilt. "Henry, everybody knows Ben Lee."

His anger bowed at the corner of his mouth. "You know what I'm asking."

"I do. And it's none of your business. Good night and don't get yourself killed." She got out of the car and walked away.

Standing in front of the Mt Pleasant Hotel waiting for the bus, Henry and Ben watched as a team of workers demolished a rundown clapboard building to make way for Mt Pleasant's new municipal park across the street. Donnie Tyler be-bopped toward them. His newsboy cap tilted to one side, the kid was oblivious to the blowing freeze.

"What do you want?" Ben asked. He puffed warm air into his gloved hands.

Ignoring Ben, Donnie asked, "Hank, got a minute?"

"Sure." Henry stepped away from his brother and huddled in the cold with Donnie.

Donnie extended his hand. "I wanted to come shake your hand and wish you luck."

Henry placed his free hand on his best friend's shoulder. "Go over to the office and tell Mrs. Jones you're there to pick up the collection journals. She'll be expecting you. If a renter challenges you, show them the letter I wrote. Just do like we always do."

Donnie nodded. "You gonna write to me? Tell me how bad the food is and all?"

"Sure."

"'Cept he can't read. Ain't that right, monkey brains?" Ben

interrupted.

"Ben, just once, can you be civil?" Henry asked.

"Just banging on his chops. Right, Donnie?" Ben lightly tapped the side of Donnie's face.

Donnie said nothing.

"What time is the bus scheduled to be here?" Ben asked. "Colder than hell out here."

"Hank, I'm takin' off. You take care of yourself," Donnie said. He rushed across the street and walked down the hill to Court and Main.

"Where's he off to?" Ben asked.

"He collects the house rents for dad," Henry said.

"He does?" Ben pulled his handkerchief from an inside breast pocket and wiped his nose.

"He's been doing it with me for over a year. You leave him alone, Ben."

"What? I haven't done anything to the little monkey."

Henry stood taller and pointed a finger at his older and much bigger brother. "You stay away from him and you stay away from his sister Violet."

"Ah. So *that's* what this is all about. It's all clear to me now," Ben said. "Poor Henry. His pickaninny girlfriend dumped him so he went off and joined the big, bad Army."

"Shut your ignorant mouth."

"I've tasted that honey," Ben whispered. "Believe me, she's too much woman for a scrawny kid like you, little brother." He smacked his lips.

Through a veil of white anger, Henry jabbed a right hook at Ben's nose.

Ben pressed his handkerchief to his face. "Son of a—."

As the smoky bus pulled up, Henry pointed at his brother and

     MELISSA POWELL GAY

said, "If I hear from Donnie that you've mistreated Violet, Sarah will learn the truth about how a tire landed on her roof and why she had to clean Alice Tyler's fruitcake off the seat of your britches. She'll hear all about your swing dance partner."

Ben's nose wheezed. Blood outlined his teeth. His eyes radiated enough hate to melt the icicles off the bus's rearview mirror.

Henry got on without looking back. He didn't care if he never saw his brother or this town ever again.

CHAPTER 9 NOW
FALSE IMPRESSIONS

Iris opened her eyes, happy to see the puffy, cloudlike water stain on the ceiling. She was in her own bed and it was Saturday, the day of Jonnie's fancy soiree. Going to Jonnie's for the evening was a welcome reprieve. Iris looked forward to an evening of passable drinking wine and hors d'oeuvres that hadn't been taken from a frozen cardboard box then deep fried to annihilation.

Plus, Iris was eager to hear more about Jonnie's plans for expanding her family's vineyard enterprise. But first she needed to get through the entire day without encountering a crisis that might require duct tape or the emergency room. She dressed in her boot camp yoga togs, preparing for battle with the retired Marine in Matilda Park.

Leaving her mom at the kitchen table eating corn flakes, she found Vinnie and Ludie by the back steps watching Heyu dig a hole for a chew toy Bert had brought him from California. There was something different about Vinnie, but she couldn't place what it was. Today, he wore cargo shorts and a Fallam County Chamber of Commerce T-shirt that stretched across his chest.

"What's on your calendar today?" she asked him as Ludie went into the house.

"I'm here to fix the toilet in your mother's room. Then I'm meeting the demolition crew at number one." Since several houses were planned for renovation, they had decided to number each house.

"Fix the toilet? A plumber was here the other night. What's wrong with it now?"

"It's clogged. I shut the water valve off last night and locked the door so she wouldn't try to use it. Can I go in her room now?"

"Yeah, she's up. Hey, thank you guys for watching her while—."

From inside, Ludie yelled, "Vinnie! Get in here!"

Iris and Vinnie rushed into the kitchen to find his wife tiptoeing in a growing pool of water at the landing of the back stairs. Water flowed from tread to tread like a waterfall Slinky. "I was going upstairs to get Miss Elizabeth's glasses and water started gushin'," she said.

Vinnie raced up the stairs.

"Mom, have you been washing diapers again?" Iris scolded. Squeezing by Ludie, she followed Vinnie up the stairs. With a couple of jabs with the plunger, Vinnie managed to unstop the overflowing toilet in the hallway bathroom. What looked like white peas swirled around the bottom of the bowl.

"What the—?" Iris asked. She reached in and pulled them out. "Oh, good Lord, Vinnie, she's gone and flushed her good pearls down the commode."

A few more plunges and they managed to rescue Elizabeth's double strand of pearls and the broach Mr. Henry had given to his mother that was later handed down to Elizabeth. In Elizabeth's bedroom, Iris took inventory of her mother's jewelry box and tried to see if any other pieces of value were missing. She'd have to sift through the pasta shell necklaces and the Elizabeth Taylor-Avon collection to retrieve the good pieces and put them in her daddy's gun safe with the medallion. The medallion. Five days had gone by and she hadn't heard "boo" from the Louvre or, for that matter, from Parisian lover boy, Mr. Manny Pants.

At noon Ludie prepared sandwiches for everybody. Vinnie sat as Iris and Ludie helped Elizabeth into her chair. Heyu found his usual spot under the table.

With everyone settled and munching potato chips, Iris sniffed. "What's that smell?"

Ludie scrunched up her nose and said, "Pee-yew. What *is* that?"

"I didn't do it," Elizabeth confessed.

Vinnie pointed downward and said, "I found him crawling through a spilled trash can in front of the Grove Street Inn an hour ago."

"Heyu!" Iris said as she put her head under the table. "What's gotten into you? You know better than to mess with the trash. Come on." She stood at the back door and said, "Go sit in the mudroom. We'll get you a bath this afternoon."

With his head hung in shame, Heyu slunk out to the mudroom and sprawled over the worn coir mat.

Back at the kitchen table, Iris asked, "Ludie, can you hang out with Mom tonight?"

Ludie stopped chewing on the mouthful of ham sandwich stuffed in one cheek.

"We had plans for tonight," Vinnie spoke for her.

Ludie's swallow was audible as she gulped at her iced tea.

"Oh, OK, no problem," Iris backtracked. "I've been invited to Jonnie's for — that's right, you two were probably invited, too. I'll call Bert."

As the old Lee luck would have it, Bert was off on one of her

          MELISSA POWELL GAY

church bus tours and not expected back until Monday. Without backup to her backup, Iris sat in her father's reading chair with last week's *Fallam County Citizen*. Elizabeth sat next to her, a lavender scented Heyu curled up in her lap snoring. A strong, late afternoon sun cast shadows of floating leaves and branches over the highly polished wooden floor.

Iris said to Elizabeth, "Want to hear what's happening in Fallam County?"

Elizabeth smiled.

"Here's something. Artie English's boy Travis got his daddy's old job. He's been appointed president at the bank." Iris showed Elizabeth the story's photo of a man who used to slide down her foyer stair rail. In the picture, a grown-up Travis stood beside a man in a double-breasted suit and a woman with spiky black hair, shaking his hand. "Who's Ella Stone Parker?" Iris asked Elizabeth.

"Oh, Ella? She and Todd were young friends of Ben and Sarah's." Elizabeth pointed at the paper and protested, "But that's not Ella Parker. Ella Parker wears her hair in a pageboy."

"It says right here, 'Ella Stone Parker, bank board member.'"

The foyer clock chimed six. Heyu woke from his nap, stretched, then jumped from Elizabeth's lap. He trotted out of the room.

"This is silly, Mom." Iris stood. "You want to go to a party?"

"A party?" Elizabeth asked. "Why, yes, I'd love to go to a party. Are the Parkers going to be there? What shall I wear?"

"We've been invited to Jonnie's for a wine tasting." Iris reached for her mother's hand and squeezed it. "Let's find you a party dress and go have some fun."

"What about your father? Is he going with us? I'll have to press a shirt for him."

Her mother's question rattled Iris. To recover, she pulled her mother's glasses from her face and vigorously polished them with the hem of her T-shirt. "You know Mr. Henry doesn't like stuffy parties." Iris helped her mother up from her chair.

"But that's where your father and I met," Elizabeth said. "At one of Ben and Sarah's house parties."

Iris glanced at the bookshelf across the room and spied the urn containing her father's ashes. "I'm guessing Mr. Henry would rather stay home tonight. He can keep Heyu company." Taking her phone from the end table, she texted Jonnie to say she planned to attend the party after all.

On the drive west, Elizabeth read aloud each road sign they passed. Iris congratulated herself on her brilliant idea. Normally, Elizabeth stayed home because public places proved too noisy and confusing for her. Iris predicted an evening with Jonnie's family, a lifetime of familiar faces, was bound to be a comforting experience for her mother.

Getting out of the car, Elizabeth protested. "This isn't Sarah's house. I thought we were going to Ben and Sarah's to see Ella and Todd." Iris helped Elizabeth as she slowly climbed the steep steps of the restored Bailey farmhouse. She'd given up on repeating that Jonnie and her brother, Wyatt Bailey, had invited them to a beginning of summer get-together.

When Iris opened the door, a blast of happy conversation and docile jazz greeted her. Elizabeth's grip on her hand tightened.

"Iris." Ludie excused herself from a pair of couples and reached for Elizabeth's other hand.

Confused, Elizabeth pulled away from Ludie.

"I'm glad you guys came," Ludie said.

"I bought Muhammad to the mountain," Iris muttered as she surveyed the Baroque flower arrangement on the hallway table.

"Muhammad? I thought your boyfriend's name was Manny? Is he parking the car?" Ludie asked. She stood at the door looking out past the painted porch and down at the vehicles crowding the circular drive.

"Where's Jonnie?" Iris asked.

"She's around somewhere. Try the den." Facing Elizabeth, Ludie added, "We found some kittens at the dumpster earlier. Want to come out back and see them?"

"I guess. Is Ella out there?" Elizabeth asked.

"Who?" Ludie asked.

"I bet she is, Mom," Iris said. "Go find her and say 'Hi.'"

Iris found her way to the new addition consisting of a grand family room with a low, beamed ceiling and a view of the farm and rolling acres of vineyards. The place was crawling with people Iris had trouble recognizing. Picking up a glass of red wine from a tray on the spacious marble counter separating the den from the country kitchen, she sipped. The sip implied somebody had bottled Wyatt's Christmas fruitcake. She spotted Ethan Quinn holding up a corner on the other side of the den. He looked good.

Iris had known Ethan since her time in the womb. While their daddies cured rural boredom with nocturnal enterprises, their mammas commiserated over the phone and in person as each attempted to locate a roving husband. Until high school, Ethan's arm slung over her shoulder felt like the protection of an older brother. They kissed once, in the hay barn on her father's farm. For a day or two she had sensed a warming passion, but eventually the feeling was overpowered by her need to leave Mt Pleasant and to find her own place in the world.

Upon his return to Mt Pleasant, Ethan asked Jonnie out on a date. One night after a bottle of Malbec, Jonnie confessed to Iris that the whole "dating Ethan" thing wasn't working. Her business schedule and his long hours of chasing deadbeats left little time for intimacies. Thinking about it now made sense to Iris. Her friend always insisted on separating her professional life from her personal one. With Jonnie's desire to carry the Bailey Farms' two-hundred-year legacy forward, Ethan made a better vintner partner than a sometime lover.

She watched Ethan as he talked with the man standing beside him. Without the dopey Andy Taylor law enforcement uniform, he passed for what every woman wanted, broad-shouldered and well-groomed. As she made her way toward him, she noticed he was dressed better than she was, pleated linen and a raw silk camp shirt. A sprinkling of silver now threaded through his tight dark curls. Underneath the curls peeked a broad, white forehead. His face below the shade line of his Stetson was tan and clean shaven. When their eyes met, she felt it, that hint of long-suffering love for her. Smiling at her, his ears blushed. Yeah, she thought, she still had that effect on him. She could fall in love with this man. Approaching him, she lifted her glass, about to congratulate him on the merger of the two farms' vineyards, but *ting, ting, ting,* someone interrupted by tapping silver against crystal. "Everybody, gather 'round. The Baileys have an announcement." A tipsy Wyatt stepped in front of the stone hearth. "Jonnie? Somebody find Jonnie. Ethan. Where's Ethan?"

Ethan excused himself to take a place beside Wyatt. The silence in the room amplified the delighted squeals of children at play outside on a summer night. Her second sip of the house wine had Iris looking for a place to set the glass. She wished she had Wyatt Bailey's faith in the Fallam County grape. She'd tasted a lot of wine in her travels and the only thing a Fallam County grape was good for was Bert's jelly. She watched as Jonnie took her place beside her brother. Had Jonnie lost weight? The woman actually glowed.

"Today is a very happy day for us here at Bailey Farms. If he was alive, today would have been our father's ninety-fifth birthday. A toast to Dad."

Iris lifted her glass then pretended to sip the wine.

"Now, I'm the oldest male of our family." Facing Jonnie, he said, "But we all know who wears the pants in this family."

A polite titter rippled through the room.

"But we also know that Jonnie is a traditional woman and she's asked me to make the happy announcement." Lifting his glass, he added, "Big Sis, I love you."

Jonnie's head tilted as her tight lips spread across her face. Jonnie and Ethan both were a head taller than Wyatt.

"Today, our family announces that our beloved Jane Cameron, or Jonnie as Daddy nicknamed her," he winked at his big sister and continued, "has accepted a proposal of marriage to Ethan Riley Quinn. A Christmas wedding is planned." Wyatt turned to face his future brother-in-law and said, "Welcome to the family, brother." Facing the room, Wyatt raised his glass and shouted, "To the lovely couple. May the love you are feeling now remain in your hearts always." Turning to face the blushing couple, he backed into the crowd and prompted everyone to join him in applause.

A shocked Iris watched Ethan place his arms around Jonnie's waist and back and kiss her like he didn't care if anyone was watching. And Jonnie responded. As if the moment had been rehearsed, the couple dipped as they finished the kiss.

Hoots and Rebel yells muffled the numbing betrayal and embarrassment that enwrapped Iris. Why hadn't Jonnie said something to her about this? Here she'd just fantasized a romp in the memory hay with Ethan, for crying out loud. She shouldn't have come. The universe had laid out road blocks so she wouldn't — the trip out West, no sitter for Elizabeth — yet she had heeded neither. Heat rose from her chest as her heart quickened. She needed fresh air. Pulling on the sleeve of the man who smelled of cedar shavings standing next to her, she handed him her glass and went to find Elizabeth to take her home.

 MELISSA POWELL GAY

CHAPTER 10 NOW

I 'ON'T KNOW

Iris heard buzzing at her ear as something pressed against the side of her leg. Opening her eyes to pitch black, she searched for the lamp. Then, *clink, splat*. Now the buzzing was on the floor. Feeling for her leg outside of the covers, she discovered a fuzzy ball of wire. Somewhere in the room, the phone stopped buzzing.

"Heyu. I'm not a pillow." She pushed his dead weight away from her sweaty body.

The buzzing renewed. Her hand felt its way to the bedside table again. This time it found the lamp's switch. As light hit the room, her eyes squinted at the *drip, drip* of black coffee wicking from a table scarf. Recovering the phone from the floor, its display silently alerted Iris to the day and time, Tuesday, 3:09 a.m. The recent call list revealed a message waiting from area code 423.

Pulling at her damp pajama top, she noticed the absence of the constant drone of the A/C unit in the window. She leaned against the edge of the bed and listened to the message.

"I'm Officer Walton. Please return my call." The last word was pronounced "cawww." Elmer Fudd must have fat-fingered a wrong number. Deleting the message, she tossed the phone on the bed and went looking for something to sop up the spilled coffee.

Tamping a towel over the stained carpet, snippets of Saturday evening rolled through her head as they had all day Sunday and Monday: Elizabeth's protest as the kitten she was holding was ripped away, laughing faces, Jonnie and Ethan holding glasses in a toast, Elizabeth driving them home. No, wait, that last one she must have dreamt. She rubbed her face. How could her two closest Mt Pleasant friends betray her like that? She'd brooded all day Sunday, expecting Jonnie to call with excuses and apologies. But she'd received not one word, not a single peep. On Monday, she tried to cry but couldn't. She drove out to Mr. Henry's farm and shot at the hay bale.

Falling back on the bed, she spread her arms and legs over the covers. The phone buzzed underneath her. Looking at the display, she recognized Officer Fudd's number.

"Look, Elmer, you've got the wrong number. Stop calling—."

"I'm Officer Walton. I'm lookin' for a Mrs. Iris Lee."

"This is Iris Lee. Who are you?"

Beeps and radio chatter confirmed Officer Walton's line of work.

"Knoxville Police, ma'am. We got a young man here who claims he belongs to you."

"I'm sorry, I live in Virginia. You've got the wrong number."

"This young man, just a boy, actually, says you're his guardian," Officer Walton insisted.

"Pal, you've got the wrong person. I'm not a 'Mrs.' And I don't have any children."

"You are Iris Lee of Grove Street, Mt Pleasant, Virginia?"

"Is this some kind of scam?"

"Ma'am, the boy was found inside a locked up Fast N Go. He says Mrs. Iris Lee of Mt Pleasant is his legal guardian. You need to

     MELISSA POWELL GAY

come down and get your boy or else we're going to have to lock him up with the adults for the rest of the night."

"Sir, I've never been to Knoxville."

"Ma'am, I'm telling you that this boy claims he belongs to you."

"What's his name?"

"Says his name is Jake. Ain't got no ID on him," the officer said.

"I'm sorry but I don't know anyone by that name. You've got me mixed up with someone else." She disconnected the phone and pulled herself from the bed. "Heyu, I don't see how people live with teenagers."

He rolled onto his other side and sighed.

She found a pair of cropped leggings and a racer back tank top in her chest of drawers. Might as well go for a run, since there was no chance of getting back to sleep. Her running routes took her all around Mt Pleasant, always ending at the Victorian ironworks water fountain in the middle of Matilda Park. She sprinted the quarter mile around the fountain, searching for Marine Mike. Catching her breath, she realized he wouldn't be there for another hour. She followed the walkway over to Court Street. Jonnie's car was parked in front of the Bailey Building. Stepping out into the street, she searched for lights in the third-floor apartment windows but found none. She reminded herself to call Jonnie to see if she'd heard any news from Benny about — then it hit her. The kid in Knoxville, Tennessee, was probably Damian Lee, Bennie's grandson.

After several phone calls to California and Knoxville, Iris pieced together what had happened. Damian, a.k.a. Jake, left Benny's house midday on Friday with his friend Doug. According to Doug, they were headed for Las Vegas. But Doug changed his mind and left Damian with his thumb in the air at a Nevada truck stop.

At the Knoxville Police Station, Damian claimed he caught a ride with a family on their way to Cherokee National Forest — a straight shot across Route 40. Something didn't smell right about his tale but Iris didn't really want to ask too many questions in front of Officer Walton and the juvenile correction officer.

Hours earlier, upon discovering where her nephew was, a hysterical Sarah had pleaded for Iris to drive to Tennessee to retrieve him. Iris didn't see what the fuss was all about. The kid had managed to hitchhike across the lower forty-eight on his own. Therefore, she reasoned with Sarah, he could probably find his way to the local airport and fly back to L.A. without much trouble. But Sarah appealed to a higher court. Bert called Iris to ask if she needed somebody to ride with her to get the child out of jail. That's how Iris found herself driving, with Heyu riding shotgun, four hours down Interstate 81 to shuttle the kid twenty miles to the local airport.

"Let's get something to eat," she said in the station's parking lot.

Damian shrugged a nonverbal consent.

As they sat in the car eating fast food, Iris caught Damian slipping fries to Heyu, now in the back seat. "Please don't do that," she said. She pinched her nose and added, "Fried food gives him gas. S. B. Ds. Silent but deadlies."

Damian snorted.

"His name's Heyu. Why did you tell the police your name is Jake?"

"I 'on't know," he said. He plugged his phone into the power outlet.

"Do you prefer 'Jake' to 'Damian'?"

Not responding to her question, he scrolled sites on his phone. "Southwest Airlines has a direct flight to L.A. leaving Dulles Airport tonight. Can you take me to Dulles?"

Her jaw dropped. The nerve of this kid. Where does he get off on treating her like his own private taxi service? She pointed at her windshield and said, "Dulles is seven hours that way." She waved at her side window and added, "I can drop you off at the bus station."

"Fine," he squeaked.

Hearing the fear in his reply, she refrained from asking him why he told the police she was his guardian. Blowing out a tired breath, she said, "Where to? Greyhound or Grove Street. Those are your options."

A continuous begging grunt floated from the back seat.

"Or, I could drop you off at a rest stop on 81. You could hitch a ride to Dulles from there," she said. She prayed he wouldn't call her bluff.

He busied himself with stuffing empty wrappers into the fast-food bag. "I guess I'll ride with you awhile." He scrolled over the map on his phone. "Roanoke, I'll get off there and hitch to Dulles." Looking straight ahead, he stuffed earbuds in his ears, dismissing her.

"Suit yourself," she said. He was a Lee, all right. He was stubborn, unable to ingratiate himself to anyone, especially his own family. Why didn't he just come out and say he'd come to spend time in Mt Pleasant?

The two hundred and eighty mile ride home was quiet and gratefully odorless. As the car turned off the interstate and headed for home, Iris didn't bother waking the sleeping runaway.

After breakfast on Wednesday morning, Iris' phone reminded her of the homeowner association meeting that evening. Turning the calendar alarm off, she watched Vinnie poke at the window A/C unit with a flat-head screwdriver. He used the bottom of his T-shirt to wipe sweat from his brow. She forced her eyes to remain on his face and not his exposed and very buff abdominal region so close to the proximity of an unmade bed.

"Your hair!" she shouted. "You cut off all your braids." Vinnie's bohemian tentacles enhanced his romantic mystique and endeared him to every Mt Pleasant woman, young and not so young. Female renters approached Iris daily requesting a visit from Vinnie to fix their broken whatevers.

Vinnie waved a hand over his short curls.

"Why'd you cut them off?"

"Ludie says if I'm to be taken seriously as a businessman, I shouldn't have dreadlocks."

"Can't argue with that advice," Iris said.

Pointing at the electrical outlet with the screwdriver, he said, "You should think about rewiring."

"Why not? Add it to the list. Bad plumbing, drafty windows, leaking refrigerator. Just like its owners, the house is falling out of warranty."

To accommodate Damian, who had slept on the sofa in Mr. Henry's library, Iris had two choices: clean out the "guest" bedroom, which was her mother's designated sewing room crammed with a lifetime of hobby detritus, or box up Mr. Henry's few personal effects.

Putting Damian in Mr. Henry's bedroom won out. She emptied her father's chest of drawers of socks, underwear and sweaters in the first cardboard box. She set a dried-up leather valet box filled with tie pins, cuff links, several Timex watches and a Big Ben pocket watch in the second box along with a pile of belts and suspenders. She wasn't ready to toss anything out, no matter how useless. She feared she'd no longer feel his presence if the things he used every day, like his shaving kit littered with loose styptic pencil nubs, were carted off like so much unwanted stuff. Opening his closet, she was confronted with a life's worth of shirts, trousers, jackets, overcoats and his wedding suit. Piling shoes and boots on top of his Army trunk, she pushed the boxes inside and locked the closet door. "I'll go through it all later," she said to herself. "I can't now." She swallowed down the lump in her throat as she hooked the skeleton key on its nail at the top of the door frame.

She checked the single drawer in the bedside table and discovered a deck of cards, a copy of Charles Lindbergh's autobiography and a silver dual picture frame of her parents on their wedding day on one side and her first-grade portrait on the other. She sat on the bed and had a good cry. She left the book in the drawer. Maybe Mr. Henry's ghost would inspire Damian to read a book.

Doing what he did best, Damian ignored everyone and everything by spending the morning on the front porch with his head over his Android, occasionally holding it up as if to snag a random cellular signal. By late afternoon he was sitting on the sidewalk curb in front of the house.

Bert arrived in time to prepare an early supper of sweet peas floating in a buttery cream broth and cornbread. After Bert's brief prayer of thanks over the food, Damian got up from the dining room table and went into the kitchen. He returned with a bowl, corn flakes and a plastic milk jug from the refrigerator. He poured cereal and milk into the bowl then turned the backside of the cereal box so he could read its content. The stillness of the dining room amplified his munching. Iris stared at him, willing him to see her displeasure. She held her temper because she knew if she spoke of his rude manners, he'd only smirk, implying that he'd won the battle. She watched him as he gulped the last of the milk from the bowl, pushed away from the table and left the room; the jug of milk and cereal box abandoned.

Lucky for Damian, her phone reminded her again of the evening meeting at the inn.

When retired New York transplant Joe Turner converted the mammoth Victorian a couple of doors down from the Lees to a small inn, he and the Lees' next-door neighbor, Mr. Wingfield, created the Grove Street Historical Society. The Society, as it came to be known, met once a month at alternating homes along the stately street of early twentieth-century houses. As she walked to the inn, Iris recalled Mr. Henry grumbling about Joe badgering him to attend the gatherings. "Passel of busybodies with a license to snoop around in their neighbors' drawers," he'd complained on more than one occasion. Now, Joe badgered Iris to not only attend the gatherings but to host one. She'd be ready for him tonight when he inquired as to the availability of the Lee house for next month's meeting. She'd be able to report with sincere conviction that the Lee house plumbing wasn't up to handling all the flushing required of the Society's members. Silver linings, Iris, she reminded herself, always search for the silver linings.

Much like her current circumstances since leaving her executive position at the bank, Iris was bored with the Society. How many times and ways could a group talk about dog poop receptacles and sidewalk repairs? They sat around talking about what should be done but never acted on any of the ideas. The circular debate caused Iris' eye to twitch. But, like that movie where the character relived the same day over and over, she went to the meetings and hoped for different results.

Entering the inn, Iris heard creaking floors and crowd murmurs from the back of the house. The meeting would be heavily attended because planning was underway for the Society's main event, the Matilda Park Fourth of July Parade and Picnic. The Society had adopted the park. Members mended benches, picked up trash and tended the flower beds.

"There's Mt Pleasant's prodigal daughter," Candice Garland greeted Iris at the sign-in table. George and Candice Garland were retired academics and proud members of the Green Party. Most

     MELISSA POWELL GAY

county residents ran the other way whenever they saw George and Candice because the pair couldn't offer a simple "hello" without working into a casual greeting their belief in the imminent apocalyptic fate of nature and all mankind, even in off-year election cycles. They were as rabid as Pentecostal snake-handlers, Mr. Henry used to say.

"How's our favorite capitalist's daughter this evening?" George asked.

"Oh, I managed to evict at least a dozen people today, mostly babies. And you? How many young people have you convinced to strive for mediocrity this week?"

"Now, now." He shook his finger at her then pointed at the refreshment table. "Have you tried the Baileys' co-op chardonnay? It's actually quite good."

"I don't drink on a school night," she said.

Their laugher mocked each other.

Iris glanced around the high-ceilinged room. Among the usual clique was the town's appointed mayor, Robert "Kooch" Kaluchi, dressed in his Big and Tall suit complete with cuff links and a gold cross draped over his tie's Windsor knot. Until a couple of months ago, Kooch's firm managed her father's properties. Then she fired him. Hiring Vinnie Quinn as a replacement was panning out. Proving himself as a skilled carpenter, the Adonis with a tool belt showed much promise as a project manager as well. Iris and Jonnie were working on a master plan to bring Lee Properties into the twenty-first century. In the next few months, she'd decide if she was going to stay in Mt Pleasant or hand things over to Vinnie and leave for the real world again.

"Everybody, find a seat. We've got loads to cover this evening," Joe announced. "Mayor Kaluchi's here to help us with our parade and picnic planning. And, we've got really, really good news about the pooper-scooper project."

An hour later, as George Garland preached the gospel of using bio-degradable doggy poop bags, Iris rose from her chair, moved to the back of the room and stood next to Joe. She felt the stares of Mr. and Mrs. Wren, who lived on the opposite end of Grove, boring into her forehead. Before the meeting came to order, they'd cornered her with questions about what they called her "low-income encroachment" project, which abutted their property. The bank's newest president, Travis English, was married to their daughter. He must have given them a heads-up on her loan applications.

Scrolling the pictures on her phone, she stopped at the one she'd taken of Damian sitting on the front porch with Heyu. "Meet my cousin's grandson. Bert's nephew. He's staying with us for a few weeks."

Joe chuckled. "I see he got the Lee jug handles."

Noticing how the picture accentuated the boy's ears, she whispered, "Yeah, I see what you mean. Can we chat for a minute?"

In the front parlor, Iris continued, "His parents aren't in his life so he's got an attitude."

"Parents got nothing to do with it. Bad attitude is part of being a teenager. Trust me, I raised three boys," he said.

"This kid is a trouble magnet. Doesn't matter where he is, it finds him. Can you keep an eye out for him? You see him doing something he shouldn't be, shoot me a text."

"Will do. Want me to ask the others to watch out for him?"

"Actually, I'd prefer you didn't. You know how they get." The Society tended to exaggerate and overshare whatever they witnessed in the name of vigilance. She wouldn't want their distortions to fulfill Bennie's prophecies of Damian's predestination for perdition.

"Yes, I do." Joe rolled his eyes. "How's Mrs. Lee?" He asked

     MELISSA POWELL GAY

as he plumped a pillow on the parlor settee. On several occasions before Iris returned to look after her folks, Joe had herded the wandering woman back to her home.

"She's … had better days. Thanks for looking out for her and pop."

"Don't mention it," he said. "You know, once I got past that crusty outlaw snarl of his, I was able to see that your dad was a truly fair person. I mean, really, he treated everyone the same."

"Yeah, with contempt."

"No, I mean he helped people. He really, really helped people. When I was short on cash and needed a new van, the bank wouldn't extend my credit. I thought seriously about closing this place down. Then one day, out of the blue, I get this letter from Tanner Ford telling me my van was ready. I finally figured out what he'd done. When I got enough money scraped together to pay him back, he told me to save the money and use it to buy the next one. Best lesson in equity building I ever got."

"I'm told he did a lot of that. His idea of philanthropy, I guess. He didn't do it for the attention, that's for sure."

"Yeah, I can see that now. It got me thinking about how I could help others. Do you know Miss Wanda?"

"Cares for homeless ladies?"

"Yeah," Joe said. "She needed a van for shopping and getting her clients around. I gave her the van when the time came for me to upgrade. Now, I'm looking for other ways to help. You know, we should do something to recognize his contributions to Mt Pleasant. Don't you think?"

"No, I don't," she replied. "If I learned anything from my father's life, I've learned that helping others help themselves is what makes us decent human beings. Crowing and tweeting about taking a can of soup to a cocktail party for a community pantry only exposes how foolish we really are."

"Iris, you're a philosopher," Joe joked.

"Nope, just Henry Lee's daughter," she said. "Thanks for keeping an eye out for Damian."

She slipped out the front door and stood on the sprawling porch. Guests of the inn talked softly while rocking in wicker chairs. The faint scent of cigar smoke and honeysuckle curled in the air.

From the inn's porch, Iris could see the backside of the town's safety command center. Ethan's cruiser was parked in the spot reserved for the chief. She decided to drop by to let him know about Damian and his circumstances.

She knocked on the metal door frame. While on his phone, he waved her in and pointed at the banker's chair in front of his desk. Waiting for him to wrap up his call, she surveyed his office. Ethan Quinn was as neat as a stack of clean, folded laundry. Every book, softball trophy, and framed citation was polished and in its place. The crown of his Stetson balanced atop a narrow occasional table next to the office doorway, the place it belonged whenever it wasn't on his head, no doubt.

They shared a similar upbringing, raised by strict, often ill-tempered fathers. However, being a boy-child, the belt was rarely spared on him. Iris guessed the whippings and a stint in the Army made Ethan obsess with control over his surroundings. Maybe he didn't tell her about his engagement to Jonnie because of how her own loud reaction would affect his ordered life. Was she really that crabby?

Hanging up the phone, Ethan leaned forward in his chair, which squeaked under his weight.

"What happened to you Saturday?" he asked.

"Had to get Mom back."

Folding his hands on the desk, he said, "Iris, we wanted to tell you, but—."

"Hey, no worries," she interrupted loudly. "I'm happy for you guys. Congratulations." Not wanting to trip the light fandango around their convoluted relationship and his pending marriage to her best friend, she rushed to change the subject. "I came by to talk with you about something else."

He nodded for her go on.

"Did I ever tell you about Bennie's family?" She leaned across the desk and shared a photo of Bert and Sarah and her family that she'd taken at the airport. She watched him as he viewed the photo. Back in his Andy Taylor's, her name for his polyester uniform, he was her old friend, her big brother again. Date Ethan Quinn? What was she thinking?

He looked up from the photo. "So Bennie finally accepted Bert as his sister?"

"Just barely," Iris said. "Bert and his daughter Sarah have hit it off." She scrolled to the next picture, the one of Damian on the porch with Heyu. "This is Bennie's grandson. He's visiting. He's got a wild streak in him."

"That comes honest," Ethan grinned.

"He's known to Orange County Police. Petty stuff. Bennie wanted to get him out of L.A. before the gangs got to him. You keep an eye out for me?"

"I'll try. How old is he?" Ethan asked.

"Fourteen going on 25," she said. "He's at that age where he's seeing what he can get away with. Hitched from L.A. to Knoxville. Fell asleep in a convenience store and got locked in. Owner found him, called the police."

Ethan grinned again. "Sounds like something I'd have done at that age."

"And there's something else," she said. "His parents are sort of

M.I.A. His mom, Bennie's other daughter, is in rehab for the second time, and his daddy is in a gang. He's Mexican."

"I see."

"I'm thinking of asking Vinnie to let him shadow him around while he's here. You think he'd be OK with that?"

"Why you askin' me? Ask Vinnie."

Iris hesitated. "I never got the whole story about Vinnie's mom. Did he spend much time with his mother's family?" While stationed in Texas, Ethan had married a woman named Lupida from across the border. He never shared with Iris why the two divorced or why Vinnie, along with his wife Ludie, moved to Mt Pleasant and now lived with his father. She assumed he had done it for the opportunities but never wanted to pry into Ethan's life outside of Mt Pleasant just as he never asked about hers. Staring into his clear and honest green eyes, she was confused, again. What did she actually feel for this man?

Ethan looked away.

"Tell me it's none of my business," Iris said, "but I thought that since they both have a Mexican parent they would have something in common."

"I'm no social worker, but a boy, especially a fourteen-year-old, needs a positive role model in his life. Being Mexican ain't got anything to do with it. If he can, I'm sure Vinnie'll help out. What's the boy's name?"

"Damian," she said. "Bennie's not the world's best grandfather. When I was there, he ragged on about the deficiencies of people with darker skin pigment."

"That sounds like him."

"Sarah, the boy's aunt, and her family treat him like a pariah."

"That's sad to hear."

"Don't feel too sorry for him. The little punk gives as good as

     MELISSA POWELL GAY

he gets. Unfortunately, he's inherited the Lee sulk. Aside from berating me with the silent treatment for not driving him all the way from Knoxville to Dulles so he could catch a direct flight back to L.A., he's maybe said three words since he's been here."

Ethan laughed. "He's gotten under your skin."

"Little twerp has the manners of a sloth."

Ethan laughed again. "Welcome to parenthood."

"Any advice on how to interact with a teenager with L.A. street cred?"

"You've got the right idea, asking Vinnie to help out. But don't try to force them to find common ground in their Hispanic background. Without being from that culture it could backfire on you. For once, I agree with Bennie Lee. Mt Pleasant's a good place for him to work things out for himself."

"Thanks for the advice," Iris said.

"What's the word on the general's medal? Jonnie said you weren't successful in donating it to the French museum."

"Long story. I decided to have Sotheby's sell it for me," she said.

Tapping the picture of Damian on her phone, he asked, "Is it secured?"

"It's locked up in Mr. Henry's gun safe." Iris stood and walked to the doorway. Facing him, she added, "You and Jonnie had better invite me to your wedding, even if the plans call for elopement. That's all I've got to say about that." Then she left.

Back at the house Iris poured herself a glass of iced tea, then opened her laptop while sitting at the kitchen table. Before she forgot, she wanted to dash off an email to her Sotheby's contacts about auctioning the medallion. The library foundation ladies called on her for a contribution and she wanted to follow through with the proclamation she'd made in Paris: sell the medallion and give all the proceeds to the new library building fund. Searching for her

Sotheby's contact information, she noticed the file icons on the laptop's screen had been moved around. She opened a file containing financial information and noticed the file's last open date showed today's date. She hadn't used her computer all day. Someone had hacked into it. Who could it be? She retraced her steps, realizing that her computer had been in the house ever since she'd returned from Paris.

Maybe Damian used it. She tapped at Mr. Henry's bedroom door before opening it. Light streaming from the hallway revealed an empty bed. A few minutes later she stood in the middle of Mr. Henry's library wondering where the boy had gone. An hour later Iris was driving on Route 220 toward Roanoke, stopping at every truck stop and restaurant looking for a fourteen-year-old kid with a wiry haired dog.

CHAPTER 11 NOW
GROVE HOUSE RULES

The groaning step, fourth from the bottom of the staircase, woke Iris. Someone was coming up the stairs. The dawn peeping through her bedroom window spotlighted the baseball bat propped in the corner. Ready to play ball, she stepped into the hallway. No one was there. Quietly, she slipped into Mr. Henry's room, next to hers; no Damian. Back in the hallway she gripped the bat high over her head, heart racing and ready to swing. She paused to listen. Splashing water alerted her that the intruder was in the bathroom.

"Damian is that you?"

No answer.

Splashing water echoed from the tiled room. Her breathing calmed, she walked toward the bathroom, more curious than scared.

She faced the entrance. "Where've you been?"

Heyu turned from his upstairs water bowl and stared up at her.

"You left the house last night. You didn't call, you didn't leave a note." Laughing, she propped the bat against the wall and reached down to ruffle the fur around his neck. "Pee-yew, whose garbage bin did you crawl into this time? I guess you know this means you're getting another bath. Is Damian with you?"

Heyu shook from nose to tail, then ran between her legs and out of the room.

Washing her hands at the sink, she called out to him, "Don't even think about sitting on any furniture until you get a bath, mister." She called for Damian from the top of the stairs but, still no answer. When she went to her bedroom to dress, she smelled Heyu again. Cowering on her bed, he sneezed, then nuzzled into her pillow. Now she understood her old man's rule on why dogs stayed on the porch. The bedclothes were covered in grime and reeked of garbage can. But she couldn't stay mad at him. With Jonnie getting married and Manny chasing other women, Heyu's status had been bumped from shotgun rider back to best friend. She commanded him to follow her down the back stairs. "And where has that partner in crime of yours, Damian, gone? Huh? Has he run away, or is he hiding from us?"

Banishing Heyu to the backyard, she checked her phone for messages from Damian and found none. To search for clues about where he might have gone, she tripped up the stairs and into Mr. Henry's room.

"Mom! What are you doing in here?"

Elizabeth, with a cloud of white hair scattered in every direction and her nightgown on backward and inside out, stood in front of the opened gun safe, holding the awkward medallion her father-in-law had given her. "What is this thing doing in your father's gun cabinet?"

"Put it back, Ma. We're keeping it in there so nobody can steal it," Iris said.

"I don't see why anybody would want to steal that thing. It's ugly as sin," Elizabeth said.

   MELISSA POWELL GAY

Ignoring her mother, Iris surveyed the room. The kid was a slob. A crumpled comic book and a lonely sock peeked out from under the unmade bed. Candy wrappers and an empty sports drink bottle loitered around the trash bin. His backpack was wedged between the wall and her father's rolltop desk. She realized her trip to the truck stop was a stupid move. If Damian was running away or going to Dulles Airport, he'd have taken his stuff with him.

"Mom?" she asked as she looked up from the pack. But Elizabeth had left the room.

How did the gun safe get unlocked? Iris remembered tugging on the latch handle to make sure it was secure when she moved Damian into the room the day before. Someone had opened it. Bile rose in her throat. She envisioned the internet headlines, "Guardian forces teen to sleep with guns." She was going to jail for reckless child endangerment, no doubt about it.

A list of all the guns was duct taped to the inside safe door along with a pencil nub dangling from a cotton string. Systematically, she compared the hand guns, rifles and shotguns to the list scrolled out in Mr. Henry's immaculate cursive. Twenty-seven of them were there. All but Mr. Henry's favorite, his Army-issued Colt .45. Iris remembered using it but she didn't remember putting it back into the safe. Maybe it was still in her car. Or, maybe she did put it back and Damian took it. But how did he get the combination to the safe? She recalled the rearranged icons on her computer. Did he hack into her computer and steal the combination to the safe? That combination was stored in the same electronic file as all of her financial account passwords, on the same Word document.

Still distracted, Iris poured corn flakes into Elizabeth's cereal bowl as Vinnie pushed his ultralight hand cart into the kitchen. Two new A/C units were strapped to the cart, one for her room and one for Elizabeth's.

"I found a good deal for you when I was at the hardware store picking up supplies yesterday." He handed her the receipts and a list of expenses for her to approve. Elizabeth coyly smiled at Vinnie as he sat next to her and across from Iris. He updated Iris on repair and maintenance jobs. Then he offered her his pen to initial the items on the list.

Returning the pen with the list, she said, "I went by the station and saw your dad yesterday."

Vinnie stuffed the paper and pen into his beat-up leather commuter bag.

Good Lord, here she was about to repeat Damian's juvenile transgressions, perhaps tainting his future by revealing his unfortunate circumstances. She was no better than the neighborhood watch snoops. There was no "smoking gun," so to speak, that proved Damian had taken Mr. Henry's gun, had broken into the safe, or had rearranged the icons on her computer.

"You went by to see my dad?" Vinnie prompted.

"I asked your dad — Bennie's grandson Damian is staying with us for a few weeks and I asked your dad if you'd be interested in hanging out with him."

"Hanging out?" Vinnie asked.

Flustered, she got up from the table to put the milk away. Leaving out the part about the two sharing a Hispanic heritage, she went on, "I have no earthly idea what fourteen-year-old boys do with their summers. What they like. What do you think of the idea of him shadowing you for a few days? You know, show him what an honest day's work is like."

"What does he like to do?"

Leaning over the butcher's block that divided the kitchen, she puffed her cheeks and slowly shook her head sideways. "Beats me.

     MELISSA POWELL GAY

Your guess is as good as mine. I know he likes his phone. He sleeps with it."

Vinnie's smile turned up on one side. "I've got to go over to Franklin County to get some lumber. Maybe he'd like to hang out at the lake's beach. Kids hang out there. Looks like it's going be a nice day." Vinnie stood to leave.

"That sounds perfect," Iris said. Fidgeting with a kitchen towel, she unfolded then refolded it while saying, "The only problem is I've kinda lost him."

"*Que?*" Vinnie asked.

"He's not here. When I came back last night from seeing your dad, he was gone. His aunt says he does that a lot."

"Want me to help you look for him?" Vinnie offered.

She waved him off, "No, you need to get on with your day. But you could give me some pointers on where he might be."

"Aye." Vinnie scratched the back of his head then snapped his fingers. "You know the rusty chin-up bars on the back side of the challenge course? Next to the tire swings?"

"Yeah."

"The park shed is behind them, near a grove of trees. The trees buffer the park from Main Street. I've seen kids hanging out near the shed." He hunched his shoulders and added, "Smoking pot."

"Yeah, I know the area. You think he could have hooked up with some local kids?"

"It's possible. Check the high school courts. I wouldn't worry, he can't get into too much trouble in Mt Pleasant."

"Bert's coming over to sit with Mom while I go look for him. Thanks for the tips about the park and the school. I'll start there."

"I'll keep an eye out for him." He turned to Elizabeth and said, "Miss Elizabeth, a pleasure seeing you again."

The old lady smiled as she lifted her hair away from her face with the back of her hand. Even her mother, half out of her mind, was enchanted by the young man. Iris thanked him with a nod.

A few minutes later, Mr. Henry's Olds plodded up the driveway. Iris met Bert at the carport. "Mom's in the kitchen," she said. "I'm going to drive over to the park then to the basketball courts by the high school."

"Ah, don't worry about the poor boy, Iris. He'll find his way home sooner or later."

"That's easy for you to say. You're not responsible for him. From what I've heard, social services doesn't look too kindly on adults allowing their children to roam the streets all night."

"Give him some room, Iris. He'll be home for breakfast," Bert said. "He's not a bad kid."

The thought of the missing gun and the fact that someone had tampered with her computer rankled her again. She got up in Bert's face. "You might think differently when he shoots another kid with Mr. Henry's wheel gun!"

"What's that suppose to mean?"

"He broke into my computer and got the combination to Mr. Henry's safe last night and stole his .45." There, she said it out loud. She was accusing Damian, a mere boy, of grand larceny.

"My word," Bert's eyes swelled. "I'll go with you."

"No! I need you to stay with Mom. I'll call you when I find him," she said as she started down the driveway. Turning back, she called to Bert. "See, this is why I didn't want to get involved with the Bennie Lee Drama Show. If anything happens to anyone, I'm responsible."

Her anger exploded. She was mad at Bert, furious with Bennie, resentful of Jonnie and Ethan, unforgiving of Manny and his affair with his Miss French Bootie Shaker. Why couldn't she just go back to processing mortgages for New York real estate dowagers

     MELISSA POWELL GAY

and negotiating leases with Texas tycoons? That work was so much easier.

From Court Street, she turned right on Main and drove north past the corner of the Bailey Building. The Main Street entrance to the park veered right. Her car slid into a space and she walked into the park. Following the gravel trail to the backside acreage, she spied the park shed, a little red cedar-siding box sitting on concrete blocks. Her anger still fuming, she increased her pace to a slow jog.

Focused on the shed, she didn't see the walker coming toward her. *BAM!* The full frontal collision caused her and the other person to fall backward.

"Oh, oh, oh," the woman groaned as she rolled on the trail. "My head, my head."

Shaking out the stars, Iris scrambled up and helped the older woman to her feet, then she brushed herself off. Her single mission of finding Damian trumped the white pain on her forehead; she struck out again at a quick clip toward the shed.

"Well, I'm just fine. Thanks for askin', you butthead," the woman called after Iris. "Idiot! Watch where you're going next time!" she screeched.

"Sor-ry," Iris called from the trail as she kept going.

When she made it to the shed, she scanned the area for kids Damian's age. Toddlers were playing in the grass on the other side of the tire swings with a couple of teenage girls standing by. One was preoccupied with her phone while the other braided her hair.

Iris approached the hair braider, "Excuse me, were you here in the park last night?"

The other girl raised her head from her browsing trance.

Iris asked, "Hi, I'm looking for a kid named Damian. Have you by any chance met a new guy here in the park? Last night?"

"We aren't allowed in the park after dark," the first one finally spoke, her rolling eyes implying that this fact was as obvious as the blue in the sky.

"Were you here at all yesterday? Did you meet a boy named Damian?"

"Our parents say we can't talk to the kids who hang out near the shed," the second girl said.

"Why's that?"

"'Cause they do drugs," again, the eye rolls.

Great, Iris thought, in town less than twenty-four hours and the kid's committed grand larceny and discovered where the shiftless hang out.

"If you meet a boy about your age hanging out here, dark curly hair and brown skin, brown eyes, floppy ears, goes by the name of Damian, tell him Iris is looking for him and for him to call her."

The two, like cats, slowly wandered away in opposite directions and circled the toddlers, loudly encouraging them not to play with the brown things buried in the sandbox.

Iris walked over to the shed. The door handles were strapped with a chain and padlock. She called out his name and waited. The chatter of the children echoed back to her from the grassy playground. Sighing, she gave up and found her way back to her car. Her head was pounding now. She flipped the car's visor down and lightly patted the growing red knot on her forehead with her fingers.

"OK, Iris," she said to the knot, "you're a fourteen-year-old kid who is absolutely convinced you are smarter than anyone over the age of thirty. Where would you go if you weren't hitchhiking on I-81?" She started her car and drove the mile or so over to the county's only high school. All the courts, basketball and tennis, were empty. No one was around at the track or soccer fields, either. Making a U-turn in the bus parking lot, she drove back to the center of town, parked in front of Chunky's, and fed the meter. Midmorning and the place was hopping with the breakfast club on their way to court across the street.

Iris sat at the table under the front window sipping a cup of Chunky's high-test. The view included the Main and Court Street intersection and the ever-faithful Memorial Solider of the Confederate Veteran. She watched people come and go as she chewed on a biscuit. Where was he? What if he was hurt and needed help? What if he shot someone? How did parents of teenagers manage to stay sane?

Her phone lit up with Bert's number.

"He just came in the back door. See, I told you, sweet pea. Just give the boy some room."

"I'm going to stop by Jonnie's office for a few minutes and will be home soon. Tell him not to leave the house."

Claire Brown, Jonnie's assistant, escorted Iris to the second-floor conference room in the back of the building, with its view of Matilda Park's fountain. The fountain reminded her of New York's Central Park. She yearned to be back in her old life; working outrageous hours all week, then spending every minute of every hour during the weekend indulging in things like a day spa mud bath or flying to London for a weekend just because.

"Good morning," Jonnie said. "What happened to your head? You look like you stepped on a rake."

"Collided with a crabby fossil," Iris replied. "Can I use your conference monitor to talk with Manny? Internet connection at Grove House is too slow."

"Sure," Jonnie said as she sat at the table. "But we've got a meeting in here in twenty minutes. Iris, something's wrong. You want to talk about it?"

Avoiding what she thought was the obvious — Jonnie failing to tell her that she was getting engaged to Ethan, Iris said, "Bennie's grandson is visiting for a few weeks."

"I know. Ethan told me," Jonnie said. She blushed at the reference to her intimate relationship.

In the quietness that followed, Iris figured out that her best friend wasn't going to offer an explanation or excuse on why she hadn't told Iris personally about the engagement, acting like the whole thing was none of her business. Well, it was her business. Ethan was in love with her, not Jonnie, and had been since they were kids. To Iris, the news of their engagement was a betrayal by both Jonnie and Ethan.

Iris said, "His name is Damian and he ran away last night."

"What?"

"He's back at the house now but he stayed out all night. Fourteen years old. Honestly, Jonnie, the child needs some serious adult supervision. His Aunt Sarah says he's O.D.D. Whatever that means. And having never been a parent, I'm not exactly qualified for the job."

"Iris Lee," Jonnie said, "you managed how many people when you were at the bank? Thousands?"

"It's not the same."

"Suck it up. Don't let the kid control the situation." She tapped on her e-tablet and said, "Now, when do you want to review last month's 'I' and 'E' numbers? Income's up, expenses are way down. Firing Kaluchi's firm really helped your bottom line. I hadn't realized how much he was costing you. At this rate, Lee Properties will be able to pay off its tax debt by the end of the year."

Rubbing the knot again, Iris said, "I don't want to talk about that today. My head is killing me. Did Bennie's lawyer contact you about dropping the lawsuits?"

"Haven't heard a peep. Why?"

"The weaselly vermin." Iris relayed to Jonnie her trip to L.A., Bennie's terminal condition, and her terms for allowing Damian to come for the summer.

"Golly, those are some, eh, unique terms." Jonnie raised an eyebrow.

"You weren't there. He was being his usual horse's butt in front of everybody."

Jonnie shook her head. "From what you've said, sounds like he's got a right to be grouchy. If I was diagnosed with brain cancer, I know I wouldn't be in a very happy mood."

"You don't get it," Iris argued. "Because of what's happening to him, you'd think he'd have a different outlook on things like family. Called his own daughter a whore! And I'm not even saying what he called you."

Jonnie folded her arms and leaned back in her chair. "Iris, I've told you before, you two will never get along. Just let it go."

"I will as soon as he drops his insane lawsuit," she complained.

Knocking on the oak table, Jonnie said, "As soon as I hear from Ulysses, I'll let you know. Make your call to Manny. Say 'hello' for me." She stood to leave.

"It's not going to be that kind of call, I'm afraid," Iris said. While looking out the window at the park's fountain, she told Jonnie about her encounter at the Paris hotel, about seeing Manny and a woman, one much younger than herself, latching onto each other in broad daylight.

"Are you sure it was him?" Jonnie said.

"I'm sure enough. But even if it wasn't him, what kind of relationship do we have? Really?" She rubbed at road rash on her palm from the fall in the park. "The last time we actually saw each other was the day before last Christmas."

"Hear him out. There's probably a reasonable explanation why he was with this woman. A co-worker maybe?"

"Does a co-worker usually ram her tongue down an associate's ear?"

"Take all the time you need. We'll find another place for our meeting. Call me later if you want to do dinner this week."

"Why didn't you tell me?" Iris blurted.

"Tell you what?"

"In the spring you said you and Ethan decided you didn't have time for a relationship. I come to your summer party and find out with the rest of Mt Pleasant's clueless that you're getting married."

"So that's what's eating at you." A slight laugh, then Jonnie said, "He proposed. I accepted."

"Is this some kind of merger?"

"Excuse me?" Jonnie said. She hugged her e-tablet.

"You don't have time for a relationship so you're getting married instead? Is it because you just want to be married to somebody and he happens to be available?"

Jonnie's cheeks reddened. A strand of white hair caught in her blinking eyelashes. Without a word, she left the room.

"That's what I thought," Iris said to herself. "She's not in love with him."

Jonnie reappeared in the doorway. "What did you say?" Wagging her finger at Iris, she said, "You're not going to make this about who I care about. This is about you, Iris With-the-Perfect-Hair Lee. You've been jilted by a — what is Manny to you, anyway? A part-time boyfriend who calls you up for a play date whenever it suits him?" Gripping the arms of the conference chair, Jonnie planted her face inches from Iris'. "Why and who I choose to marry is none of your concern." Jonnie pushed away from the chair. "If I didn't know you any better, I'd say you're jealous. But I do know you and you don't have enough empathy swirling around in that pint-sized body of yours to care about a drowning stray cat much less your best friend's happiness. Turn the lights off when you're finished." And she left.

Iris wedged her hands between her legs and thought about what Jonnie said about their friendship, about her relationship with Manny.

They'd agreed from the beginning that it was an open relationship. Clearly, from what she saw in Paris, Manny had moved on. Could she? She took a deep breath and dialed his international number. All of her angst for naught, she got a call block signal. She hung up and called his sister, Mary Margaret.

After an obligatory "How are you doing? Fine, and you?" exchange, Iris asked, "You know Manny and I never got a chance to meet up in Paris. Have you talked to him lately?"

"Yeah, he's back in the states," Mary Margaret said, "or he will be by the end of this week. He said he tried to meet up with you a couple of times but you weren't available."

That never happened, Iris thought.

"He said he's got a new boss, she's younger and he's helping her get settled in."

I bet he is. She told herself not to care, to leave it behind. To Mary Margaret she said, "Ask him to call me. Tell him it's about St. Barts."

Along with another couple, Iris and Manny had a standing reservation for a week on the island of St. Bartholomew. Their third year of renting a luxury villa was up for renewal and Carol and Beau from South Carolina were emailing her to confirm whether she and Manny were in. A deposit was needed if the group still planned to meet up the week after Christmas. If she broke up with

Manny now, who got custody of the week in St. Barts? More important, who got custody of Heyu?

Back at Grove House she found everyone napping. Heyu was curled up in a dirt bed he'd scratched out in Elizabeth's kitchen herb garden while Elizabeth and Bert dozed in chairs in the sunroom off the kitchen. She tiptoed up the stairs and spied Damian splayed out on his belly on Mr. Henry's single bed with his earbuds plugged in and his phone cradled in his hand.

Iris silently thanked the universe for the new A/C unit in her bedroom window as cool poofs of air wisped over her. Each day she dedicated an hour or so culling through boxes of ancient business papers she'd discovered in Mr. Henry's bedroom closet, tossing out the mundane. Anything with his handwriting or signature made it harder for her to chuck into the burn pile. Today, she leafed through a shoebox full of random, loose photos of buildings in various states of construction. Few of the photos had people in them. One showed a young Mr. Henry standing beside a black man in a wheelchair in front of a newly constructed The Shops of Mt Pleasant. She set it on her bedside table to show to her mom later. Another one, a Polaroid, depicted a baseball bat nuzzled in a blanket. She didn't want to know what *that* was about. Tossing the Polaroid back in the box, she set the shoebox aside and opened the last of the storage boxes. On top was a proposal Mr. Henry and Kooch Kaluchi's management firm had pitched to the county for a new library the previous year. She thumbed through it. They had proposed to gut the old movie theater and rebuild. Reading the vision statement, she heard her father's voice. He spoke of a library being more than a repository of books but a common meeting place where community ideas grew and thrived. "Henry Lee could write," she murmured.

The medallion's purpose was now even clearer to Iris. She'd

failed in Paris because the cursed thing was meant to ignite the restoration of a once-vibrant town. She tucked the proposal in her business tote bag and called the bank to schedule an appointment with Travis English.

Before she left the house, she taped a note on the leaky refrigerator. It read:

Grove House Rules for the Under Aged and Petulant

Walk Heyu twice a day

Do your own laundry

Keep bedroom clean at all times

NEVER touch the gun safe, its contents, or someone else's personal computer

Shadow employees of Lee Properties four hours a day, four days a week

If staying out all night, let someone know.

FORWARNED: The first time you take a ride in the back seat of a police car, you're on a plane back to L.A. At your own expense. No exceptions.

CHAPTER 12 NOW
STORM'S COMING

Mr. Henry and Artie English established Fallam County Community Bank in the 1990s when a newly minted national bank stepped in one day and bought the two competing local institutions. Both businessmen believed in the need for a locally owned depository to support small businesses and local development. At least that was what the newspaper surmised. Mr. Henry refused to deposit his own money in an institution that sucked all the earned profits out of the county and transferred them to the bulging coffers of New York bankers who were, in his eyes, no more than a higher class of Las Vegas gamblers. He created the bank because he needed a place to park his cash. He hired Artie, the laid-off president of one of the consumed banks, to manage the business.

The new venture was a success. Many county residents and independently owned businesses left the national chain and moved their money to FCCB. After the bank offered common shares to the investing public, Mr. Henry sold his stock. As was his goal all along, the bank was now owned and operated by the community it served.

Travis English, Artie's son and current president of FCCB,

greeted Iris in the lobby. He was a carbon copy of his dad. He even dressed like him, Iris thought. To hide his short arms, Travis folded the cuffs of his button-down shirt underneath the sleeves. His blond hair mixed with silver hosted a sizable cowlick on his forehead, conveying a sense of openness to his customers.

As they shook hands, she said, "I'm here to talk about the new library."

Sliding his hands in his pockets, he waved with his elbow. "Come on back." Past the two teller stations and down a fluorescent lighted hallway, Travis' office shared a glass wall with the computer room.

"What's the total on the new library fund drive?" she asked as she sat.

Travis tapped at computer keys, "Let's see. As of last night's postings, we have two million and some change."

"That's all?" she asked.

"Times are hard, I suppose."

"Mr. Henry's proposal estimated the cost of the land and building at twenty million." She pulled it from her bag. "Do you know why they rejected the proposal?"

"They didn't like the site. They want to put it somewhere in the county."

"But Travis, seventy percent of the county's population lives in Mt Pleasant. Last time I checked, cows don't read."

"Augie Young thinks those number are going to flip in the next twenty years," Travis said.

"Augie Young?"

"You remember the baseball player Gus Young? Played for Detroit. Augie's his son. He's a county supervisor."

"Twenty years? So for the next twenty years the people who live in town will have to drive out to East Jesus to take their kid to story time? That doesn't make sense." The failure of the proposal explained her father's amplified crankiness over the last few months of his life. The new library was to be Mr. Henry's legacy, his gift to Fallam County. The missed opportunity of working with him on such a noble effort saddened her.

Travis was saying, "… meeting minutes from last September. I believe they're on record saying they'll split the capital costs with the foundation. That's when we decided to launch the campaign." He played with a paperclip. "So, less the two we already have, we need about eight to get started. Then, somebody's got to motivate the supervisors to sign off, allocate their funds."

Iris lightly tapped the knot on her head, it was getting bigger. "You got any ideas on how we can raise that kind of capital?"

"Bank's done all it can. We've agreed to carry the cost on the construction account."

"Does the library foundation have a couple million laying around to spare?"

He hesitated. "You'd … have to ask them about that, Iris."

"What we need are a couple of cash happy, nerdy patrons who read murder mysteries."

"Our 'go-to guy' was usually your dad," he said quietly. "We're having some folks over Saturday night for Pen's birthday. Couple of 'em sit on the foundation's board."

"Maybe you can ask them," Iris suggested.

"It would mean more coming from the daughter of Henry Lee," he said.

She'd failed in Paris, she'd failed with Manny, and, in a way, she'd failed at having a relationship with her father. Iris Lee wouldn't fail again. She sighed. Begging people for money wasn't her idea of a fun Saturday night. When she'd left her finance job, she swore she'd never again wear four-inch heels, Spanx, or control top pantyhose.

     MELISSA POWELL GAY

Conceding herself to the cause, she sighed then asked, "What's the dress code?"

Travis laughed. "It's a cookout. The imported beer is the fanciest thing going. Come on by and grab a burger." As he escorted Iris to the lobby, Travis added, "Jonnie and Ethan will be there. Did you know they were engaged? Pen said Jonnie told her last week over lunch that they'd planned to elope, but Wyatt found out about it and insisted on a Christmas wedding."

So every gossip in town found out Jonnie was engaged to the guy who still carried a torch for Iris. How much longer was she going to stay here and take the shunning, she half-joked to herself. As she walked back to Grove House, Iris reasoned that her paranoia was justified because the entire town had colluded against her when no one, not even Jonnie, told her Bert's story.

She found Damian still sprawled on the bed and drooling on his pillow. In her room, she opened up her laptop to check for messages. When she entered her password, the screen went blue and the computer shut down. She pressed the power key again. When she keyed in her password, the screen replied with an invalid password message.

"What's going on?" she murmured. She tried to log on again, same result. Someone had hacked her computer and kicked her out. "Damian!" she yelled. When she didn't get an answer, she ripped the laptop's power cord from the wall socket and carried it into Mr. Henry's room.

Damian's head was lifted off the pillow, his puffy eyes blinking.

"Give it to me?" she demanded.

His eyes blinked some more.

"What's the new password?"

Ignoring Iris, he looked around the room as if he was still asleep.

"Time for you to get up, anyway. Bert's making lunch."

His face crashed back onto the pillow.

"OK, you're not hungry. But you're going to give me the new password."

His voice muffled from the pillow, "I didn't change your password."

"Right," she said. "Mom logged onto my laptop and changed the code. What's the new password, Damian?"

Silence from the bed.

"All righty, then. Get up. Pack your things. I'm taking you to the airport."

He rolled over on his side, facing the wall. "I didn't change it," he insisted.

"But you hacked into it. Didn't you?"

Her question went unanswered.

"You broke it, you fix it." She tossed the computer on the bed thanking her stars that she had saved all of her important files onto an external drive days before. However, it was still a nuisance. "Get dressed. Meet me downstairs and we'll talk about the new house rules I've posted on the refrigerator."

Downstairs, Bert hummed her favorite hymn as she chopped and stirred. Growing up, Iris always knew what day of the week it was by the chicken dish placed on the table. Must be Thursday, Bert was making chicken salad sandwiches. Elizabeth sat at the table staring out the window at nothing.

"Your angelic nephew hacked into my computer and now I can't get into it," Iris complained to Bert.

Knife in hand, Bert looked up from her task of cutting sandwiches in two. "What happened to your head? Looks like someone whacked you good. Oh, Ludie called. She ain't gonna make it this afternoon for cleaning. She'll talk to you tomorrow."

They both looked up when they heard the *thump, thump, thump* of Damian's sizable sneakers descending. He set his backpack at the foot of the stairs. Dressed in a Lakers jersey with swingman shorts, he opened the refrigerator and grabbed the orange juice. After a generous gulp from the carton, he tossed it back inside and wiped his mouth on his arm as he read the Grove House Rules posted on the refrigerator door. He belched.

Open-mouthed, Iris and Bert had just witnessed the worst violation of refrigerator etiquette in Grove House history.

Who raised this child? Iris thought.

Bert pointed her long serrated blade at Damian. "That's not the way we drink orange juice or any other beverage in this house, young man. We use a glass." Again with her knife, she pointed at the kitchen table set for the midday meal.

Damian mumbled, "Whatever," as he sat across from Elizabeth.

To lighten the mood, Bert proclaimed, "Hallelujah! You're just in time for some of my famous chicken salad." She placed a platter of sandwiches in the center of the table and sat next to Elizabeth and across from the kid.

Iris sat next to Damian as Elizabeth extended her hand across the table and said, "Hello, I'm Elizabeth Lee."

Damian ignored her as he reached for a sandwich.

Bert tapped his hand. "Wait for the blessing." She closed her eyes and turned her palms to the ceiling. "Let us thank our Lord for food when others are hungry; for drink when others are thirsty; for friends when others are lonely. Amen, my Lord Jesus!"

During the blessing, Iris watched the kid flash the universal teenage eye roll, then reach for his iced tea. His impertinence reminded her that he had yet to account for what he did to her computer or what he did with Mr. Henry's gun. However, lunch with her befuddled mother wasn't the place to have a conversation about theft, so, as Bert lifted the platter to offer Damian a sandwich, Iris asked him, "Now that you've read the house rules, do you have any comments? Objections?"

His mouth already full, Damian shrugged his shoulders.

"I take that as 'no'." In reference to Damian doing his own laundry, she added, "You have any questions on how to operate the washing machine, talk to Ludie. And I mean it about the staying out all night part. I get it that you want to hang out with other kids, but you've got to let us know you're alive and haven't been kidnapped by some pervert."

Damian snorted. His eyes squinted with amusement.

"What she means, sweet pea," Bert added, "is that we care about you and would hate it if anything was to happen to you."

Damian spoke through a mouthful of lunch, "OK."

"OK? OK, you'll text me when you plan to stay out all night? Tell me who you're with?" Iris asked.

Damian reached for his second sandwich and attacked it.

"I got a text from our construction manager, Vinnie. He'll be here in a few minutes. You're shadowing him this afternoon. If you're nice to him, he'll drop you off at the beach by the lake so you can hang out and make some new friends."

"K."

And, as if on cue, a horn sounded from the direction of the driveway.

Damian wrapped one of the sandwiches in a paper napkin and pushed away from the table.

Standing, Iris said, "Let me go with you to introduce you to Vinnie."

"We already met," Damian said. As he stood, he gulped down the rest of his iced tea and again wiped his mouth with his bare arm.

"When?" Iris asked.

"This morning," the kid said. "He gave me a ride home from that convenience store past the high school?" He lifted the backpack and slung it over one shoulder.

"Louie's?" she asked.

He tossed a shrug at her.

"Don't forget, you've got to figure out what you did to my computer to cause it to eat my password."

"I fixed it," he said. "I put it back in your room. You should change your password. A-B-C-1-2-3 is kind of lame."

She followed him out the door and into the backyard. "What did you do with it?"

"I told you I didn't change your password. It looks like you've got a virus of some kind."

"I don't mean the computer," she said as she grabbed his arm. "What did you do with the revolver you stole from the gun safe?"

"I didn't steal no gun," he said. He lifted his arm to free it from her grasp and hefted his backpack.

"Yes, you did."

"No, I didn't."

Another horn toot.

"After stealing my rental car in California, you expect me to believe you? Look, give it back and we can forget it happened," she said.

In corporal defiance he turned and walked away. Iris followed him. She went to the driver's side and said to Vinnie, "Drop him back here or call me if we need to come pick him up."

She waved at Vinnie as his truck backed out of the driveway, then she checked her car for the missing gun. It wasn't there.

Back in the kitchen, the faucet dripped on dirty dishes in the sink as Bert read the *Fallam County Citizen*. Fixing the leaky spigot had already been added to the list. At least once a day, she or Ludie had to mop up defrosted water leaking from the base of the clanking refrigerator working overtime in the un-air-conditioned kitchen. It belonged in the Smithsonian with the rest of the mid-twentieth-century appliances.

"Where did Violet's boy run off to?" Elizabeth asked.

"Who?" Bert asked.

"Violet Tyler's boy. Where did he go?"

"You mean Damian?" Bert asked as she stacked the sandwich plates. "The boy that was just here?"

"Mom, you know Damian. You met him yesterday. He's Megan's son."

"Megan's son?" Elizabeth fondled the top button of her summer blouse. Her face revealed that she was quite certain she didn't know anyone by the name of Megan.

Facing Elizabeth, Iris enunciated, "He's Ben-nie's grand-son. Your great-nephew."

Startled by her daughter's loud voice, Elizabeth changed the subject. "What happened to your head? Looks like you were whacked with a baseball bat."

Iris rubbed the swollen knot. "Let's get you in the sunroom so you can finish today's crossword puzzle." She helped Elizabeth up and guided her by the elbow into the sunroom.

Back in the kitchen, Iris asked Bert, "Where does she get these ideas about people from ancient past?" Referencing Elizabeth's question about Violet Tyler, she said, "I didn't know Violet had a son."

"She didn't," Bert said as she swished soapy water around in the sink. "What *did* happen to your head?"

"Collided with a jogger in the park," she said. "More collateral damage courtesy of our guest." Iris asked, "Did Mom and Violet know each other?"

   MELISSA POWELL GAY

"Who?" Bert asked.

Bert's tone told Iris that her cousin was pretending she didn't understand the question. Iris repeated, "Did your mother and my mother know each other?"

"I guess they knew one another. 'Cept I don't think neither of them ever went out of their way to have tea together. Vee wasn't the afternoon tea sort. She preferred rye whiskey at midnight."

Iris felt the aloofness as Bert used her mother's nickname. Bert rarely talked about Violet and never referred to her as "Mom" or "Mama" in an endearing way. "I'm sorry, Bert. I didn't know," Iris said.

Standing at the kitchen sink, steam rising from the water, Bert sniffed and wiped sweat from her forehead with the back of her hand. "That's all right, sweet pea. Vee lived the life of a Billie Holiday song. Or, at least, that's what she wanted people to believe, that nothing ever went her way."

"When Mr. Henry was in the hospital, Mom thought he was there visiting Violet. What was their story?"

Bert paused to think about Iris' question. "Because of what happened between your uncle and Vee, I think your daddy felt responsible for her. That's what Uncle Donnie used to say."

"Aside from the obvious, what *did* happen between Uncle Ben and Violet?"

"I don't rightly know the whole story, Iris. I know your daddy had a soft spot for her. She could do no wrong in his eyes. I suppose in his own way he loved her, but the times being what they was—"

"You mean because she was black and he was white?" Iris asked.

"You best talk to Donnie about this, Iris. I'd just get it all wrong," Bert said. She shook dishwater from her hands and dried them on her apron, signaling to Iris that she was finished with the subject. "You should put some ice on that head of yours."

But Iris kept up her inquiry. "Is it painful for you to talk about?"

The older woman sighed. "It's like this. You know how you felt about your daddy? All frustrated 'cause he ignored you? Well, that's how I felt about Vee when I was young. She didn't have nothing to do with me. Like seein' me reminded her of her sin."

"Bert, don't—."

"'Cept I know for a fact," Bert interrupted, "you was what made the light shine in those black eyes of your daddy's."

"But to think that your own mother felt that way—."

"Iris, once I learned how to shut out all the hurtful feelings inside of myself, I was able to see her as just another person in this world, nothing more. And when she passed, I didn't mourn her 'cause she meant nothing to me."

For consolation, Iris said, "Mr. Henry loved you like a daughter. He was gruff with you but you know as well as I that it meant he cared."

Bert grinned. "Yeah, sweet pea. I know your daddy loved me. He cared about what happened to me. That's why it always upset me so when y'all fought. 'Cause I loved you both and it hurt me to see y'all hurt each other."

Iris felt awkward and graceless in these infrequent tender moments. She never knew what to do with them: write them down, save them for a memoir. And how should she react to the other person? She was incapable of displaying deliberate acts of kindness such as hugging; she was a Lee, after all. But why was the sentiment of love, a word everyone else's family threw about so often and so freely, the hardest one for her to show, the hardest one to feel, the hardest one for her to use every day, to hand out, and to give away?

Abruptly, Bert pulled herself from the foggy stillness and walked toward the back stairs. "Let me get upstairs and get that boy's dirty clothes. Might as well do a load of laundry for Ludie

     MELISSA POWELL GAY

while I'm here. You got anything that needs washin'?"

Iris responded, "Don't sabotage my attempts at parenting. Let Damian do his own laundry!"

Just as she stuck her hands into the dishwater to finish the noonday task, her phone vibrated across the butcher's block. She stretched to see Manny's face on screen. With a wet finger, she tapped the answer display and said, "What?"

"Did you call me?"

"Carol, Beau, St. Barts. You in?"

Their phone conversations were always like this one, short like the infamous New York minute.

"Ah, let me check my work schedule."

No surprise there, Iris thought as she envisioned Manny and Miss Francy Pants rubbing noses.

"It's looking tough."

"I'm not sure I can go, either. I'm hosting a guy from L.A." No need to divulge Damian's age or relationship to her, Iris thought.

"I see. Can we find someone to use it or schedule another time? Or get our money back?"

It wasn't about the money. Manny's family owned real estate in D.C., a lot of it. She'd met him through his sister when Mary Margaret was a property manager and Iris' banking client. He was stalling on the real reason why he couldn't go. Or didn't want to go.

She answered, "I'm not sure I'd have the time to play social planner." She waited for him to volunteer coordinating things with Beau. After all, the whole outing had always been Beau and Manny's thing. Iris played the plus-one to make a foursome.

Dancing around the pending commitment, they both ignored the missed Paris rendezvous altogether.

"Let me get back to you," he said. "I'll call Beau and see if we can reschedule or just cancel this year."

"You do that," Iris said.

Later, Iris stood in the foyer and called for Heyu to join her in their evening walk around uptown. When it wasn't raining, the pair started at the end of her father's driveway and followed Grove Street down to the Grove Street Inn. At the inn they either followed Grove all the way to Eastend Street and looped back or took Court Street over to Main.

In the spring, while Mr. Henry was in the hospital, the two had taken the Court to Main option and walked south on Main all the way to the hospital to visit him. Sometimes she smuggled Heyu into Mr. Henry's room for a visit. After the old man's death, the two had kept to the scheduled walk as a memorial to him. Since her return from Paris, whenever they took the Main Street route, they'd pass the hospital and go as far as Elder Home, the assisted living community her father had visited daily and where Donnie Tyler lived.

Calling for Heyu from the carport, she surveyed the backyard for his wiry fuzz. As the days grew longer and hotter and with no air conditioning downstairs, Heyu'd gotten into the habit of scratching out a shallow bowl in the cool dirt for long naps; the favorite places to dig were underneath Elizabeth's sunroom or in the backyard under a maple tree.

At the entrance to the driveway, she whistled for Heyu but got no response. "Suit yourself," she mumbled as she turned left. Approaching the inn, she noticed the gathering storm clouds. If she quickened her pace, she'd have enough time to take Grove to Eastend, survey Vinnie's demolition at their first house and be back at Grove House before the storm arrived.

The grand houses along Grove Street were sealed up with everyone tucked inside in the comfort of cooler air. As she turned the corner at Eastend Street, a distant whirring lawn mower popped then died. Kids chased after one another in the middle of the street while adults leaned on parked cars. She walked to the end of the long two blocks where a Lee Property construction dumpster took up most of the front yard of a bungalow. Standing on the porch, she saw the outline of a shiny new padlock and hinges bolted to the paneled front door. She cupped her hands around her eyes and tried to see through the grime on the front window. Progress was being made. In only two days, Vinnie's crew had ripped out moldy carpet and linoleum, plumbing and out-of-code wiring, and painted over cabinets. A dusty trash bin sat in the middle of the front room, laths caked with horsehair plaster sticking out of it.

"Iris? That you?"

She heard the clink of a Zippo lighter, and turned to see the glow of the lighted end of a cigarillo floating in the dusky, thick air. Thunder rumbled as she joined Uncle Donnie on the sidewalk.

"Sounds like a storm's on the way."

"Yeah, weatherman says storms'll be rolling through here all night," he said. His index finger, with its oversized dark nail, hooked over the cigarillo. His right eye squinted as his thin lips pulled on the wooden tip. The wind stirred fumes of burnt cherry tobacco and ganja around their heads.

"Give me a hit on that," she said as they both gazed at the sad little house. As she hacked out noxious smoke, thunder cracked and the wind picked up. She asked, "Think you can make it back to Elder Home before the storm breaks?"

"I've been caught in storms before," he said. He chuckled quietly. "Reminds me of the time me and your daddy tried to hop a train." He laughed a little louder. "We was trying to haul a case of 'shine over to Hotel Roanoke for a politicians' meetin'. Special order for your Uncle Ben."

"Come over to the house and tell me about it," Iris said. "I'll drive you home." But it was too late to make a run for Grove House. As fat raindrops fell sideways, Iris and Donnie took cover on the porch.

"I can't tell you that one, I'm too old to go back to jail. But I will tell you about the time the law was chasing after Henry when the '37 Olds threw a rod."

　　MELISSA POWELL GAY

CHAPTER 13 THEN

RIDIN' IN THE RAIN

The rain poured into the night. Henry feared that the creek at the bottom of the hill had most likely flooded over the hard-top on Willie Creek Bridge. As the bands of water fanned against his faithful '37 Olds coupe, the wipers proved worthless. He stuck his head out the window for a better view and the drops pinged at his face. Switching to high-beams worsened visibility, the light reflected off the wash of rain. Speeding well over the limit, he was feeling his way down the steep grade rather than driving it. Ever since he could see between the spokes of a steering wheel, he'd driven all the roads in Fallam County and knew every dip, curve, bridge and low shoulder like the back of his hand.

As the car approached the bridge, lights flashed in his rearview mirror. Adrenaline rushed through him as he goosed the gas and prayed that the creek was still in its banks. The bald front tires slammed into the steel tie that connected the road to the bridge's asphalt track, the impact and subsequent compression caused him to bite his tongue. The tires managed to wade through the high water and the engine pulled the car up the opposite hill. Two squad cars followed. On the next decent, Henry pressed harder on the gas and took a curve so fast he felt the left side of the car slightly lift off the road. The first squad car spun off the curve and down an embankment. The second took its place behind the Olds.

The coupe knocked and pinged as it pulled itself up another long, slow hill. Henry glanced in the rearview and, for reasons he wasn't going to take time to figure out, the second squad car had stopped. Black smoke followed in his wake. He had to get off the hardtop and onto a dirt road before the engine froze up and bail out the cases of Franklin County's finest rattling around in the trunk.

Hauling for Donnie's friends Odis and Odell, Henry was running late on a Saturday night delivery to the Lickin' Hole because he had looped through downtown Mt Pleasant. He wanted to ask Violet if she'd go with him but his brother's car was parked in front of her new beauty salon. Ever since Henry had returned to Mt Pleasant from serving in the Army, Donnie nagged at him to forget about dating his older sister because "every white man she ever messed with either ended up in prison or dead." But Henry couldn't leave it alone. His heart had some unfinished business with Violet Tyler.

Too much smoke poured from the front of the faithful jalopy, it was a goner. Henry scanned the road, then took a sharp right onto a private drive, the Quinn farm. A quarter of a mile down, the trees gave way to the farm's cornfield, where stalks were high enough to hide a broken down car and a few cases of moonshine.

The rainy deluge continued as the car fishtailed in the muddy ruts made from Hilbert Quinn's tractor. The engine knocked, then wheezed out its last breath as the car slid sideways and came to rest in a soggy ditch. Gravity pulled the door open and Henry jumped out. Racing to the center of the drive, he arrived in time to see flashing lights rush by on the county road. Only then did he taste the metal tang of blood seeping from his throbbing tongue. What a ride, what a rush!

Quickly, Henry heaved a wooden crate out of the car's trunk and dragged it into the middle of the cornfield. He repeated the effort until all the cases were neatly lined up between two rows of corn. Throwing his Army parka over his shoulders, he walked in the rain and practiced what he'd say to any driver who stopped to offer him a ride in the middle of a soggy summer night.

"It was a set up," Henry spoke harsh and low to Donnie as the two stood in the shade of the wooden awnings of Booker T's. He deposited a nickel and reached for a soda from the outdoor cooler.

"I don't know about that, but I do know Odis and Odell are mighty upset their stuff didn't make it to the Hole last night," Donnie said.

"Either somebody wants to see my hind parts cooling off in jail or the O. Brothers had better watch their backs." Henry gulped down half the bottle of orange soda.

"I'm in a world of hurt, too. I vouched for you. They don't mess around." Donnie smiled at a pretty young woman as she got out of her car. He tipped his straw fedora as he opened the store's Rainbow Bread screen door for her.

"Those clowns aren't going to mess with you," Henry said.

"Only reason they ain't gonna mess with me is 'cause I'm standin' in front of Booker T's talking to Ben Lee's brother."

"What do they think happened?" Henry asked.

Donnie shrugged. "That you stole their hooch."

"Cut the crap. You know I wouldn't steal anybody's stuff. If I wanted to make real scratch from bootlegging, I'd be working for Pops Young." Finishing off the soda, Henry burped and then slipped the empty bottle in the returns basket. "Any idea what we should do?"

"Yeah, go back and get the cases and take them over to the Hole," Donnie said. He sat on a bench then leaned against the store's clapboard siding and swung one leg over the other. "You sure nobody can see the car from the road?"

Henry sat next to him. "I pulled brambles over it and hid the hooch in a cornfield."

Donnie slapped his leg and laughed. "You got some nerve, Henry Lee."

"The old coupe is busted up pretty bad. How am I going to get the stuff over to Roanoke?"

Donnie pointed at the shiny new Olds sedan parked next to the gas pumps. "That sweet honey of a thing's got plenty of booty space."

"You know there's no way on God's green earth I'm taking my mother's car on a 'shine run."

They both waved at the woman as she sashayed back to her car and drove away. "Elder Saunders' baby girl," Donnie volunteered as he waved again.

"You like her?" Henry asked.

"Yeah, but her daddy don't like me." He turned to Henry and said, "I'll take the coupe off your hands if you ain't got no use for it anymore."

Henry tore the foil from the top of a cigarette pack and tamped one out. He rolled it between his forefinger and thumb. With his forearms on the tops of his legs, he leaned forward and squinted at the Lee family's latest auto acquisition. Scratching at three-day chin stubble, Henry grinned at Donnie and said, "I got an idea." He got in his mother's car. With his elbow hanging out the window, he called, "You coming?"

"Woo-wee, we're ridin' in style now, Cap," Donnie whooped as the back tires spun in the gravel parking lot.

    MELISSA POWELL GAY

On the drive over to Hodge's Garage, Henry explained his plan to Donnie. Henry would borrow Turnip Hodge's tow truck and he and Donnie would go over to the Quinn farm. After they got the car hitched and towed out of the ditch, they'd put the cases back in the trunk. Then they would tow the wreck and its contents all the way to the Lickin' Hole. In broad daylight.

As the new Olds skidded to a stop in front of Turnip's place, Donnie asked, "What are we gonna do if Mr. Quinn sees us?"

"Brother, every fool knows a Fallam County farmer is feeding his pie hole with a plate full of fried squash and green beans this time of day."

Stuffing a bill in Turnip's oily coverall breast pocket, Henry promised the mechanic a gallon jar of O. Brothers' peach brandy upon their return if Turnip agreed it was best not to tag along. "I'll have your truck back before the supper hour," Henry assured him.

And the plan to go unnoticed was almost a success.

That evening at supper, Allen Lee asked Henry, "What's wrong with the Olds?"

Stalling, Henry politely asked his mother to pass the buttered potatoes.

"One of my clients saw it parked in front of Hodge's Garage this afternoon. You know I'm not paying someone else for an oil change on a brand new car."

"Oh, that," Henry said, "I borrowed it to drive over to the garage. Had to hire a tow truck to pull the coupe out of a ditch on Willis Creek Road."

"What happened?"

"Blew a rod. Pretty sure the engine's cooked."

"What? How did that happen?" The old man complained.

"The car is ancient. It's got over—."

"I don't care how many miles it's got on it. You take care of things; they take care of you."

Henry mouthed his father's last proclamation. He knew it by heart. Might as well get this over with, he thought. "I gave it to Donnie Tyler."

"You did what?" Allen asked his seemingly belligerent son.

"It's not worth the effort it would take to scrap. Last time I took it in for inspection, I had to beg Turnip not to fail it." He left out the part about bribing the greaser with a gallon of moonshine.

"You just gave my car away?"

"Mr. Lee." With her small hand, Matilda patted her husband's. "As I recall, you gave the car to Henry for his birthday. What he does with it is his business."

Mr. Lee's lips flattened as he shot a frown at Henry. He nodded acquiescence to his wife as her demands usually proved fair and realistic.

"Henry, be a dear, and help me clear the table," Matilda said.

In a show of gratitude, Henry dried the dishes while his mother washed. "Thanks for that," he quietly said.

With her hands covered in soapsuds, she played patty-cake on his cheeks. "Next time you come to the table, you shave and put on a clean shirt." She smiled and added, "For me?" With an unsteady voice, she continued, "Since M. Ellen's not here to do it, you can drive me over to that new dress shop on Jefferson Street tomorrow morning. Then we'll stop by Mr. Mark's jewelry store to have my watch repaired."

Later, too hot to sleep indoors, Henry lay with his hands cupped behind his head in the backyard's damp grass. Stars illuminated the night sky. When he was younger, his big sister M. Ellen would take his hand and lead him outside. Lying on a blanket, she'd pointed at the constellations. She talked about sailors and compasses and finding true north. Not until he was much older did he realize she was speaking of faith and not science.

In her last year of high school, when Henry was fourteen, M. Ellen went away to boarding school in Richmond. The following Christmas she married a medical doctor ten years her senior. As Southern Baptist missionaries, she and her husband left for China the following spring of 1947. The mail from the other side of the world was sporadic but each of M. Ellen's letters was dated a week apart. One reported the couple settling in Shanghai. Another brought news of her husband attending to missionary staff and congregants while she kept busy helping in the school within the confines of the mission. Another reported that they had applied to transfer to another mission, one further inland. M. Ellen posted a letter dated Wednesday, September 8, 1948, announcing that she and the doctor were expecting their first child the following January. This was the last letter the postal service delivered to Mt Pleasant.

While M. Ellen wrote letters to her anxious family, young Henry left the local high school to became a day student at the University of Virginia. He discussed the politics of the civil unrest in China with older students, veterans attending college on the GI Bill. In the evenings he and his father listened to the news for reports of fighting between the Communists and the U.S.-backed Chinese Nationalists. The family's light faded bit by bit as each day passed and news of M. Ellen failed to arrive in the mail.

His mother cried. Mr. Lee, after getting no help from the mission board in Richmond, pestered the county's man serving in the House of Representatives to find his daughter and her young family. The politician's reports were never encouraging. Henry felt the need to act but, like so many of the decisions he'd made so far in his young life, his parents weren't too pleased when he announced he had quit college and enlisted. The U.S. Army invited Henry to report to basic training the first week of January 1949. Thus, his mother cried some more.

The following December, Henry was bound for home instead of China. The youngest son of Allen and Matilda Lee later learned that the same representative who had been unsuccessful in locating his sister was responsible for pulling him out of his place in line to go fight the Communists in Korea. Where Mr. Lee had failed, Matilda had prevailed in keeping a second Lee child from falling off the end of the Pacific Ocean, never to return to her.

Searching the skies on that hot summer night in 1951, Henry watched a falling star arc across the darkness. He envied M. Ellen. She never questioned her place in the world. She held fast to her beliefs and acted in their name without fear. Because of her unfaltering faith, she was content with a life of service, comforting many who were lost. Every day since his return from California and his aborted term of military service, he'd struggled with comforting only one lost soul, his grieving mother. Unlike his brave sister who had found her North Star to guide her all the way to China, he feared he'd never find his own to propel him out into the world. Trapped by obligations to family and place, he felt hopeless. His course was already set, his life's work predetermined the day she had left.

CHAPTER 14 THEN

NEW LEASE

Bootlegging and driving cars fast was a popular pastime in Fallam County. The cat-and-mouse chase with local police and federal revenuers juiced up slow Friday and Saturday nights in a place where the choices of entertainment were shooting dice or attending church potluck suppers, with nothing in between.

Henry Lee and Donnie Tyler excelled at the sport. With Henry at the wheel, Donnie played salesman as the pair delivered O. Brothers' brew to half the roadhouses and nip joints in the tri-county area. On occasion, special deliveries took them to remote hotel resorts up in the Appalachian Mountains. Honey's Hut, a nip joint on the Fallam-Franklin County line, was where they got their delivery orders and where they went to unwind after a long night's run.

A week after the Willis Creek bridge incident, Henry found Donnie playing cards in a back room at Honey's. Henry sidled up to him and whispered, "Otis have any ideas on who might have sicced the law on me?"

Donnie tossed in his ante. "Nope."

Henry found Vee standing at the bar with her friend Naomi.

He ordered a beer, then tossed his Army field cap on the bar.

"Vee, I'll see y'all later." Naomi's shoulder brushed Henry's as she walked away.

Vee was in her cups. "Big time operator!"

"Want a ride home?"

"Why you always feel the need to rescue me?" Putting his hat on her head, she cocked it to one side. Her eyes half-closed, she pressed against him and whispered, "If you want to do something for me, buy me a drink."

"Another one?"

She pulled away. "Why do you care how much I drink? Besides, got to do somethin' while I'm waitin' for him to come get me."

"He's not coming tonight."

"How you know?" she asked.

"Because I just saw him," Henry said. "How's Baby?"

Her eyes narrowed. "Where? Who was he with?"

To Henry, Vee seemed more concerned these days about her lover's whereabouts and things he was doing without her than she did about the well-being of her own daughter. Donnie said she was spending most of her time carousing and too little of it in her shop. Customers were complaining to him. Since Baby's arrival, Henry had seen the change in her. The light in her smile had vanished. "He's at the folks' house. With Sarah," Henry said.

Her mood changed. She tugged at a curl and winked at Henry. "Let's go dancing. We haven't danced since the night I met you. Remember? Lord. When you was kissing on me, Ben saw it and got so jealous, he threw you to the floor." She laughed at him.

So he took her dancing. And more drinking.

They sat at a bar in a noisy dance hall. Vee'd found her second wind and was pouring her charm all over an out-of-towner. Closing his eyes, Henry listened to her sparkle on about some new TV show about kids. He heard her say to the man, "I've got a baby girl."

While stationed in Oakland, California, Henry received a long-distance collect call from Donnie late one night. Vee was pregnant.

"I just wanted you to know, Cap, before you shipped out."

"Ben the father?" Henry asked.

The line popped and crackled.

"That would be my guess," Donnie replied.

Henry was going to be an uncle but he wasn't sure how he felt about it, given who the father was. "Send pictures when it's born."

"I'll do that. You be safe," Donnie said. He hung up the phone in Aunt Skeeta's hallway.

When Henry came home from the Army, he quietly renovated the run-down train station, making the upstairs a cozy apartment for Vee and her new baby. He gave her money for beauty salon equipment and rented the entire building to her for the price of a monthly haircut.

Now, the pair were stumbling up the outside steps to the apartment two hours before dawn.

As he opened the door for her, he asked, "Where's Baby?"

"I took her over to Alice's so I could have some peace. Why? You want her to come live with you?" She tugged at his sleeve and said, "Come on."

He followed her into the bedroom. The iron bed from her room at Aunt Skeeta's was shoved catty-cornered on the opposite side of the room. She unzipped her summer dress and shimmied out of it. She turned on the bedside lamp, then draped a scarf over its shade. Her back to him, she clasped her hands behind her head and arched her back. "Unhook me," she said.

At sunrise, he awoke to his mistake. His mind fogged with drunken memories and shame, he got dressed and left a sleeping Vee.

Henry stayed out until sunrise most nights because he could no longer bear the muffled cries coming from his parents' bedroom. His mother had become inconsolable after the disappearance of M. Ellen, the family's greatest treasure. To add to his own misery, he resented the humiliation they'd caused when their influence had separated him from his brothers in arms. How was he to become a man if they insisted in meddling in his life?

Running moonshine hauls for the O. Brothers barely covered his bar tab. He needed a day job to buy a new set of wheels and to rent a place of his own. He thought about applying for work in one of the furniture factories over in Franklin. But others' seniority would relegate him to the evening shift, which would have interfered with his nighttime pursuits. Several homebuilders had offered him jobs, and working outdoors appealed to him. However, factory work and homebuilding both came with bosses. Henry Lee and bosses rarely saw eye to eye on things that mattered.

His parents wanted him to go back to the university and finish his degree but, in his opinion, he'd learned all he could stand from egghead professors. He'd argued with his father that a piece of paper wasn't going to make any difference; a man had brains or he didn't. His father suggested that Henry "read the law" as he'd done as a young man and work for the Lee law firm. But to Henry that would mean more bosses, and the worst kind: relatives.

Being the youngest of the three Lee children, Henry had resisted his mother's coddling when he could. He'd received daily doses of bullying from his older brother, to which Mr. Lee turned a blind eye. Now in his twenties, Henry figured he'd had his life's share of being told what to do and vowed to earn a living working for himself.

Along with the real estate within the corporate limits of Mt Pleasant, the Lees owned a farm in the eastern part of the county. A terrain of rolling hills, the fields had lain fallow for a generation. Henry's grandfather grew tobacco, wheat, corn and hay, and raised cattle. So, lying low after the Willis Creek washout, Henry decided to lease the homestead from Lee Properties and give farming a try.

The boarded-up house required mostly cosmetic improvements with one exception. There was no indoor plumbing. He succeeded in the task of installing a water pump in the kitchen in spite of his brother's meddling and critical eye.

One late afternoon in early September under the shade of the pole barn, Henry was changing the oil on a half-dead tractor that his new neighbor Hil Quinn lent him. Ben supervised while running his mouth about a case he'd settled out of court. The two had never discussed the Lickin' Hole incident in which Ben's dignity had been publicly cold-cocked by a pimply teenage brother and that shameless black woman, even though most residents mentioned the dramatic episode whenever telling strangers about the town's most notable brothers.

"Why are you here?" Henry asked Ben.

"The old man wanted me to check on you. See to it you haven't burned the place to the ground," Ben mocked.

"You can see that the house is still standing, so I guess you can leave."

"Hold up, little brother," Ben said, his hands in the air. "I'm just trying to help you out. Jeeze, why do you carry that big chip around on your shoulder?"

"Because you have to ask, I'm not going to explain why I do," Henry mumbled to himself as he searched for the oil rag to wipe his hands.

"What?" Ben asked.

Ignoring the question, Henry wiped his hands on his Army khakis. He headed across the field toward the house. As Ben approached the porch, Henry came out with a beer and sat in one of two mismatched wooden chairs. He gazed past his brother at the sunset over violet hills, hoping Ben would get in his overpriced sedan and leave. But he knew better. Ben wanted something.

"Offer your guest a beer?" Ben asked as his climbed the three steps.

"Help yourself. In the icebox," Henry said as he flipped his Zippo and lit a cigarette.

Fastidious and vain with his grooming and clothes, Ben removed his suit jacket and hung it over the back of the second chair, then rolled up his starched shirt sleeves. "I don't see how you stand living in this rathole. Every time the wind blows it reeks of old man Quinn's pig sty. Or is that your new plumbing system I smell?" He tee-heed as he patted at his oiled hair, then went inside to fetch himself a beer. Back outside on the porch, Ben extended his pinky finger as he sipped. Pointing with the bottle neck, the cocky lawyer droned on about what Henry should do with the front porch. Ben always ran his mouth too much when he wanted something from others. How his clients must suffer for it, Henry thought.

"What do you want?" Henry interrupted his brother's tips on home renovations.

Ben rubbed the sweating bottle against his jaw, then said, "What are you doing out here? Come back to work for the old man. He's driving me crazy. He treats me like I'm sixteen. Won't listen to any new ideas I have. He's stubborn about doing things his way."

"So you mean you don't like being told what to do?" Henry asked. He lit another cigarette with the butt of the first one. Along with the tobacco smoke, Henry's comment blew right over his brother's over-anointed head.

"Light one of those for me, will ya?" Ben said. "I've got all these great ideas on where to take the business. The money we can make. He's … he's slowing things down."

"What sort of ideas?" Henry asked. He stacked one Army boot over the other against a weathered porch column, balancing the chair on its hind legs.

Ben looked out into the weedy yard. "I want to open an office in Roanoke. Get a higher class of clients." He belched and tossed the empty beer bottle into the yard.

Ben wasn't the brightest bulb on the tree. In fact, Henry was as surprised as Ben when it was announced that his older brother had passed the bar exam, allowing him to practice law in Virginia. "Do you have any clients in Roanoke?" Henry asked.

"Not yet, but I'm working on it," Ben said. "Sarah wants to move. She's had her fill of Fallam County rednecks."

Henry held back his commentary on his sister-in-law's desires to escape the lifestyle of Rebel privileges by simply moving from one Southern locale to another. However, the beer made him bold. Rubbing his chin, he mocked, "And living in the same town as her husband's mistress and misbegotten daughter has nothing to do with her desire to move."

"You little shrimp turd." Ben's foot kicked a back leg of Henry's chair. Henry and the ladder-back crashed to the floor. The big guy bent over Henry and spit out, "From what I hear, the brat could be yours as well as anyone's." Placing his hands on his knees, he leaned over and exhaled cigarette smoke into Henry's face. "Henry, stop wasting your time scratching at the dirt and running with niggers."

Lying on his back, Henry squinted through the smoke and waited for it and his brother's words to dissipate into the dusty air.

"Get up, you big cry baby. Did you hurt yourself?"

Henry pulled himself up and righted the chair, his brother's insult still ringing in his ear. Then it came to him. He jabbed a finger into Ben's chest and said, "It was you." His brother had set the law on him for hauling hooch. "Was it because I was haulin' for your client's competitor? Huh?"

Ben's beefy arm brushed Henry's hand away.

"You ratted me out to the law." Lowering his head, Henry rushed at Ben's middle and tackled him to the floor. With arms and legs flying, Ben managed to pin Henry, holding him at his wrists.

Henry spit at Ben and yelled, "Get off me." He bucked with his torso.

Pressing a knee into Henry's chest, Ben said, "Say 'Uncle,'" and laughed. "Say 'pretty please.'"

"Get off me, you coward."

Ben's eyes filled with fire. He drew back and punched Henry in the nose. "That's payback for the day at the bus station."

Henry spit blood on his brother's white shirt.

Ben stood and brushed at his shirt. "Ah, hell. You're paying me for a new shirt, buddy row."

Henry lay on the porch pressing his shirt sleeve against his nose. "Stop denying it. Baby is your child."

Ben brushed at his trousers. "I don't know where you get these demented notions. I'm a married man. How could I father a child with another woman?" He tucked in his shirt and straightened his tie.

"Yeah, that logic's going to win your case every time, counselor," Henry said as he rolled to his side, then stood. He demanded, "What do you want?"

"Henry. We're brothers. Let's make peace." Ben reached to put his arm around Henry but Henry elbowed him away. "Why are we

     MELISSA POWELL GAY

fighting? We should be working together. Dad's going to need your help when I move my practice to Roanoke."

"I'm not a lawyer. I can't file things or stand in front of a judge for somebody."

"All I'm asking is for you to look after the properties. Is that too much to ask? To help your parents out? Bets will see that he gets to court when he needs to and see to the filings," Ben said.

Elizabeth "Bets" Jones, the old man's secretary, ran the business with the efficiency of a Swiss train. But Henry waited. There had to be more. This request was nothing new. The old man pestered Henry about working for the firm every time he walked through the front door at Grove House.

"And I can sweeten the pot for you." Ben squinted at the western view.

Here it came, thought Henry.

"I was thinkin' when you moved back to town, we could turn this rathole into a poker lodge. I supply the booze and the clients, and you run the place. We split the take," Ben offered.

Dumbfounded, Henry stared at his brother.

"Don't be such a prig, Henry." Throwing Henry the charmed gaze, the one he used to warm judges' hearts, Ben softened. "Think about it? There's serious money in it." He kicked the second chair. It collapsed onto the gritty floorboards, landing on top of his suit coat. "Ah, hell."

Henry watched his brother brush the garment the way their father's prissy tailor did. Once again, his family was running his life. "Tell Dad I'll help out. But I'm not moving back to town."

"Fine," Ben said. "You can manage things from here."

"You don't get it. I'm not running a shot house in our ancestors' homestead."

Descending the steps, Ben said, "We'll see. Hey, I got some

things in the trunk for you to store upstairs. Mom's not taking Mr. Stanley's latest news too well. Dad made her box up all M. Ellen's stuff." As he hefted the family's old phonograph from the back seat, he added, "Dad said to do whatever you want with this. All the records are in one of the boxes." Later, as he got in his car to leave, Ben said to Henry, "Time for you to get into the game of life, brother. You can't hide out here forever."

At midnight, Henry opened another beer as he listened to the scratchy moans of Sister Rosetta's electric guitar and sorted through the boxes of M. Ellen's books. One box, sealed with packing tape, sat alone in the corner. Inside were his sister's personal effects, recovered by the mission board. Upon delivering the box, Congressman Stanley stated that the United States government was unable to confirm M. Ellen's whereabouts, alive or otherwise.

CHAPTER 15 NOW

SCREAM FOR ICE CREAM

Thursday evening's storm hustled in a smothering quilt of clouds, leaving the following day's stilted air intolerable and typical for Mt Pleasant's summer weather: humid, hot and hazy. To cool down, Iris decided to take a drive out to the farm to search for her father's missing gun. She loaded Elizabeth into her SUV and cranked up the air conditioner. Standing in the backyard, she called for Heyu and waited. He loved the farm and wouldn't miss an opportunity to sniff out every square inch of the barn. Iris worried. Heyu hadn't come home the night before.

Neither had Damian. Bucking her refrigerator code of conduct, the ear-budded post-millennial hadn't texted or called with his overnight sleeping plans. At their regular morning meeting, Vinnie confirmed that Damian was dropped off at the lake park around four p.m. the previous day. Vinnie'd made him promise to call Iris about his evening plans.

As Iris drove along the wet county road, she smiled at the memory of the stories Uncle Donnie had shared the night before of Mr. Henry running into a ditch by the Quinn farm and hiding the moonshine in the cornfield. Having known Donnie Tyler all of her life, she knew him to be a man who kept the record straight. However, the cherry cigarillo laced with ganja must have clouded his memory. As the rain poured over the roof of the Eastend house, she howled with laughter and cried "foul" when he claimed the pair stole moonshine from one bootlegger to sell to another.

"Clover Hill," Elizabeth read from the approaching road sign. "Why are we going to Clover Hill?"

"We're not going to Clover Hill, Mom, we're going to the farm."

"The farm? Whose farm?" Elizabeth looked worried.

Iris had already explained to Elizabeth three times in the car that they were on their way to Mr. Henry's farm for fresh-made strawberry jam. To cover the farm's property taxes, the Lees leased their fields to a neighboring farmer who kept them in soy beans and corn for his cattle. The farmer also put in a sizable vegetable garden and ran a roadside stand from June until November, when the collard greens came in.

Elizabeth read the marquee of an approaching strip mall, "Louie's Gas-N-Go. Farmer's Feed and Supply. Valley Ice Creamery. Can we stop for ice cream?"

"Sure, we can stop on the way back," Iris said.

"On the way back? From where?"

The gun wasn't in the barn. In the creaky loft, faint scents from other ages reminded her of days climbing hay stacks while her dad "checked on things," whatever that meant. Cicadas shrilled as she gazed out at the hazy view from the second story. To her far right on a mild slope an ancient oak brooded over the family cemetery, reminding her that she had yet to bury her father's ashes. The private road passed the oak and ended in front of the toolshed on the far side of the house where Elizabeth sat in the car listening to smooth jazz and, no doubt, dozing in the cooler air.

     MELISSA POWELL GAY

The rust of the tin roof on the farmhouse matched the color of the clay and stone footings of the gray clapboard, two-story structure; the box leaned toward the west while the porch and its roof managed to hang on. With four rooms on each floor divided by a hallway and stairs, the house had been home to at least three generations of Lees and now it provided refuge for birds, mice and squirrels. Since coming back to care for her parents, she'd not been inside it.

Behind the toolshed, she checked around the hay bale stack with the bull's eye target. The gun wasn't there either. Unlocking the toolshed, she poked her head into the oily smelling outbuilding and scanned over a room full of cobwebs, Ball jars and rusty mounds of hand tools but saw no glistening nickel-plated metal objects. The sudden movement of something black slithering away underneath a coil of hemp rope caused her to jump, banging her forehead against the door.

"Sun on a beach," she yelled as she snapped shut the padlock. She sighed and patted the injured knot on her forehead. "Where could I have put the stupid thing?" She'd check Grove House one more time. If it didn't turn up, she'd call Ethan to report it, dreading his accusations of Damian's possible involvement.

With jam, squash, and green beans loaded in the back, Iris checked for traffic before pulling onto the county road in front of the farmer's stand. Her phone buzzed with an unfamiliar number.

"Yeah?" she asked.

"Can you come and get me at the lake?" It was Damian.

"I'll be there in ten minutes. Meet me in the parking lot," Iris said to Damian.

As they passed the strip mall, Elizabeth said. "I thought we were going for ice cream?"

With her eyes on the road, Iris asked, "Why is it you can remember I promised to take you to get ice cream but you can't re-member me telling you we're going to the farm?"

She circled the full parking lot a couple of times. Still no spac-es and no Damian, she double-parked behind a car covered with bumper stickers.

Elizabeth read aloud, "'I break for unicorns,' 'No offshore drill-ing,' 'What Would Scooby Do?'"

"Mom, you stay here and read the bumper stickers. I'll be right back."

"I thought we were going to get ice cream?"

"I'm going to find Damian so he can go with us."

Her T-shirt wicked up the thick humidity as she scanned the parking lot for a Lakers jersey with bare arms as thick as toothpicks. Following the path to the beach, she came across a group of boys loitering around picnic tables under a pavilion. She smelled burn-ing weed. Not seeing the boy, she called out, "Have any of you guys seen Damian. Ah, Damian Lee?"

The tallest, and perhaps the oldest, stared at her like she was a curious rash. Appearing to be in charge of things, he called out, "Yo! L.A. Jake. Your ride's here."

Amid the snorts, crutch grabbing, and catcalls, Damian popped out of the crowd and, with one shoe in his hand, limped over to Iris.

"What happened?" she asked.

"Busted up my ankle," he said as he hoisted his backpack on his shoulder.

"Yo! L.A.'s ah-rite. You should 'a seen it. Tried a back flip off the pavilion roof," the boss kid said.

More snorts and snickers.

Extending her arm to offer assistance, Iris said, "Let me help you." The boy smelled like an abandoned gym bag filled with un-washed socks.

"No, I can walk by myself."

"Looks serious. Let's go have it X-rayed. Do you have insurance?" she asked.

"I 'on't know."

"Of course you don't know," she said as she draped his arm over her shoulder and slowly walked as he hopped to the car.

A call from the hospital's waiting room to Bennie's daughter Sarah confirmed Iris' assumption of Damian's lack of medical coverage. When Iris suggested someone in Megan's family take the time to register Damian for California's free health care program for children, Sarah sobbed on about her family obligations and how impossible it was for her to do *everything*.

"Sarah, slow down. Breathe. You've got to learn that when somebody brings up a problem it's not always yours to solve at the exact moment it's mentioned."

"I just can't. I just can't take on another responsibility. There's no way. I don't have the bandwidth. I've got my own family to look after and Megan is being released from rehab next week and her counselor thinks it's a good idea for her to reconcile with Daddy and Daddy doesn't want her in the house because she steals things and he's getting worse instead of better like his new doctor promised and I have to supervise his nurses because he doesn't trust strangers in his house. I mean, what's the point in hiring professional caregivers if he wants me to be there all the time, too?"

Iris waited for Sarah to wind down. The girl was excitable like her father. Not wanting to start her up again, Iris refrained from sharing Damian's recent escapades, aside from the sprained ankle. Yet, Iris knew the sound of a good sob story when she heard one. Although she probably wasn't aware she was doing it, Sarah was goading Iris to offer to take on the guardian's responsibilities of a feral fourteen-year-old boy with a teeming abundance of pheromones.

"Can you please keep him at least until Thanksgiving?"

"We agreed to two months," Iris pushed back, wondering how in the world she would survive *that* amount of time. After a pause, she said, "Tell you what. You make sure he gets on a California health plan by next week and he can stay until Labor Day. If not, he's back in L.A. the middle of August. Fair?"

"I don't see why he can't just—."

Iris pressed, "Fair?" And added, "By the way, my lawyer still hasn't received any correspondence from your dad about our agreement to drop his lawsuits."

"What lawsuits? Daddy hasn't mentioned anything about lawsuits to me."

"Just pass the message along to him, will ya?"

Elizabeth and Iris sat in the waiting room as one of the medical staff fitted Damian with a foot brace. The curly headed nurse, the one who helped Mr. Henry ease into the Sweet Hereafter, waved at them from the hallway that led to the rest of hospital. As she got closer, her smiling face shifted to concern.

"Miss Lee, has someone attended you?" Cricket Bowles asked.

"What?" Iris asked.

"Your head? What happened? Were you in a car accident?"

"No. Why?"

Elizabeth offered her medical opinion. "Looks like someone hit her with a baseball bat. Doesn't it?"

"Are you OK?" Nurse Cricket asked.

"Oh, that. I ran into … some …. I'm fine."

"It's really swollen. You should put an ice pack on it. Want me to get you one?"

"I'm fine. We're waiting for my cousin. He sprained his ankle."

Nurse Cricket waved and turned to leave. Then she twirled back around and pointed at Iris and asked, "Don't you have a beagle-looking kind of dog? Frizzy fur? He walks with you past the hospital sometime?"

"Yes. Have you seen him? He didn't come home last night."

"I saw him yesterday, late afternoon, before that big storm. He was by his-self. Which is the reason I noticed."

"Where?"

"You know that road by the high school, leading to Fallam Farms subdivision? That's where I live. He was just walking along the road like nobody's business."

"If you see him again, tell him Iris said to come home."

Back home, Iris helped the patient ease into Mr. Henry's reading chair in the library. He lifted his new ortho-walking boot as she pushed the oversized ottoman under his leg. Damian's long toes stuck out of the foot brace. Iris opened the front windows and turned on a standing osculating fan she'd dug out from the closet under the foyer stairs.

Elizabeth folded her petite hands and stressed, "He shouldn't be sitting in Henry's chair. You'll just have to get him up when your father comes home."

"You're right, we'll move him when Mr. Henry comes home," Iris said. She blotted at sweat trickling over the bruised knot on her forehead with the sleeve of her T-shirt. As the fan whisked a blade of hot, steamy air her way, Damian's bacterial funk charged up her nose. "Ah, we're gonna have to hose you down, son. Think you can make it to the backyard?"

CHAPTER 16 NOW
PARTY AT TRAVIS AND PEN'S

That evening, Iris sat in her parked vehicle across the street from Travis and Pen English's vinyl siding mansion in the county's newest housing development, Quail Ridge Hollow Estates. She twisted the vents in her idling car so cold air washed over her face and watched as Ethan and Jonnie entered the house. The last time they had spoken she'd accused Jonnie of marrying a man she didn't love. Maybe she'd skip the cookout. Maybe she'd troll this part of town for Heyu. He'd been gone for two days now.

Stalling to get out of the car, she scrolled through her voice mail messages and replayed one from Sotheby's Fred Kitter. The auction house had approved featuring the medallion in their upcoming Christmas catalog. Fred added that several institutions and private investors, one of which was represented by their pal *M.* Lambert, showed interest in bidding. The medallion needed to be cleaned and photographed for its twenty-first-century debut. He advised her to contact Sotheby's Virginia agent, Syke Darcy. He'd pick it up and transport it to New York.

Caregiving and homeownership had dominated all her time for the past two days. Along with the pain in his ankle, Dami-

     MELISSA POWELL GAY

an suffered withdrawals from no internet access and a lost phone. She encouraged him to give reading a try and found some ancient *National Geographic* magazines for him to study. And the curse of bad plumbing had returned, as well. All Saturday morning, Iris enjoyed the close company of Plumber Ed while the two pulled a pair of vintage Liz Taylor earrings and a small comb out of Elizabeth's toilet. With all the distractions, she'd forgotten to call Mr. Darcy. Reaching his voice mail as she watched other party guests stroll up the front walkway, she left a message for him to call her.

She looked around the street. Maybe she'd leave. No one had seen her arrive.

She flipped down the visor and switched on the mirror light. The swelling on her forehead had morphed into a purple-blue bull's eye. Her hair begged for a trim, a salon wash with some sweet smelling coconut product and a blowout. With dark circles under her eyes, her reflection appeared tired, unengaging. She didn't feel as old as the reflection portrayed but, boy, did she look like she'd ridden down a hard road. Maybe a swipe of lipstick would help. Nope, all that did was accentuate the tiny vertical crevices above her upper lip.

During the past year, Iris had felt her identity slipping away, fading like the rest of her New York and Richmond relationships. Who she was no longer seemed relevant. Were all her accomplishments behind her? Was she to sit around like Mr. Henry and read the newspaper and wait for the stroke or heart attack with her name on it to knock at the door? Quite literally that was what had happened to him. He answered the door to a summons with his name on it and stroked out right there on the foyer floor.

What was the point? She turned the key in the ignition.

Then her eyes locked with those of another guest, Walker Davis. He waved, waiting for her to join him. Aside from being Penelope Walker Wren English's great-uncle and godfather, Walker Davis, who lived and worked in Richmond, had been her father's stock broker and financial adviser.

Busted, she pressed the button for the car window. "Mr. Davis. Good to see you."

"It's good to see you, too, young lady." His droopy lidded blue eyes wanted to know what happened to her forehead. He waited for her explanation.

She turned the car off, stuffed her phone into her purse and got out.

As they strolled up the walkway to the Englishes' front door, he said, "Listen, I've not had a chance to pay my respects to your mother. How is she, by the way?"

"Right now she's upset she no longer has unlimited access to the ice cream."

The old man chuckled then turned solemn. "I'm truly sorry about what happened to Henry."

"Why?" Iris asked. "He wouldn't want your pity, Mr. Davis. He knew it was his time."

"I—I—I meant I'm sorry I didn't get by to see him in the hospital before he died. He's been on my mind a lot lately."

"How so?" She asked.

Ringing the doorbell, he said, "Let's have lunch next week. Are you still in Richmond? We can meet in my office downtown and go for a nice lunch at the club afterwards." He clapped his hands together, "But now, we've got a birthday to celebrate."

As the door opened, cooler air, bluegrass music and laugher invited Iris and Walker Davis into the party.

"Uncle Walker, Miss Lee," Pen English said as her long, elegant bare arms wrapped around her favorite uncle's middle. "Did you come together?"

"No, we just arrived at the same time, Penny. Stop trying to set me up with younger women." He pecked her on her cheek. "I've got a fantastic present for you in the car. Let's go get it."

The pair joined hands and left Iris at the threshold.

"Come on in!" Travis called. "We're all out back." He touched his own forehead and said, "It's looking worse."

Like most new homes, the back of the Englishes' opened up to a covered porch composed of pressed concrete, ceiling fans, stainless steel appliances and a flotsam of plastic furniture. The thirty or so guests, appearing lively and heading toward inebriation, didn't seem to mind the lingering summer heat. She recognized a handful of Grove Street residents and the innkeeper, Joe Turner. The newly engaged couple held court in a canopied three-person swing in the overlandscaped backyard.

"Beer?" Travis offered her a green bottle.

"Thanks. Nice place," Iris said.

"It makes Pen and the kids happy," Travis said without much enthusiasm. "I'd be happy in an old farmhouse with the nearest neighbor a couple miles away."

"You hunt?" she asked him.

"I was going ask you if I could hunt Mr. Henry's farm next season."

"Did he not allow you to?"

"He did. I didn't know if you liked that kind of thing or if you were an animal-rights type."

"As long as you're hunting for game and not for sport." Taking a sip of the cold beer, she saw a familiar face across the room. A man, the one with the Salvador Dali mustache posing with Travis in the newspaper story she'd read aloud to her mom the day they went to Jonnie's party, was talking to a tanned lady with white lips and straw hair. "Say Travis, who is that?"

"Oh, let me introduce you—."

"No, just tell me who they are," she insisted.

Travis turned his back to his guests and said, "The man is Bill Yates. Retired banker. Just moved into a place on the lake. He's looking to make investments. Maybe you can ask him to donate some of his money to the library."

"Since you know him, I'll let you ask. Who's the tanned lady standing next to him?" Iris asked.

"Pen says she's one of Ruth Kaluchi's friends from Richmond. They came out together, whatever that means."

"Debutantes," Iris said. Mr. Yates smiled at her from across the covered patio, one of those smiles that made a person want to take her skin off and wash it. "You want to point out the library foundation members and I'll start shaking hands."

"Sure," Travis said. Pointing with his beer bottle, he said, "Do you know the Garlands? They live up the street from Pen's mom and dad. They announced at the fundraiser kickoff that they have put their house in a trust for the library. When they die, the place goes to the foundation."

"You know their mortgage on that place is probably upside down, right?" she asked.

"No way. How do you know that?"

"Mr. Henry told me that George Garland came to him for a loan." What she didn't repeat to Travis was that her father told her Garland's credit cards were maxed out and he'd spent all the house's equity. Mr. Henry called the house donation a "Clinton move" referring to the news report of the Clintons deducting their used underwear as a charitable contribution on their federal income tax return.

"I liked your father," Travis said. "My dad said that without him, the bank wouldn't have happened and most of the businesses in this town wouldn't have made it. Kept *my* dad in bacon. He was a special guy."

"That's what everybody keeps telling me," Iris said as she sipped. Saint Henry's deeds were morphing into urban legend. He told *her* the bank was formed to keep his money away from New York financial shysters.

The noise level escalated as more guests arrived. She waved at Ethan as he passed her on his way to get another beer. Raising her voice, she asked Travis, "Who else from the foundation is here?"

Travis pointed with his beer. A woman with spiky black hair, her back to Travis, was waving her arms in a one-way conversation with the Kaluchis. "That's Ella Stone Parker. And your best prospect. Her husband just passed and she inherited a pile of money."

"Great day," Iris said. "What did Mr. Parker do to earn his fortune?"

"Not much of nothing. He inherited it. Railroad and coal mine stock. And of course you know Ruth and Kooch. She's got a trust. They're moving up to Winchester next month. He's got a job with a startup. So if you're going to tap them for a contribution, you better do it quick."

"Introduce me to Mrs. Parker, will you?" Iris asked.

As Iris and Travis approached Mrs. Parker and the Kaluchis, the host extended his arm to bring the group together.

As they got closer, Iris saw the black and blue knot the size of a John F. Kennedy half-dollar smack in the middle of the woman's high forehead.

Mrs. Parker's lips curled into a snarl. "You?"

Iris leaned into Travis and whispered, "I don't think I'm the one to ask Mrs. Parker for money."

"You! You're the moron who ran into me." Mrs. Parker pointed her manicured index finger at Iris. "You didn't stop to see if I was all right. To see if I needed anything. Where were your manners?"

"You seemed fine," Iris tried to explain herself.

The room grew silent enough for everyone to hear the high, lonesome cry of a fiddle streaming from the ceiling speakers.

"Do you have any idea of the pain you've caused me, missy? I still have a migraine."

Walker Davis joined the circle and interrupted Mrs. Parker's lament of injustice. "Ah, knock it off, Ella, it's just a bump on the old bean. Take a couple of aspirin and get over yourself." He laughed, then asked, "What? Did you two knock noggins?"

The escalating tension evaporated with Davis' silly question. The party resumed and the conversation level crept back up to yelling.

"Mrs. Parker, I'm Iris Lee," she said, rubbing her sweating hands on her slacks. "I apologize if our collision hurt you. I assumed you were fine when we started walking in opposite directions."

Travis chuckled. "I guess you two literally bumped into each other."

"Hey, Iris. Nice third eye," Kooch Kaluchi added.

"Shut up," Iris and Ella said at the same time.

In mock surprise, Ella said, "Yours looks worse than mine."

For the next hour or so, Ella warmed to Iris as they each cracked on the other with bad head-knocking jokes and puns. Finally, Iris'd had enough, she thanked Travis and Pen for their hospitality and waved goodbye to Ella, who was now party yelling at Bill Yates.

Ella shouted over the roar, "You need to have your head examined," and hee-hawed at her own joke. Iris pretended to laugh as she waved, then left the party. Outside, the ringing in her ears got louder. The thought of the tub of ice cream tucked under Bert's frozen chicken casseroles in the basement freezer calmed her.

Out of habit, she parked her car close to the front of the house instead of in the side carport where Mr. Henry used to keep his car. The front entrance was easier to maneuver at night. A light from the front window indicated Damian was probably still up.

An envelope addressed to her was taped to the solid oak front door. She ripped it open. A single piece of paper was inside, but the light was too dim for her to read it. She unlocked and opened the door and followed the light into the library. Damian wasn't in Mr. Henry's chair. She called out to him but got no response. She went through to the kitchen but found no one, so she climbed the back stairs, calling for him again. At the top of the stairs she noticed the light in Mr. Henry's room and went to say good night. But there was no Damian. She knocked on the half-closed hallway bathroom door and asked, "Damian? Are you in there?" She pushed the door but it wouldn't move.

In spite of the hot stuffiness of the hallway, the stillness of the house chilled her spine and gave her goose bumps. She tiptoed to Elizabeth's room and heard the old woman snoring like a band saw, harmonizing with the new A/C window unit that Vinnie had installed. She closed Elizabeth's bedroom door and silently walked to the bathroom. Pushing, the door finally gave way to a room of tropical turmoil; wet towels littered the floor and several personal hygiene products a teenage boy might try to mask his musk occupied every surface. But no Damian.

Dazed, she noticed the letter from the front door envelope crumpled in her hand. She unfolded it and read:

We got him If you ever want to see him again leave $1000 CASH — small Bills — in brown envalop behind mail box in front of Groove hotel by 6 AM tamarra No Tricks No Police Your being watched.

"Hey, Iris," Ethan answered in a loud voice over party noise. "Where'd you go? Why did you leave?"

"Someone has kidnapped Damian and is demanding a ransom. Please come to the house right away. No lights and sirens."

CHAPTER 17 NOW

LOST AND FOUND

Iris invited Ethan and Jonnie into the library. With the couple's heads together, they read the ransom note as Bert placed a tray of iced tea on an occasional table under Elizabeth's painting of Fallam County hills. When Iris alerted Bert of the kidnapping, Bert pressed "pause" on her recorded nighttime soap opera and bolted over to Grove House.

"Lord in heaven," Bert cried as she poured the iced tea. "Who would do such a thing to that poor child?"

Iris glanced at the time on her phone; it was still early in L.A. Running her hand through her hair, she thought about what she'd say to Bennie and his family. Over the noise of the standing fan, she said, "There's no other option. We've got to find him. *Tonight.* Ethan, call out whoever you need: county police, state troopers, the FBI."

Looking up from the letter, Ethan said, "I know you're worried and all, but let's take our time and think this through. When was the last time you seen him?" He patted his breast pocket for the tools of his trade, his pen and notebook, and came up empty.

Pointing with her chin at Mr. Henry's chair, Iris said, "He was sitting right there, reading, when I left for Pen's party. Bert, was he here when you left?"

Fanning herself with a folded newspaper she'd picked up from the ottoman, Bert said, "Once I got Elizabeth in the bed, about 8:30, I come down the back stairs. I called out to 'im. I said, 'Good night, sweet pea.'" Tears filled her eyes.

Jonnie comforted Bert. "Just take your time." She pulled out a pen and a crumpled envelope from her purse and handed them to Ethan. "Here, write on this."

"I said, 'Good night, sweet pea,'" Bert repeated, her voice strained. "I didn't hear back so I figured he was caught up in whatever he was reading. I just left out the back door."

"Was he in the library when you went up to tuck Mrs. Lee in?" Ethan asked. He wiped sweat from the side of his face with the napkin Bert had handed him then gulped his iced tea.

"He was. I brought him some ice cream so he didn't have to hop all the way to the kitchen to get it. See." She went over to the reading table between the Morris chairs, picked up the empty bowl and two glasses and placed them on the tray with the tea pitcher. "Oh, Lord, what's happened to Megan's boy?" She hugged herself around her waist.

"Hop to the kitchen?" Ethan asked.

"He sprained his ankle while he was at the lake," Iris offered. "He's recuperating in here so he doesn't have to use the stairs. He's wearing one of those clunky ortho boots."

Ethan cupped Jonnie's envelope in his large hand and began scribbling as he asked, "Physical description? What was he wearing when you last saw him?"

"Five-five, hundred pounds-ish. Dark hair, floppy ears. Mostly arms and legs. He's got a scar over his left eyebrow. He was wearing a basketball jersey, baggy shorts." Recalling the boy's appear-

      MELISSA POWELL GAY

ance, her heart quickened. "We've got to find him tonight, Ethan. I wouldn't know what to say to Bennie if we can't find him."

"You got any idea who may have wanted to do this?" he asked.

"He's only been here a few days," Iris said. "Unless, maybe some of his new lake buddies are pranking us." She chewed on a thumbnail.

Pushing her hair back with her reading glasses, Jonnie offered, "There's something about this note that doesn't feel right to me."

"The thousand dollars?" Ethan asked.

"Seems low. Don't you think?" Jonnie said. "Not that I know the going rate for a kidnapped child."

"I thought the same," Ethan said. He stood, placed his hands on his hips and scanned the room. "Iris, Bert, y'all notice anything out of the ordinary in here?"

"The bed pillow's missing," Bert said. She pointed at the ottoman. "He used a pillow to prop up his foot. And Miss Elizabeth's striped throw blanket ain't here, either."

"She's right," Iris confirmed. Piling her hair on top of her head with one hand, she fanned her neck with the other. How did Mr. Henry and her mother live through Virginia's humid summers without central air?

Iris paced. Partly because she didn't want to make eye contact with Jonnie, doing so meant facing the elephant she'd created when she accused Jonnie of not loving Ethan. But mostly she paced because she was shaken. Had someone come inside her parents' home and abducted Damian? Being cooped up inside the stifling house, waiting on him and putting up with his silent swagger aggravated her to no end, sure, but he was just a wise-acre kid with misguided ideas on what the world owed him. Who would want to do him harm?

"Can y'all check his bedroom? See if the pillow and blanket are up there?" Ethan said as he stepped into the foyer and pulled out his phone.

"Are you calling the state police?" Iris asked as she followed him.

"I'll get Vinnie and Ludie to drive by the lake park beach to see if he's there," he said.

"I'll check on Miss Elizabeth and look in his room for the pillow and blanket," Bert offered as she lumbered up the front steps.

Jonnie held up the ransom note and spoke softly so not to interrupt Ethan's phone conversation. "Something's off about this. The bad spelling. The handwriting. It feels like the author is a young person or someone not very bright." She slipped her glasses back on her nose and went for a close-up of the bruise on Iris' forehead. "Oh, my," she said. Handing Iris the note, she said, "Here, read it again."

Slighted by Jonnie's nonverbal commentary on her mishap with Mrs. Parker, Iris said, "Well, duh. Does kidnapping someone require a college degree?"

"No," Jonnie said, "I'm saying the note doesn't seem … credible."

Iris read the note aloud and argued, "Or, maybe they meant it to sound like that. To throw us off."

"Perhaps," Jonnie said. "Do you think Damian could have written it?"

Iris inspected the handwriting. "I've never seen his handwriting. He seems to be a pretty smart kid. Annoying, but bright. But he's got that Lee pride, so he wouldn't want anyone to think he's illiterate not even if it was a joke." The tension melted a little in her neck. "I don't think Damian wrote this. Besides, why would he?"

"The money?" Jonnie asked.

"He's got money. I gave him some cash. Besides, he's going to work for Vinnie while he's here."

"Maybe he needs more, for something he can't tell you about," Jonnie suggested.

"Extorting money from me when he could just ask for it? I'm not buying it."

"Ethan said that his dad's in a gang."

"What are you saying?"

"Like father, like son?"

"Ah, come on, Jonnie. Give the kid a break. He's only fourteen."

"Which is the average age of newly inducted gang members," Jonnie argued.

Ethan came and stood behind Jonnie. Hearing them squabble, he busied himself with scratching on the crumbled envelope.

"You're wrong. He wouldn't do this," Iris insisted. She handed the note to Ethan as Bert returned to the room.

"Fine!" Jonnie loudly responded.

"Y'all need to keep it down. Miss Elizabeth's trying to sleep," Bert said. "The pillow and the blanket ain't in his room, Mr. Quinn."

Ethan informed everyone that he had dispatched Vinnie over to the lake to see if a kid fitting Damian's description was running with the punks who terrorized the park every summer. He suggested that everybody refill their iced tea glasses and retire to the front porch, where a body might catch a cool breeze and a smoke while waiting for an update from Vinnie.

Iris saw in Ethan's eyes that he felt the same as Jonnie, that Damian was a hard-core urban gangbanger come to stir up and school Mt Pleasant's naïve hooligans on the advantages of fraud and larceny. She'd have none of that. Aside from dispensing an oversized can of lippy teenage disrespect and staying out all night without telling anyone, the kid wasn't that bad. Of course, there was the gun safe break-in and the missing gun. But he'd denied taking it and, right now, she believed him. She now regretted betraying him, telling Ethan about his unfortunate circumstances.

As the evening melted into the wee hour, the oppressive heat retreated. No one was talking. Iris watched the red dot of Ethan's cigarette zigzag. Ethan and Jonnie were nestled in the wide veranda's wooden glider, his arm stretched along the top of the bench's back. Bert snored softly in Matilda Lee's wicker rocker. Iris's tailbone ached from perching on the stone pedestal at the top of the slate steps.

Jonnie pecked Ethan on the cheek, stood and stretched. "It's late. I've got Sunday school in the morning. I'm sleeping at the apartment tonight. I'll leave my vehicle here." Tapping the tip of his nose, she added, "In case you have to go in hot pursuit of the bad guys."

Ethan stood and offered, "Want me to walk you up there?"

She answered with a lingering kiss on the lips.

Iris looked away.

"Where's Heyu?" Jonnie asked as she descended the front steps.

"Out on a county tour," Iris said. "Someone saw him over by the high school on Friday. He'll come home when he's ready."

Jonnie disappeared behind the front walkway's lamplight into the darkness as her lilting "Good night" floated back to them.

Iris listened to the night noise. In harmony with the cicadas, Bert's snoring kicked up a notch. The glider rhythmically moaned as Ethan rocked it with his feet.

"What did you two have a fallin' out about?" Ethan asked.

"Ask her," Iris replied.

"I did," he said, "but she doesn't want to talk about it."

Her face hidden in the shadows, Iris worried. Iris' petty accusation of Jonnie's compulsion to bind herself to a man before some arbitrary marriageability deadline may have permanently scarred their friendship.

A groan from Bert interrupted the night noise as she pulled herself up from the rocker. Without a word she stumbled across the veranda and went inside.

Iris slid into the glider and said, "I'll take one of your smokes."

Ethan offered the cigarette and a light.

"I was gonna call you on Monday about something. I think someone has stolen Mr. Henry's revolver." She coughed.

"The Colt?"

"I can't find it anywhere. I've traced my steps from the last time I remember using it. It's not in my car or at the farm. I've turned the house upside down."

"When did you discover it missing?"

"Earlier this week I was in Mr. Henry's room and I noticed the gun cabinet ajar. Everything was in its place except the Colt."

"Do you recall the last time you fired it?"

"Yeah, before I went to California, I took it down to the farm and fired off a few rounds. But I'm positive I cleaned it and put it back in the safe. And don't say Damian took it."

"I wasn't. But since you brought it up, did you ask him?" he asked.

"Claims he didn't take it and I believe him," she replied.

Ethan's phone buzzed. "Yell-o? Un-huh. Thanks. I owe you one, bud."

"So? Was that Vinnie? What did he say?" she asked.

Snapping his phone back in its case clipped to his belt, Ethan rested his ankle on top of his knee. "He didn't see him. He asked around, but nobody's seen him tonight."

"What do we do now?" Iris asked as she muffled a yawn.

Standing, Ethan pressed his hands into the small of his long back, then stretched his arms over his head. "I'll park Jonnie's van on the street and watch to see if anybody messes with the inn's mailbox."

"I'll go with you," Iris insisted.

"No reason for both of us to lose sleep over this." He brushed a strand of hair away from her bruised forehead. "You need to watch where you're going."

She backed away from him.

"Try not to worry. He'll turn up. You said yourself that he's been known to disappear for a spell without telling anybody."

"But the note."

"Get some sleep. I'll call you if anything develops."

Iris went inside. Trying to forget the feeling of Ethan's touch, she circled the downstairs and discovered Bert asleep on the sunroom's rattan sofa. As she reached for the pull cord on the small table lamp beside the matching chair, she noticed the chair's cushions missing.

Bert stirred.

"You awake?" Iris asked.

"Too hot to sleep," Bert said. She sat up and patted the sofa's middle cushion.

Iris sat next to her. Together, they stared at the chair with the missing cushions.

"Where're the cushions at?" Bert asked.

"Ludie's on one of her Tasmanian devil cleaning tirades again," Iris said. "Yesterday she washed down the ceiling and all the jalousies out here. She must have taken the cushions home to clean."

"Hmm." After a few seconds, Bert asked, "You want me to call Bennie? I know you don't like talking to him."

"Let's wait until the morning. See what Ethan turns up." Iris rested her head on the back of the sofa and blew out a puff of air. Staring at the beadboard ceiling, she asked, "How was it with you two when you were young? When did Bennie learn you were his half-sister?"

"I don't know. We never spoke," Bert said. She stuck her fingers in her heather gray curls and massaged her scalp. "He probably figured it out on his own. His mother acted like I didn't exist. We'd be alone in a room and she'd walk out. If I had to guess, she never talked about me to her only child."

"So you two never did, like, normal brother-sister things?"

Bert's eyebrows shot up. "Remember that prissy grown-up doll you had?"

"Miss America Barbie! He stole her. I know he did," Iris said.

"I walked in on him by mistake while he was playing with it in the bathroom," Bert said. "Girl, if looks could kill, I'd of died on that day. That boy was nothing but spoiled rotten evil. Caught him spittin' in my coffee one time. But I forgave him. And my mamma. And Ben Lee. And look what the Lord provided me in return, two beautiful nieces and their families."

"Bert, if you saw a pile of manure in the street, you'd ask, 'Where's the pony?'"

Bert chuckled at Iris' claims of her optimistic hopefulness.

"Tell me how Mr. Henry and Uncle Ben ended up where the other wanted to be."

"What do you mean?"

"Daddy told me he went out to California with no intentions of returning. And Bennie claims his father was the rightful heir to the business here in Mt Pleasant, that his father was forced to leave. Why the switch?"

"Sweet pea, I'm done talking about that man. The doctor told me to stay away from things that cause my blood pressure to rise. Talk to Uncle D. He does a better job of rememberin' those times."

Out of the blue, Iris asked, "Do you want this house?"

"What? Nah. What I want this fussy old house for? Your daddy fixed me up a nice place on Eastend. Ain't nothing here for me but sad memories and reminders of people like Ben Lee and our granddaddy. 'Is is your house. Why you ask me that?"

"I figure you have as much right to the place as any of us." Iris stretched out and propped her feet in Bert's lap.

"This ain't about me, is it?" Bert rested her hands on Iris' feet. "What's bothering you?"

Iris wasn't sure how to verbalize the gloomy aura surrounding her entire body. At times all she wanted to do was walk away from her life, and all the things in it, and go live in a yurt in Outer Mongolia. Her old life was gone, she wasn't getting it back and the new one showed no promise, just a day-to-day endurance. Finally, she said, "I'm losing people. A father I never really knew. My mother. And now this."

"We'll find him," Bert said. "Stinker's probably run off with some of those new friends of his." The doubt in her voice wasn't missed.

They listened to the tree frogs for a minute or two.

"For the past two years, Manny and I went to a Nats game in D.C. around the Fourth of July," she said. "He hasn't called to ask me to go this year."

"The Retail Merchants' softball league has a game every Friday night over at Peter's Field. Remember? They play while ridin' on donkeys for the Fourth of July game," Bert offered.

"Not quite the same as watching the boys of summer run the bases, Bert, but thanks for the visual. I—just—I don't belong here anymore."

"'Course you belong here. This is where you come from, where you were born. Your daddy wanted you to have this house, to live in it," Bert insisted.

"It's not about the house. I feel like I don't belong to Mt Pleasant anymore."

"You feelin' blue 'cause Jonnie's marryin' Chef Quinn?"

"No, it's not that." How did Bert always know?

"A person can't hide heartbreak, sweet pea," Bert said. "You always wear yours in your eyes." She patted Iris' feet again. "Besides, he ain't the man for you, anyway. Move your feet, I'm going home." She hefted herself up from the sofa and added, "Be happy for Jonnie. She finally got her a man who ain't afraid to let her do all the drivin'." As she wobbled out of the room, she said, "Call me as soon as you hear anything."

No use going upstairs to bed, Iris' mind was throwing off bottle rockets. Bert was right, as always. Ethan wasn't for her. She'd just make the both of them miserable. Stretching out on the creaking sofa, she tried the meditation exercises she'd learned while practicing yoga in Richmond. Richmond? She hadn't spent a night in her own home for over four months. She missed her little air-conditioned crow's nest with its views of the river and downtown skyline. She missed sitting on the small balcony with Heyu. Where was he, anyway? Unlike her, he seemed to have adapted to Mt Pleasant and its pace. When she finally got around to moving back to Richmond, would he come along or would he move in with Bert or Vinnie or move back in with Manny?

Manny. She pictured herself with him at the top of the black diamond trail at Lake Tahoe's Heavenly Ski Resort looking out at all the shades of blue: the sky, the lake, the powdered snow. She conjured up the icy, dry air and the snow trapped inside the back of her jacket from a tumble on the first run of the day. For that one moment on that mountaintop, in a place called Heavenly, no less, she had been content with her life. Had Manny ever been satisfied with their relationship? Judging from how he acted in Paris, he wasn't beating down the dogs of discontent to sustain it. In her meditation, her hips and knees swayed side to side as her body lightly floated down the ski run.

She'd lost Manny, too. She promised herself that before she formally ended their relationship, she'd ask him if he remembered that day and if it had made him happy.

"Ah!" Iris started. Her heart was pounding against her chest, as if it wanted out. Soft clinking floated through the open jalousie windows, the next-door neighbor's wind chimes hidden by the Virginia creeper and trees. As she swallowed, she tasted the acrid remnants of last night's borrowed cigarette. She got up from the sofa and went in search of the time and something to drink. The kitchen spigot jerked and spit as she held a glass over a sink full of dirty dishes. Humming as if its gears were stuck, the Westclox told her it was almost sunrise and only twenty-four minutes before the kidnappers' deadline of 6 a.m. A bolt of nervous current tingled through her core as she recalled the previous evening's events. After gulping down the sweet Mt Pleasant tap water, she lugged herself up the back stairs to change out of her party clothes and into shorts and a T-shirt. Tiptoeing to the second-floor window in her mother's room, she spied Jonnie's van through the lace of tree leaves.

Muggy air engulfed her as she strolled down the driveway. At the entrance, she peeked around the mammoth chestnut tree and down toward the mailbox in front of the Grove Street Inn. No one was around. Across the street, the windows in Jonnie's car were closed up tight and Ethan was not at the wheel.

"Where is he?" Iris whispered. She pulled her phone from her back pocket and called him. The call went to voice mail. Calling Jonnie, she got the same result. Darting across the street, she hid behind the vehicle while scanning the street again, still no one. Jogging in the opposite direction of the inn, she rushed down the alley behind the Bailey House Library and the law offices and came out onto Main Street. She trotted around to the front of the Bailey Building and buzzed the intercom mounted on the front of the building. After a second or two, she buzzed again, holding the button down and looking up into the camera mounted over the doors. No answer.

Next, she set out for the police command center behind the courthouse and town municipal building across the street from Jonnie's place. At the front desk, she inquired if Chief Quinn was in the building. The desk officer, a young woman with her chest flattened by a Kevlar vest, shook her head in the negative. Iris asked the officer to call Ethan on the radio, but the young woman protested. "All Sunday emergencies and callouts, we're supposed to get ahold of the deputy chief." In another line of inquiry, the desk officer asked, "What happened to your forehead?"

With annoyed impatience, Iris waved her off and left. Outside, the day was getting brighter and warmer. She dialed Ethan again and left a message. Quickly, she retraced her steps back to the chestnut tree. As she jogged up the driveway, she decided to get in her car and cruise by the inn to see if she could see any shady characters lurking around. She bounded up the front stairs to retrieve her purse and keys and to check on Elizabeth, who appeared to be in dreamland still.

Descending the back stairs, she heard the refrigerator door slam. She cautiously peered from behind the wainscot paneled stairwell. At the kitchen's butcher block island, the bowed backside of Damian Lee perched on Bert's scuffed-up barstool, his sweaty, bed-head hair spiked in every direction. Swinging his ortho-booted foot, he was showing intense interest in the side panel of a cereal box.

"Damian?" she cried.

He started. The spoon in his hand clinked against the cereal bowl.

"Are you OK?" she asked as she rushed to him.

He picked up the spoon, tightened his arm around the bowl and resumed reading.

"How did you get here?" She tried to get closer to him, but he pushed her away with his elbow. Relieved, yet confused, she continued to pepper him with questions. "Who are they? Do you know them? How did you get away? I've been worried sick. We've got Ethan and Vinnie out looking for you."

Damian looked up from his breakfast and grunted out a familiar, disinterested "hey."

Outside, the rumblings of a vehicle echoed inside the carport. Still stunned, Iris went to the back door, where she saw Vinnie walking on the stone path toward her. She welcomed him inside and said, "Look who's home from the hill." The two stood in front of Damian while Iris put her hands on her hips like the anxious parent she was becoming.

Damian acknowledged Vinnie with an "*Hola.*"

Vinnie nodded.

Iris asked Vinnie, "Have you seen your dad this morning? I can't get him on the phone." While Vinnie leaned against the butcher's block watching Damian eat, Iris called Ethan again and left a third plea for him to call. "Damian, are you sure you're all right? Did they hurt you? Where did they take you? Do you know where they are now? We need to have Ethan send a squad car around and have these thugs arrested."

Looking at Vinnie, Damian said, "What's she talking about? *Bruja loca.*"

Vinnie's faced darkened as he asked, "Where were you last night?"

"Dude, this place is like an oven. I took some cushions from the sunroom and slept in the back yard." Damian lifted the bowl and slurped down the milk dregs. "We got any bacon? I'm starving."

Forgetting about her bruised forehead, Iris smacked it with her palm. "You. Spent. The night. In the backyard? Didn't you hear me calling you?" She wanted to grab him by his arms and shake him until his teeth rattled, but she restrained herself by stuffing her hands into her armpits. "I can't stand this."

"We thought someone had taken you," Vinnie said with true concern in his voice.

"Taken me? Where?" Damian asked.

"Someone left a ransom note at the front door," Iris added.

"I didn't see anybody," Damian said.

"What time did you go out to the backyard?" Iris asked.

"I'on't know," Damian said. The shoulder shrugging was back.

"Was Bert still here?" Iris asked.

"I'on't know," Damian said. "Why you asking me all these questions. I didn't have anything to do with taping no note on the door."

"We didn't say you did," Vinnie added in. "Check the attitude, Jake. This is serious and someone is in a lot of trouble."

Vinnie was stepping up. Iris liked it but why did he just call Damian "Jake"?

"Did any of those jerks at the lake have anything to do with this?" Vinnie asked.

Damian shrugged.

"Answer me. Do you know if they did this?"

"I don't know," Damian shouted back.

"Did you see anyone around the house last night?"

"Why are you yelling at me? I didn't do anything."

"Yes, you did," Vinnie said. "You've been disrespectful to Miss Lee. And ungrateful for her hospitality. Now apologize for your smart mouth."

"But—."

"Now!"

Wow, Vinnie was wound up about something, Iris thought.

"I'm sorry," Damian murmured.

Vinnie grabbed Damian by his arm. "Tell her you're sorry you caused her to worry."

"I'm sorry."

He tightened his grip on the kid's arm. "Now, thank her for letting you stay with her and for taking care of you."

The words "thank you" squeaked out of Damian.

"Iris?" A shaky voice called from behind Iris and Vinnie.

The three turned to see Elizabeth Lee in a shower cap and her birthday suit.

"Iris, I can't find my pink bath tub."

CHAPTER 18 THEN

COLD NIGHTS

An anxious pounding roused Henry. In the darkness the glass doors of the parlor's wood stove glowed orange. Judging from the chill in the air, the burning wood had peaked hours ago. His dry mouth reminded him of the evening's drinking.

"Henry! I know you're in there," a woman called out. And there was the pounding again.

A young child whined.

"Henry, you gonna let me and my baby freeze out here? Open this door."

He sat up in the middle of the musty mohair sofa, then waited a second for the spinning in his head to stop. On the three-legged table next to the sofa, he felt for the shadeless lamp and pulled its chain. The harsh light revealed the bachelor state of his grandparents' homestead. He stubbed his toe on a beer bottle, which rolled across the bare floor and clanked into another one.

"Henry!" The late night visitor insisted.

"Hen-wee," a child's hoarse voice mimicked.

"Hold your water. I'm coming," he said to himself.

Now the pounding was more deliberate. "Henry Lee. You better come open this door."

Turning the key in the lock, Henry opened the front door. Instantly, he lifted his arm to shield his eyes from a headlight's glare streaming from the front yard. Two silhouettes stood on the porch. "Vee? Is that you?"

"No, it's Lana Turner," Violet Tyler said. She pushed her way passed Henry and into the parlor. Almost four-year-old Baby Tyler followed behind, carrying a brown paper bag as big as she was. Vee snapped her finger and pointed. "Baby, climb up on that sofa and go to sleep."

Baby managed to scale the sofa with the bag in tow. The shoeless trouper sat upright and closed her eyes. She found sleep before Henry finished stoking the fire with more wood. She whimpered as Henry eased her down and covered her with the warm folded quilt he had been using as a pillow. Then he joined Vee in the kitchen across the hallway.

Absentmindedly, he patted his shirt pocket searching for his smokes. "Strange time for a social call," Henry said. "Who's in the car?" He nudged the kitchen curtain just enough to spy on the unfamiliar car parked right at his porch steps. "What time is it, anyway?"

"We closed down Slick's Pool Hall about an hour ago." Standing in the middle of the kitchen with her coat still on, she lit a cigarette and tossed the spent match at a full ashtray on the cluttered farm table. She asked, "You got any brandy?"

Henry smelled the wrong-doing on her. "What happened to your lip?" he asked.

"Give me a drink and I'll tell you." She was drunk.

Reaching into the back of his grandmother's pine cupboard, he retrieved a half-gallon jar of O. Brothers' peach brandy. He gripped the jar by its lid while searching for a clean glass in the cupboard, finding only teacups. Making room on the table for the dainty china, he poured the brandy.

Vee jerked the jar from his hand and drank straight from its lip. "Woo, that'll grow hair on your tongue." She lightly patted her swollen upper lip. Snapping her fingers at the jar lid, she said, "Hand it here," and screwed it back on.

A horn tooted and someone from the yard called, "Vee, y'all coming?"

Another voice hooted something, followed by laughter.

"Sounds like a traveling New Year's Eve party. Y'all heading back to your place?"

Pointing at her busted lip, she said, "Your brother did this to me. In my own home. I'm gettin' sick and tired of this." Cradling the jar of moonshine, she staggered to the front door and yelled back at Henry, "I'm done with the Lees."

Following her, Henry called, "Vee, wait."

"Tell him to stay away from me, Henry," she cried out as her high heels clacked on the wooden steps. As she stood by the opened car door, she called out to him, "And tell him it's high time he looked after Baby. I cain't do it no more."

At Vee's proclamation, hoots and cackles exploded from within the car. A woman's voice cried, "She gone and done it now."

Standing in his stocking feet, Henry felt the frigid night settling into his bones. He watched as the taillights glided along the farm's long drive past the family graves and then disappear over the hill.

In spite of who she had become, he still loved her.

Back inside, Henry shoved more wood into the stove. Standing over Baby, he watched her sleep, her little fists raised above her head. Her innocence beamed from her round face with its pointed chin, his sister M. Ellen's chin.

A gust of winter air rattled window panes and stirred dusty drapes. He sat at the end of the sofa and picked up the book he'd found in the box of M. Ellen's things that the congressman had delivered to his parents. A worn copy of *The Spirit of St. Louis*, wrapped in brown paper and tied with string, had been addressed to him. Inscribed on the title page was "Henry, find your True Star. All my love, Ellen." An unopened letter, which had not been posted but tucked in the back of the book, was the cause for his nightly drinking. Enclosed was M. Ellen's sweet sixteen locket and a single sheet of folded writing paper. Her husband wrote of his wife's death from childbirth, with clinical detachment.

For weeks, Henry alone carried the weight of knowing his sister's fate. He hesitated whenever he tried to show the letter to his parents. The Godless manner and tone of her husband's words on the gruesome news would set his mother into a deeper spiral of despair. Let her have another day of hoping for her daughter's return, he rationalized.

He tried to read the book but the words had no meaning. He pressed his thumbs into his eyes. His mind was restless from the night's drinking and Vee's visit. Tomorrow, he resolved, he'd show them the letter. He looked over at a sleeping Baby. And how would he ever tell them about her?

He stretched out on the floor in front of the woodstove. To calm his mind, he closed his eyes and traveled back, as he had done many times before, to the boarding house and Violet's iron bed. He conjured up the whisper of that first touch, the quivering of his body against hers. Sensing he was about to say things she didn't want to hear, she'd pressed her fingers against his lips. He wanted to say how beautiful she was, but saying this would only make her cross. So instead, he'd taken her hand away and told her about Donnie's encounter with a stray dog in a train car they'd hopped.

     MELISSA POWELL GAY

Embellishing the story of her brother's misfortune had made her laugh.

But, now, over time, the booze and abuse had stripped away what virtue she had and replaced it with rancor and self-loathing. He willed his mind to picture her full-bronze nakedness as he'd seen her that night but the memory was fading.

The following day, New Year's Day 1954, Henry transported a hungry and shoeless Baby to Alice Tyler's kitchen on Eastend Street. Baby's grandmother was relieved to see them. She served both of them bowls of stewed tomatoes and black-eyed peas. Over coffee, Mrs. Tyler rocked a sated Baby to sleep as she and Henry talked quietly.

"Henry, we all know how much you care for Violet. All the stuff you done for her and Baby. But you need to let her go, son. The Devil latched onto that child when she was sixteen and he ain't done messin' with her yet."

Henry bowed his head.

"Me and her daddy done told her a thousand times she better quit the hard livin' or else she gonna die young. But she cain't or don't want to." She reached across the table for Henry's hand. "Don't let her pull you down with her, son. Walk away. Just walk away."

"I'm trying to," Henry said, "but it's not easy."

"Child, cain't you or nobody else help her now." She squeezed his wrist. "She's got to love herself and accept God's grace on her own. You cain't do those things for her."

Henry pulled his handkerchief from his back pocket and swiped at his eyes.

"That's right. You go on home and have a good cry, then you get on with your life. Find yourself a pretty young white girl, y'all make Miss Matilda some grandbabies. That would lift everybody's spirit." She looked down at Baby, who was rubbing sleep from her eyes. "Ain't that right, Baby?"

The child grinned at her grandma. "Grandma, can I stay at your house? It's too noisy at Vee's and I lost my shoes."

"Yes, you can, sweet pea. You can stay here as long as you want." She kissed the top of the child's head then said to Henry, "And Mr. Henry can come and visit you here anytime he wants."

CHAPTER 19 NOW
LOST AND MISSING

Barbara Roberts and Sukie Rose, two of Iris' high school classmates, snickered as she passed their booth at Whiskey Grill, the new restaurant that earned five stars from locals for its haute cuisine of meatloaf and mac and cheese. Before the evening's end, she'd have to quell all assumptions that dinner with Walker Davis was a date. With Barbara and Sukie, gossip was an Olympic sport and they had the gold bangles to prove it. Iris' personal relationships were already convoluted enough without people thinking she was stepping out with a man old enough to remember battle tales from the mouths of Confederate veterans.

Curious about why the fossil wanted her to visit him in Richmond, she had invited Mr. Davis to join her for an early Sunday dinner in Fallam County before he ended his weekend visit with Pen and Travis. With all the excitement swirling around in Mt Pleasant, she explained to him over the phone, she wasn't sure when she'd make it to Richmond again.

On top of all the other circus acts at Grove House, an hour after she'd invited him to dinner she discovered her family's priceless heirloom was no longer in its box. Like her father's revolver, the medallion had gone missing from the safe.

She asked Bert to stay at Grove House with Elizabeth and Damian while she dined with Mr. Davis. Swearing he had no knowledge of the ransom note, Damian stammered through a stack of denials when she asked him how he knew the note had been taped to the door. Her trust in him was waning. Under the threat of sending him back to live with his grandfather, he'd finally admitted to hacking into her computer and trolling around in her files. He also confessed to using the gun safe combination he'd found in the file marked "password" to open the strongbox. But his protests were adamant. He claimed he took nothing from the safe.

Iris longed for a stiff drink, something with ice. Her head was spinning from all the chaos and the purple knot on her forehead. Ethan continued to ignore her persistent calls. The motive and culprit behind the ransom note remained a mystery. Mr. Henry's gun was still missing, and, now, the medallion had disappeared. How much anarchy could one unemployed banker, who lived with her eighty-year-old exhibitionist mother, take? She gave thanks for Davis' silence as she closed her eyes and sipped her first gin and tonic of the summer.

"Your forehead seems to be getting better," Davis offered. His smile revealed a healthy set of veneers. "I hear the fried bass is worth the extra cholesterol." He fished his readers from his pink gingham shirt pocket and opened the tri-fold menu. "My treat."

During dinner, he talked about his college days with Henry Lee and others. "Of course, what rated as a prank when we were at the university doesn't come near what these kids pull today. I hear about them because I'm on the executive board."

Throughout the meal, Iris listened quietly as the UVA senior alumnus dropped names from the university's aristocracy annals.

Getting the waiter's attention, he pointed at his empty cocktail glass and asked for a refill. Pushing aside his dinner plate and finishing his third glass of wine, Davis drew in a breath and asked, "Do you remember the Dot-com bubble back in the late nineties? Of course you do, you're a banker. And a damned good one, your father told me."

Trying to be as polite as her mother at a church social, Iris folded her hands in her lap.

"Near as I can tell, your daddy saved me from financial ruin. Heck, he kept the entire firm from going under. After he turned down a seat on our board, we put him on retainer as an analyst."

"I see." Iris shook her head to the waiter's query for another drink as he placed the after-dinner cocktail in front of Davis.

"Late nineties, he just stopped trading. Called me up one day and told me to cash out all his stocks and buy gold. I told him he was crazy and he told me—."

"To mind your own business." Iris finished the old man's sentence for him.

Holding his head up to look through his readers, Davis replied, "Near as I remember, that's about what he said. We all lost our shirts. Henry put some of his portfolio back into the market just in time for the 9/11 downturn. But he faired a sight better than the boys on Wall Street. So when he came to me in the second quarter of '08 and told me to sell off all my bank stock, by God, that's what I did. He didn't have to tell me twice, no ma'am." Jabbing an index finger at the table, Davis continued, "Henry Lee was a financial wizard. I'd match him to anybody Wall Street wanted to put up. He had a mind like a steel trap."

"You know, he didn't have a computer and the stock data came from a day-old *Journal*," she said with a pinch of pride.

Davis laughed. "And damned if I was going to tell our other clients I got my trading tips from an ill-tempered hillbilly who studied the markets from his Appalachian easy chair." He finished off the cocktail and waved his credit card at the waiter. "The others won't admit it but our firm wouldn't have pulled through that last bear market without his advice. And he never once crowed to me or anybody else about it. That's the honest truth. I wanted you to know that."

Honest truth, Iris thought. What was truth if it wasn't honest? She said, "I appreciate you sharing that story with me. But that's not why you wanted to talk, is it?"

"Travis told me you're interested in helping with the new library," he said.

"About a year ago, Mr. Henry told me he was disappointed that the county turned down a proposal for plans for a new building. I want to help get it back on track."

"Without violating my fiduciary duty to the foundation or naming names, I suppose I can tell you most of the money they've managed to raise for the venture came from a single anonymous contributor. I thought you should know."

"How much did this single donor give?" Iris asked.

"I'd say at least ninety percent of what's been collected," Davis said. "He set up a trust with the firm and made yours truly the executor. Travis assumes that role in the event of my retirement or death. The trust is very specific on its instructions on how the money will be allocated. Only after the foundation has raised over half of the funds required to build a new facility can the monies be disbursed."

"What you're saying is he wanted that money to be used for a new building."

"Exactly," Davis slurred. "And believe me, all those biddies on the foundation have tried to get their hands on it for a number of other things. My fear is that when Travis takes over, they'll hoodwink the youngster into a spending spree. And that's not what your father wanted. He wanted this place to have a real library, not a hand-me-down full of books about a single topic."

"I see," Iris said. "Any advice on how I can help?"

"Convince the county to appropriate funds for their share of the capital."

"You mean, like, launch a PR campaign?"

"Ha, I was going to suggest you bribe a county supervisor, but a PR campaign will work," Davis said. "I know a few firms in Richmond that would be happy to oblige——."

"For a fee." Again, Iris finished Davis' sentence for him.

"Well, they're not coming all the way out here to Hicksville for nothing," he assured her.

As the old man dropped names of managing partners of Richmond's advertising elite, Iris noticed her classmates waltzing toward her table. Perhaps she could put the gossip team of Roberts and Rose on the case.

"Barbara. Sukie," she called out, "You know Walker Davis, Pen English's uncle? We're here to talk about the new library."

"New library?" Barbara asked. "I thought that plan got axed. Ella Stone told me about your little run-in." Smiling, Barbara tapped her own forehead. "Yours definitely looks worse."

"Are we getting a new library?" Sukie asked. "We need one. There's only one computer for the internet." She shimmied her shoulders. "The book selection's pretty lame, too."

Davis swayed as he stood to offer the chatty ladies a seat at the table. "We're discussing plans to launch a publicity campaign. Let county residents know about the building plan," Davis said.

"Are you two interested in helping?" Iris asked.

"This might be the three margaritas talking, but I'd love to help out," Barbara volunteered.

"Me, too!" Sukie added.

Iris said to Davis, "Looks like we've got our PR team. What do we do next?"

At the end of her Monday morning workout with Marine Mike, Iris jogged by Jonnie's office and asked Claire to print a few fliers. She'd created a "Reward Offered" flier for information leading to the return of Heyu. She planned to post them around town. Six days and he still hadn't shown his mug for dinner. She worried about him.

Iris dropped by the *Fallam County Citizen* on South Main Street to place a lost and found ad. Janis, the clerk at the front desk, read aloud from one of the fliers. "'Re-ward. A hundred dollars.'" Looking up from the flier, she said, "Cha-ching. Did you check with animal control, doll?"

"No, but that's a good idea. Thanks," Iris said.

"You better do it fast 'cause if the dog catcher picked him up, he's liable to be ethan-ized."

"What? You mean euthanized?" Iris asked.

Janis warned, "If it was my dog, hon, I'd go by the animal shelter real quick."

"He has a microchip implant, so if he's picked up they should be able to contact the owner." Oh, *merde*, Iris thought, Manny's name and number were encoded on the chip. If animal control called him, she'd be in the dog house. The two hadn't spoken since the St. Bart's vacation conversation. If Manny found out Heyu had run away, he'd blame her for it, which some might see as an accurate claim. What did Davis call it? The honest truth? The honest truth was it *was* her fault. Because of all the commotion with Damian, the plumbing eruptions, and no A/C, she'd ignored him. Like a neglected teenager, Heyu had run away from home.

"You OK?" Janis reached for Iris' hand. "I don't know if they got chip readers, hon. I'd get over there anyway."

"You're right, you're right," Iris said. She paid for an ad. Her plans to file a report with the police on the missing medallion had to wait. No way was she going to allow Heyu to be "ethan-ized."

Iris and Damian rode to the animal shelter south of town and next to the landfill. On the ride over, she asked Damian if he remembered the last time he saw Heyu. He responded with one of his nonverbal grunts. At the shelter, a cute, pony-tailed redhead about Damian's age greeted them.

"Hi!" she lisped. Her smile revealed a grill of thin wire with pink rubber bands. "Welcome to Fallam County's Shelter for Friends. Is this your first visit?"

"It is," Iris replied. Seizing the teachable moment on civil introductions for Damian, Iris extended her hand and said, "My name is Iris Lee."

"I know you," the girl said. "I read all about you and the civil war medal in the *Citizen*. My dad made me do a research paper on it for school."

"And you are?"

Pointing at her name tag, she said, "Tabitha Jean."

"Tabitha Jean, this is Damian Lee."

Damian blushed. "Hi," he said meekly. Without his phone to use as a shield to his personal space, he suddenly showed intense interest in the pet spaying and neutering brochures at the counter.

Iris recounted the story of the runaway and gave a flier to Tabitha Jean.

"It's just Tabitha or Tabby, you know, like the cat," the girl said, then, looking at Heyu's mug, cried, "Aww. Poor little fella."

"Do you know if he's here?" Iris asked. "He's wearing a blue collar with a brass medallion, his name's on one side and my phone number's on the other. And he's got a chip implant."

"Let's look at the log," Tabby said. Behind the counter she keyed her query. "What breed?"

"He's a mix. Beagle and schnauzer."

Tabby slurred, "A schneagle," then giggled.

Damian laughed, too.

"There's no Heyu Lee registered here."

"Can we post a flier?" Iris asked. "And can you call me if he shows up here?"

"Sure, we've got a bulletin board in the hallway. You may have seen it when you came in. Follow me." She flashed her bedazzled grill at Damian. "And, if you'd like, I can post it on our online bulletin board, too."

Again, milking the teachable moment for all its worth, Iris stared at Damian and said, "Thank you for being so helpful, Tabby."

"No problem. Y'all want a tour?"

Iris hesitated.

"The director says we have to give everyone who comes in for the first time a tour of our kennels. You know, in case you want to adopt a roomie for Heyu."

"Thanks. But—."

"That would be awesome," Damian interrupted.

Iris blinked. The boy actually articulated an idea using a complete sentence. Suddenly, he appeared genuinely interested in something that wasn't on his phone or the back of a cereal box. During the tour, Iris watched him steal glances at Tabby, revealing another kind of truth: It's always about the girl.

Iris and Damian spent the rest of the day posting fliers around town. Along the way, she confessed to stories of underage offenses that she and the rest of the Grove Street kids committed. Pulling into the driveway at Grove House, she made him laugh when she

     MELISSA POWELL GAY

told him about Bennie overestimating the number of cherry bombs required to blow the mailbox off its pedestal. In her afternoon revelry, she left out the bits where the boy's grandfather, in his own youth, terrorized any kid younger, smaller or slower than the rest. Why dwell on it? It served no use for Damian, except for guilt by association.

Sitting in the driveway, she felt Damian's thick defensive wall crumbling a little around the edges. From recounting her teenage shenanigans, she came to realize why Damian acted out. He was bored. Bored just like she was every summer while living in Mt Pleasant. He needed something to occupy his time and mind.

"Damian, this isn't L.A. so there's not much to do around here for fun. Do you like working with Vinnie?"

He shrugged.

"I noticed on the bulletin board that the shelter is looking for volunteers. Would you like to wash pound puppies and hang out with the winsome Tabby?"

His eyes gave him away. He liked Tabby. The two had experienced some type of mind meld while Tabby gave them a tour of the shelter. "Winsome?" he asked.

"Sweet, charming." Iris smiled at him. "Your peeps would say 'awesome, fine.'"

His thin lips turned up on one side to show a dimple in his left cheek, just like Mr. Henry's.

In the library they discovered Ludie and Elizabeth gyrating to the housekeeper's favorite hip-hop playlist on her portable music player. Over the deep boom-boom bass, Bert rapped along in the kitchen as she swayed her hips in front of the stove. Damian hopped onto the rickety barstool and tapped out a tattoo on the butcher's block in sync with the hip-hop ditty.

The painted portrait of Allen Lee's family, that presided from over the library fireplace, rested on the kitchen table surrounded by dust rags. A sunbeam filled with dust specks cut through the center of the portrait and highlighted the face of young Henry. For a split second from an overlapping reality, Iris saw the Mr. Henry from the portrait sitting on the barstool asking Bert if there were any of those awesome fried apple pies left over from the morning's breakfast. Shaking the illusion from her head, she took the back stairs to her bedroom, her portal to the real world, to catch up on emails and return phone calls.

"There's nothing else to tell," Iris said to a hysterical Fred Kitter. "Yesterday, I went to the safe to get it so I could take it to Mr. Darcy and it wasn't there." Telling Fred her trip to see his co-worker was canceled because of all the balls in the air at Mt Pleasant would have been easier. But, why lie? In fact, Iris' proclivity to tell *all* the truth was her greatest fault; it had kept her from advancing to the top rung of her company's ladder and, more important, ruined untold number of personal relationships. Interrupting Fred's anxious "but, but, buts," she told him for the third time, "It's not where I stored it for safekeeping."

"But what happened to it?" Fred pleaded.

"If I knew *that* we'd be having a different conversation, wouldn't we?" Social nuance just wasn't her thing. "I'm filing a report with the police. It's insured so we're covered for the resale value of the stones, at least."

"*You're* covered. What about us? We've got all that time and expense from Paris."

"You're not pinning that bill on me, Fred. Did you do what I suggested? Did you get your guys to challenge the French on their lame authentication protests?" She waited for a response but got none, which meant "no." "Send a bill to Julien Lambert. After all,

　　　MELISSA POWELL GAY

they were the ones who wanted the meeting."

"Bill the Louvre? Funny one, Iris." Then he admitted, "I've got another proposal in front of them."

Iris stayed mute on the subject of Fred's expenses. Her credit card had racked up its share of Parisian hotel and restaurant tabs.

"All right, I'll see if accounting will write it off to new business development. But Iris, going forward, we've already dropped a load of cash on marketing buzz. The entire winter sale is wrapped around the romance of Marie Antoinette having the medal made for her beloved Louis." Sounding lost, he asked, "What do I tell the art director?"

"Tell them to relax and eat some cake," Iris said.

"This isn't funny."

"What's the cut-off date for the catalog publication?"

"I don't know," Fred said.

The comment reminded her of Damian and his mumblings. What was it with people and their refusal to participate in the fate of their own prospects? "What's your plan 'B'?" she asked.

"I don't know if there is one," Fred said.

"Let's give it a couple of days. I'll call you."

"Couple of days? Iris, this thing needs to be resolved ASAP."

"Give me to the end of the week."

After another hesitation, he said, "I guess we can wait a day or so. I'll call you on Thursday. Where are you, anyway? Sounds like you're in a hip-hop club."

The disco booms vibrating from below abruptly stopped and Iris heard the muffled sounds of her family gathering in the dining room below. When she joined them, they all tore into Bert's new chicken enchilada recipe, one recommended by Damian. For the first time, she saw him smile and she was pleased to see it because it was Mr. Henry's smile, too.

CHAPTER 20 NOW
FILING THE REPORT

The humidity had retreated. Leaving Damian and Bert with the supper dishes, Iris decided to walk over to the police station to file her reports of stolen items. When the front door opened, a pink envelope fell to the floor. This time the note inside read:

We thought we had a deal. The price just went up to $2,000 dollars If you ever want to see the mutt again leave the money in the trashcan beside the red shack in the back of the park. TO-nite. No tricks. Wer watching.

The ransom envelope included a Polaroid of a caged Heyu appearing sad and confused. Iris was stunned. How could she have been so dense? The ransom wasn't for Damian. It was for Heyu. Heyu was kidnapped. Actually, in the eyes of the law, he had been dognapped, but either way, someone had taken Heyu from his family.

Iris sprinted all the way to the police station. Rushing past the front desk, she stormed into Ethan's office, which was filled with uniforms and suits. "Ethan! It's Heyu. The ransom note. It's for Heyu!"

The room clammed up. Quickly, she counted four, five pairs of vigilant eyes staring at her. And Vinnie, he was sitting in a folding chair off to one side and away from the others. Someone bumped into her backside and she heard them say, "Chief, I tried to tell her you was tied up."

Ethan stood and said, "That's OK, Darrell. Iris, we're in the middle of something here. Why don't you go with Officer Crouch to the front and wait 'til we finish up?"

"But someone's been kidnapped!"

Ethan hooked his thumb in his pants' pocket and cleared his throat. He nodded at one of the suits and said, "Excuse me a minute." Taking Iris by the elbow, he escorted her into an empty conference room. "What are you talking about?" he asked.

She jerked her arm away from his hold and said, "If you'd answer my calls or listen to my messages, you'd know."

Placing his hands on his belt, he looked down at her and said, "Tell me again." His eyes conveyed that her credibility with him had diminished. The ruckus she'd caused when Damian disappeared had backfired when the teen had miraculously reappeared the morning after she'd badgered Ethen into calling out everybody except the National Guard to search for and rescue him.

"Stop looking at me like I'm one of those church ladies crying about some homeless guy peeing on the park hydrangeas."

"Calm down. Tell me what's wrong," he said. He motioned for her to sit in one of the chairs along the room's wall.

"Calm down!" she accused. She walked the length of the room to a narrow window. Turning to face him, she tossed her hands in the air and said, "There's something really, really weird going on at my house. And you're ignoring it. You're not taking me seriously. Just like we didn't take Mr. Henry seriously."

"How can I help if you won't tell me what's got you so riled?" he asked in a raised voice.

She stared out the window at the painted brick back of the courthouse and tried to visualize how all the turmoil swirling around her was connected. Was Bennie still trying to get his hands on the medallion? And what about those guys who came by to see Mr. Henry back in March when she and Ethan found him half out of his mind and waving his pistol around?

"Iris?" Ethan prompted. "I got an office full of lawmen waiting for me in the other room."

"You remember that Sunday I called you in a panic? It was right before daddy died. He claimed some low-lifes were trying to get in the house?"

"We checked that out and couldn't find anybody to corroborate his story."

"But later on, when Mr. Henry was in the hospital, we decided that because of Bennie's claims and his internet scheme to get the medallion, someone may have actually tried to break in."

Ethan looked at his watch.

"Something stinks to high heaven," she said as she took a marker from the tray and drew a line across the conference room's whiteboard. "In March, Mr. Henry says two, he called them boys, came to the house claiming to be property assessors. Remember? He'd gotten his Colt out and loaded it? Right there in the house!" She marked a short vertical tick at the left end of her time line. "Last week I discover the gun safe open and the pistol missing." She made another slash through the timeline.

"Where you going with this?" Ethan asked.

Thinking out loud, she continued, "So, Saturday night, I come home and there's a ransom note taped to my front door." She slashed the timeline with another tick and wrote "ransom note" underneath the line.

Looking at his watch again, Ethan said, "You said something about a kidnapping?"

"Just stay with me. In the note, they failed to mention that the extortion was for my *dog*. Because I couldn't find Damian that night, I assumed the note was about him." She tossed the second ransom note and the Polaroid on the table near Ethan. "These guys aren't the brightest bulbs on the Christmas tree." She made another tick and wrote "ransom note-2."

Ethan picked up the note and the photo and asked, "Where exactly did you find these?"

With that question, she felt he was back in her corner. "In an envelope taped to my front door. Just like the last one."

Ethan grunted. Then he said, "Somebody is pulling a prank on you, Iris." He tossed the note on the table but continued to stare at the photo of Heyu.

"Then explain why the medallion is missing." With dramatic flair, she slashed another tick mark through the timeline between 'ransom note' and 'ransom note-2.' "I discovered the medallion missing a couple of days ago, but when Heyu didn't come home, I'd forgotten all about it. Tonight, I thought I'd come up here to report it missing and that's when I discovered the second note."

Ethan rubbed the back of his neck. "I'm sorry, Iris. I don't see the connections. But you can file a report on the dog and the medallion. I'll send someone to your house to take a statement."

"Dang it all, Ethan. Somebody has broken into my house. Twice! Stolen my daddy's favorite gun, the one he flashed around in March, and a priceless piece of art. Now, they've got the nerve to kidnap the dog and demand ransom money. And all you can say to me is 'file a report'?"

His face shaded red as a single snort eked out.

"It's not funny." She tapped at his rock-hard shoulder.

"Can you hear yourself?" His eyes watered as he fought to contain an eruption. Straining, he said, "'They got the nerve … to … kidnap the dog.' Sounds like a country-western song." He plopped into a conference chair and pointed at the photo, unable to stop the involuntary snickering.

"I'm glad I can provide you with a little entertainment tonight." She picked up the note from the table. "Guess I'll handle this on my own."

A quick rap at the door came as one of the deputies poked his head inside the room. "Chief, it's been five minutes."

Ethan stood. "Tell them I'll be there in a second." Turning to Iris, he placed his hand on her shoulder. "I'm sorry I laughed, the picture, the way you said it." He took a deep breath to calm himself. "Look, I know this is serious. Stay here. I'll send a deputy in to take a statement." And he left.

Iris paced the length of the conference room debating whether to stay or go.

"Mrs. Lee?" A deputy, in full uniform, stood in the doorway. "Chief said I was to take your statement about a theft in your home."

She recognized the young man as the deputy who delivered Bennie's lawsuit summons that day in Jonnie's office. The same deputy who had delivered the same summons to her father minutes later. The summons that had provoked her father's stroke.

He held up a clipboard and pen. "We need you to fill out this form and—."

She jerked them from him and sat to complete the form.

"You know, Chief's pretty busy right now. He ain't got time to be a private security detail and all—."

"Shhh," she spat. "If I need your opinion on my relationship with your boss, I'll ask. Until then, keep your trap shut."

Deputy Hunter Jones stood by the door staring at his boots.

CHAPTER 21 NOW

LEE CURSE

The plan to apprehend Heyu's kidnappers called for Deputies Jones and Spratton to stake out the park's garden shed that night. Ethan insisted Iris go home. He assured her that his guys were capable of catching a small time petty thief. He'd call her when they rescued Heyu.

Iris found Bert and Damian playing checkers in the sunroom.

"Well?" Bert asked. "Did they find him?"

"Ethan's got a team watching the park shed," she said as she plopped into a chair.

Damian pulled at the soft hair that was trying to be a beard on the side of his face, his eyes intent on the game.

"I told Damian I'd teach him how to drive. He claims he already knows how," Bert announced. "I told him as soon as he gets his driver's license, he can have Mr. Henry's car."

Recalling her stolen rental in California, Iris really didn't want to know the circumstances of how he'd learned to drive; better to focus on learning when he was legally qualified to get behind the wheel. "When's your birthday?" Iris asked.

"December first," Damian said.

"Well, I'll be. Ain't that something, Iris," Bert said.

"What?" Damian asked.

"That's your Uncle Henry's birthday," Iris said. "Your grand-dad's uncle," she squinted. "Guess that would make him your great-uncle."

The kid shrugged. "So."

"Follow me," Iris said.

Damian hobbled behind Iris and Bert as they led him into Mr. Henry's library. The family portrait was back over the fireplace mantel after one of Ludie's epic cleaning episodes. Pointing at the taller of the two sons, Iris said to Damian, "That's your great-grandfather. Bennie Lee's dad. He moved out to California. What year was it, Bert?"

"Ben Lee and his family left Virginia the year Jimmy Carter ran for president, nineteen and seventy-six," Bert said. She hugged her bosom and mashed her lips together as if to keep from saying something else, maybe something not so nice.

Damian grabbed at his elbow as he looked up at the picture.

"The other son," Iris pointed at her father, "is Henry Lee, my dad. You and he share the same birthday." She switched on the light over the portrait. "And you guys share a lot more. You've got his eyes, his hair, mouth, and you're smart like he was. And, unfortunately, you inherited the Lee curse."

"Lee curse?" Damian asked.

"You got the jumbo wing flappers." She grinned as she pinched one of his ears.

He swatted at her hand.

"As your grandfather is fond of reminding me, he's the oldest of our generation. You're the oldest of your generation of Lees."

"But I'm not a Lee, I'm Damian Rodriguez," he protested.

"The copy of the birth certificate your Aunt Sarah sent me says your last name is Lee." Grabbing his chin, she forced him to look at her. "But it doesn't matter if it's Lee or Rodriguez or Smith or Bozo. You're Bennie's grandchild. *That* makes you a Lee."

If he were there, Bennie would argue with her by insisting the child was illegitimate. But Iris wanted to make this right. There would be no more family secrets in this house. For too long the Lee pride had refused to acknowledge its acts of bigotry and shame. In her small way, Iris wanted to make it right for Damian and any future siblings or children.

He pulled away from her and said, "Whatever."

Iris sighed.

"Son, don't you be disrespectful," Bert said. "You can't disrespect somebody who's trying to help you."

"All right, so I look like some white dude who used to live here. I don't see what the big deal is." His plastic boot in tow, he lumbered to Mr. Henry's chair. With his elbows on his knees, Damian leaned over the ottoman just as Mr. Henry had a thousand times while he read the newspaper spread out before him.

In her preaching stance, Bert stood over him ready to dole out family judgment. "When I was your age, my daddy acted like I never existed. Just like your granddaddy wants to do with you." Pointing at the portrait, she heaved to hold back tears. "And—and that man, that man Henry Lee, he saw to it me and my family got what we needed. Now his daughter wants to do the same for you."

Damian responded by lowering his head and picking at his cuticles.

"Don't make me be ashamed to know you, Damian Lee."

Another shrug.

"What was that?"

"Yes, ma'am."

"That's what I thought you said. Let me go get you some ice

cream before you go on up to bed."

Iris sat next to him in the opposite Morris chair. "Sarah called me earlier. She said that they had to ask your mom to move out of the house because she was using again."

Hope struggling on his face, he asked, "So she went back to Surf's Rehab?"

"I don't think they know where she is. Your grandfather disowned her."

"What do you mean 'disowned her'? Like, he's not paying for her rehab or her medicine? So she can get better?" His voice cracked. The stoic, pint-sized punk with gang connections melted into a puddle on the floor revealing the real Damian Lee, a boy who craved a mother's love.

Iris worried. How was this boy going to deal with the fact that his mother was a junkie who cared for only one thing and was lost not only to him but to the entire family? And that, Walker Davis, was an honest truth.

The clanking air conditioner woke Iris. The alarm clock glowed four-sixteen. She stared into the darkness, missing the gentle pressure of Heyu against her leg. Bert's handling of Damian's sullen indifference and the unintended implications of taking in the child rattled around in her head. She wasn't prepared for what Bert was suggesting, taking on the responsibility of caring for a child.

Dressed in her workout clothes, she left a note on the kitchen table and set out for the park to find Marine Mike. Instead, she discovered Ethan sitting against the base of a magnolia tree, its low limbs muffling his loud snores. She pressed a sweating water bottle against the side of his face. He jumped.

"Any kidnappers yet?" she asked, handing him the cold water.

Uncapping the bottle, he glugged down half its content, then

     MELISSA POWELL GAY

smacked his neck. "Nothin' out here but me and a swarm of mosquitoes. You know, Iris, things were all quiet and peaceful like until you moved back to town."

"What can I say?" she said. "Be thankful I'm not a psycho killer come to seek retribution for the wrongs done unto me when I was living here."

"Is that suppose to be funny?"

"Who said I moved back?"

"I'm sorry. I assumed you were living here now. How long are you staying?"

"I wish I knew the answer. Part of me wants to run away before the roads are blocked and I can't escape. But something about this place tugs at me to stay."

"I felt the same when I was truckin' back and forth between here and Texas. I'd lived in Texas for so long, it almost felt like home. Plus, Vinnie was there."

"He's a good egg," Iris said. "Why was he at your office with those suits?"

"He's helping us out with something. That's all I can say." He sipped at Iris' water. "The only thing I miss about Texas now is the food. You'd think us Virginia rednecks would know how to refry pinto beans. I'd give anything for a plate of San Antonio *migas* right now."

"Maybe later we can go over to Chunky's. He's got a decent egg burrito."

"Ain't the same," he said.

Bert was right, Ethan was Jonnie's man.

As if he was reading her mind, he asked "Are you and Jonnie ever going to make up?"

"I said something really ugly to her. I wouldn't be surprised if she never spoke to me again."

"I wish you two would go on one of your spa trips and make up. She's been impossible to be around lately. She threw a wine bottle—."

"Shhhh."

Footsteps, coming from the direction of the Main Street parking lot, got louder as they crunched over the gravel path. Crawling to the outer perimeter of the magnolia's canopy, Iris nudged aside a leaf and spied a lanky, hooded figure stopping in front of the cedar shed.

Over her shoulder, she whispered, "Someone's headed for the back of the shed." But the chief of police was gone. Scrambling after him, she headed for the walkway and tripped over its railroad tie border. On her way down, someone near the shed yelled, "Hey, you. Stop!" Arms in the air, her body committed to a full dive over the gravel lane. As she body-surfed across the stones, someone rammed into her ribs and fell across her back. Without a word or cry of pain, the bounder rolled and sprinted away. Before her brain had a chance to report all the damage, one of Mt Pleasant's chubbier constables landed on top of her.

"I got him, Chief," the deputy called out. To Iris, he spat out, "Show me your hands." Straddling her, he gathered her wrists behind her back and cuffed them. In a swift jerk, he yanked her up by the cuffs and then spun her around.

Pain like stabs of a thousand switch blades arced along her shoulders and down her arms. As she teetered in front of the deputy, she noticed his name badge: Deputy Jones. Her stomach heaved then spewed its contents out over his leather high-tops. She blacked out.

Flashing colors floated over her eyelids as she tasted a mix of bile and dust. She heard voices, some loud and some close to her ear. Then the pain was back, burning and throbbing everywhere. She feared that if she opened her eyes the agony would somehow intensify. Her fists, clutched close to her body, felt sticky and wet. But nothing beat out the pain in her right shoulder. Or, was it her left?

"Iris?" someone whispered near her ear. "I'm Jack. EMT. Can you hear me?"

She smelled peppermint and sandalwood. Her eyelids fluttered.

"That's good. That's good," he assured her. "Can you open your eyes for me?"

She obeyed. Through the cloud of pain, she saw an out-of-focus face outlined by an aura of sunrise.

"Keep your eyes on me," he said. "Can you tell me where it hurts?"

She moved her arm. Electric shock ripped across her chest in sharp, white bolts. She sucked in, paused, then howled out a few choice words she'd learned from Ludie, her gutter swearing housekeeper. Then normal breathing returned. Everything came back into focus. Her gaze landed on Jack EMT's bonnie blues. They smiled at her.

"Looks like you might have yourself a dislocated shoulder," he said softly. "I'm going to wrap you up and take you to the hospital. Can you stay with me?" With intimate tenderness, he wrapped gauze around her shoulders. The calming voice of Jack EMT soothed her pain on the blurred ambulance ride to the hospital.

Her left arm in a black neoprene sling, Iris sat in a wheelchair at the entrance of the emergency room. She and Nurse Cricket were joking about the frequency of her visits as Ethan pulled up in his squad car.

"I got this, Cricket," Ethan said. "Iris, let me take you home."

"Bert's on the way over." She winced as she shifted in the chair.

"Iris, on behalf of the entire squad and Deputy Jones, I'm sorry as I can be about this. But I told you we'd take care of things."

"Did you find Heyu?" she asked.

He removed his straw Stetson and banged it against the side of his long thigh. He shook his head and said, "I got the kid. Name's Roscoe Young. Vinnie says he's the one who rides herd over the lake gang. Cut him loose but I've got somebody watching him. What's the verdict on you?"

"Dislocated shoulder." She held up a bandaged right hand, "Five stitches. You think this Roscoe Young could be working for Bennie?"

"Too early to know for sure."

"I guess Vinnie told you about Damian hanging out at the lake. That's my fault. I encouraged him to get out and make friends."

"You can't blame yourself for that. A kid's mistake is his own doin'."

Recalling Damian's talents for cracking computer passwords, she asked, "Could Damian be in on this?"

"That's one theory," Ethan said.

"Or, maybe they coerced him," Iris said as they watched Bert and Damian pull up in Mr. Henry's Olds, Damian behind the wheel.

CHAPTER 22 NOW

MAKING UP

Barbara Roberts and Sukie Rose were on it. In only three days, the pair managed to froth up the ire of a dozen or so commando readers who were disappointed in Fallam County's failings to support the printed word. A meeting was called at the Bailey Library on Wednesday evening and Iris was invited. Under the pretense of helping her get around, she asked Damian to tag along. Since the discovery of his possible connection with the suspect in Heyu's kidnapping, she wanted him close by at all times.

As they crossed Grove Street and walked along the side of the library, Iris recounted to Damian the legend of Judge John Bailey and his father's Gilded Age mansion. The three-story greystone, at Grove and Court, was once Bailey's private home. It housed the judge's collection of rare books and Confederate artifacts and a hodge-podge of paperbacks and faded copies of classic American and Western European literature. Jutting out over the porch gable, the county flag and Bailey's family crest floated on a breeze. A brass plaque next to the door welcomed visitors to Fallam County Library Main Branch, causing most who entered to wonder where the other branches were.

The meeting preamble was taken up with inquires about Iris' sling with its attached pillow and Damian's plastic boot. Halfway through the agenda, Iris thought about the bottle of pain pills on her dresser. Her entire body throbbed. Her shoulder, her stitched hand, her ribs where the fleeing suspect kicked her, every part of her body begged to go home and stretch out on her new memory foam mattress.

"Iris, what do you think?" Barbara asked.

"About what?"

"Should we go straight to the residents or petition the county supervisors?"

"Yes," Iris replied. "I'm not trying to be a smart aleck, but you need to do both. Your campaign focus has two points: educate residents on the library plan itself and convince the county manager to propose what's called a general obligation bond resolution to the supervisors."

"But what about all those basshole Republicans who think we don't need a new library because we've already got one?" one of the organizers asked.

"You call this a library?" someone added.

"No, it's the main branch," another smirked.

"Most conservatives think in terms of greater need versus cost," Iris said. "Make sure your message addresses costs for *not* building a new facility."

Sukie said, "Iris, you've got experience doing this kind of thing. Can you run it for us?"

"'Fraid not," she said, "conflict of interest. The county solicited my father's company to buy parcels for the site. Check the board of supervisors meeting minutes from last September."

"Where do they want to put it?" asked a volunteer named Maria.

Apparently, Superintendent Augie Young wanted it in his district, but she didn't say this. Instead, she said, "The question you all should be asking is, 'Where do the citizens of Fallam County want it?'"

"Oh, wow! That's a fantastic idea," Barbara exclaimed. "We could get the kids involved and have a voting contest and print up T-shirts."

"And we could have a 'Name the Library' contest," another organizer chimed in.

After the meeting, despite her pain, Iris walked to the other end of the block to Jonnie's office and knocked on the glass door. Looking up at the security camera while she pressed the intercom button, she called, "Jonnie? Are you in there?"

"Who's Jonnie?" Damian asked.

"Jonnie Bailey. Her family owned the house the library is in," she said.

"They must be rich," Damian said as he followed her back down Court toward Grove when the buzzer drew no response.

"I saw Tabby at the meeting. Why didn't you talk to her?" Iris asked.

"Do you think she likes me?"

"It's not about what I think, Damian. Why don't you ask her?"

"Can I drive your car over to the shelter tomorrow?"

"No."

"Can I drive the Olds?"

"No." The inquiry reminded Iris that with her bandaged hand and bum shoulder, she was unable to drive herself. "Ask Ludie to drive you over."

The next morning, the rotary phone rang while Iris, Elizabeth and Damian were having breakfast. Iris labored over to the phone and picked up the heavy receiver with her bandaged hand.

"Is 'is the number I call to report on seein' that mutt hound?"

"It is. Do you know where he is?" Iris asked while making eye contact with Damian. Pain spiked through her injured hand. She wanted justice for Heyu but feared Damian may have had a part in the crime.

"I seen him over on the main road headed to the lake last Saturday."

Iris waited for more information.

"He was by his-self."

"That's all you've got?" she asked. "You saw him walking along the side of the road?"

"No, ma'am. He wont walking on the side. He was walkin' down the *middle*. Like he owned it. Like he knew where he was going to. I honked at him 'til he moved over."

"Did he seem all right?" Iris asked.

"Fine, as best as I could tell. When do I get my reward?"

"I'll get back to you." She hung up without getting the caller's name and number.

The phone rang again.

A mousey voice said, "Hello? I'm Madison and my bru-dder said I should call and tell you I saw your puppy."

Iris heard giggles in the background.

The little girl added, "Bubba says your dog's name is Prince Albert and you better let him out of his can. Bye-bye." The background giggles echoed across the phone line until the disconnect signal replaced them.

Calls of Heyu sightings peppered the entire morning, so much so that they contradicted one another. Sam Holland saw him at the top of Craggy Hill while Princess Crook swore he was running with a pack of mutts on the opposite side of the county. Callers were keenly interested in how to retrieve their reward for information on the hound's whereabouts. But some were sincere in their efforts to help Heyu get back to where he belonged. All the calls gave Iris a comforting sense that Heyu was in the county somewhere and that he'd be home soon.

By two o'clock, Iris switched on the answering machine to filter the calls. Around three, Jonnie arrived with a box of fresh garden vegetables and a sweet pea and onion casserole. Iris was relieved to see her friend.

"Time for a glass of tea?" Iris asked as Elizabeth hovered behind her.

Glancing at her watch, Jonnie said, "Sure, I've got a few minutes."

"Mom, show Jonnie to the sunroom while I make us some tea," Iris said.

As Iris handed Jonnie her drink, Jonnie asked, "Where's your house guest?"

"Who? Damian?" Iris replied.

Jonnie fanned her face with one of Elizabeth's *The Upper Room* devotional magazines and sipped her tea.

"Ludie drove him over to the animal shelter. He's decided to volunteer there," Iris said. "He doused himself with deodorant and aftershave and put on his best basketball jersey to go bathe muddy strays."

"Ah, the fair Tabitha Jean," Jonnie said.

"You know it's *always* about the girl," Iris said.

"Have you met her dad?" Jonnie asked. "Nice guy."

"Nope, we met Tabby when we took some fliers over to the shelter. I believe I witnessed love at first sight. Damian is smitten."

Elizabeth sat quietly and listened as Iris and Jonnie talked about everything but the topic both were avoiding. Iris gnawed on her friend's ear about overflowing toilets, living with a nonverbal teenager and Heyu's disappearance. Jonnie commented on the fading bruise on Iris' head, then rushed into wedding plan minutiae. On and on, the bride-to-be went.

Iris interrupted. "I'm sorry."

Jonnie crossed her arms and arched one of her perfect eyebrows.

"About what I said about you not being in love with Ethan."

"Iris!" Elizabeth blurted out. "Another woman's love for her man is none of your business."

"Oh, Miss Elizabeth, I'm sure Iris meant well."

"No, Jonnie, she's right. It's none of my business. I don't know what got into me that day. I'm sorry for being so callous. It's the Lee way, as you already know."

Leaning forward, Jonnie said, "Apology accepted. But, now I have a confession." Tugging at an earring, she added, "To be honest, I'm nervous about getting married. Maybe that was what you were sensing and misread it."

"You're too kind to say that but, no, it was all me. Wrestling with my green demons and making a horse's ass of myself."

"Iris! Watch that smart mouth of yours," Elizabeth said.

Jonnie pulled at the sides of her skirt then placed her hands in her lap. "What I'm saying is I've been on my own all of my adult life. What if I'm not wife material? What if I mess things up?"

Iris snorted. "You? Mess things up? Jonnie, you're the 'fix-it' queen. There's no way you would allow your own marriage to fail."

"I do love him, you know. I've loved him since the first grade, but when he started following you around like a love-sick puppy in high school, I figured, well, I decided that was that. He was in love with you. Then and there, I promised myself that I was going to find a man who looked at me the way he used to look at you."

"Jonnie, I had no idea. All these years? Why didn't you say something?" Iris pleaded.

Leveling her hand at Elizabeth, Jonnie smiled and said, "Like your mother says, a woman's love is her own affair."

"For the love of Pete's sake," Iris said. "One of these days, Jane Cameron Bailey, I'm going to make you sit down and tell me about every last one of the secrets you and this whole town have been hiding from me." To avoid an emotional reconciliation, one with possible awkward hugs, Iris changed the subject, signifying the matter as resolved. "Are you going to the Fourth of July parade?"

"Oh, I love a parade," Elizabeth said. "Henry and I like to sit near the fountain. I hope we have fair weather this year."

CHAPTER 23 NOW
CHICKEN WIRE AND PORT-A-POTTIES

Iris was watching Plumber Ed thrust his bare hand down Elizabeth's toilet when she felt her phone buzzing in the front pocket of her madras shorts. She stuck her tongue out at Manny's picture as it smiled back at her. She'd been avoiding his calls because she feared he would ask about Heyu and she didn't want to lie about the dog's whereabouts. But this was his third call in the last few hours without leaving a message.

She sighed. Her swollen fingers, poking out from the bandage around her hand, pressed the answer key. "Iris Lee." She felt the hesitation on the other end.

"Iris?"

Hearing him say her name almost caused her knees to buckle. Her body missed his, ached for it.

"I've been trying to reach you all morning."

"Phone service out here is spotty."

"Where are you?"

"My folks'. Helping out with some home renovations. What's up?"

"We're supposed to talk about St. Barts?" His habit of talking up like a fifteen-year-old was once endearing. Now, it grated against the pounding pain in her shoulder.

"Did you talk to Beau?" she asked.

"Bit tricky. He and Carol are still in Bangkok," Manny said.

"Now that's something I don't see everyday," Ed butted in. He held up a single white kid leather glove, water dripping from its fingers and into the toilet bowl.

Iris had seen enough. She stepped over Ed's toolbox and found her way out into the hall. The day was heating up and the smell of baking cedar wafted down from the attic. She waited for Manny to continue.

"I'm in the States for a few days," he said. "We're all here at Sandbridge. Why don't you come down for the Fourth? Bring Heyu. Mary Margaret keeps asking about him."

Iris leaned against the banister and looked down at Ludie polishing the round table in the foyer. "I don't know if I can make it. My guest from L.A. is still here."

"Oh?"

The faint disappointment in his voice sparked a mote's worth of guilt for her false implication. "What have you decided about St. Barts?" she asked.

"I don't think I can swing it. I've got too much going on. I've got to be in Paris on the sixth and I'm not sure when I'll get back to the states." He paused. "About Paris. I'm sorry we didn't get a chance to see each other."

"I am, too," she said as she recalled the young woman tugging at Manny's earlobe. She waited for him to offer a make-up date, another get-away rendezvous for her to turn down. But he didn't. Their romance was crumbling down into the ash heap of lost loves.

"I've got to go. They're calling me. We're sailing the Back Bay this afternoon."

In his wordless way, Manny had just dumped her. The breakup declaration was in what he hadn't said. He didn't say, "I miss you." He hadn't tried hard enough to coax her into coming to the beach by asking, "Are you sure you can't come?" He didn't offer another option like, "Let's go sailing by moonlight." He left her holding the phone to her ear without saying goodbye.

She wasn't going to cry, that's what people in love did. She was no longer in love with David Emmanuel Scott, she declared. And if he wanted Heyu, he'd have to walk over her dead body and get past Ethan's squad of tobacco-chewing gumshoes to get him, possession being nine-tenths of the law and all that. However, she didn't actually have possession of Heyu at the moment. Ethan had dropped by the night before to say that the Young boy slipped through the squad's dragnet. He feared she'd most probably never see Heyu again. So, no, losing a part-time, cheating boyfriend wasn't going to cost her any tears. Not now, anyway. She had too many other worries.

The disappearance of General Jubal Early's medallion unnerved her. She and Ludie had turned the house upside down looking for it. Like Heyu and her father's gun, it had vanished. Fred Kidder's boss's boss called and threatened to cancel the upcoming Christmas show if she didn't produce the artifact by "close of business." The vice president of Sotheby's also hinted at possible legal action for the recovery of their expenses associated with the sale of the medallion. Iris wished she'd never laid eyes on the stupid thing.

Back in Elizabeth's bathroom, she was greeted by the plumber's backside. Today, his T-shirt informed her that Ed was a "Turd Herder." Amid his grunts and groans, he tossed his tools into an oversized metal chest. As he stood, he said, "Mrs. Lee, somebody is stuffing everything but the kitchen sink down that there commode." He pulled a bandanna from his back pocket and mopped

     MELISSA POWELL GAY

his face.

"So, it's working now? You got it all out?" she asked.

Ed stopped midwipe and said, "Hon', this commode is closed for business." He shoved the business end of the snake auger into Iris's face. "Look at this. See that? The pipes are rustin' out. I'm surprised they haven't already busted and flooded the room below."

"But we can still use the hallway bathroom. Right?"

Ed pulled a stick of gum from his shirt pocket, stuffed it in his mouth then said, "You can if you want to make your second floor a swimming pool. Look it, hon', whoever crammed that mess in the master toilet did you a favor. Any day now you'd've come home and found that pretty pink bathtub on top of the dining room table."

Iris adjusted the sling pillow under her arm and asked, "How long will it take to repair?"

"I can't do it now. I got another call. Plus, this here's a two-man job. Best I can do is next week, and that's if I can get Mole to come with me."

Iris stared at her phone, hoping it had the answer to her problems. How was she supposed to care for a wandering woman and a cagey teen with no toilets and no running water in the house? As Ed's truck backed out of the driveway, she scrolled her phone's contacts list for the Grove Street Inn. "Silver linings, Iris," she reminded herself. "The Lee crew is going on a 'Stay-cation'."

Joe Tuner answered.

"Joe! I need two rooms for three days, maybe four."

Joe didn't have any rooms, but he invited her and the others to his annual "after the parade" cookout. Checking with hotels out on the interstate and along the lake road, she discovered every place was booked because of the upcoming holiday. Jonnie had a full house of relations and their families coming in to celebrate their annual get-together. Iris thought about carting everybody off to

Richmond to stay in her condo but Damian resisted when she finally reached him at the shelter. He wanted to stay for the Fourth of July celebrations and begged her for a ride to the hardware store. More chicken wire was needed for the Shelter for Friends' parade float that Tabby and the other volunteers were building.

Leaving Elizabeth with Bert at her Eastend Street bungalow, Iris and Ludie drove over to the shelter to pick up Damian and Tabby. As she merged onto the highway, Ludie buzzed through a litany of enterprises she was pursuing since she and Vinnie had moved to Fallam County. "Miss Lee, Vinnie and I are so grateful for everything you've done for us. You and Mr. Quinn and Miss Bailey are going to be our first house guests when we finally move in. The house should be ready by the end of August."

In exchange for managing the maintenance and renovations of Lee Properties, Iris gave the couple a rundown rental house, two doors down from Bert, to restore. She'd come to rely on the couple. Without their daily assistance, Iris was sure she'd be back in Richmond staring at the high ceilings of her condo and Elizabeth would be wandering around at Miss Wanda's Home for Gentle Ladies. She was grateful for their friendship.

Ludie drove like she cleaned house, with clumsy determination. Iris popped one of her special Tylenols, then pressed her feet against the car's floor. "Careful with the road shoulder, Ludie, I think the county would appreciate you leaving some of the gravel where it is." Iris said.

Ludie guffawed. "Miss Lee, you're funny."

"There's something I keep forgetting to ask Vinnie. Maybe you know the answer. Why was he hanging out in his dad's office with a bunch of Feds the other night?"

Ludie's elbows locked up and her grip on the steering wheel tightened. Eventually, she answered. "Sometimes he works as a

translator, you know, sometimes the people in the jail don't understand English. Vinnie volunteers to help them out."

"Wow! That's something I didn't know about him. What about
you? Do you speak Spanish?"

"No, but being around Vinnie all the time, I can pretty much
understand what he's, what's the word?"

"Conveying?" Iris offered.

"Yeah, what he's conveying."

"How about his mother? Do you guys ever have a chance to talk
to her? Is she bilingual?" Iris asked. "Watch out!" she cried as the
car veered toward a roadside mailbox.

Ludie corrected the car's trajectory with a stiff jerk.

"Pull over," Iris commanded. "Focus on the road, will ya. I've
already been to the hospital twice this month. I'm not interested in
going a third time." Iris was confused. Vinnie's close proximity to a
federal agent or Ludie talking to Vinnie's mother clearly rattled the
nervous housekeeper.

With the grace of a charging rhino, Ludie landed the SUV at
the entrance of a rural driveway. The tires skidded over loose gravel
before they jerked to a stop.

"Remind me to call a cab the next time I ask you to drive," Iris
deadpanned. Taking a shot in the dark, she asked an open-ended
question. "What's going on?"

Ludie hid her face in her shaking hands. For a second the only
sound was the idling motor. Then raw sobs flooded out of her as
she wailed like a biblical wretch. The noise took over all the space
and air inside the car.

Never believing she'd ever borrow words from her plumber,
Iris said, "Hon'," and tried to console Ludie by patting her on the
shoulder with her bandaged hand.

The sobbing contractions intensified.

"You want to talk about this?" Iris asked.

"No! No! No! I can't. I can't. Please don't make me." Her turned down flattened bottom lip revealed teeth in a pool of spittle. Holding her fists to her chest, she rocked as she sat behind the wheel, eking out, "I promised. I promised. I can't tell. Don't make me tell you." She pulled away a strand of hair snot-glued to her cheek. A prominent scar, round like a cigarette burn, glowed pink on the back of her trembling hand.

What had this child been through in life? Knowing Ludie was probably aching for one, Iris suggested, "Let's have a smoke." Leaning against the back of the car, Ludie puffed away as traffic whizzed by. Iris waited.

Ludie hocked then spit into the red dust at her feet. "When we were living in Santa Fe, a friend of ours, his name was Odie, got me a job cleaning houses. One of the customers is the world's *numero uno* a-hole. I'd call him worse but I promised your mom I'd try to give up cussin'."

Iris waited as Ludie took a long drag on her smoke.

"Those Feds were in Mt Pleasant asking Vinnie about Odie and his customers," Ludie said.

Iris watched a farm truck wobble by, knowing she had no right to ask Ludie to explain herself. She tried a different tack. "Does Ethan know what you can't tell me?"

Blowing smoke, the skittish anorectic nodded, then ground out her cigarette with her flip-flop.

"That's all I need to know." And it was. Her life was complicated enough without getting entangled in Ludie's hillbilly tragedies. She was comforted by the fact that Ethan, their mutual protector, had whomever this *numero uno* a-hole was in his cross-hairs. "Let's go get Damian and Tabby and see about that chicken wire."

Back in the car, Ludie heaved in a gulp of air and wiped at her

     MELISSA POWELL GAY

wet face. "I'm sorry about making such a fuss. That hard cry was like a nasty ole hairball, it needed to come out."

Tabby's teenage exuberance appeared to be diluting Damian's boy gangsta machismo. He actually squealed when she asked Ludie to stop at Louie's Gas-N-Go for ice cream. Watching the budding love birds ogle each other as melting ice cream drooled over their fingers caused Iris to dread the adult conversation she needed to have with him about all things missing. No room for denial, all three Lee treasures: the gun, the medallion and Heyu went missing the week Damian had arrived. By choice or under duress, either way, he was involved.

The previous evening, when Ethan had sat in the front porch glider drinking iced tea and updating Iris on his failed plan to follow Young to Heyu, he wanted to question Damian. Iris refused. The boy was, after all, her charge and if he was involved, she wanted to know before an officer of the court questioned him. Frustrated, Ethan hinted that Young was connected to a gang of New Mexico rough riders. Since Damian had been seen with Young, he was implicated in the dognapping and worse. Ethan invited her to bring him down to the station for an informal chat. Iris cautioned Ethan. Hauling Damian down to the jailhouse and accusing him of theft and extortion would produce the opposite of the Chief's desired results. Ratting out his new friend, or worse, making a confession, wasn't something a kid with Damian's creed was inclined to do.

"That boy needs to learn there are consequences to his actions, Iris. The sooner the better. You know what road he's headed down. If I don't talk to him before tomorrow night, the next knock on your door will be a couple of FBI boys." Ethan put on his hat and walked away.

Licking her own ice cream cone, she listened as Tabby and

Damian flirted under the patio table's umbrella. How could a kid whose voice still cracked be messed up with hard-boiled scum the likes of which Ethan dealt with every day? The thought gave her goose bumps. If he was involved, what was his motive? Why would he purposely want to cause harm to Heyu? The two hit it off instantly on the ride home from Knoxville. Could he have been involved then changed his mind and wanted out? Could he have been coerced by Young and the other kids? Or, maybe, just maybe, he was telling the truth and didn't have anything to do with the thefts.

Roscoe Young, almost an adult in the eyes of the law, was tied to Heyu's ransom and Damian knew this boy. Iris recognized the young man in a picture Ethan showed her. He was the smart mouthed boy who spoke of Damian's diving skills the day she went to fetch him, the day he sprained his ankle. Damian had access to the safe where the gun and the medallion were but he denied taking them. Maybe the Young kid bullied Damian into steeling the gun and the medallion. But did that really make any sense? Why didn't they take the other weapons? With her half-eaten ice cream cone, she took a one-handed lay up shot at the trashcan and missed. She'd run out of time. She had to confront Damian with what Ethan suspected.

Pushing a cart with the side of her lame hand at Duncan's Hardware, Iris nodded as Tabby chattered on and on about why she and her dad weren't taking a summer vacation this year on account of her job at the shelter. Damian and Ludie had followed one of the red vested associates to load the wire into the SUV.

"That's nice," Iris said to Tabby who had moved on to why she and her dad had left her boozy mother. Surrounded by the smell of ages of salt treated lumber, hemp rope and oily nails, the cart lead her to the plumbing aisle. And there they were, her solution to her water closet woes-bedside waterless commodes. She and Tabby

    MELISSA POWELL GAY

watched as another helpful associate climbed a ladder and retrieved two, complete with folding arms and toilet paper holders. At the checkout counter, she paid for the commodes and the chicken wire with her credit card, the one she used to purchase Broadway show tickets and 5th Avenue shopping sprees. How her life had changed.

CHAPTR 24 THEN
LOVE AND BABY

When Henry went to work for his father in the fall of 1953, Ben got his wish. The Lee Properties management company paid for a new office suite in the National Building, downtown Roanoke's hot new, and only, skyscraper. The company also made a down payment on a railroad executive's overpriced Greek revival with a valley view from its veranda. Washing Fallam County's red dust from the panels of their new station wagon, Ben and Sarah set out to live a privileged life among the city's modern, gilt-edged elite. Sarah hosted afternoon bridge games and baby showers while Ben, the son-in-law of a judge, played golf and accepted board appointments. Back home in Mt Pleasant, Henry helped his father phase out his law practice and managed the upkeep of all the buildings and rental houses Allen Lee had amassed over the decades.

Once the handsome couple settled in, social protocol called for an open house. One spring evening the following year, Mt Pleasant family and friends from the lower rungs were allowed a peek inside Ben and Sarah's new world of groomed acquaintances and chintz draperies. With contrived gentility, the affair featured bourbon laced with fresh mint in Jefferson cups, iced tea sweating in lead crystal glasses and fancy finger food. Henry's attendance was mandatory as driver and footman for his parents. After an exhausting round of introductions, the over-gracious hostess parked the three in the library on a pair of settees under a painting of crossed sabers entwined with corded sash and Confederate battle flag. On a wood-paneled wall, an empty custom-made shadow box hung waiting, as Sarah mentioned, for Jubal Early's Civil War artifact that Ben would inherit one day. Whispering in Henry's ear, Matilda commented on the flagrant boldness of the room's décor as Mr. Lee discussed national politics with a federal judge. His parents settled, Henry excused himself. He weaved among guests, who were shouting and blowing smoke at one another, and found his way to the kitchen.

"Look out, coming through." To avoid a collision, a young woman raised a serving tray above her head. Henry held the butler's door and watched as the small, trim figure found a path through party gadflies. Embarrassed, he looked away as she caught him watching her.

Upon her return to the kitchen, she extended her hand and said, "Elizabeth Carter."

Henry's past girl troubles started with a pretty one offering her hand. He slipped his hands into his pressed chinos. "I'm Henry."

"Henry, as in Sarah's brother-in-law Henry?"

To which he replied, "You must be Elizabeth as in 'You have to meet my best friend Libby.'" As he followed the brown-eyed girl to a table full of party food, he said, "I've come to raid my brother's liquor cabinet. Ben would never serve the good stuff to Mt Pleasant teetotalers."

Elizabeth giggled. "I wouldn't know. I'm a teetotaler myself."

A blue sapphire ribbon held in place with rhinestone bobby pins kept a thatch of rich brown strands away from her sweet face.

She was pretty in a creamy, wholesome kind of way. Her youthful countenance suggested he ask her what grade she was in at school. But a stolen glance at her woman's body as she reached across the table hinted that she was old enough to handle men's advances. He blew out a long breath to distract his thoughts and surveyed the spread of cheeses, dips, crackers and celery sticks. "I don't believe Mt Pleasant's great unwashed have ever eaten food prepared in this way. Where are the potato salad and ham biscuits?" He picked up something that looked like a beef lollypop.

Henry's question provoked an unexpected reaction. Breezy laugher filled his ears, a laugh that had not yet known profound sorrows. Years later, when he recalled hearing her laugh that first time, he marked it as the moment he decided he wanted her by his side for the rest of his days.

"What's so funny?" He laughed along with her.

"Sarah said you had a sarcastic wit," she said.

"Why? Because I prefer ham biscuits to canapés? Must have taken you awhile to make these." He held up the half-eaten meat stick as an exhibit.

"Me? Oh, no. I didn't make those." Spreading her arms over the feast, she added, "All this was catered. I can't boil water without burning the pan," she said. "I think you'll find the good bourbon in the butler's pantry." She removed the apron Sarah lent her earlier and tossed it on the counter.

From that day forward Henry and Elizabeth lived their lives as a couple. Henry's dark moods and her unconventional, sometimes feminist, views on everything from politics to child rearing occasionally caused their relationship to stray from its path of devotion. However, until his dying day, Henry adored his blissful dove Elizabeth.

In the summer of 1954, they walked down the aisle at Mt

     MELISSA POWELL GAY

Pleasant Methodist Church six weeks after Elizabeth told Henry she was pregnant. The newlyweds settled into the Lee farmhouse and Elizabeth transformed the makeshift frat lodge into a home and nest for their new arrival. The honeymoon was cut short when Matilda Lee died unexpectedly, prompting Henry and Elizabeth to move to Grove House to care for a grieving Mr. Lee.

The first Grove House Thanksgiving dinner without Matilda was a somber occasion for everyone. Everyone except Ben. For Ben, Henry and his flakey wife moving to Grove House meant the return to gambling, drinking and other adventures a married man cared to enjoy in the backwoods of Fallam County. Taking Henry aside after dinner, Ben ordered his little brother to reopen the farmhouse. Then he slapped Henry on the back and stuffed a hand-rolled cigar into his shirt pocket. Henry had been expecting his brother's request to convert their family's birthplace into a playpen for Ben and his toadies. Becoming a husband and an expectant father bolstered his confidence; Henry had a plan to outmaneuver, thus stand up to, his brother without resorting to childish fisticuffs.

"I have neither the time nor desire to pick up after that shiftless horde of idlers you call friends," Henry said as the two sat in front of fireplace. He handed the cigar back to his brother. With attempted bravado, his voice warbled when he added, "They want to gamble and whore around, take it to the other side of the railroad tracks or down Old Lick Road."

"Come on, Henry, get off your church horse. Stumpy Quinn already told us he'll keep his boys from sniffing around. Pay one of the company's lackeys to keep the place up and be done with it," Ben said. He sat back, struck a match on the sole of his shoe and sucked on the cigar.

Gaining confidence, Henry said, "No. I've rented the place out to one of Tom Tyler's nephews and his family. Vee's daughter Baby is going to live with them. They move in on the first of December."

"Why you little," Ben threw the spent match at the fire. "Leave it alone, Henry."

"No. I won't," Henry pushed back.

Ben shook a finger at Henry. "Why I ought to deck you right here, you little squirt. You think you know better than me."

"Stumpy Quinn might be able to tell his own men what to do but he can't keep Feds from poking around. If your little operation was ever raided, it'd drag the Lee name through the mud."

Ben blew smoke into Henry's face then said. "Boooooy, that little bleeding heart Eleanor Roosevelt you've hitched up with has drained all the good sense right out of you."

Henry clenched his jaw. As usual, Ben was goading him. Past experiences taught him that a jab at his brother's kisser only gave Ben cause to play the victim. Henry focused on the waning fire.

"You want to know what's going to shame our family's good name, little brother?" Ben asked quietly. With eerie calm, he poked at Henry's arm as he said, "Renting out the birthplace of your granddaddy, a colonel who served with distinction in the Army of Northern Virginia, to a pack of coons."

Henry responded with equal composure. "And what? Ignoring the birthright of your own child and beating her mother senseless whenever the mood strikes you gets us Family of the Year?" Maintaining eye contact, Henry willed himself not to flinch.

Storm clouds passed over his brother's eyes, then dissipated. Ben smiled and said, "Ah, wittle Hen-wee still mad 'cause big brudder stole his girlfriend. Does Mrs. Roosevelt know you're still in love with the county's hottest ticket in the love game?" Ben's powerful hand clamped around Henry's wrist and squeezed.

"Cut it out." Henry tried to free his arm.

"Let me tell you something. Violet Tyler gets what she asks for.

     MELISSA POWELL GAY

Now, you go tell that Tyler boy he needs to find another place to raise all his brats."

Henry yanked his wrist free from Ben's grip.

"Here now, what's all this?"

The brothers turned to see the old man leading Sarah and Elizabeth into the drawing room.

"Henry, what's the matter?" a worried Elizabeth asked.

"Tell them, Ben," Henry said as he rubbed his wrist. "Share with the rest of the family your plans for the farmhouse."

"Get your stuff, Sarah. We're leaving," Ben said.

"Henry?" Elizabeth repeated.

Ben brushed passed Sarah, almost knocking her down.

Sarah called out, "Ben. Wait," and ran after him

"Henry? What have you done to make your brother so angry?" The old man asked.

Ben had folded, leaving Henry to worry over what he should tell their father. Still rubbing at his wrist he recalled the night Vee showed up at his door, the hatred and violence on her face burned in his memory. And Baby, without coat or shoes, was standing by her side in the cold, raw air. The next day, Henry had delivered Baby to a much relieved Alice Tyler. From time to time, Henry dropped by to check on Baby. During one such visit, Henry met a Tyler nephew and his wife. They had taken Baby to live with their large family in a tar-paper shack out in the woods of the southern part of the county. When it came time to move to Grove House, Henry offered Andy Tyler the use of the farm in exchange for its upkeep and a small percentage of the crop's income, enough to cover the property taxes.

"Henry? What's going on?" Elizabeth was at his side.

"Ben and I are at odds about what to do with the farmhouse now that we're no longer living there."

"Elizabeth, can you leave us?" the old man asked.

Rubbing her swollen belly, Elizabeth kissed her husband's cheek and retired for the evening.

"Henry, are you ever going to learn to stand up for yourself?"

"What are you asking?"

"Your brother has run roughshod over you since you were boys. You're about to become a father. No child wants a doormat for a daddy. Sit down, son. What were you two arguing about?"

"Ben wants the farmhouse … as a second residence," Henry said as he sat beside his father. "But I've already rented it out to Andy Tyler. He wants to try his hand at raising tobacco."

"Tom Tyler's son?"

"His nephew," Henry said. "The place is idle and Andy is a willing renter."

"Son, we can't have coloreds living in Colonel Lee's house."

"What difference does it make if he's colored? He wants to rent the place. Growing up, you always told us to treat everyone fair and square," Henry said.

"If your brother wants the use of the house, let him have it. Rent Andy the land to farm," the old man said. "Now, I think that's fair. Don't you?" He sniffed the cigar his oldest son had given him then said, "Hand me a match, boy."

"Oh, so you must have meant fair and square and separate," Henry said as he lit his father's cigar.

Focusing on the stogie, Mr. Lee said, "Condescension is a haughty cloak, boy. It never looks good on its owner. Do as your brother asks."

That night as they lay in bed, Henry told Elizabeth about Violet Tyler leaving her daughter at his doorstep and him helping the Tylers make a home for Baby.

"Oh, Henry. That poor child," Elizabeth said. He felt her arm

     MELISSA POWELL GAY

move as she rubbed her belly. Then, out of the dark came, "Are you her father?"

His bride's unambiguous insight caused Henry discomfort. Rolling away from her onto his side, he said, "No. Ben is."

Fearing the unknown more than the consequences of the answer, Elizabeth asked, "Are you still in love with her?"

"I may have loved her, a long time ago."

"Perhaps, because you loved her, you feel a duty to care for her and the child since your brother won't. Is that what the two of you were arguing over when we came in?"

He rose and towered over the bed. "Baby's family needs a home. Ben doesn't need another place to sell bootleg. That's what we were arguing about. Don't ever ask me about Violet Tyler again." He slipped from the room.

The honeymoon was over and the marriage had begun, Elizabeth thought. How was she to compete with a bond as strong as first love? Rubbing her belly, she said to Phillip, Philippa if it was to be a girl, "Let's pray he will love you as much as he loves Baby." She thought about going down to the kitchen for another piece of pumpkin pie but the baby was still for once so she dozed off to sleep.

In the early morning Henry awoke from a restless night in the front seat of his car. He drove down the county road thinking about a cup of Luzianne's at Andy's. His stomach soured at the thought of telling Andy's wife that the house was no longer available. After pulling into the yard, he watched a gust of wind lift a loose end of tar paper from the corner of the two-room cabin, revealing raw wood and mud. During his time at the farmhouse, Henry had wired it for electricity and installed plumbing for the kitchen. He and Andy were planning an addition for an indoor bathroom. The heating oil company was scheduled to install a burner in the second floor hallway to keep Baby and her cousins' bedrooms warm. The place was a palace compared to the leaning shack before him.

Several pairs of young eyes appeared in the cracked window as a fact occurred to Henry. Baby was a Lee. She had as much right as her father to live in that farmhouse. With renewed cravings for a warm cup of chicory, he got out of his car and went inside to ask Andy and Melba if they needed help moving their stuff into their new home.

On a balmy Wednesday afternoon in September 1964, Sarah Duncan Lee walked briskly down the hallway of the shiny new Fallam County hospital gripping the hand of her four-year-old son, Bennie Jr. As they approached, Henry sat a little straighter and winked at the towheaded boy and called him Cracker Jack because that's what the kid always asked for whenever Henry took him to Booker T's for a treat.

Staring at Henry, the tyke pulled on the plastic nose of his stuffed hound dog tucked under his arm.

"Say hello to your Uncle Henry, Bennie," Sarah said.

"No!" He hid his face in the folds of his mother's skirt.

Henry said, "It's kind of you to come. Mrs. Duncan getting along all right?" The judge's widow lived with her daughter and handsome son-in-law.

"Mom's fine. Any word yet on Libby and the baby?" Sarah perched on the edge of the waiting room sofa with her back straight and ankles crossed.

"Doctor says she's right on schedule," Henry said.

"I dropped off a tuna casserole at the house. It's nice of that colored girl to stay with your father so you can be here with Libby."

"Bert's been a comfort for Elizabeth. She helps out after school," Henry said. Sarah's calling Bert "that colored girl" irritated Henry.

His sister-in-law knew good and well who Bert was, but he didn't fault her for her feigned ignorance.

"Ben sends his love. He's sorry he can't be here. He's got a big day in court tomorrow."

"That's kind of you to deliver his message." Henry went along with the charade for the sake of Elizabeth's fondness of Sarah. Once Bert started working for Elizabeth after school and on weekends, Ben avoided most family events.

Sarah mashed her lips together. Her fingers fidgeted with her purse handles. She patted the empty space on the sofa and called for Bennie to join her. As he climbed up beside his mother, she said, "Sweetie, you're going to get another cousin today. Someone you can play with when you and daddy come to Mt Pleasant. Won't that be fun?"

"Can we play with my toys at Miss Vee's 'partment?" the boy asked.

Henry's eyes widened at the child's question.

Sarah laughed nervously, "Sure honey," and, as if she needed to explain for Henry, she added, "Daddy sometimes has to go to Miss Vee's to get a haircut and you and your cousin can go with him and play together." She pulled a coin purse from her handbag and sang, "Bennie, honey, be a big boy and go down the hall and ask that nice nurse to help you buy a pack of Nabs from the vending machine for Mommy." She wasted no time as Bennie hop-skipped down the polished hallway. "Don't give me that look, buster. It's all your fault. If you hadn't let that … that … Tyler family move into the farmhouse, he wouldn't be spending all of his time at her place."

Henry had heard it all before. For months after the Tylers moved in, Ben cried a river over his younger brother's "flagrant disregard of father's ruling" on the farmhouse's use. Henry bided his time. And when Ben came to him to borrow money to buy a membership in a new private county club, Henry offered Ben a personal loan with the condition that he'd quit his bellyaching about the farm. Years later, Henry had yet to get his money back and Sarah had become Ben's proxy to lord over Henry the injustice of his actions.

"It's just not fair to us, Henry," Sarah complained. "Ben wants to restore the place and use it for a retreat for the family. I think it would be good for him. For us."

Henry leaned back in his chair and crossed his arms over his chest. "Doctor said it might take awhile." He closed his eyes to pretend sleep. Talking with Sarah required more restraint than he had energy for at the moment.

Whenever Sarah visited Elizabeth and Henry at Grove House, she took the opportunity to share with her country relations the fortunate lifestyle her family enjoyed as a result of her loving husband's success in the courtroom. Elizabeth believed every word. Henry considered the woman delusional. Brother Ben kept his wife distracted with garish gifts while running with the criminals and cowards he sometimes represented in court. Often tempted to inform Sarah of the actual source of her husband's seemingly infinite income, he refrained because of the discomfort it would cause Elizabeth.

"Mr. Lee," the nurse said softly. "She's ready for you now."

Rubbing sleep from his eyes, Henry noticed that Sarah and Bennie were gone. Following the nurse through a maze of hallways and rooms, they reached Elizabeth's. His wife, looking haggard, held a tiny swaddle of pink flannel close to her chest.

"She's beautiful, Hank," Elizabeth marveled. "Look at our own little sweet pea. Iris Hazel."

But all Henry saw was his wife. Taking her head in his hands, he buried his tears in her thicket of auburn locks and kissed them. They had almost lost her, twice, to miscarriages, each time a boy.

She had persuaded him to try again.

"Want to hold her?" Elizabeth asked.

"I'll hold you both," he said. He wrapped his arms around Elizabeth as she squeezed her baby tight.

The infant wailed.

"Oh, no," Henry whispered into Elizabeth's ear, "Another lawyer."

"Wisenheimer," Elizabeth playfully patted the side of his face. "Can you take her for a minute? I'm tired."

Before Henry could lift his daughter from her mother's arms, a nurse swooped in and carried the babe away. Henry stayed at Elizabeth's side, watching her sleep. Before he left the hospital, the doctor assured him of Elizabeth's recovery but recommended she not give birth to any more children. At home, the place blazed with light. In the dining room, Bert and the old man were eager for news of the family's latest addition.

"My first granddaughter!" Mr. Lee exclaimed.

Amid the old man's renewed pleas for his son to consider naming the child after her grandmother Matilda, Henry searched Bert's face for a response to the unintended slight. He watched as she quickly stacked up dishes on a tray. He followed her into the kitchen. "Forgive him, Baby. He doesn't know," Henry said.

"I've asked you to call me Roberta or Bert. That's my name," she said. "That woman who give birth to me calls me Baby and I want nothin' to do with her or that stupid name."

Henry nodded. "I'm sorry, Bert." Tilting his head to get her attention, he continued, "That name suits you. You're growing up to be a strong woman, Bert Tyler." Unpracticed at handing out compliments, he reached for a plate on the tray to mask his uneasiness.

She jerked the plate from his hand and placed it in the sink.

"Bert, come outside," he said. He motioned for her to follow him to the back porch.

"Why? So the old man won't hear us talking about his other granddaughter?"

"Don't get smart mouthed," Henry said.

She crossed her arms over her growing breasts and harrumphed.

To get through what he wanted to say to his niece, Henry stared out at the night sky searching for M. Ellen's guiding star. Eventually, he said, "Listen to me. The old man was born in the last century. He lived his entire life believing what he was taught as righteous. He's a lost cause. I'd forget about him if I were you." Henry forced himself to face Bert.

"What if I was to tell him?" Bert insisted.

"I'd advise against it. The pain of the telling would be on you, not him," he paused then went on, "Because of who he is, he can't see you as anyone but one of Andy Tyler's chaps."

Bert's face glistened with tears.

Handing her his handkerchief, he said, "Hey, you see me crying because I didn't get what I wanted in life?"

"You got a mama and daddy who claim you and say they love you," Bert sniffed.

He laughed at her naiveté. "Believe me, having a daddy who controlled every part of my life isn't what I'd call a happy childhood. And love, my father never used that word with me. But you, Bert Tyler, have more people who claim you and care about you than anyone in this town."

Bert blew her nose and sat on the top step. "Andy and Melba's my kin but they ain't my mama and daddy."

Henry sat next to her and lit a cigarette. Squeezing the butt between his thumb and forefinger, he counted on his other fingers, "They raised you right, put clothes on your back and food in your mouth. A roof over your head. Made you go to school when you didn't want to. In my book, that's what a mama and daddy do."

"'Cept they don't treat me like all the others," Bert whined.

"See, now you're just looking for ways to feel sorry for yourself. And I find that tiresome."

After a minute of reflection, Bert said, "Tell me about the baby. Does she take after her mama?"

A grin tugged at the corner of Henry's flat lips. "Natural selection saw to it that she didn't get my ears."

"Praise goodness, I know Miss Elizabeth is grateful for that," she said.

And that was the last time Henry and Bert discussed their familial connection. The expression "I love you" was never exchanged between them.

CHAPTER 25 NOW

ELIZABETH SPEAKS

Iris and Ludie left the kids at the shelter to finish decorating the parade float. On their way back to town, they listened to the weather forecast: hot and hazy with a high probability of afternoon thunderstorms. They found Bert, with Elizabeth, rocking on her front porch. Donnie waved from the sidewalk as Ludie parallel parked.

Before they got out of the car, Iris said, "Ludie, whatever happened in Santa Fe, you and Vinnie need to trust Ethan to help sort it out."

Ludie looked away, offering neither explanation nor excuse.

"Do you own a gun?" Iris asked.

Ludie laughed. "We live with a cop who used to be in the military. But Vinnie doesn't like guns. He wrestled in high school."

"What about you?" Iris asked. "The boys aren't any good to you if they're not around."

"I can take care of myself," Ludie assured her.

"It's a hot one today," Bert called out as they stepped onto her porch.

"Bert, why don't you let Vinnie's guys install central air for you?"

     MELISSA POWELL GAY

Iris asked.

"Sweet pea, I've lived over sixty years without wearing a sweater in July and I don't plan on startin' now," Bert said. "I can't stand to be cold."

"Me neither," Donnie chimed in. "At the Elder Care, they keep the thermostat on arctic freeze."

"Y'all want some tea?" Bert asked.

"No, thank you. I'm meeting Vinnie over at the house," Ludie said, waving goodbye.

"Stiff wind gonna come along one day and blow that girl right up in the air if she don't put some meat on her bones," Bert said as they followed Ludie's lopsided gait down the sidewalk. While Bert served tea, Donnie lit up on the top step. Iris leaned against the banister.

Seeing her mother slip into a cat nap, Iris asked, "Bert, when Dad was in the hospital, Mom kept saying he was visiting Violet Tyler. Exactly what was their relationship?" She spied Donnie's cautionary glance at Bert. "Hey, I've forgiven you guys for hiding the family drama in the closet and not telling me about it. But I'm not the little kid anymore. I'm actually in charge of my family now. So, if you wouldn't mind, I'd appreciate it if you'd answer my question."

"What you want to know?" Donnie asked.

"Why you want to dig up old hurts?" Bert fretted.

"Now, Baby, that's not for you to judge," Donnie insisted.

"Baby?" Iris squinted.

"That's what's on my birth certificate. My mama, she was too busy running the road and drinking to name me."

"So, how did you end up with 'Bert?'" Iris asked.

"I believe," Donnie said, "Mr. Henry and Andy's wife decided she needed a name more fitting than 'Baby Tyler.'" Donnie said to

Bert, "Mr. Henry said he asked you what you wanted to be called and you said 'Eartha.'" Donnie took a hit off his cigarette, then continued. "But Melba suggested you take the name Roberta after your daddy Benjamin Robert."

Bert chuckled, "I wanted to be a singer like Eartha Kitt." She added, "But I like my name because Mr. Henry liked it."

"He liked it 'cause it helped remind the Lees who you were," Donnie said.

A rumble of distant thunder interrupted the awkward silence.

Changing the subject, Bert complained, "We don't need any more rain. Weeds already takin' over my pole beans."

"I'm confused," Iris said. "Henry liked Violet. So, did Ben steal her away?"

"You could say that," Donnie said.

"Chile, the jealousy between your daddy and his brother was as old as Cain and Abel's. Those two competed for everything, including my mama's attention. My grandma told me that Vee told her those two fought over her constantly."

Donnie ground his butt onto the concrete step. "You got to mind who's telling the story. Vee tended to puff up her feathers."

"Mom said she was pretty," Iris said.

"A lot of men thought so," Donnie said. "She and Ben were mad for each other. Know what I'm sayin'? They'd be hangin' on each other one minute and tryin' to kill each other the next. I reckon today they'd lock Ben up for punching her around like he did. But she gave as good as she got. Two peas in a pod, those two."

"How did she die?"

"Cancer."

Another rumble of thunder, along with a cool breeze, seeped into the conversation.

Bert sniffed, got up and went into the house.

"I guess she doesn't like hearing about this," Iris said.

"Would you? Neither one of those sorry excuses ever recognized her as their own, that I know of. She would'a told me if they had."

"So, Bert was a love child and dad was in love with his brother's lover?"

"Sweet pea, your daddy wont in love with nobody 'cept your mama. And that's a fact."

"Why did Ben leave?" Iris asked. "Jonnie told me he left because he was in trouble with a judge. Do you know anything about that?"

"Ben threatened me. Henry told him to leave and never come back," Elizabeth said.

They stared in surprise at Elizabeth. Her arms wobbled as she pushed herself up from the rocker. "He was a liar and a bully. Took what pleased him. Your father was the only person who would stand up to him."

Bert's wind chimes jangled.

"Mom?" Iris asked, not sure what confused her more, her mother's accusations or her speaking more coherently than she had in months. "You never told me that." She latched onto the old woman's elbow to help steady her.

Elizabeth tilted her head to get a better view of her daughter. To everybody in town, Ben Lee was a man of the community. But your father knew what he really was, a poser," Elizabeth said.

"What's that supposed to mean?" Iris asked.

"I don't talk about it because I don't want to hurt Bert's feelings." Cupping her hand to her mouth, she whispered, "She's Ben's daughter, you know." Raising her voice, she said, "I'm hungry. What are we having for dinner?"

"Mom—," Iris tried.

"Iris, don't." Bert was back on the porch. "Come on, Miss Elizabeth, let's get you home."

"No!" Iris exclaimed, hair floating in the swirling breeze. "We're not going anywhere until I get some answers." Thinking about what waited for her at home, no water, no bath, no toilet for the next who knew how long, Iris exploded. "I'm getting sick and tired of people changing the subject every time I ask about Dad and Uncle Ben." Her excitement caused her to twist her arm and pain shot through the shoulder, driving her fury. "First, Jonnie tells me he left because he lied to a judge, then, Bert, when we were in L.A., you tell me he was chased out by his moonshiner clients. Now, Mom says *Dad* forced him away from his home because he was nasty to her? Which is it?"

"Why are you yelling, Iris?" Elizabeth asked.

"I'm not yelling." Lowering her voice, Iris said, "I'm frustrated." She squirmed under the hot shoulder sling.

"It was the medallion," Bert blurted out. She eased back into her rocker.

"What?"

"Elizabeth and your daddy said that Ben was obsessed with it," Bert said.

"Oh, he was, all right. His pot boiled over when he learned Mr. Lee had left it to me," Elizabeth said with the clarity of one with total recall.

"Mom, why didn't you tell me this?" Iris whined.

"You never asked," Elizabeth replied simply.

"But, remember when we were cleaning out your closet and we found it in your coat pocket?" As Iris spotted confusion in her mother's face, she said, "Never mind." Her shoulder and her stitched hand ached for another aspirin.

Bert picked up the story, "The day after they put Mr. Lee to rest, I was staying with you while your mom and dad went to the lawyer's office. Mr. Henry come home and got in his car and drove away without coming inside. Well, after he left, here come your mama and Ben and his wife in their car. Sarah stayed in the car. When Ben and your mama came inside, he started yelling and cursing. You remember that, Elizabeth?"

Elizabeth nodded. "He called me the 'C' word."

Iris and Bert went wide-eyed from that comment.

"But you stood up to him. Didn't you, Elizabeth?"

"I did."

Bert helped the story along. "Ben followed your mama up the stairs. But she managed to lock herself in the bathroom. He was pounding on the door and screaming at her. Saying if she didn't give him the general's medal, he was gonna tell Henry about what happened between them."

"What!" Iris shrilled.

"It was nothing. I kissed him once," Elizabeth said. "Now, can we go? I want ice cream for dinner."

"Mom," Iris said, "you vamp."

"Hush up, child," Elizabeth scolded in a husky voice.

Bert continued. "Then Sarah went up the stairs and started yelling at Ben to stop beating on the door and to get in the car. She wanted to leave. Those two were the yelling-est people I ever knew," she said. "Thank God and baby Jesus, she came in when she did. Ben had 'bout ripped the door frame away. If he'd gotten to Elizabeth, there was no telling what he might've done. Man was plumb out of his mind."

"Why don't I remember any of this?" Iris asked.

"I made sure you was playin' in the backyard, sweet pea," Bert said. "No sense in a child your age hearing such family ruckus."

"Ben was a poser," Elizabeth repeated. Her hand lapped over the other on her tummy.

"He and Sarah left. Walked right passed me. I never saw him

again," Bert said.

An anxious Elizabeth blinked and spoke as if she'd just awoken from her nap in the rocker. "Iris, we need to get home before it gets dark."

They reached home before the storm arrived. Standing in the frame of the front door, she felt the pressure of the storm as if suspended underwater. Above her, the wind flowed through Elizabeth's giant chestnut tree, retreating then surging again like a tidal wave. Thick with moisture, the heavy air muffled distant sounds of slamming doors and barking dogs. She hoped Heyu found shelter, wherever he was.

Elizabeth came to her daughter's side. Closing her eyes and lifting her face to the wind, she asked, "Can you smell it?"

"Smell what?" Iris asked.

"The smell of summer, the sweetness of rain drops melting on hot pavement."

Iris closed her eyes, hearing the wind-surf surge again. "The wind in the trees sounds like ocean waves," she whispered.

"Shhh," Elizabeth said calmly.

They listened as the gusts became louder.

Then, *CRACK*!

Iris opened her eyes as a violent blow twisted the limbs of the chestnut tree. Its roots bobbed to the surface then dangled while the tree rose up into a wind spout long enough for lightning to harpoon its greatest limb. As if underwater, the leviathan sank weightlessly, taking power lines with it as it landed across the driveway.

"Glory to God!" Elizabeth cried. Holding her hands to her lips as in prayer, she called out over the wind, "Hosanna in the highest!"

Confounded by the day's inconveniences, Iris howled as the wind picked up again, "Holy sky fairies!" The fall of the mighty chestnut meant they'd go days without power. She put her good

     MELISSA POWELL GAY

arm over her mother's shoulder and watched as hailstones bounced among the fallen limbs and leaves.

Iris and Elizabeth spent the night on the sun porch with all the jalousie rolled out to allow what cool air could be had to find them. Aside from the heat, her mother's passive snoring managed to keep her awake most of the night. Just as Iris made it to sleep's edge, Elizabeth's fluttering lips quietly *flapped, flapped, flapped, flapped.* At sunrise she lay on her flaccid air mattress and stared at the ceiling. Damian never made it home.

"Hello?" an unfamiliar male voice called from the backyard.

Iris leveraged the elbow on her good side over a sofa cushion and pushed herself up. Flexing her fingers, she felt the stitches tug in her hand. Readjusting the shoulder sling, she caught a whiff of body odor.

"Hello?" The male voice called again.

Iris tiptoed through the mudroom and out the back door. A shirtless young man donning a lime safety vest, stood in jeans and boots on the walkway. Swinging from his powerful hand was the biggest chainsaw Iris had ever seen. She squinted at the guy and rubbed at her bedhead. "Who are you?"

"Enrico," he said, "but everybody calls me Hank."

"And you're here because?" Her tongue reminded her she needed to brush her teeth.

"Vinnie sent us to cut up the tree," Hank said. "I got a generator in the back of my truck, if you want to hook up your hot water heater."

If I had some water to heat, Iris complained to herself. "No, thanks. I'll pass. But I could use a charge for my phone." She followed Hank around the house to the downed tree.

"I saw the power guys down by the hotel. They should be at your place soon," Hank said as he stuffed his ears with plugs.

"Wait a minute," Iris said. "I'd like to have this tree milled. Can you trim the limbs and just roll the trunk away from the driveway?"

Hank scratched his head.

"I'll help you move it," she offered.

He pointed at her shoulder sling and smiled. "Ho-K. We'll do that." As if on cue, another worker appeared. Simultaneously, they ripped their saws into action. With sadness, Iris watched, thinking of her father and what he may have thought about the loss of the tree. Her parents were so proud of their stewardship of the last remaining chestnut tree in Fallam County. Gone was the tree and with it the world of Henry Lee.

Amid the noise of the wailing saws, the reporter from *Fallam County Citizen* stepped around a pile of limbs. "Miss Lee," he nodded. "Chunky said you lost your chestnut tree. Thought it would make a good centerpiece for the storm coverage."

"Sure," Iris said.

"What happened to your arm?" he asked.

Thinking of Heyu and the paper's readership coverage, she said, "Let's meet up at the Early Riser for breakfast tomorrow and I'll tell you all about it."

CHAPTER 26 NOW
FOURTH OF JULY PARADE AND FIREWORKS

Mt Pleasant's Fourth of July celebrations hadn't changed since Iris was a kid. The town merchants, what was left of them, hosted a parade and community barbecue in Matilda Park. The parade started at the high school and crawled down Main Street, passed the hospital and around through the downtown shopping district then returned to the school. The lineup included merchant floats, the high school marching band, antique cars filled with local officials and teen queens, Uncle Sam and Betsy Ross on stilts, and veterans led by a drum and fife corps from the middle school as kids on bikes weaved through it all.

Sukie and Barbara waved at Iris as they rolled by in Sukie's red mustang convertible with a poster board attached to the side that read: *Let's All Read at Fallam County's New Library*. The speed at which the pair had kick-started the new library campaign impressed Iris. Ella Stone Parker, the woman with railroad millions, the one who butted heads with Iris in the park, waved from the back seat. Iris saluted with her bandaged hand. Rumor had it that the funding referendum was expected to be voted on, and approved, at the next meeting of the all-male board of supervisors. The old girl network was alive and well in Mt Pleasant.

At the Main Street entrance of the park, Iris hoisted herself onto the seat of a park bench for a better view of the next float.

"Ma'am, I'm going to have to ask you to get down off the bench, please." When Deputy Jones recognized her, he said, "Mrs. Lee. How's the shoulder?"

"Wrestled any helpless women to the ground today?" She'd given up on correcting him on the fact that she was not as "Mrs.", was not married nor had ever been.

"I said I's sorry about that," he replied. "But you really need to get down from that bench. It's not there for people to stand on."

Iris whistled her best New York taxi call as the Shelter for Friends float rolled by. The signal caught Damian's attention. He and Tabby were finding their way around a large *papier-mâché* Labrador. His arms in the air, Damian waved frantically at her and called out something Iris couldn't make out.

"Mrs. Lee, I don't want to have to come up there and take you down," Deputy Jones shouted, "but I will if you don't get off."

"Go fight crime somewhere else," she said. "Damian!" she called out and waved with her free arm. The bruised ribs reminded her not to do so.

Standing at the back of the float, Damian and Tabby jumped up and down, excited about something. Then Iris heard, "Heyu, Heyu!"

Her eyes followed the direction of their pointing fingers to the park's trailhead. All the park visitors were packed on the sidewalks, watching the parade. The trail was empty of pedestrians, except one lanky, black jeaned, hoodie-wearing dude pulling a leash with Heyu on the other end.

"Heyu!" Iris cried. Watching him fight his captor, Iris realized

     MELISSA POWELL GAY

he must have heard her whistle. She whistled again as loud as her busted ribs allowed, then called out, "Heyu!" Jumping from the bench to scramble after him, she collided with Jones, who, apparently, was making good on his threat to "come up there and take you down." Landing on top of the deputy, Iris rolled away and bounded toward the trailhead after her friend, the cries of prior injuries be damned. Clutching his utility belt, the deputy lumbered after her, commanding, "Hey, you, stop!"

Hoodie-guy darted left on the path leading to the shed. Gaining on the dognapper, Iris heard Heyu's howls of pain as he was dragged through the gravel. Surprising both the hooded thief and Iris, Deputy Jones appeared in front of them, blocking the path. The once high school defensive linebacker charged, leaping into the air. Dropping Heyu's leash, the thief calmly stepped to the edge of the path, allowing the full momentum of Jones' charge to find an unintended target. The weight of Deputy Jones' doughnut gut crushed down on the twenty-two-pound captive.

Heyu's howls of agony echoed throughout the park.

Iris' protector instincts kicked in as she shoved the moaning deputy to his side and pulled Heyu from underneath. He yelped when she tried to pick him up.

"Iris!" Damian called as he hobbled in his boot-cast. Tabby and a man followed behind.

As Heyu whimpered at her feet, she leaned over the moaning deputy and yanked his baton from his hand. "Where did you train? Police Academy for Dumb Asses?" Hefting the club in her bandaged hand, she said to Damian, "Ask Tabby to call the vet on her cell phone and stay here with Heyu."

"Where are you going?" he called after her.

"To find the miserable toad who would drag a helpless creature over a pit of gravel," she replied. Deep in the park woods, she paused, unsure which way to go next.

"Over there," someone behind her called.

She whipped around to face the man who had followed Tabby to Heyu's rescue. Dressed in dark blue running shorts and T-shirt, he looked familiar, but she wasn't sure where she'd seen him before. Maybe one of Marine Mike's workout sessions? She followed him along the path bordering the park, cresting the hilltop behind the town cemetery.

"He's gone," the runner said. "Probably in his car driving away by now."

Iris tapped the club against her leg. The hooded thief wouldn't have had time to get across the cemetery before they topped the hill, she thought. The coward was still in the park.

The runner's voice interrupted her thoughts. "Ah, you all right?"

Ignoring him, she turned back on the trail and raced toward sounds of the gathering barbecue party. A detour through the playground took her to the park's maintenance shed.

"Where are—."

"Quiet," she whispered. Quickly, she surveyed the area and discovered a gravel rake propped against the wall of the shed. Leaning the baton against the shed, she signaled her plan to the jogger. Squatting, they held either end of the wooden rake at ankle height in front of the shed door. Then, she called out, "I know what I saw. I saw two rattlesnakes crawling in that shed window this morning."

The jogger tugged gently, Iris felt power from his grip and something else from his royal blue eyes. Where had she seen those eyes before?

He joined in. "Must be after the rats that live in there."

"One of them was at least ten feet long, I swear," Iris added.

The door swung open and out flew their quarry. Iris recognized him as one of the kids at the lake with Damian. Seeing Iris, his

     MELISSA POWELL GAY

sweaty face registered surprise, then, tripping over the rake, he belly-flopped onto the path.

Dropping the rake, she picked up the baton and pressed her knee into the stunned boy's back. Her rage grabbed control and it wanted to wail this kid for what he'd done to Heyu.

The jogger pressed a hand on her arm and said quietly, "Iris, I don't think you want to do this."

"Get out of my way," she cried. "This is between Hoodie Boy and me."

The jogger grabbed her wrist and lightly squeezed. When their eyes met, her grip on the baton loosened. "He's just a kid," the man said softly.

Calmer now, she lowered the baton and said, "Fine. Help me take him back to Deputy Dog so he can make an arrest." Now aware of the baton's weight in her hand, she cringed at what she might have done to another human being.

Taking the baton from her, the runner quietly said, "I can do that." Grabbing the boy by the arm, he pulled him up and said, "Come on, you. Let's get this sorted out."

As they hiked back in silence, she stopped on the trail and mumbled, "Damian." Before the day was over, he was going to give her the truth even if she had to drag it out of him with threats of jail time in Mt Pleasant or L.A. She'd let him decide where he'd spend the remainder of his summer.

The county's only vet and Tabby huddled over Heyu as Damian stood a few steps away. Off to the side of the trail, Deputy Jones rotated his shoulder as he talked on his phone.

With a firm grip, the runner held onto Hoodie Boy's arm as he handed the deputy his club and said, "I believe this belongs to you."

"Thank goodness, Dr. Jim was on the float with us," Tabby offered.

"Broken front left leg," the vet said. "His weight's down. Infested with fleas and ticks. Bring him over to my office and I'll X-ray his leg and set it in a cast." He extended his hand to Iris and said, "Jim Alfred."

After shaking the vet's hand, Iris squatted next to a shivering Heyu and scratched him behind his ear. Wiping away a grimy tear with her bandaged hand, she whispered, "Glad you made it home, buddy." Then she motioned for Damian and Hoodie Boy to sit on the ground in front of her. Quietly she said, "The true character of a man is found in the way he treats others, including those in his dominion." Gently patting Heyu's head, she asked them, "How would you like someone to put a collar around your neck and drag you down the middle of Main Street?"

Both of them avoided her eyes.

"I didn't think so. We're going to the police station to have a chat with the chief about this. And boys, he's not going to be in a very good mood because we'll be disturbing his family cookout."

Deputy Jones interrupted, "Ah, Mrs. Lee, the chief's off today. He's not to be called in unless it's an emergency."

Iris stood and pulled her phone from her pocket. Staring at Jones, Iris talked to Ethan. She said to Jones, "Let's get the suspects in your cruiser. Chief's on his way."

Damian objected, "But, I didn't do—."

"Zip it," Iris interrupted.

Hoodie Boy snickered.

Pulling at the arm of the jogger, Tabby said, "This is my dad."

The jogger nodded and said, "Jack Duval."

Finally recalling where she'd met the jogger, Iris said, "You're Jack EMT."

"I am," he said. "How's your shoulder?"

"Good," she replied. Actually, the thing was freezing up on her.

"Let me and Tabby take Heyu to the vet while you sort out—

what needs sorting out," Jack offered.

The boys rode in the back of Deputy Jones' cruiser the two blocks to the jailhouse. Sitting up front, Iris asked, "What's the sentence for dognapping in Virginia?"

"Up to ten years," he replied.

They waited in a conference room for the chief to arrive. From giant windows, they watched the chief, dressed in his Andy Taylor shirt and blue jeans with a gun clipped on his Texas belt, get out of his big ride. Ethan requested that the boys be placed in separate interview rooms and sent Deputy Jones to invite Hoodie Boy's parents to come to the jail.

After conveying her side of the story in Ethan's office, Iris said, "So I guess you were right. You should talk to Damian. He knows something about the kidnapping."

Ethan grunted as he chewed on a toothpick.

"The gun and the medallion are still missing. I've been trolling sites that sell that type of stuff. Nada. Anything on your end?"

All business, he said, "Nothing I can share. Let's go talk to Damian."

The boy seemed smaller now. Shoulders hunched, his dark eyes followed Ethan as the chief and Iris entered the room and sat across from him. Iris noticed that Damian could use a haircut. She'd ask Ludie to take him to Bubba's tomorrow.

In his calm way, Ethan folded his hands on the table and waited for the boy to speak.

"I didn't have anything to do with it," he cried.

"With what?" Ethan asked.

"With taking Heyu."

"But you know who did," Ethan stated with confidence.

Damian looked away.

"Damian, tell the chief what you know," Iris said.

They sat quietly, waiting for the boy to speak. Clearly, Ethan was comfortable with silence as he crossed his arms over his chest and stared at Damian. Iris fidgeted while Damian picked at the hem of his jersey.

A tap at the door and Deputy Jones' shaved head popped in and said, "Chief, the parents are here."

Not giving up on his concentration on Damian, Ethan said, "Show them to my office."

"Roger that." Jones knocked twice on the door frame with a knuckle.

Ethan waited another minute, then sighed. "I'm going to go talk to the other boy and get his story. Here's your chance to tell your side of things."

Damian dug in by burying his hands in his armpits. "I didn't have anything to do with taking Heyu."

Ethan left the room.

Iris went to Damian's side and said, "Look at me. Did one of the boys at the lake take Heyu?"

"It wasn't my idea," the boy peeped out.

"Then who?" She eased into the chair beside him. "Who took him?"

"I ain't a snitch."

Iris gritted her teeth and tried again. "You're not snitching if you tell me. I'm not the police."

"Yeah, but—."

"No 'yeah, buts' about it, Kimosabe. Tell me what you know about who kidnapped Heyu or you're spending the night in jail and you'll be on a plane back to L.A. tomorrow morning."

The last threat hit its mark. Damian's eyes widened.

"That first night I was here I couldn't sleep so I walked over to the park and that's where I met Flea and T-Ball. When they found out where I was staying, they wanted to know if you had anything worth stealing." He paused and pressed his fingers into his palms.

"What did you tell them? Did you tell them about the gun cabinet?"

"I said the only thing you had worth stealing in that old house was the dog. I told them how smart he was and all. But I didn't think they'd steal him."

Iris ran a mental movie of the inside of her father's house, viewing it through Damian's eyes. The kid was right. To anyone who hadn't spent a lifetime in those rooms, the place looked like a run-down theater set for a Tennessee Williams' play.

"Then what happened?" she asked.

"I found the code for the gun safe in your computer and cracked it open."

"Was anyone with you?"

"No." After a pause, he added, "The guys said they shot at rats down at the lake with their BB guns. So when you asked Vinnie to take me to the lake, I got the Colt out of the safe and took it with me. I meant to return it. I swear."

Restraining her temper, she pushed away from the table and stood. "You *got*?" She kicked at the chair. "You *got* the Colt out of the safe?"

"I stole the gun from the safe," he admitted.

"If you wanted to shoot at rats, all you had to do was ask. We've got a barn full of them down at the farm. So where's my father's gun now?"

Damian stalled.

"We were all at the lake taking turns with the Colt."

Iris felt her skin go cold. What if Damian or any of the other kids had gotten hurt? Or worse?

Damian continued his story, something about the boy gang

standing on top of the pavilion, taking turns shooting the Colt into the water. "… then Coe showed up."

Iris asked, "Coe?"

"Flea's big brother. T-Ball's cousin."

"He climbed up on the roof and yanked the gun away from T-Ball. When I tried to get it back, that's when he pushed me in the lake."

Iris rubbed at her face. "Damian, is that how you lost the medallion? When you went in the water?"

"What? No," he protested.

"Tell the truth. Did you take the medallion from the safe?"

Damian gazed past her.

She tried scaring the truth out of him. "The thing is worth a lot of money. If you took it and the police charge you, you go back in detention."

Damian took on his thousand-yard stare, pulling at the fuzz on the side of his face.

She tapped the back of his chair. "Answer me."

"Why should I? No matter what I say, you won't believe me." He placed his arms on the table and lowered his head.

Voices rose and fell outside the room. Chairs scrapped across linoleum. Iris opened the door to a command center full of activity.

"What's going on?" she asked the front desk clerk.

"The FBI's here," she said.

"Mrs. Lee?" Deputy Jones was standing in Ethan's office doorway. "Chief needs to see you."

Jones, another deputy, and a suit with aviator sunglasses propped on his head stood in a semicircle in front of Ethan's desk.

"What's going on?" she asked.

"Thomas 'T-Ball' Scruggs confessed to the dognapping. He and Markus 'Flea' Young, Roscoe Young's younger brother, wrote the notes and took the dog. There's no proof Damian was involved," Ethan reported.

"Damian took Mr. Henry's gun out of the safe. Says Coe Young took it from him."

"That'd be Roscoe Young, Chief," Deputy Jones offered.

"The boy who ran me down in the park the other night?" Iris asked.

Ethan nodded, then asked her, "And the general's medal?"

Iris shook her head. "Claims he didn't take it."

The nervous suit, wearing too much cologne, cracked his knuckles and said, "Here's a scenario, Quinn. The suspects we're after hired the boys to get the dog out of the way so they could enter the house to steal the valuable artifact."

"Who are you?" Iris asked.

"Iris, meet Matthew Tagert, FBI," Ethan said. "Agent Tagert is part of a team investigating a ring of home invaders who go after high-end stuff like family silver, artwork."

"Your chief's report landed in our daily sweeps in the Richmond office. We'd like to interview you about your missing valuables." He offered his hand.

Iris saluted him with her bandaged hand. She waited for the jumpy agent to do all the talking.

And that he did. His cryptic tale, full of federal acronyms, described caustic home invaders tearing through the South like Sherman on his march to the sea. Tagert finally got around to asking his first interview question. Holding up a printed copy of a picture of the medallion, he asked, "When did you notice this missing?"

"The time line is in the report," Ethan offered.

Iris said, "About two weeks ago."

"Any other items of value missing from your home?" Tagert asked.

Iris pleaded with her eyes for Ethan to answer.

"A vintage Colt revolver," Ethan said.

"The timeline fits." Tagert appeared eager to move ahead, with what, Iris wasn't sure. "The Lee kid tells them where the safe is and what's in it, and the local punks get the dog out of the house allowing the perps I'm after to waltz in."

Ethan's expression showed little confidence in the agent's theory. "With all due respect, I'm not seeing it." Addressing the deputies, he asked, "You guys hear anything on the street or from other commands about unusual break-ins?"

Both men shook their heads. "Just the usual minor stuff at the lake near the county line," one said.

"OK, let's check in with the other counties."

"Dad has a collection of guns that would make General Patton swoon," Iris said. "An American Revolution Ferguson, the Colt, couple of semiautomatics. If your guys did break in, why didn't they take those?"

"They're smart. They only take what they have orders for or what they can sell within twenty-four hours." Tagert shook one leg, then the other. "When can I talk to Mr. Scruggs?"

"He's in Interview Room 1 with his parents. Jones, take Agent Tagert to meet Thomas and his parents." Ethan held Iris back as the others left the room. "Iris, between you and me, I don't agree with Tagert's assessments. Can you think of anyone outside of your family who has had access to your house?"

"Aside from the family, Vinnie and Ludie, the only other people who've been around are servicemen. The plumber and the guys who delivered my new mattress," Iris said.

"Ed?"

"Unfortunately. Know any other plumbers?"

"He's the best there is. I don't think he's inclined to go snooping

     MELISSA POWELL GAY

around people's gun safe's. He's a scout master over at the Baptist Church."

"My money's on Damian's new friends," Iris said. "Let me know what happens."

"Take Damian home," he said.

"I'm sorry that we ruined your holiday," she said.

"Let's stay in touch," he said and headed for Interview Room 1.

When she went back to the conference room to fetch Damian to take him home, he was gone.

CHAPTER 27 THEN
ANGEL'S GIFT

Driving west on Eastend Street, Henry listened to the six o'clock news reporting Vietnam's daily body count and home-grown riots. The world was still mad. Hot and tired, Henry smelled of dried sweat, sawdust and oil grime. A soak in his tub would put things right.

He spotted Violet Tyler in front of her mother's house. He veered to the curb at the exact place he had given her the pin and asked her to run away with him years ago, when they were children.

Wearing a halter top and a flared skirt, her skin glistened with a sheen of summer sweat. She bent into the car, folding her lanky arms over the open window. She smelled of peaches and vanilla.

"Henry, stop looking at my titties," she teased.

He forced his eyes to meet hers and gasped. "Who hit you?"

"I ran into a door. How 'bout let's ride over to Honey's Hut for an ice cold beer."

"Can't. I'm expected at home." She didn't need to know that he'd promised Elizabeth he'd stay away from Honey's after Donnie had piled him on the doorstep one night when he was too drunk to get himself home. "Is that some of brother Ben's handiwork?"

Avoiding his question, she asked, "How about a ride to my place then?"

"Hop in."

As the car turned to go downtown, she said, "I see your wife and little girl around town sometimes. Mama tells me your little girl's smart like you."

Because she had refused him, she had no right to talk about his family, his life without her. He accepted her compliment with a grunt and left it at that.

Pursing her full lips at a tiny gold compact, she applied tangerine lipstick then air kissed her reflection. Watching the town whiz by, she said, "Town biddies be lit up tomorrow. Talking about seeing Henry Lee driving the town floozy around."

"Stop it."

She laughed at him.

In front of her beauty salon, Henry spotted Ben's car. "Looks like you've got a customer."

"He can wait." She slid across the seat, her hand finding his leg.

"Just say the word and I'll see to it he never touches you again," he said.

She sighed then slid back to her side. "Like you said, looks like I got a customer." As she got out of the car, a breeze swirled her skirt around her bare legs.

He watched her sashay across the street, the spell she still held over him awakening his dormant desires. He needed something to stop the cravings, so he pointed the car toward the county line. At Honey's he signaled for a shot of Tennessee mash. Ignoring calls for him to join a card game, he threw back the drink and then walked out.

At home in the tub, Henry splashed water over his face. A breeze stirred as Elizabeth came into the room, folded linen in her arms. Placing a towel on a wooden stool, she dipped a facecloth into the water then wrung it out over his shoulders.

Handing her the soap, he asked softly, "Where's Iris?"

"She's over at the Baileys." Pressing herself against his arm, she gently rubbed his chest and stomach with the soapy cloth.

"Close the door," he said quietly.

In the stillness of summer's dusk, the lock clicked. She slipped out of her cotton shift, then her bra and panties. He relaxed his arms on the rim of the tub and watched as she raised her arms to tie her hair on top of her head with her blue ribbon. The ivory creaminess of her torso contrasted with her suntanned and speckled arms and dark nipples. He stirred as she straddled him. Her back arched as his calloused hands cupped her small breasts, then encircled her waist. Their rhythms created swells in the milky water. Splashes from the overspill went unnoticed.

The night was humid and they lay naked and apart under a cool sheet. He stared into the darkness as he listened to her contented breathing, the sleep of the innocent. How different they were: Violet with her exotic African beauty and reckless passion and Elizabeth with her unawares radiance, insight and kindness. He still desired the one but cherished the other. He loved them both.

At eighty-eight and sound of mind, the old man still insisted on weekly outings to church on Sundays, and on Thursdays to the barbershop then lunch with a quorum of inactive barristers. On this Thursday, the day before the Fourth of July, Mr. Lee commented on Elizabeth's latest culinary catastrophe as Henry drove him to the barbershop. "Your Elizabeth is a right smart gal but her cooking isn't up to your mother's standards. If something isn't done, we'll all soon be dead of ptomaine poisoning."

The cooking critique was the same every week, and it gave

Henry small pleasure to respond with comments such as, "She did provide full disclosure the night we invited you and Mom to her apartment for our engagement dinner. Her fried Spam with shrimp cocktail sauce is still my favorite."

"Did you notice the fried chicken last night? It was burnt on one side and raw on the other."

"I thought it was delicious," Henry said. "Best chicken I've ever eaten."

Henry's replies were never heard. He could have said Elizabeth cooked for the Queen of England, but the old man had selective hearing when it came to his second son's opinions on anything. Mr. Lee's conclusion of his judgment on Elizabeth's cooking always ended with "Now, Ben's wife, Sarah, she can cook. She makes the best tuna salad casserole, bar none."

Henry never bothered to enlighten his father to the fact that Sarah employed a maid who also did all the family's cooking. What would be the point?

While the old man spent the morning jawing with Mr. Phips and his oldest son, Bubba, Henry went round to the office to check in with Bets Jones, the office manager. Except Bets had yet to stack the suppliers' checks neatly on his desk for him to sign like she always did on Thursdays. Bets Jones was dead. Henry discovered the loyal employee of over forty years slumped at her desk, black coffee spilled on the open accounts payable ledger.

With the sanctuary windows opened to capture an occasional cross breeze, the putrid lily pollen filled the air, giving Henry a migraine. His "summer suit," as Elizabeth called it, itched to high heaven. He closed his eyes to focus on the minister's eulogy. Bets never spoke of any family. Elizabeth helped with the obituary, stating that Bets worked tirelessly for Allen Lee and spent Sundays solving The New York Times crossword puzzle.

Sitting beside his brother, Henry heard Ben hack to clear his throat then blow his nose. His brother appeared truly bereft. Humbly, Ben offered to help out at the office until a new girl was hired. Indeed, citing his superior personnel management skills to their father, he offered to find Bets' replacement.

At the gravesite, Henry helped his father sit under the funeral tent, then stood behind him. The minister's prayers spoke of service and sacrifice. Henry reflected on his own service. To his father, he was just another Bets Jones. However, Bets had more freedom than he ever did. She could have left her employer at will and never been harassed to return to the drudgery of ledgers and adding machines. His exit, on the other hand, was thwarted at every turn. His family had pulled strings to retrieve him from the Army, they had shut down his efforts at tobacco farming and summoned him to Grove House to care for his father after his mother's death. Standing on hallowed ground, Henry had an epiphany: Ben would always be their father's favorite son and he was slave to them both. Then and there, he declared to himself that if he was bound to Lee Properties for perpetual servitude, things were going to be done his way from now on.

The next week Henry sat at Bets' desk opening the mail and soon realized the extent of her competencies. He was drowning in paperwork and phone calls. Ben's offer to help consisted of a trail of gum-chewing teenage girls from the stenography class at the high school. None of them was qualified. By the end of July, he was exhausted from the double duty, pulling his hours on job sites, then redoing all of Bets work the gal of the day managed to mess up. Fortunately, an angel came to his rescue. Angel Farthing.

Angel was one of the young men who left Fallam County with dreams to chase. Two years later he returned without his legs and a head full of tropical nightmares. When Henry introduced him to Ben and Mr. Lee as Bets' replacement, Angel, who was a friend of one of Donnie Tyler's nephew's, was not judged by the bookkeeping certificate he'd obtained on the GI Bill, but by the color of his skin.

The old man asked Angel, "Are you an honest man?"

To which Angel replied, "Sir, not to sound like a smart-ass, but shouldn't you ask my references that question? I mean, begging your pardon, sir, but I could tell you a pack of lies that sound as truthful as a sinner's confession on Saturday night. Sir."

Annoyed at the young man's impudence, Ben asked, "What he means is, can we trust you?"

Angel said to Ben, "From your question, I reckon you've never served. My commander and my best friend trusted me to cover them from a shit storm whiles we were in country." Pointing at the space where his lower legs and feet used to be, he said, "I left these behind in exchange for my buddies' lives." Angel's wheelchair squeaked as his powerful arms readjusted his weight.

Henry realized he was going to like working with this brother in arms. The Vietnam vet relished playing his pity card to shame those who asked inane questions. Hooah!

Agitated, Ben persisted. "A lot of cash goes through this office, boy. You can appreciate we wouldn't want to hire someone who is … easily tempted."

Angel looked at Henry and asked, "Did he just call me a thief?"

"No, no, no, Angel," Ben protested. "No one's calling you a thief. But you have to agree that this job requires a high degree of trust and discretion."

"Mr. Lee," Angel said to the old man, "I'll promise to carry out my duties as ordered by my superiors. Sir." He saluted him. Turning to Ben, he added, "There's no way I can run off with your money. I ain't got no legs."

Two of the three Lee men failed to see the humor in Angel's argument.

At dinner that evening, Henry was determined to prevail in the hiring. This was his first effort at taking charge of the business. If the old man objected to his hiring of Angel, he'd leave Lee Properties and look for opportunities elsewhere. He had all his arguments lined up in his head. A high school graduate, Angel received high marks in bookkeeping at a local trade school. His commanding officer bragged about his bravery and intelligence. And, saving the best argument for last, Lee Properties needed to do its part by hiring a war veteran.

"And none of the young women your brother referred have worked out?" Mr. Lee asked after Henry stated his defense.

"I don't think any of us realized how much work Bets actually did for us, Dad," Henry said. "With the new strip mall keeping me busy, I don't have time to do both. Those young girls are just not mature enough to take on the responsibilities of running an office on their own. I need someone who's not afraid to take charge."

"He's a bit unorthodox," Mr. Lee said.

Henry said nothing, anticipating the "but." It never came.

Before leaving for work the following morning, Henry said to his father, "Angel starts working today. I've offered to pay him what we were paying Bets. We're building an entrance ramp and making alterations to the office so he can get around."

"It's your decision. Let's pray that it's not a bad one," Mr. Lee said.

Over the next few months Henry and Angel settled into a routine. The Friday before Christmas week, Henry poured two fingers of bourbon for himself and his office manager as Angel locked up the ledgers in the vault. With Angel's arrival, things had turned around for Lee Properties. They had managed to finish the year in the black and won a construction contract to build the county's new school board offices out on North Main next to the new four-lane highway.

Henry discovered that his new assistant not only had a photographic memory for numbers but he was also a human calculator. Angel never bothered with an adding machine to tally rent receipts and expenses. He computed compound interest and return on investment ratios like most signed their name on a check. Effective in job estimates and collecting overdue accounts receivables, Angel struggled with small talk to those who visited or called the office. To the chagrin of his brother's "I told you so," Henry hired Dolly, a recent high school graduate recommended by Ben, to answer the phones and talk to walk-ins.

Henry raised his coffee mug and said, "A toast to a good ending of a bad year."

"Cheers," Angel said.

"Have you given any more thoughts to going to college?"

"I don't know," Angel said. "I'd have to quit my job here. I need the jack. My disability check barely covers rent."

"I've been thinking about that." Henry poured them both another shot. "What if you worked here at nights? You could go to school during the day and do the numbers at night. When you finished school, you could take on other clients."

"And that wouldn't make you mad?" Angel asked.

"It's only a matter of time before the bank makes you an offer I can't match. Let me help you get set up as a bookkeeper and you can make as much or as little money as you want. And be your own boss."

Angel laughed. "I'm glad you said that. I was losing my mind from boredom." He clinked his mug to Henry's and said,

"Thanks, brother."

"If you fall behind, I'll have to let you go. But I don't have to tell you, the world's got bigger plans for Angel Farthing."

"I 'preciate that, man." After a pause, he said, "I need to show you something."

Henry followed Angel into the back room where the supplies and old files were stored.

Angel breathed out a nervous sigh. "My smart mouth tends to get me into trouble. But since you seem to want to take a chance on me, I'm takin' one with you." He pulled a ledger from a metal bookshelf. "Reach in there and pull out the book wedged in the back."

Henry pulled the ledger from its hiding place and set it on a center table.

Angel opened it and said, "One day, I was late to work. Before y'all hired Dolly. I saw your brother leaving the office. When I came in here to make coffee, I noticed the journals were out of order. Sixty-five was in front of sixty-four." He opened the book and continued, "You can fire me now for being a snoop but something tells me you don't know about this. Looks like ledgers for inventory, sales, deliveries. Bootlegging is my guess. But look at this. Pay offs. With initials by each one."

Henry took the book from Angel and quickly read down the list. Ben was buying influence from most of the local officials in a three-county area. This wasn't too bothersome to Henry because bootleggers buying off crooked officials was common and usually expected. Yet, the practice was one of his father's pet peeves. No, what turned Henry's blood cold was the list of "JDs." His brother was bribing judges.

"You going to call him out on this?" Angel asked.

Henry gnawed at his thumbnail.

"And there's something else," Angel said. "I found this the first week I was here. I just assumed y'all were running a scam on The Man."

"What are you talking about?" Henry said still reeling from learning his wife-cheating, mistress-beating brother was also an extortionist.

"When I first started working here, Ben came to me and offered to take all the deposits to the bank. Said he did it for Bets and he didn't mind doing it for me on account of me being in a wheelchair. But I told him y'all hired me to do a job and I could do it as good as anybody." Angel opened the safe and retrieved the current ledger and set it on the table. "I went back two years and, for the life of me, couldn't get the cash receipts to balance with the weekly deposits. But look here," Angel turned the opened book to Henry. "Since I started making the deposits in August, the bank receipts tie back to the ledger. See."

"That explains our positive cash flow this quarter," Henry mused.

"Like I said, I thought maybe y'all were in on a tax scam—."

"No, we aren't," Henry insisted.

"And there's something else," Angel said.

Henry nodded for him to continue.

"Did you know there are three bank accounts at the Mt Pleasant bank?"

"No, we've only got two. One for expenses and one for our credit line," Henry said.

"While I was at the bank one day, Candy asked if we were interested in converting our savings account to a mutual fund account. I told her she must be mistaken. The savings account was probably Mr. Lee's personal account. She said, 'No, it's titled as Lee Properties.'"

"Let me guess," Henry said, "Ben is the only account holder."

"Yep. I bought Candy some flowers the following week. I explained to her that my boss 'Mr. Lee' had asked that a copy of the statement get sent to the office and I forgot to ask her to do it earlier." Angel rolled over to a file cabinet and pulled out a folder stuffed with bank statements. Placing them next to the secret ledger, Angel used a pencil to trace payments made to "JD's" on the ledger to withdrawals from the bank account."

Henry was speechless.

"Hey, man, you really didn't know about all this?"

"No," Henry said. His gut groaned. His knee bobbed up and down. "Make sure Dolly doesn't have access to the statements or the safe. Keep a watch on her. And keep all of this to yourself. I need some time to think about what to do."

A few days later on Christmas Eve after the old man and Iris were tucked in for the night, Henry and Elizabeth sat together on the parlor sofa enjoying a few minutes of peace. She snuggled against him as he wrapped his arms around her.

"Are you cold? I can build a fire," he said.

"It's too late. Besides it would be our luck for Iris to come downstairs and accuse us of trying to roast Santa Claus." She pulled the sofa throw over them and resettled in his arms. "You've been quieter than usual tonight. What's bothering you?"

Not answering right away, he placed his chin on top of her head and breathed in her scent. He debated whether to tell her of Angel's discovery, thereby spoiling Christmas for her. Instead, he asked, "What do you think of turning this room into a library? Build some bookshelves along that wall, make spaces for some of your paintings, add a sunroom to the back."

She pushed away from him and said, "Really? You want to go ahead with the plan?"

"Sure. Let's get started after Christmas," Henry said.

She kissed him then whispered in his ear. "Let's make our own fire."

"We better make it quick. Wouldn't want Santa to drop in on us." He slipped his hand under her sweater and unhooked her bra.

The Lee holiday celebrations closed each year with a Christmas Night walk on Grove Street, a tradition of delivering presents to neighbors started by Matilda. Elizabeth and Sarah insisted that the family continue the ritual to honor their mother-in-law's memory and to enable their children to spend time together as cousins. Amid the excitement of gathering packages and bundling up in scarves, hats, gloves and snow boots, everyone watched as Elizabeth descended the front stairs in a knee-length sable coat.

"Elizabeth!" Sarah exclaimed. "Oh, my goodness."

Elizabeth twirled, then gathered up the collar. "I got it at an estate sale for a song."

"Honey, look at Elizabeth's coat," Sarah said as she tugged on Ben's sleeve. "You have to get me one."

"I see you're wearing the medallion," the old man said as he leaned against his cane.

"Yes, doesn't it look grand pinned to the collar?" Elizabeth asked. Taking Mr. Lee's arm, she guided him to his parlor chair near the fire. "Are you sure you're OK to stay by yourself?"

"I'll stay here," Henry volunteered.

"No, daddy," Iris protested. "You have to pull me on my new sled."

"I'm fine. Go. Have a good time," Mr. Lee said. "I know the Wingfields have a special treat for Iris and Bennie."

"Come on. Let's go," Iris cried, pulling on her father's hand.

Later when the cold wind blew them all back inside, everyone sat around the fire as Elizabeth served hot chocolate before Ben and his family started out on their drive home.

"Elizabeth's been helping me research the origins of the medallion," Mr. Lee said.

"Dad, did you forget that you wanted me to have that?" Ben asked.

"I didn't forget. However, Elizabeth and I are playing history detectives. We're trying to see if my client Miss Sorin was who she said she was."

Elizabeth jumped up from her perch on the arm of Mr. Lee's chair and retrieved the pendant from the lapel of her coat. Using the ribbon threaded at the top, she placed the pendant around her neck.

"But we know who she was," Ben grumbled. "You told us. She's Jubal Early's illegitimate daughter. He gave his war medal to her mother." Elizabeth pawing all over his Civil War artifact and using it as fashion jewelry clearly frustrated Ben.

"That's what Bella Sorin claimed. But, if it was the general's, where did he get it?" Elizabeth asked. "It's a mystery."

"No, it's not a mystery. And, it's not some cheap department store necklace for you to wear to a church social. It's an authentic Civil War artifact. Put it back where you found it," Ben ordered.

Sitting on the sofa with Iris, Henry looked up from their card game. "Ben, there's no cause to be so nasty. She's just trying to help Dad out."

Bowing her head, Elizabeth took the medallion off and folded the ribbon around it. "I sent a sketch of it to the Confederate Museum in Richmond. We got a letter back saying it wasn't a Confederate design. They said it looked nothing like any of the medals awarded by the Army of Northern Virginia." Henry heard the hurt in her voice. How he loathed his brother.

Seemingly oblivious to the tension, the old man took Elizabeth's hand in his, and said, "They suggested we contact the Brits. Elizabeth is helping me with correspondence to the chief curator at their national army museum. We're having such good fun. Aren't we, Elizabeth?"

"Wow, helping with translations from American to British English," Ben smirked.

"Cut it out, Ben," Henry shouted.

"One day, Henry," the old man sang. "Just one day, can you not argue with your brother?"

To clear the room of its anxiety, Elizabeth rose and announced, "Iris, it's past your bedtime. Let's go, sweetheart." She took a complaining Iris by the hand and the pair left the room.

Later that evening, Henry discovered Elizabeth sitting in bed, fidgeting with the sheet's hem. To console her, he placed his hand on her shoulder. "He's a giant bag of green puss that can't stand to see anybody else have a success, Elizabeth. Ignore him."

She asked, "Why does he have such a fixation on that stupid broach?"

Unbuttoning his shirt, Henry said, "He's been fascinated with it for years. The old man used to tell us stories about General Early. I'm sure most of it was made up to keep us interested in our history lessons." He took his shoes off and stripped down to his skivvies. "Why?"

"When we were walking down the street tonight, he was downright vile toward me. Called me the 'B' word. Said if I didn't put it back, he'd—he'd—well, he'd complain to your father."

"He's obsessed. You know that shadow box he had built into his library wall? When he inherits the medallion, he plans to mount it in the box. Show it off to his history pals."

"But, Henry, weren't you listening? Your dad and I have historic proof it's not a Civil War medal," she said. "For all we know it's war booty."

He lifted the covers and slid in beside his wife. "And that, Mrs. Lee, is why he deserves to have it." His lips nuzzled at her neck.

"What? So he can make a fool of himself?"

"Exactly."

On the first business day of 1970, Henry called up the office supply store and ordered their latest model photocopier. Because of Lee Properties' gold customer status, they delivered it the same day. After saying goodnight to Dolly and Angel, Henry pulled the secret ledger from its hiding place and copied every page, front and back. Then he lit a cigar and settled down at his father's rolltop desk to think about what the discovery meant to him and his family.

CHAPTER 28 NOW

COME UP FIGHTING

Iris mulled over Damian's disappearance as she walked home from the jailhouse. He reminded her of a feral cat she and her college roommate tried to coax into their first-floor dorm room freshman year. No amount of canned tuna persuaded the long-haired tabby they'd named Fufu to come inside. Her roommate's boyfriend suggested that life for Fufu probably felt safer among the dumpsters than having to forage through the clothes and crusty, unwashed dishes littering their room. As with Damian, no amount of coaxing was going to persuade him to come in from the callous street until she got her own house in order. She promised herself that the next time she saw him, she'd apologize for the hard words at the jailhouse and offer him a place to stay for as long as he wanted it. The time had come to get serious about renovating Grove House.

An unfamiliar car was in the driveway. The frame for the license plate advertised a Richmond Cadillac dealership.

"Iris," Bert whispered as she hovered at the front door. "There's a Mrs. Holly from Richmond come to see you. Said she was in the neighborhood. She claims she's friends of the Kaluchis and Mr. Darcy, that little white-haired fella with the bowtie who came here to talk about the medallion."

"What does she want?" Iris asked not caring who heard.

"She won't say, only that she wanted to speak with you. She's in Mr. Henry's liberry."

Elizabeth and the visitor, the woman standing next to Travis' new customer Bill Yates at Pen's birthday party, were sitting on the sofa talking about the chestnut tree. As Iris entered, Mrs. Holly stood and introduced herself, insisting on being addressed by her Christian name, JoRena. Gold accents sparkled from her bangles on both over-suntanned wrists and her lamé high-heeled sandals. Everything about her straight white teeth, sharp features and streaked straw-blond head reeked of old Virginia family, fundraising galas and horse stables. Her perfume even smelled like money.

"Your mother has been telling me all about the loss of your tree," JoRena said. She straightened her stars and stripes silk blouse over her white slacks.

Iris, never one for small talk, repeated her question, "What do you want?"

Flattening a French manicured hand to her chest, JoRena stammered, "Well—I—suppose—I." Raising her chin, she continued, "We didn't get a chance to introduce ourselves at Pen's birthday party." She extended her hand.

Iris held up her bandaged one.

"Anyway, Syke Darcy is a family friend and he shared with me the story of your discovery. While I'm here visiting Ruth and Kooch, thought I'd drop by."

"For?" Iris was in no mood for parlor games.

JoRena's eyes darted around the room as if she was expecting to see the flashy pendant on display like a Chihuly glass sculpture. She beamed a debutant's smile at Iris, code for "I get what I want when I set my mind to it." "Here's the thing," she said, "I'm a descendent of several Civil War heroes and, because of my heritage, I collect war-era artifacts. I'm interested in buying yours. But before I do, I'd like to see it? May I?"

"The medallion is not a Civil War piece, dear," Elizabeth interrupted. "Check your records at the Confederate Museum. They confirmed that for us in 1969."

Iris raised an eyebrow at JoRena.

"But you said in the article that Jubal Early—," JoRena stammered.

Gently guiding JoRena by her slim arm to the front door, Iris said, "If you're interested in placing a bid at the auction we have scheduled in December, I suggest you contact Mr. Darcy or Sotheby's directly."

As she watched JoRena's runway strut glide down the drive, Iris recited her license number to Bert who scribbled it on a pad. Using the last bit of power on her phone, she dialed Mr. Darcy and left a message on his answering machine. Had Mr. Darcy encouraged this woman to come see her? If so, it didn't make sense. It would cut out Sotheby's, and Mr. Darcy's, commission should Iris decide to sell it to her directly. "Hamlet, something's rotten in the town of Mt Pleasant," she said aloud.

"What's that, sweet pea?" Bert asked as she handed the pad to Iris. "Donnie came by and told me what happened in the park this morning. Where's Damian and Heyu?"

"Damian's off brooding somewhere. Heyu's at the vet's." She picked at the dirty bandage on her hand. "What did Mom mean when she said the museum confirmed the medal wasn't from the Civil War era?"

"If I ever did know, I don't remember now," Bert replied as she followed Iris back into the library.

"Mom?" Iris sat next to Elizabeth on the worn sofa. The afternoon sun highlighted dust motes and the cloudy rims of Elizabeth's eyes. Iris took her mother's hands and asked softly, "What else can you tell me about the medal Allen Lee gave you?"

"Where did that nice young lady go?" Elizabeth asked.

"She left but she wanted to know about General Early's medal. You said the Confederate Museum confirmed it wasn't one of theirs. What else can you tell me about it?"

"I hid it where Ben wouldn't find it," Elizabeth said.

"We know, you hid it in your mink coat pocket," Iris said.

"No, I hid it in my bathroom." She giggled. "Somewhere Ben would never think to look." She offered Iris her glasses and said, "Sweetheart, can you clean these for me? I'm having trouble seeing."

FBI Agent Tagert's question about when the medallion was stolen swirled around the image of the open gun safe. Iris visualized Elizabeth in the room, holding the medallion. "Mom, remember the day we were looking at the things in Mr. Henry's safe and I asked you to put the medallion back inside it?"

Without her oversized plastic glasses, Elizabeth appeared as wee as a house mouse. She blinked then rubbed at her chin with her finger tips, signaling to Iris she couldn't answer the question. Iris placed Elizabeth's glasses back on her face.

"So, we'll check the bathroom, again," she said to herself. Before she went searching for treasure in her mother's bathroom, Iris went to Mr. Henry's room. Scanning it, she noticed Damian's backpack stuffed underneath the rolltop desk. His clothes were folded and neatly stacked on his unmade bed. She checked the gun safe again with no luck.

When she was little, her father renovated the en-suite bathroom and installed a massive pink enameled tub large enough for two people. Light once blocked by the chestnut tree revealed the rundown state of the room. She remembered swimming in bubbles in the huge tub, where Elizabeth's plastic bathing chair now sat. The distressed room had worn out its style and usefulness. Like her stitched hand wrapped in soiled gauze, the room needed a change.

Plowing through the medicine cabinet and vanity drawers, Iris struck out, no medallion hidden in a box of Kotex circa 1970. Giving up, she walked into her mother's bedroom and, seeing her jewelry chest, she rummaged through its drawers. Fondling her mother's pearls, another thought occurred to her. This time she recalled Vinnie fishing her mother's exotic pearls from the toilet bowl in the hallway bathroom.

"SHASAM!" She cried out. That was it! The master bath's pipes weren't rusted out. Surveying the room for something to stick down the toilet, she grabbed a wire hanger and bent it. Back in the bathroom she stuffed it down into the toilet, but quickly realized it wasn't long enough to reach beyond the toilet bowl's trap.

"Iris?" Bert asked.

Iris jumped. "Cheese and crackers, Bert. Didn't anyone ever tell you not to sneak up on a person?"

"I been calling. You didn't hear me?" Filling the door frame, she asked, "What are you up to now?"

"I think I know where the medallion is. Do you know where Mr. Henry keeps his plumbing tools?"

Bert studied a frazzled Iris, then the bent clothes hanger jutting out of the toilet bowl. Placing the outsides of her wrists on her hips, she shook her head. "Check the basement. That Mr. Darcy's on the phone. Want me to tell him to call you back?"

Ah, the miracles of rotary dial telephones, they still worked when there was no power. She whispered a thanks to Mr. Henry for keeping the old phone as she hurried down the back stairs.

"Mr. Darcy," she said, catching her breath.

"Miss Lee. I assume you called to say you've found your misplaced artifact?"

She paused before she rushed into the story of her mother hiding family jewels in an unlikely place. "Ah, I'm still working on that but we should know something by tomorrow."

"Oh, wonderful. Mr. Kitter will be glad to hear the good news."

"The reason I phoned was to inquire about someone who visited me today."

"Oh?"

"Do you know a woman by the name of JoRena Holly?" Iris stretched the phone cord to the butcher's block to make herself a peanut butter and honey sandwich. Four o'clock had come and gone and she'd missed the park barbecue.

"Yes, Mrs. Holly is a client of mine. Isn't that a coincidence. How do you know her?"

"I don't. She knocked on my door out of the blue with some tale about knowing you and wanting to see the medallion."

"Miss Lee. It's company policy. We never discuss one client's business when advising another. I know JoRena but I've *never* said anything to her about your plans."

"Thank you," Iris said. Abruptly disconnecting Mr. Darcy, she jiggled the receiver hook, waited for dial tone and dialed 9-1-1. From the kitchen window, Iris watched Bert clip roses in the backyard flower garden as she waited for the desk clerk to patch Ethan into their call.

"Ethan, I've got a lead for the FBI agent."

Babble sounding like a backyard barbecue drifted from the weighty handset.

"Give me a minute," she said and set the receiver on the butcher's block. She circled the downstairs searching for the note pad with Mrs. Holly's license plate number. She found Elizabeth sitting on the library's sofa wearing radio headphones, like the ones Damian sometimes wore, and conducting with her index fingers. No time to stop and figure that one out, Iris scooped the pad from the foyer table and made her way back to the kitchen. "Thanks for holding."

"Iris, I don't think—."

"This won't take long," she said. She recounted seeing JoRena Holly at Pen and Travis' party, then the woman popping in un-announced with a yarn about knowing Mr. Darcy and asking to see the medallion. Being her father's daughter, Iris didn't believe in coincidences. "Travis didn't go into a lot of detail on his new client Bill Yates but he said he recently moved into the area. I saw the two talking to each other at the party. Don't you think Agent Tagert might find these two characters interesting? For the case he's working?"

"Iris, he's already left the area. I don't think two people talking at a party—."

She interrupted by reciting the Cadillac's license plate number. "Something's not square, Ethan. I can feel it. The hair on the back of my neck is standing straight up."

"Ah-rite, I'll pass this along through channels," he said.

Iris felt the disinterest in his response. "Listen! I'll bet you the price of a new Stetson that there's something to this. Call him as soon as you hang up with me."

"Wait a minute," Ethan said. "If the medallion is not in the gun safe and you believe the clowns Tagert's tailing are sniffing around asking you about it, that means they don't have it. Which means someone else took it."

"Gotta go. Have fun at your party." She hung up the phone before he had a chance to ask any more questions. Imagine the ribbing she'd get if Mt Pleasant and the entire art world found out she allowed it to be flushed down a toilet. At least she'd found it.

Pulling his calling card from her shorts pocket, Iris dialed Dr. Alfred's office.

"You just caught me leaving," he said. "You're calling about Heyu Lee."

"Yeah, how's he doing?"

"With that young Tabby Duval as his caregiver, I think he'll get through. She helped me set his leg. She and her dad took him over to the shelter for a good worming and a bath. You might check there."

"Thanks for being there," Iris said. "Mail me your bill?"

"It's been paid."

"By who?"

"Jack Duval. Said he'd catch up with you."

Hanging up the phone, Iris pictured Jack Duval hovering over her in the park. "Hmmm," she said. And that's all the time she had for such musings. She dialed the animal shelter.

"Shelter for Friends," a young voice answered. No, Heyu Lee wasn't an overnight guest and no, Tabby and her dad weren't there. They said something about going to the high school football stadium to see the fireworks.

She hung up and said to no one in particular, "I don't think someone in Heyu's condition would find fireworks very amusing tonight."

With her arms full of flowers, Bert entered the kitchen. She asked, "You've been talking to yourself all afternoon. What's going on? Have you heard from Damian? Is Heyu gonna be OK?"

"What? Oh, yeah, Damian's friend Tabby and her dad have Heyu. Hopefully, he'll be here soon."

Placing the flowers in a vase of water, Bert asked, "Are you ready to go?"

Iris shrugged with a question on her face.

"Remember? Joe Turner invited us to his cookout," Bert said.

"You guys go ahead, I'll catch up later," Iris said. She wasn't going to stop obsessing about the medallion in the toilet until she got it out. "Save me a hot dog," she called after Bert and Elizabeth from the front steps. The empty driveway reminded Iris that Ludie still had her car.

Inside she stood in the middle of Mr. Henry's library and paused. Surveying the room, she envisioned it with new furniture, painted ceiling beams and woodwork. No, this was still his room. She picked up scattered newspapers around his Morris chair. He wasn't finished with this room, not yet, and she wasn't ready for him to leave.

What was she doing? The medallion, right.

Descending into the damp basement always gave Iris sensations of spiders crawling up her legs. At the foot of the steps, she swung her arm until she found the bare light bulb suspended from the low ceiling and pulled the chain. No light, no power. Back upstairs, she grabbed a small flashlight off the kitchen table.

Something thumped in the front of the house.

She called out, "Damian?" Hair on her free arm rose as she quietly circled the front rooms and peered out of the dining room windows at the front yard and empty driveway.

Back down in the basement she scanned the back wall with the flashlight. Near the mismatched washer and dryer, Bert's freezer dripped water from a rusted corner. "Nothing like the smell of thawing chicken casserole on a hot summer's day," Iris said to keep her mind off whatever might be lurking in the dark corners. The light beams found the backless shelves that bisected the basement front and back. Iris never ventured to the front side, the dirt floor side where all her childhood monsters slithered and hopped. An old rock'n'roll song about a bullfrog named Jeremiah popped into her mind.

On the shelves, glass jars of fruits and vegetables, jams and relishes, most leftover from another era, waited patiently for the chef. Rusty topped paint buckets, a shoebox filled with twist ties and clothes pins, and other junk not fit for a yard sale crammed in next to the neat rows of preserved food. Distracted about what she'd do with the hoarded mess, she felt the sugar rush from the honey sandwich. Spying her father's green metal toolbox, she was reminded of why she came to the basement. She opened it to find the basic home repair kit of hammers, screwdrivers, pliers, and in the bottom, a plumber's auger. "Jackpot!" she murmured.

Struggling with the toolbox and flashlight while climbing the stairs, she heard footsteps overhead. Someone was in the house. Sweat trickled down her back as she shivered. Instinct warned her not to call out this time. She quietly set the box on a step midway up the stairs. Flicking the flashlight off, she continued her ascent. As she reached the kitchen, she spied her father's gun poking out from the belted waistband of the backside of a pair of camo-cargo shorts slinking up the back stairs to the second floor.

Later, each time she thought back on the incident, she shuddered at how close she had come to peril. But in the moment, all she felt was raging indignation. Its energy guided her. She softly lifted the phone receiver and dialed 9-1-1. She prayed the armed lizard, now stomping overhead in his dirty white socks and plastic slide-on thongs, was too occupied to hear the spin of a rotary dial phone. Stretching the cord halfway down the basement stairs, she whispered into the handset for Deputy Crouch to dispatch police to One Grove Street because of a burglary in progress. She grabbed a hammer from the toolbox on her way back up the stairs.

As Iris balanced the handset on its back on top of the wall

phone, Damian, without his ortho-boot, came skulking through the butler's door. Surprised to see her, he clutched his backpack to his chest.

"Someone's upstairs!" she whispered. "Go out the back. The police are on their way."

Damian's eyes widened.

Iris turned to discover the cause of Damian's shock.

"L.A. Jake." Roscoe "Coe" Young stood with Iris' pain pills in his right hand. "You and Flea not telling me straight, little brother. Where're the big jewels at?"

Iris caught Coe's eyes, bloodshot blue, assuming he was high on something and not in his right mind. In spite of warning bells going off in her head, she poked the bear by asking, "Are you the jackass who threw Damian off the pavilion roof and into the lake?" Managing to position herself between the two boys, she almost hurled from the larger boy's body odor.

He grinned down at her. "I told those boys to keep off the roof or else somebody's liable to get hurt. Didn't I, Jake?"

"Give me my daddy's gun," Iris demanded. She gripped the hammer, raising it as high as the pain in her ribs allowed. The hammer's light weight finally registered. She'd grabbed her mother's upholstery tack hammer instead of the ball peen.

He backed away and pulled the Colt from the back of his shorts with his other hand. His edgy eyes widened. "What if I don't?" Laughing, he pointed the gun, gangster style, at the hammer and said, "You going to hammer me? With that?" His mocking laughter took over the room.

"Put the loaded gun on the counter and leave this house," Iris commanded. She nodded at the handset resting on its back on top of the phone's base. "The police are listening, Roscoe. They're recording this conversation. They're on their way right now."

"Lady, you wack," Coe's voice cracked. He dropped the gun and the pills into side pockets of his camo shorts. "Come on, Jake, let's go."

Still clutching his backpack, Damian backed into the butler's door.

Coe stepped forward and raised his hand, "I said, let's go, you little rabbit fart."

Iris charged at Coe and before her hammer found its mark, his willowy but powerful arm blocked it. Raising his other arm, he punched her injured shoulder. Seeing red then white, she dropped to the floor as she howled in pain. The white quickly went black.

CHAPTER 29 NOW

STILL LOOKING

Someone's cool hands were cupping her face.

"Iris. Iris?"

She opened her eyes to a worried Jack EMT staring back at her, Tabby and Deputy Jones leaning in behind him. "My shoulder," she moaned. "I think it went out of joint again. Oh, just shoot me now." She turned her head and threw up the honey and peanut butter sandwich. Everything went black again.

She dreamed she was in Paris, chasing Manny and his young *amie* down an alley. At the end of the alley, her father appeared dressed in his ancient leather car coat and fedora. Taking each man by an arm, the young woman looked back at her, laughed, and declared, "*Vous ne pouvez pas venir avec nous.*" But she *would* come with them, Iris tried to call out. But she couldn't speak. Unable to move, she discovered her feet buried in Bert's green bean patch. The vines bound her to the red clay. She whimpered as the three faded into a misty distance.

She woke to a view of ceiling tiles. Wrinkling her brow, she focused on where she might be. Her feet were tangled up in a sheet and she heard beeping. She turned her head toward the sound and

Ethan's mug filled her view. "Where am I?"

"ER."

"What time is it?"

"About eight. How are you feeling?"

"Did you get the lunatic?"

"Was is Roscoe Young?"

She nodded and asked, "did you get him?"

"No, but he won't get too far. We found his plastic sandals in your backyard. What happened?"

Iris pushed at her hair and noticed a clean bandage on her hand.

"We need a statement from you. What happened at your house?"

"*I need* to go home," she pulled herself up. What did happen at her house? Had Damian come with that cowardly bacterial funk or, like her, was he just unlucky enough to be in the house when Roscoe decided to break in?

"Jack Duval's little girl, the one who likes to talk, she said Damian told her Roscoe Young stole his phone. We're tracking it now. Let's hope he's got it turned on."

"Did I see Jack Duval in my house, or was it a dream?" she asked.

"Yeah, he and his daughter were knocking on your door when my guys showed up, responding to your 9-1-1 call. Tabby, is it? Told us about knowing Damian. It doesn't look good for him. I fear he's got himself mixed up with some pretty nasty punks whether he wanted to or not."

"Where is he?" Iris asked as she sipped water from a plastic cup Ethan offered.

"Was hoping you'd tell us," Ethan said.

"He was with me when that gonzo freak pulled my daddy's gun on me. That's all I remember." Ethan motioned to help her but she waved him off. "I got this."

Ethan tried reason. "Maybe you should rest a little longer. You've gone through a lot."

"You should stay right there, young lady," a man, younger than Iris, in green scrubs coaxed. His name tag read "Dr. Dwyer."

"Is anything broken?" Iris asked.

"Doesn't appear so. We're ordering new X-rays. I strongly advise you stay overnight," Dr. Dwyer recommended.

"Nope, I've had enough for one day. I'm going home to my messy house with no running water and no electricity. Ethan, if you can't give me a ride home, call me a cab."

"It's your health," the doctor shrugged. "But I want you back here tomorrow morning."

"To do what? Give you more money for tests I don't need?" She recognized Mr. Henry's voice in her own. She slid from the bed.

"Actually, there's somebody here to see you," Ethan said. He helped her into a wheelchair and rolled her to the ER entrance.

Tabby, with Heyu in her arms, and Jack Duval were waiting on the bench outside the lobby, the same bench where Iris and Heyu had waited for Mr. Henry to get better. Tabby placed Heyu in Iris' lap. A shivering Heyu whimpered as he sniffed and licked at her salty face. A fluorescent green cast covered his front leg. In the background of their happy reunion, Tabby chattered about what a brave patient Heyu had been, giving a much too descriptive commentary of the crawly things attached and growing on and inside his body.

Jack interrupted the verbal surge by taking Heyu from Iris' lap and handing him back to his daughter. "I think she gets the idea, Tabby,"

"Was I alone when you found me?" she asked Jack.

He nodded.

"Thanks. Again." As she used her sort-of good arm to get out of the chair, she asked, "can you give me and Heyu a ride home?"

He smiled. "Here, let me help." His light touch on her elbow guided her to his vehicle.

At the house they were greeted by Bert's hand-wringing. She followed Iris from Jack's van to the front porch with boundless questions. "Why did you leave the door wide open for anybody to waltz right in? Who got sick all over the kitchen floor? And why didn't you clean it up? What's going on, sweet pea?"

"Where's Mom?" Iris asked.

"She's on the sun porch listening to music on headphones she said Vee's son gave to her. Power's still out. Why don't you bring Elizabeth to my house and y'all spend the night?" She extended her hand to Jack, "I'm Bert."

After the introductions, Iris took Bert aside and, in a low voice, told her what happened after Bert and Elizabeth left for the cookout.

Inside the light was fading. The place felt haunted as Bert led them through Mr. Henry's library and into the kitchen.

"Tabby told me about your electricity problems. Sounds like you've fallen into a large bucket of bad luck lately," Jack said.

"It's a large bucket, all right," Iris said as she lit a candle in a tall hurricane lantern on the table. "Can I get you something to drink? Hot bottled water? Flat soda?"

They stood for a moment without talking as Tabby's chatter fluttered in from the sun porch. She and Bert were making Heyu his own pallet.

"We lost power when the storm ripped our tree from the ground," she said. After a few minutes of small talk, Iris said, "I'm exhausted. I'm going to turn in."

"Here, let me." His gentle touch rested at the small of her back. "Looks like a sleepover," he said as they entered the sunroom.

     MELISSA POWELL GAY

"We're living the life of gypsies," Iris said. "We're sleeping out here until the power is restored." The camping lantern she'd gotten for Christmas the year she tried Girl Scouting illuminated the room enough to reveal the sagging air mattress and crumpled bedsheets.

Wearing her newly acquired headphones, Elizabeth sat on the sofa asleep. Bert took them off and eased Elizabeth onto the makeshift bed, then covered her with a sheet.

"Where did Mom get the headphones?" Iris asked.

"Damian gave them to her. We came by here before the parade," Tabby offered. "He told me he traded his laptop for them. He thought your mom would like them."

"Bless his heart," Bert said.

"What do you mean 'Bless his heart?' He didn't have a laptop to trade," Iris said thinking of her own computer, which Damian had hacked. "The sunny beach!"

"What is it?" Jack asked.

"You guys wait right here. I'll be back in a second." Using a flashlight, Iris hobbled up the back stairs and into her bedroom. Panning the room with light, she winced as she felt Jack at her back. Why did she care what he thought of her dirty underwear and stinky workout clothes all over the floor?

"What's wrong? Can I help?" he asked.

"I've got to find my laptop. If it's not here, I'll have to cancel all my credit cards." She waded through the clothes to her bed and sat.

Jack sat beside her. "If it's any help, I spent some time with the boy yesterday. He didn't come across as the computer stealing type."

Iris' sarcasm raised an objection. "Really?" Then she added, "Sure, he's all Mr. Nice Guy around you because he wants to date your daughter. He broke into my computer and stole the code to the safe … ah, jeeze … Damian. Don't make me think you did this."

"What?" Jack pleaded. "Did what?"

"If he got the code for the safe out of my computer, which he did, he most likely has all my other user names and passwords." She opened the drawer on the bedside table, no laptop. Standing, she scanned the room with the flashlight. "Close your eyes if you don't want your retinas burned by bedroom bedlam."

"Ha!" he flirted. "Nothing can scare me. I've got a teenage daughter. Where do you keep it when you aren't using it?"

"The last place I used it," she said. She handed the flashlight to Jack. "Hold this." One-handed she lifted the bed covers and shook. A running shoe clomped to the floor. "Honest, I'm usually a neat person." She scratched at her dirty hair. "Maybe it's on my father's desk." Taking the flashlight from Jack, Iris led the way to her father's room and spotlighted the desk. She felt the heat of Jack's body as she pointed the light at the end of the desk and the wall, where Damian kept his backpack. The pack was gone. Handing Jack the flashlight, she said, "Point at the desk." She tugged at the tambour door on the desk but it was locked, so was each drawer. "Point it at the safe. Over here." The safe's door handle was horizontal instead of vertical to the dial. She tapped at her lips.

"What?" Jack asked.

Upon closer inspection, she noticed the number at the top of the dial was the last number of the combination. She always spun the dial back to zero whenever she closed the safe, something she'd watched her father do many times. She pulled on the handle and the door opened. "Hmm," she said.

"What is it?" Jack asked. The flashlight weakened.

"Someone broke into the safe. Again."

Jack shook the flashlight and its beam brightened, catching the chrome flash of Iris' laptop. "Another mystery," she said as she pulled the computer from the widest shelf. "Here's my laptop."

"Good," Jack sounded relieved.

"Nope," Iris said as she wrapped the power cord around the computer. "I didn't put it there." Together they sat on the single bed. Jack opened the laptop, allowing her to press the power key. After she pecked out her password, the screen flashed and the computer died. "Arrr!" The computer battery needed charging.

"What?" Jack asked the third time.

"I've got to find a hot spot so I can recharge the computer and change all my passwords."

"Are you sure?" Jack asked. "You really think that young man'd hack your accounts?"

Not wanting an almost total stranger to know too much of her family drama, Iris blew out a puff of exhausted air and said, "Look, all this nonsense has interrupted your holiday time. I really appreciate what you and Tabby have done. I'll work this stuff out tomorrow." Once she got Jack and Tabby out the front door, she'd walk down to Joe's to use his Wi-Fi.

Jack stood and offered his hand. "Have you eaten?"

Iris handed him the computer and stood on her own.

"Let's get you to Burger Doodle. I think they have Wi-Fi. Tabby's been begging me to take her there all day. How about it?"

"That's not the safest place to change a password to your bank accounts," she stalled.

"You're welcome to come to our house," he offered.

She hesitated, then said, "Burger Doodle works. Besides I wouldn't want to deprive Tabby of her fries. I could use a bite myself."

With Bert's urging, Iris, Jack and Tabby set out to the local burger joint. After getting Iris past the log-on screen, Tabby nibbled on French fries and talked enough for all three of them. Iris managed to peck out new passwords for her online accounts. When she finished, she excused herself to go to the bathroom.

The mirror's assessment was brutal. Brash lighting accentuated every single gray hair. After splashing cold water on her face with the hand in the sling, she peered into the mirror and noticed stray eyebrows that should have been plucked two weeks ago.

Noise floated into the bathroom as Tabby entered.

"Are you OK?" Tabby asked. "You look kind of pale."

"I'm fine," Iris said. Via the mirror, she found Tabby's face and said, "Thanks for taking care of Heyu. You saved his life."

"I just did what I love doing. Daddy said it would be all right if you and your mama wanted to come over to our house to use the shower."

She laughed. "Tell him thanks, but we're not as helpless as we look," pumping soap from the dispenser, she added, "or smell."

"Let me," Tabby said. She pumped some soap on a damp paper towel and dabbed at Iris' face. As she washed, she said quietly, "Jake wouldn't have taken your computer, Mrs. Lee. He's a nice boy."

"Jake?"

"That's what Damian said he wanted me to call him," Tabby said.

"Did he say anything to you about what happened at the lake, how he hurt his foot?"

"Just that some bully threw him off the pavilion roof."

"Did he say anything to you about the medallion? You know, the one you read about in the newspaper?"

"No," Tabby said. "But I know he wouldn't steal from you." She looked at Iris with her innocent eyes.

Like her father's, Tabby's eyes were as blue as the sapphire colored ribbon that dangled from Elizabeth Lee's dressing vanity. Hers conveyed the goodness and purity only a child understood. Honest truth, Iris thought. How was she to explain to Tabby all the trouble

Damian was in without destroying the child's faith in the boy?

"Tabby, has anyone talked to you about boy-girl relationships?"

"I learned on the internet how a girl gets pregnant or STDs if her partner doesn't use a condom."

Iris' eyes widened. "Right." She thought a minute before she continued. She believed it was in the little redhead's best interest to know about Damian's situation. But she wanted to do it without passing judgment on his past actions. "Tabby, there are two types of guys. There are men like your dad and Mr. Quinn who look out for others, who try to help out in anyway they can." She thought of her own father and his secret philanthropy. "Like your dad bringing me here to use the Wi-Fi. It's just in their nature to think of others first. Then there's the rest of them. Don't get me wrong, they're mostly good men but they're not always able to think past what they're going to have for lunch."

Tabby played with a locket on a chain around her neck. She said, "You mean all they think about is themselves."

"Something like that," Iris said. "Until he reveals to you which type he is, I'd suggest you keep your heart in that locket. Do you understand what I'm trying to say?"

"I think so. You're telling me Jake is trouble and I shouldn't hang out with him. But Mrs. Lee, my woman's intuition is telling me he's one of the good guys."

"I see. What does your dad say?" Iris pushed the bathroom door open with her backside and nodded for Tabby to lead.

"He thinks we're too young to date," Tabby said.

"What took you so long?" Jack asked. "I was getting ready to send the waitress in to make sure you hadn't fallen in."

"Not funny, Dad," Tabby sulked.

Back home, after Bert and the Duvals had left, Iris lumbered up the back stairs with her Girl Scout lantern and her father's toolbox. In semidarkness, she shoved the rusty plumbing auger down the dry toilet and reeled it back onto its spool. No medallion. She hobbled back to the sunroom and lay on her air mattress. Elizabeth's soft snoring and the day's trapped heat kept her from sleep. She got up and pulled the flaccid air mattress, a sheet and her pillow out to the backyard. Once settled under the bright sky, she closed her eyes. Whimpers drifted out from the sunroom. She got up again and brought Heyu out to her bed. As he pressed his backside against her leg, she thought about Tabby's locket. It was the locket Mr. Henry had given her on her tenth birthday. He told her that it had once belonged to his sister, M. Ellen and that it had been all the way to China and back. She fell asleep wondering what she thought about Damian taking it from her childhood treasure chest and giving it to Tabby.

     MELISSA POWELL GAY

CHAPTER 30 THEN

A BROTHER WRONGED

Henry waited in his car for someone to come out into the yard. Reuben Young's coonhound was barking its fool head off. Its front claws scratched at the car door where the window was rolled down. The hound snapped at him, spewing drool all over Henry and the door. *BAM!* Henry wacked the dog's snout with the compact billy club he kept under the driver's seat. Snarls turned to cries and then whimpers as the beast retreated behind the house.

"You leave my dog alone, Henry Lee," a woman shouted from the steps.

Henry called back, "Mr. Young said he wanted to see me."

The woman, in jeans and a Henley T, waved him inside. "He's in there." She nodded and disappeared into the back of the house to sounds of a daytime soap opera.

"Henry Lee," a phlegmy voice called from the front room.

The rank odor of unwashed bedclothes layered with liniment flooded Henry's nostrils. A string of blue smoke curled up from Pops' Camel burning in an ashtray.

"Somebody said you were looking for me." He remained standing because he didn't want to stay any longer than he had to.

"Sit down," Pops commanded.

Out of respect for the dying, Henry dragged a chair, cotton batting oozing from the cracks of its plastic seat, to the foot of the patient's bed and sat.

The two waited for the other to speak.

"You did me a favor onc't," Pops said. With his fists, he propped himself up against the bed pillows. "You remember that?"

Henry kept silent.

"I's at that gas station next to the county line and you come up and told me you heard the Feds was planning a raid on my still up on Deer Run Hill." For the next minute he coughed and spat on a newspaper on the floor beside his bed. He wheezed on, "That's when I realized you got all the brass in your family. Your brother, he don't have much use for you." He spat again. "Reckon you already know that."

Henry's jaw tightened. Things had become tense between the brothers since Angel started making the bank deposits. Henry stared through the smoke at his brother's partner in an illegal whiskey enterprise.

"Ben Lee done good representin' me in court. And we made a lot of money together. But he owes me. You tell him he needs to come see me. I got something I want to get off my chest before I go meet my Maker."

Leaning forward, Henry rested his elbows on his knees, hands laced together.

Pops coughed. "Ah, God. I wouldn't wish the cancer on no-body." He held up a brown clay mug and asked, "You want a nip?"

Henry tipped his head, no.

"That college boy that wrecked his car down by Bottoms Crossing last winter. The day after he died in the hospital, my boy Gus come to me and told me what happened."

"The paper said he died of head injuries from a single-car crash," Henry said.

"That's what the police told them to say," Pops said. He shifted his weight again and continued his story. "Gus was at Honey's that night. Said the college boy been 'ere hours drinkin' beer and 'shine shots. Your brother and his girlfriend come in and was standin' at the bar. Gus said while he was talking to Ben, the kid come up to Vee and put his arm around her and said, 'I hear you like to show a guy a good time.' Gus said your brother turned mad as a rabid dog in July, grabbed the kid by the collar and kicked him in the pants out the door."

Henry shrugged with indifference.

"Gus said your brother made him get his pickup and they took off after the boy. They tailed him for a mile or so and then the boy's car veered off the road and down into a creek bed. Ben got Gus' bat from behind the seat and told Gus to go get the police and ambulance. Gus told me 'Dad, when I left, that kid was leaning against a tree pukin' his guts out. He was walking around, talkin', cryin' about his car gettin' all busted up.' Gus said when the medics pulled the boy out of the ditch he was unconscious and his face had been beaten in and Ben left with the police. Gus slid down into the ditch and found his bat, broke in two, covered in blood."

"What did he do with it?"

Pops' hacking was back. He spat again on the floor, then lit another cigarette.

Henry had known this man most of his adult life and knew he was a liar and a cheat. He stayed quiet.

"He brung it to me. He was scared the police would think he'd beat the kid up, what with his name on the bat and all. The week after the boy died, Ben come to see me. Wanted to talk to Gus. I told him Gus had left to go live with his Kentucky gran-maw."

"Why are you telling me this? Why didn't Gus go to the police with what he knew?"

Pops took a hit on his cigarette. "You don't suffer no fools, Henry Lee, and neither do I. Ben Lee and the law are thick as thieves. You know what he would've done to my boy if he'd come forward with that bat."

"Where's Gus now?"

"He's still in Kentucky. Wants to come home. Reckon he wants to see his old man before he goes." Another hacking fit ensued as Pops called for the young woman, Carin.

The sullen woman stood in the doorway with crossed arms.

"Bring me that box up in mama's closet."

A minute later, Carin placed a long cardboard box, like the one Elizabeth used to store her wedding gown, at the foot of the bed. "Now, git," Pops dismissed her. To Henry he said, "Go on, open it."

Lifting the flimsy lid, Henry saw a Louisville slugger, broken at the grip and nestled in an old blanket. The college boy's blood, if it was his, was now dried and black. Burned into the barrel of the bat was the name "Gussy Young .245."

"My boy was being scouted by a couple of farm teams. I blame Ben Lee for killing his chances at a career in baseball."

Henry had no defense for his brother, although he suspected Pops' story would not stand up in a court of law. "Why are you telling me this ... tale?"

"Like I said, I wanted to get it off my conscience before I go."

Henry stood to leave. "That's what preachers are for."

"Sit your ass back down," Pops commanded. "Gus wants to come home. And before I die, I want Ben Lee's word he won't cause no trouble." With shaky, liver-spotted hands, he covered the bat with the old blanket and placed the cardboard lid back in place. "Guilty or not, imagine what this would do to your family's good name if Gus ever told *his* version of what happened in a court-room."

"The way I see it, that's between your son and my brother. It's none of our concern."

"Does your daddy know about his son's," Pops paused for dramatic effect, "special friend, Violet Tyler?"

"That's none of your business and I'd advise you leave well enough alone," Henry seethed.

"Carin tells me Baby Tyler is working for Miss Elizabeth now. Does the lady of Grove House know who's ironing her husband's undershorts and fryin' her eggs?" Hairless and rheumy eyed, the old man smiled, revealing a row of jagged, tobacco-stained teeth.

Henry felt as if he was staring at the hound of hell himself.

In a low tone, one Henry barely heard, the old man hissed, "Don't make me call up Stumpy Quinn and tell him what I just told you, Henry."

Henry bluffed, "I hardly think the law would believe you. Sounds like sour grapes between two bulls who've had a falling out to me."

"We'll just have to see, won't we," Pops said. "Now, get out of my sight."

The woman was standing in the doorway again. Glaring at Henry, she said, "I think it's time for you to leave."

The old man's last words boomed after Henry as he walked out the door. "Tell that brother of yours if he knows what's best for him, he better come see me. He owes me. Owes me money and owes my son a guarantee."

Driving away, Henry reeled from the moonshiner's confession. He lit up and felt the nicotine rush to his lungs. His brother was seen as a pillar in the community. He and his wife co-chaired numerous fund-raisers for hopeless causes. Ben was a Rotary member, on the vestry at his church and a generous contributor to annual college football scholarships. But, being family, Henry knew all his brother's flaws and Ben Lee wasn't the saint everybody thought he was. But was he capable of murder?

He tossed the cigarette butt out of the speeding car, then ran his hand over his stubby flattop. He needed to think. He pulled to the side of the road and got out of his car. At times, walking along the cattle paths throughout the county cleared his mind. And now, the views of wide swatches of dried corn stalks and the orange and blue hills soothed him as he trekked along a path. He tried to conjure up happier times spent with his brother, when they were kids. But every instance Henry recalled involved Ben's ridicule and taunts, usually made with an audience of his brother's toadies. They played pranks on him. They abandoned him in the woods alone at night, threw firecrackers at his feet, and stuffed his pockets full of candy at the Five and Dime and dared him to walk out. At times he searched out M. Ellen for solace. Quoting scripture, she assured him Ben loved him. He sure had a funny way of showing it. Once, Ben and his friends took him for a joy ride on the parkway in a car they said belonged to somebody's father. The car ran out of gas in between nowhere and lost, so they encouraged him to stay in the car while they all went for gasoline. Not until the sun was setting did Henry realize what they had done. He turned the key in the ignition and watched the fuel needle inch up from empty to a quarter tank. A state trooper stopped him on the highway exit to Mt Pleasant. Only after his father promised to administer a pun-ishment to fit the crime did the car's owner and trooper agree not to press charges against the minor. Hopping over a cow patty on the path, the thought of the prank curled his lip into a smile. He had been grounded for a month. But it was worth it because he bragged to his own friends, Donnie Tyler and the English brothers, Thomas and Artie, of his daring feat of social rebellion; minus the role his brother had played, of course.

At the next summit, he veered from the path and sat on a bald patch of rock. In the waning light he reflected on the dying man's words, "Your brother don't have much use for you." It took a vengeful hillbilly to expose the honest truth about his relationship with his brother. Throughout their lives, Ben never did anything that called for Henry's affections. Not once had Ben ever shared a kind word or deed toward Henry, his wife, his child or for the sacrifices he'd made for the good of the family. Now in his forties, Henry admitted to himself that he didn't much care for his brother's company and felt no shame in his lapse of familial commitment to honor his brother. He supposed that at some point in the past he'd looked up to his older brother. But all reverence was lost the night he saw Ben, newly married, entwined in the arms of the woman he, Henry, had planned to run away with to California. What a fool he'd been.

"What am I going to do about this?" he asked the evening star. "Betray my brother or myself?"

Henry drove back to Pops'. He offered to trade the bat for his own word. He promised Pops Young that Benjamin Robert Lee would never interfere in his son's life. He peeled off ten C-notes and instructed Carin to send the boy 'round to his office when he needed more for college tuition. Henry left with the box tucked under his arm. He had to know if his brother had committed the malicious acts of murdering a young boy and ruining the life of another all because he didn't like hearing the honest truth about his mistress.

The next day, Henry drove to Ben's office in Roanoke. The place buzzed with activity: phones ringing, people walking about with purpose. A stylish receptionist held up a finger at Henry as he approached. She was on the phone repeating herself, "I see. I see."

Feeling underdressed, Henry shoved his hands in his pockets. But he'd learned from previous visits that the only way he'd get an audience with his brother was to stand at the desk until the person grew uncomfortable with his presence.

The young woman interrupted her caller, "Sir, Mr. Lee isn't available. Perhaps his associate Mr. Hardy can help. Let me patch you through."

The phone rang. Waving her finger again at Henry, she answered, "Lee Law Offices." Several calls later, she blew a strand of hair from her perfect face and rolled her hand at Henry to speak.

"I'm here to see Ben Lee," he said.

Without looking at her calendar, she said, "I'm sorry, but Mr. Lee is in conference all day. Did you have an appointment?"

"No," he said. "I'm his brother. It's a private matter."

"I'm sorry but he's really busy," she offered.

"Just let him know I'm here."

She pressed an orange button on her phone. Tucking a strand of light brown hair back into place, she whispered into the receiver.

Henry took in the highly polished twelfth floor, its view of downtown, and the girl's nervous reverence when she said, "Yes, Mr. Lee. Yes, sir. Yes, sir." With such a thriving law practice, he questioned why his brother stole from the family business, from ignorant pokes like Pops Young, and from him. His brother took from those who had no recourse. That was about to change.

"Mr. Lee can't see you today. He suggests you go by his house this evening." Ever helpful, she added, "Do you have the address?"

"I know where my brother lives," Henry said. He walked to the door but changed his mind. Back at the reception desk, he leaned over and whispered, "Tell my brother—."

The phone rang. She lifted the receiver. Henry pressed down on the switch hook. She set the receiver on the desk.

"Tell my brother that I'm across the street at the cafeteria having a cup of coffee. Tell him it's about Gussy Young and his batting average."

She stared at him, her doe eyes jittering.

"You want to write it down? Gussy Young. Batting average."

She stumbled out of her chair, disappearing down a hallway.

Henry found a seat next to a paneled window facing Ben's building. He watched as a banker stopped his brother. Ben laughed at whatever the pinstripe said then slapped him on the arm with the rolled up newspaper he carried. Ben was a different person in public; everyone looking at the exchange saw two prosperous men casually sniffing each other's coattails. As Ben turned and spotted Henry, his forehead wrinkled in contempt, his brows pressed together – the same look Henry's daughter Iris gave him when she'd done something she was told not to do and he'd called her out on it. Ben's face told Henry he'd hit a nerve with the Gussy Young comment.

After ten minutes of glad-handing at the coffee urn, Ben placed his cup on the table. Unbuttoning his suit coat, he pulled out a chair and sat across from Henry. He asked, "Henry? Why are you harassing my help?"

"Help? That girl wouldn't know what help was if it came up and bit her on the—."

"What's this about Gus Young?"

"Pops invited me for a visit. He appears awfully peeved that you won't drop by to see him on his death bed."

"Old coot. Thinks I owe him money."

"Do you?"

Winking at a table of young women, Ben asked, "Do I what?"

"Owe Pops Young money?"

"Oh, for heaven's sake, Henry. He's demented. Cancer's eating away at what brain he ever had."

"Aren't you interested in why he asked me to come see him?"

Brushing lint from a sleeve, Ben said, "I suppose he thought he could collect from you."

"So you do owe him money. How much?"

Ben clenched his teeth to keep from raising his voice. "Listen, you thick little backwater beaver, I don't owe that codger money."

Pushing his cup away, Henry said, "I'm just a messenger. Pops wants you to come see him. He's got something he wants you to have."

"What?"

"Something about a broken baseball bat." Henry let the words float around in the air between them.

"A baseball bat?" Ben laughed casually. "What? He wants me to sponsor his moonshiner's team this year?"

"Don't make me repeat the story he told me, Ben. Not here."

"I don't know what you're talking about, little brother," Ben said.

Henry recognized the denial in his brother's eyes. He'd seen Ben backpedal out of a mess in front of their parents on more than one occasion. What was the joke? How do you know when a lawyer is lying? When his lips are moving?

"What does he want?"

"He said Gus wants to come home. He wants your assurance you'll leave him alone."

"Leave him alone? What's that supposed to mean?"

"Can the Mr. Innocent act, Ben. Gus told his dad about what happened the night the college kid crashed his car."

Jabbing the table, Ben said, "That kid was mouthing off so I kicked him out of the club. He was so drunk we followed him to make sure he made it back to his dorm. That's when he ran off the road. I told Gus to go for help. If we hadn't been there, he would've

     MELISSA POWELL GAY

died alone on the side of that hill."

To Henry, Ben's words sounded like one of his client's practiced testimonies.

"That's all there is to tell," Ben said. He flattened his hand over his tie.

"He showed me the bat," Henry said softly.

"What's that?" Ben asked.

"Pops showed me the bat. It was broken in two. Blood and hair all over the barrel," Henry said. He noticed his brother slipping into his middistance stare, the one he'd take on whenever he was about to lose his temper.

Henry waited.

With a predator's speed, Ben's arm swept coffee cups, saucers, and a host of condiments off the table. He grabbed at Henry's shirt. "You little idiot. And you didn't think to get it and bring it to me?"

A cafeteria manger rushed to Mr. Lee's aid. "We'll get this cleaned up for you right away. Can we get you another coffee?"

Pushing his brother's hands away, Henry saw Ben's recognition of his mistake. Fear edged into Ben's shocked stare as he said to the manager, "No, thank you, Ed. We're finished."

Maintaining eye contact with his brother, Henry said, "You know what, Ed. I'd like another cup of that fine brew of yours. Put it on his tab. Sorry about the mess. Mr. Lee gets overanxious sometimes." After the manager left, Henry calmly reached for a photo in his coat pocket. "Elizabeth got this neat camera for her birthday. Darnedest thing, you press the button and out comes the picture. It develops before your very eyes." He set the picture on the table. He'd taken several Polaroids of the bat before he shoved it underneath the house he'd given to Bert and her new husband on Eastend Street. The spare instant photos were stuffed in a shoebox along with countless pictures of construction sites in his office.

Ben swallowed. "Game, set, match, little brother," he said. "Where is it?"

"Somewhere you've never been and, most likely, somewhere you'll never go," Henry sighed.

"Stop talking in riddles. Where is it?"

Henry leaned over the table. "You know that I know you stole money from the company. Stealing from your own family when you had plenty. Despicable."

"Technically, Lee Properties belongs to me since I'm the oldest son. So, there's no way a man can steal from himself," Ben said, seeming relieved to move onto another topic.

"I can see why you did what you did with the receipts. Sometimes cash flow gets tight." Henry paced his accusations. "What with a big house mortgage, a wife with expensive taste and a boy in private school." He waited, then said, "Keeping a mistress." He watched his brother squirm. "Remember when you raised Cain about me buying that fancy copy machine? I make copies of your new entries every week. Bribing judges, Bennie? Are you that desperate?"

Ben looked at his wristwatch. Apparently, at the advice of his own counsel, he stopped talking.

"Now this." Henry threw the picture at Ben. "You disgust me." Henry got up to leave.

"That's circumstantial evidence," Ben called out to Henry over the fray of dining room chatter. "You should turn it into the authorities."

Henry came back to the table and bent down to his brother's ear, the sweet aftershave stinging his nose. "Don't tempt me, big brother." He left with everyone wondering what the wiry little man had whispered into Mr. Lee's ear.

CHAPTER 31 THEN
GOD'S HONEST TRUTH

By the fall of 1970 Allen Lee, with little fuss, traded his cane for a wheelchair. His body was weak but his mind was still strong. Each morning, Henry found him sitting in his bed, which they had moved into the parlor, reading a law book or his Bible. His Thursday luncheons with the retired brethren of the bar, a dwindling number, were now held in Grove House's dining room. To set Elizabeth's nerves at ease, Henry hired Bert to prepare the special noonday meals. And, because Mr. Lee required more and more of Elizabeth's time, by Thanksgiving Bert had become their full-time housekeeper. Elizabeth, and the entire family, cheered when Bert took over kitchen duties and family meals.

Henry hoped his father would come to know Bert as one of the family and welcome her into his heart as he had his other grandchildren. However, revealing to the old man Bert's paternity and her parent's on-going relationship, Henry believed, was not his duty or business. Besides, his father discounted everything Henry ever told him anyway.

One night in bed, Henry grumbled about his father's blindness to Ben's indiscretions. "Surely, after all these years," he complained to Elizabeth, "one of the *venerable* burghers of Mt Pleasant has taken Dad into his confidence and told him of the extramarital dalliances of his beloved son."

Looking up from her book, Elizabeth said, "Bert and your dad get along famously the way things are."

"But he treats her like … the hired help," he blustered.

"How would you expect him to treat her?" she asked. "He's respectful toward her. Believe me, if he knew the truth, he'd want her out of the house." She put her book on the nightstand, turned out the light, and snuggled next to her husband. "Let's just appreciate that we have her with us. Don't spoil things by stirring up the ugly past."

Bending to her gentle plea, Henry pledged to himself to try and set the matter aside.

On Thanksgiving evening, as swirling leaves reminded them of winter's pending arrival, the entire Lee clan gathered for dinner at Grove House. Mr. Lee raised a port glass of Andy Tyler's wine made from Fallam County grapes and said in a wobbly voice, "To Matilda and all the blessings she bestowed on this family."

"To Matilda," everyone replied.

"Mommy, this jello doesn't taste as good as the cherry jello Miss Bert makes," Iris complained.

Everyone laughed.

"It's not jello, you baby, it's cranberry sauce," Bennie Jr. taunted.

"I'm not a baby. I'm six," Iris cried out.

"Enough, you two. Eat your turkey," Ben said. Using his napkin, he dabbed at a swollen cut above his eyebrow.

To Henry, Ben appeared more nervous than usual. He and Sarah had come in separate cars.

The room fell silent as everyone stuffed themselves with the holiday turkey spread that Bert prepared the day before. Bert had recently married Otha Swanson and the two were spending the holiday with his folks.

Amid the tinkling of silverware and complements to the absent cook, the doorbell chimed.

"I'll get it," Iris offered. She hopped off her chair and ran to the foyer before hearing her grandfather complain about rude visitors calling at the dinner hour.

Feeling cold air at his ankles, Henry tossed his napkin on the seat of his chair. He found his small daughter standing in the open doorway looking up at Violet Tyler. The child appeared mesmerized, as if an exotic queen from one of her storybooks had come to visit.

The queen was saying, "… look at you in your fancy dress. Is your daddy home?"

Henry heard the drink in her raspy voice. Wedging himself between them, he said, "Violet? What are you doing here?"

Vee's eyes shinned like glass. She cawed with laughter. "That's some welcome, Hank."

"Iris, go finish your turkey," he ordered.

"I finished my turkey." She stamped a foot and folded her arms like grown-ups did.

"Then go see what your mother's doing. Daddy's got to talk to this lady," he said.

Iris pulled on her daddy's hand and climbed the side of his leg, a game she often played.

"Ah, father and daughter," Vee said. She was swaying in her platform shoes. Her clothes sparkled as if she was headed for a night out on the town.

"Iris, go inside," Henry said. He pushed the protesting child inside and closed the door, forcing Vee to back away onto the stone veranda.

"Nice place here, Hank. Y'all all having yourselves a Norman Rockwell Thanksgiving? I'm sorry I'm late. Did you save some for me? You know how much I love my daughter's cookin'."

"Vee, you're drunk. You don't want to do this." He noticed Bennie Jr. pressing his upturned nose against the dining room window. Only a matter of minutes before everyone found out who the caller was.

"I'm not so drunk," Vee said. "You've seen me drunker." She clucked.

In the muted light she looked as beautiful as the night he'd met her. The way she tilted her head, her almond-shaped eyes pulling him into her like they always did. Her perfume whisked him back to the night Ben had stood her up and she'd made Henry take her dancing.

"He broke up with me, Henry." She was crying now.

"How'd you get here? Let me take you home." He reached for her elbow, but she pulled away.

"No!" she cried out. "He came by earlier to say he didn't want to be with me anymore. That we were finished." She pointed at the door. "I know he's in there." Raising her voice, she called, "Ben Lee, I want you to come out here and tell it to my face. You coward! Tell it to my face you don't love me anymore." Mascara stained her cheeks.

Henry ached to hold her in his arms and soak up all her pain, but knew he'd drown if he did. How different their lives would have been if she'd loved him as much as she loved his brother.

She was hyperventilating. "Help me, Henry. I don't know what to do." Slowly, she squatted, hugging her knees and swaying over her platform shoes, repeating her cry, "What am I gonna do?"

Henry glanced at the windows. Sarah and Iris had joined Bennie, all three cupping their hands against the panes to see outside. He offered his hand and said, maybe to himself, "You're going to do what we've all done. You're going to move on and find someone who appreciates you."

"But it hurts so bad. Why does it hurt, Henry?" she cried.

"Come on, Vee. Get up. We've got an audience and you're making me look bad."

She took his hand. As he pulled her to unsteady feet, she fell into his arms and heaved another round of sobs. "Why is he doing this to me? Why now?" She pushed away from him and steadied her balance. "He promised me we'd be together. He's going to California and promised to take me with him." Facing the front of the house, she screeched, "You promised! You promised me you'd take me with you."

"Here, now!" Mr. Lee was at the door. "What's all this?"

The boom of the old man's voice, a voice borne from the previous paternalistic century, shook Vee from her grieving. Henry pulled a handkerchief from his trouser pocket and handed it to her. She took it and patted her face as calmly as if she was sitting in front of her dressing table.

"Henry?" Elizabeth stepped past Mr. Lee's wheelchair. "Is something the matter?"

Thankful for the interruption, Henry reached for his wife's waist and pulled her to his side. "Vee, you know my wife Elizabeth?"

Extending her hand to Vee, Elizabeth said, "Henry, for heaven's sake. You're going to let our guest freeze out here. Miss Tyler, good to see you again."

Hugging herself in the cold, Vee said timidly, "Hello."

"Won't you come in and enjoy some of Bert's sweet potato pie? I'm sure you know how delicious it is."

"No," Vee said meekly. "I've got somewhere to be. If Henry could give me a ride."

Taking Vee by the arm, he guided her to his car and helped her in. "Which way?" Henry asked when he needed to turn.

"Take me to the shop," Vee said, "I don't feel like being thankful in public tonight."

"You've got lots to be thankful for. Your family, your business, your friends."

"I'm too tired to laugh, so shut up, Mr. Sunshine." In front of her shop, Vee said, "Come up for a drink."

Hearing the pain in her voice, Henry sensed he'd better go with her. He followed her up the exterior stairs attached to the side of the old train station.

Inside, she untied the flowing scarf from around her neck and walked out of her shoes on the way to the sofa. "Fix us a drink."

Broken pieces of a wash bowl splayed on the floor explained the bump above Ben's eye. Henry found a pint of rye among the dirty dishes on the kitchen counter and rinsed out a jelly glass. Standing over her, he offered her the drink and put the bottle on the coffee table.

Sitting up, she took it and patted the sofa beside her. "Sit with me, just this once."

"He's not available, so you come to me?" Henry asked, ashamed of himself before the thought left his lips. He remained standing.

"Don't be dumb," she said. She downed the rye and held up her glass for another. She was calm now like the eye of a hurricane. "He came over last Friday like usual. He was all excited about some trip to California he was planning. He said he was leaving that dried up goat of a wife of his. He said he'd take me with him."

"Tell me you see the irony in that," Henry said as he poured her another drink.

"Shut up." She turned quiet and sipped at the second drink. "Then I told him I thought I was pregnant. My periods stopped and I was feeling tired."

Speechless, Henry sat beside her.

The waterworks came back on as she looked at Henry. "He denied it was his. Then we decided I'd go have it … you know … taken care of." She wrapped her arms around her waist and leaned forward.

"Is it?" Henry asked. "Is it his?"

"I'm not pregnant, Henry. The doctor said I got something growing in my insides. He wants me to go to Baltimore to some hospital up there to see a specialist. When Ben came by this afternoon, I told him what the doctor said and asked him to take me. That's when he told me he couldn't see me anymore." She leaned her head on Henry's shoulder and wept.

Henry took her in his arms and rocked her. "Shhh," he whispered, "I'll take you there."

By the time Henry made it home, the house was dark with the exception of a small light next to his father's bed.

"Henry? Is that you?" His father called from the parlor.

"Yeah, Dad. Go to sleep," Henry said.

"Come in here, boy."

Henry came to his father's bedside.

"We all missed you this evening. Did you get that young lady home?"

"Yes, sir."

"Come sit next to me."

Henry yawned and stretched as he sat on the edge of the bed.

"You've been a good son. Don't think I haven't noticed all the sacrifices you've made."

Hearing this, the closest his father had ever come to praising him, Henry bent over his father and asked, "You feeling all right, Pop?" He placed his hand on the old man's chest.

"I'm fine. Pay attention to what I have to say. A colleague of mine came to me last week and confided in me that several complaints have been filed with the state bar against your brother."

"So. You've said yourself that happens all the time. Clients unhappy with a judge's ruling, looking for someone to blame. You should see his setup. He's churning through more cases in a month than you probably did in a year. It's bound to happen."

Mr. Lee grabbed Henry's hand. "Henry, stop. I know what you're doing."

"What?"

"You're trying to protect your brother, cover for him. Just like you've always done. You thought I didn't see it, but I did. There are things a man knows about his sons."

Confused, Henry pulled his hand away from his father's weak grip.

"This is something far more serious than a ruling complaint. It's a criminal matter. I asked your brother about it tonight and he flatly denied the accusations."

Henry's stomach tightened as he thought about the copies of Ben's secret ledger locked in his desk drawer and the unreturned phone call he received from the commonwealth's attorney's office earlier in the week.

"Our commonwealth's attorney has it in for your brother. Someone has whispered in his ear that your brother's offering bribes to court officials," Mr. Lee said. "Of course, it's ludicrous. The man's obviously jealous of your brother's courtroom prowess. I saw it in my time."

"Yes, it is ludicrous," Henry said. Ludicrous his father thought he really knew his sons.

Seemingly satisfied with Henry's response, Mr. Lee moved to another topic. "Your brother is obsessed with that absurd medal. Did you know he's built a shadow box for it in his library?"

Henry stared at his hands in silence, wondering who reported the bribes.

"I've been thinking. Elizabeth has been so good to me since your mother passed. I'm seriously thinking of leaving it to her."

"What?" Tired and distracted, Henry rubbed his face. He'd waited for Vee to cry herself to sleep, then carried her to her bed.

"The general's medallion. She has enjoyed it so. I think she would make a good steward for it because she's genuinely interested in discovering who gave it to the general."

"If that's what you want, Dad," Henry said. He stood and said, "Good night."

"That woman who was here tonight, she's your brother's mistress, isn't she?"

"Dad, you're tired, get some sleep and we'll talk about this in the morning," Henry said as he reached for the light.

"Son, I'm tired all the time but I'm never sleepy. Now, look me in the eye and tell me the God's honest truth. Has your brother been unfaithful to his vows of marriage to Sarah?"

Instilled in him during his upbringing, Henry, as every other Fallam County male child, was threatened with boiling water, leaches and thrashings if ever caught lying whenever a parent demanded testimony certified as "God's honest truth." So, he answered his father with, "Yes, sir. He has."

"And, in his unfaithfulness, did he father a mulatto child?"

"Yes, sir, he has. Violet Tyler, the woman at the door tonight, is Bert's mother."

An involuntary whimper escaped from his father's lips. He

stated with complete clarity, "Ben is Bert's father."

"Yes," Henry confirmed. "She's your granddaughter."

Shaking with anger and feebleness, the old man commanded, "Go to bed, son."

The next day, while everyone was away, Allen Lee summoned his attorney, John Bailey, to his home. Mr. Lee insisted Bailey bring a notary with him.

          MELISSA POWELL GAY

CHAPTER 32 NOW

IT'S GOOD TO BE IRIS LEE

Iris was determined to get everything back to normal, well, normal by Mt Pleasant standards. First, as she had for the last two days, she dialed Ethan's personal number. Damian was still missing. When she contacted Bennie about Damian's disappearance, the man flew into a rage, holding her responsible if anything happened to him. Fair enough, she thought. The old Iris would have screamed back at the maniac, reminding him of how eager he was to throw the child away like so much refrigerator leftovers.

"Hey," a sleepy voice mumbled.

"Did you find him?" she asked.

"Not yet."

"Do you think he's still with that gang?" she asked, always dreading the answer.

"Sweetheart, I just don't know," Ethan said.

Hearing the weariness in his voice, she melted at "sweetheart" and felt a little better. He was back to being her big brother. "Did that FBI agent get his man?"

"Don't know." And that was all she was going to get from him.

"I've got to go. Bert's here. She's taking Mom and Heyu to Bible school." She laughed when she said, "Heyu is the star of Lost Lambs' Bible school show-and-tell today. Call me tonight?"

"I'll try. I've got a pretty full calendar. Take care, now," he said and hung up.

And back to trying to make things normal, she walked Elizabeth out to the Lost Lambs' van that Bert had bought for the congregation. Heyu limped along behind.

"Thanks for taking Mom along today," she said as she hoisted Heyu into his car seat.

"Sweet pea, every now and then your mama and me used to talk about the things we were going to do when we retired. And volunteering for summer vacation Bible school was one of them." She patted Elizabeth on her hand and said, "Ain't that right, Miss Elizabeth?"

"'Isn't,' Bert. The word is 'isn't.' How many times do I have to tell you? You're never going to catch a new man if you don't use good grammar," Elizabeth protested.

Iris waved as they backed out of the driveway.

Later that morning, she offered Vinnie and his new number one, Hank, a seat at the kitchen table for their daily meeting. As they knocked around ideas on what to do with the chestnut tree lumber, the lights popped on and the second hand on the old Westclox started whirring again. Taking the power restoration as a good sign, they all toasted with store-bought iced tea, sans the ice.

The first house to be renovated was on schedule to be completed by the end of the month and they already had two interested buyers. Uncle Donnie had managed to coax all the squatters in the first block to move out. Iris didn't want to know how he did it, but suspected offers of weed and illegal whiskey were involved. They ended the meeting with intentions to visit Travis English the following week to ask for a second, bigger construction loan to cover

    MELISSA POWELL GAY

the remaining houses on the block. Vinnie was ready with plans and cost projections for Mt Pleasant's first affordable housing community. Iris followed them to Vinnie's truck.

Vinnie offered, "Tomorrow we can take time to work on your renovation plans."

"Have you finished at Bert's?" she asked. She'd finally convinced Bert to hire Vinnie to install central air at her house.

"That reminds me," Vinnie said. He hopped up into the truck bed and slid a decaying cardboard box onto the tailgate. "I found this while I was crawling around under her house." He lifted the crumbling lid.

Iris peered inside. "What is it?"

Vinnie brushed at rat droppings and pulled away a dry-rotted blanket to reveal a baseball bat.

Squinting, Iris read, "Gussy Young .245."

"Dad said a Gus Young from here played for Detroit in the '70s."

"He played at Virginia Tech. Drafted his sophomore year. It was a big deal, Fallam County boy hitting the major league baseball lottery," Iris said. "Did Bert say why it was under her house?"

"Cop's kids are suspicious people. Thought I'd ask you first," he said.

"How would I know?" Iris asked. "Why are you suspicious?"

Using pliers, he turned the bat at its grip. "See there. It's busted in two. Wrapped in a blanket, shoved under a house. Somebody hid it for some reason."

"Then forgot about it," Iris said.

"What do you want me to do with it?"

"Throw it in the site dumpster," she said.

"Are you sure?" he entreated with his Caribbean-colored eyes.

"Oh, all right," she said. "Put it in the garage. I'll talk to Bert about it." After Vinnie left, Iris stood over the sagging box. What-ever foul play the bat had been a part of had no place in Bert's life now. She'd been through enough. Iris decided she'd toss the thing in the trash can on garbage pick-up day.

In the hottest part of the day, Ed the plumber finally arrived with his enforcement, a pale and crusty looking soul with thick rim-less glasses sliding down his pointed nose. Didn't Ed say the boy's name was Mole? Iris perched herself on Elizabeth's bath stool as Ed bent over to unbolt the toilet from the floor. Convinced the medal-lion was lodged in the sewage pipe, she wasn't budging despite the heat and closeness of their bodies. Sweat dripping from his jowls, Ed grunted as he pushed aside the commode. He straightened his back and mopped his brow with the tail of his T-shirt. Today's shirt message, under a line of shot glasses, read "One Tequila, Two Te-quila, Three Tequila, Floor." He whipped out his trusty auger and rammed it down the sewer line.

"Ah-yeah, I think you might be on to something, Mrs. Lee," he said while sticking his tongue out at the ceiling. "There's something down there all right."

"Can you pull it out?" Iris asked.

"It's lodged in the elbow." He yanked on the auger.

"Don't!" Iris exclaimed. "If it's stuck, you'll bend it. Is there any way you can remove the pipe?"

"Ma'am, we'd have to tear up your floor to get at it," he said.

"Fine," she said. "Go for it."

"OK, it's your floor." He turned to Mole and said, "Go fetch the sledge hammer and crow bar."

As Mole pounded away at bathroom tile, Iris opened the front door to a polite deliveryman. "Package for Iris Lee," he said.

She signed for the box, surprised at its heavy weight when he handed it to her. Placing the kitchen scissors on the butcher's block,

     MELISSA POWELL GAY

she hefted the package again. Nothing on the white box indicated a return address.

Heavy boots on the back stairs signaled that Mole and Ed had hit the mother lode. Without concern for the pipe's purpose over the last forty-plus years, Ed plopped it on the butcher's block where Bert prepared meals and Iris ate her cereal every morning. Iris calmly suggested they take it outside to the rundown picnic table tagged for the recycle center.

Mole beamed an LED light at the pipe's center while Ed peered inside with one eye closed. "Ah-yeah. There's something shiny in there, all right. Mole, hand me your needle nose."

Iris stood by.

"Here it is," Ed said. The pliers pinched a small broach.

Forgetting the origin of the pipe herself, Iris snatched the broach from him. It wasn't the medallion. It was one of her mother's costume pieces she's bought herself for Christmas one year. "*Merde!*" Iris chucked the piece on the table and held her hand away from her body. "Keep digging, Ed. Check both bathrooms."

"It's your dollar, little lady," Ed smiled. Mole followed him back inside the house.

Inside, Iris struggled with her sling as she washed her hands with bleach. Then she called Jonnie to beg for a ride to the beauty parlor. With her shoulder in a sling, she had been unable to wash her hair for days.

"Come by around four. I'll take you to dinner afterward," Jonnie offered.

For the remainder of the afternoon, Iris supervised Ed and Mole as they probed and poked every inch of the sewer lines, but no more treasure was discovered. Before they left, they restored water service everywhere except Elizabeth's bathroom. Finally, Grove House was up and operational again.

Before she left for Jonnie's office, she spied the white delivery box on the kitchen island. She tore it open. Inside, whatever the content, it was bound up in bubble-wrap. Slowly she unwrapped her father's revolver. She checked the cylinder for shot. It was empty, cleaned and oiled. She searched the box for a note from Damian but knew she wouldn't find one.

"Safety first, Iris," she said out loud to an empty house. Strange, before coming back to Mt Pleasant, she craved solitude, went out of her way to find it. But now, she realized that living alone was overrated. Damian could have thrived here, she thought. She carried the gun up to her father's room.

After a few familiar clicks, the safe door fell open. When she tried to place the reveler in its designated spot, the handle jutted out. Something was wedged in the back of the cubby hole. She stuck her hand inside and pulled out an envelope. She opened it and there it was, shiny as ever, Jubal A. Early's war booty. "That's why he came back, the little stinker," she said to Mr. Henry's ghost. "He came back to return the medallion. Which he lied about taking!"

Saluting Claire Brown at the front desk, Iris found her way to Jonnie's office. Jonnie waved her in while she talked on the phone. Iris stood at the window looking out over Court Street. George Garland and his wife were standing in front of the Confederate soldier statue, shaming court visitors into signing their petition to have it removed "from this public space," citing it as offensive and racist. As she had approached Jonnie's office, he called for her to add her name to the growing list. To wind him up and hear him sing, she called back, "How many Fallam County Civil War veterans do you suppose actually owned slaves and wanted to secede the Union?" He harrumphed and accused her of misunderstanding the meaning of the vile statue's intimidating Jim Crow representation. She neglected to correct his assumption that the statue occupied public space. It was only a matter of time before Plinkus Young, the president of Fallam County Historical Society, set him straight. As clear as Mt Pleasant tap water, Jonnie's monthly business reports showed that Lee Properties, by her grandfather Allen Lee's pen, owned and had leased the square to the historical society for the tidy sum of one dollar a year in perpetuity, or until one or both parties no longer desired the arrangement. The society maintained the statue and the small garden, for a fee of course, for the statue's owner, a nonprofit organization in Tennessee. She'd take Sukie and Barbara out for tequilas one night and ask them if they had any interest in getting ahead of what most likely would become one ugly PR train wreck for Fallam County. Maybe now was the time in Lee history to deed more land to the public domain. She sighed, wondering what Mr. Henry would think about her solution. She missed her dad.

Two hours later at the new downtown place called Whiskey Grill, Iris' euphoria from a head massage, shampoo and blowout evaporated as she listened to Jonnie's distress, informing her that the wedding was off.

"But Jonnie, why? What happened?"

"I don't know what I was thinking, Iris." Jonnie paused to sip her Old Fashioned. "It would never work. Thinking we could go back to the way it was in high school."

"But Jonnie, you two are perfect for each other," Iris said.

"Stop trying to make me feel worse than I already do."

"I think you're making a mistake. Ethan really cares for you." Iris bit into her first fry.

"That's just it, Iris," Jonnie's voice rose. "He *cares* for me. There's no passion, no 'come sweep me off my feet' and 'take me away to an undisclosed mossy spot deep in the woods and ravage me.'"

"Wow, I see you've set your priorities for a meaningful relationship," Iris teased.

Jonnie fidgeted with her engagement ring and said, "I feel like I wouldn't be able to compete."

"Compete? Are we talking about a marriage or a race?"

"Lupita is here. And, worse, she's not showing any signs of leaving."

"Who?" Iris was lost. Jonnie, the barrister who ate her opponent's arguments for a snack, was whining like a six-year-old who'd had her lunch money stolen. Iris reached across the table for Jonnie's arm. "Take deep breaths. Start at the beginning."

"Ethan's ex, Lupita, showed up at our Fourth of July party. At my house, Iris!" She gulped her drink. "Claims she drove all the way from Texas because she missed her boys."

"I thought Vinnie was an only child?"

"Exactly my point. Ethan said I misunderstood what she meant."

"What's she like?"

"A younger version of you. She probably lies to her mother."

Prone to teenage gossip in their youth, Iris and Jonnie used the expression "she probably lies to her mother" as girl code for their target having zero physical flaws for them to criticize.

"She can't be that bad."

Jonnie rolled her big hazel eyes and whispered, "Iris, please. Besides, I think he's seeing her again."

"For the love of—this is Ethan we're talking about, Jonnie. Mr. Loyalty. What makes you think he's seeing his ex-wife?"

"I heard him on the phone this morning. At first, I thought it was just one of the deputies. I heard him call her 'sweetheart.' Then he pecked me on the check and asked if we were meeting for dinner tonight. Like it was no big deal."

"I don't care what you heard this morning. I know Ethan Quinn. And he wants to marry you, Jonnie Bailey. Don't give up on the one and only guy who makes your heart flutter and your toes curl. Isn't that what you're always telling me?"

"I'm so confused, Iris," Jonnie said.

"Here's what you're going to do. You're going to take your backbone out of that mega-sized purse of yours and put it back on. Then, you're going to call him and invite him up to the Bailey Building penthouse for a night cap. Tonight. Have you bought your wedding night negligee yet?"

"You know I have." She giggled.

"Guys like Ethan need to have it spelled out for them every now and then. So, you're going to put on that negligee and lounge on the sofa. Make him sit in a chair across the room. Then you're going to tell him he's the love of your life, the man of your dreams. And then, you're going to tell him what you want from him. Tell him if he wants to make love with you, he's going to have to find a mossy spot."

Jonnie giggled louder.

Iris shook her freshly coiffed mane. It felt so good to be Iris Lee again.

With her shoulder on the mend, Iris decided to drive herself to the lake the next day. She sat under the pavilion and watched kids spread blankets and set up chairs for the day's fun in the sun. She recognized one of the boys from the gang she saw the day she'd picked up Damian. He was sitting with a group of girls lounging on a quilt.

"Hey," she called out to him. "Have you seen Damian?"

The boy squinted at her.

"Jake," she corrected herself, "have you seen Jake?"

"I saw him last night. Said he was heading back to L.A. this morning."

"What's your name?" she asked.

"Flea," he said. He stood, dusted sand from his britches and walked down to the water's edge.

Iris fished her phone from her pocket and called Ethan.

A state trooper picked up Damian at an entrance ramp to Interstate 81 south of Roanoke.

At the station, Iris urged, "Ethan, let me talk to him before you pull that passive-aggressive silent treatment detective routine on him."

"Fifteen minutes," he said.

Iris found Damian staring out of one of the conference room windows. He appeared subdued, resigned. His basketball jersey was torn and muddy and his shoe laces were missing. She wanted to reach out to him, to hug him and tell him everything was OK. But she didn't. Instead, she sat at the long table and said, "Come sit next to me."

Silently, he pulled out the chair and sat. His arms and legs were covered with dirt, bug bites, scratches and bruises.

She brushed a strand of matted hair away from his eye. "We need to get you to Bubba's for a hair cut." She willed herself not to cry.

He lowered his head and folded his hands in his lap.

She sensed a calmness in him, no fidgeting body parts. "Want to tell me what happened after Roscoe knocked me out?" She waited for an answer but none came. "Damian, I want to help you, son." She paused, then continued, "I care about you. I don't care what happens to that oversized toad Roscoe."

That got a smile.

"There are always going to be Roscoe Youngs. Fact of life. You've got to make up your mind that you're going to learn how to interact with them, learn how to stand up to them."

"My mom told me to run away," he said.

"A good tactic if you're *five*. But when you're a grown man it's not your best option," she said. "Stand your ground by telling the truth. Because lying … that's the first step in becoming a Roscoe yourself. Don't be a Roscoe."

Two quick knocks at the door signaled to Iris their time alone was up. Her favorite deputy popped his shaved head in and said, "Chef's ready."

"Give us another minute," she said. Turning to Damian, she asked, "are you ready to tell the truth?"

Damian nodded then asked, "Will you stay with me?"

She gulped back the growing lump in her throat. "I'm not going anywhere."

While in Ethan's office, Damian asked for a sports drink. Iris and Ethan watched as he chugged down half.

"After I left here," he said, "I was too scared to go back to your house. You said the first time I rode in a police cruiser, I was going back to the detention center."

Iris winced.

"Honest, I had nothing to do with taking Heyu." He finished off the blue drink and wiped his mouth with his arm. "I went back to the park to see if I could hook up with Flea. Nobody was around so I started walking out of town and that's when Coe and his posse drove by. He made me get in the back seat with him. He was jacked up on rocket fuel and weed. He made Hopper take us to your house. 'Cause your car wasn't in the driveway, we figured nobody was home."

"Did he say what his intentions were?" Ethan asked.

Damian bounced the plastic bottle against his knee.

"Damian?" Iris asked.

"He said he wanted to steal all the guns and jewelry." Quickening the pace, he continued to pound the plastic drink bottle against his knee.

"And how did he know about the contents of the house?" Ethan asked.

"Flea must have told him. I told Flea about the gun safe," he turned to Iris, "and your mom's jewelry box. Anyway, he made me go with him. When we were in my room, I pretended like I couldn't open the safe, that maybe you had changed the combination. He pummeled me in the arm." Damian lifted his skinny arm and pointed out an egg-sized bruise. "I told him about your mom's jewelry box in her room and while he was rummaging around in it, I opened the gun safe and stuffed the medallion as far back in the hole as I could."

"So you had it all that time?" Iris asked.

"In my backpack. I took it when I took the gun." The plastic bottle crackled and popped as he squeezed it with his hands.

Iris yanked it from him and walked out to the common area, looking for a recycle bin. She didn't want him to see how angry she was. It wasn't the stealing that infuriated her, it was his lying. Before she reentered Ethan's office, she took a deep breath. Inside, she sat and asked, "Why did you take it?"

"I 'on't know."

Pointing her finger at him she said, "Nope. You don't get a pass with that answer this time. Tell the truth. Why did you take it?"

"Thought I could sell it to that second hand store downtown. But when Tabby talked about how valuable it was and how everybody knew about it … I knew … I had to put it back."

"Why did you put my computer in the safe?"

     MELISSA POWELL GAY

"It was right there on the counter for anybody to steal. You should be more careful where you keep your electronics. I put it in the there when Tabby and I came by before the parade so I could change clothes."

Iris looked at Ethan. "He's right. Roscoe would have walked out of the house with my computer had he seen it."

"After he hit you and you fell on the floor, Coe acted like it was no big deal and wandered into the dining room. That's when he saw a car pulling into the driveway. We bolted out the back."

"But Damian, why did you run? You didn't assault me," Iris said.

"I 'ont … 'cause you said you had called the police and they were on their way. The police would blame me for hitting you." He lowered his head in shame and murmured, "I'm sorry I didn't stay to help you."

Iris leaned over and asked softly, "And why do you think the police wouldn't believe you?"

The boy was crying now. "'Cause I don't tell the truth?"

Iris patted Damian's back. "Quinn, I believe Damian's learned his lesson. I'm taking him home."

CHAPTER 33 THEN

HIS BROTHER'S KEEPER

As the apple trees started to bud, Henry and his brother laid their father to rest beside their mother in the cemetery on the hill overlooking Lee Farm. Henry watched a hawk catch a draft as the minister murmured over the grave. Turning to the old house, which he and Elizabeth had lived in when they were first married, he felt it calling out to him. Those dusty old rooms and the Virginia hills were what tethered his life to this spot on earth.

Ben was hankering to take over the town properties. In a way, Henry was relieved. After years of dealing with delinquent rents and leaky plumbing, he hoped to start a new life for himself and his family. He thought of his short time spent in California, as he often did. He'd heard from an Army buddy in Wyoming who invited him to join his ranch operations. The man needed an agent in California. Henry had discussed the offer with Elizabeth, but she'd pleaded with him to stay in Fallam County. They fought over it. Watching the hawk float in the blue void, Henry felt it taunting him, as if it knew Henry's destiny.

After the service, he sat on the edge of the porch soaking in the unseasonably warm day and watched as family and friends moved his grandmother's kitchen table, mismatched chairs and a bench from the back porch out under the bare walnut tree for the mourner's luncheon. A tablecloth was spread and the women laid out the afternoon meal. The men huddled around cars, smoking and passing a flask or two.

Swinging her feet as she sat next to him, Elizabeth leaned into Henry. "This was always my favorite view." She shaded her eyes from the early spring sun. "We were happy here, weren't we?"

"Hmm," Henry said.

Rubbing his hands together, Ben approached them. "Bailey wants us in his office tomorrow morning, nine o'clock sharp."

As soon as Mr. Lee showed signs of breathing his last, Ben informed Henry of his plans to run Lee Properties from his offices in Roanoke; citing the building Henry and his staff occupied as unrealized rental potential. Henry was too weary to argue.

Henry dreaded the meeting with Judge Bailey. Not because of what it meant for his future employment; he was done with Lee Properties. Ben could have it all. What made Henry uneasy about attending the reading of his father's will was that it would be his final act as a loyal son. Now he was truly on his own. This excited and worried him at the same time. Starting from scratch at his age, with a family to care for, was an unpredictable endeavor.

Ben nudged Henry, "Say, when we leave here, I'm dropping by the house to get the general's medal."

His brother's guilelessness amazed Henry still. Just having buried their father, a man as good as any Henry had ever known, his brother showed no sorrow. At least he could have the common decency to pretend to mourn his death. Instead, all Ben cared about was some useless trinket to hang in his overdecorated house. "You're always beating your sanctimonious lowest," Henry said.

"What? What did I say to offend you now?"

"Excuse me," Elizabeth said as she hopped off the porch and called out to Iris to stop rolling in the dirt in her church clothes.

"She never liked me," Ben said.

"And I bet you wonder why," Henry replied. The two sat on the porch in the rockers that Henry and Elizabeth left behind when they moved to Mt Pleasant. The brothers watched Elizabeth as she brushed dead grass off Iris' dress. "We've got plans," Henry continued. "Why don't you come by tomorrow after the reading of the will." Exhausted from sitting vigil at his father's side for days, Henry needed some time alone.

After Bailey's clerk Mr. Dunkley found chairs for the brothers and their wives and a cousin on Matilda's side, John Bailey sat at his desk and rested his hands on top of three sealed packages. He started, "Before we begin, let me offer my condolences again for your loss. I considered Allen Lee a dear friend and respected colleague." Mr. Lee had recommended Bailey to the General Assembly for the post of circuit court judge. "Just as everyone here, I owe him much. Now, let me explain why there are three envelopes on my desk."

Henry felt his brother's leg pump up and down against his own. He crossed his leg to move away from him. When this was over and done, he'd be free. If he lived another forty years without seeing his brother, he'd be satisfied.

"The first package contains the original will. This one was drawn up before you two were born. Leaving everything to Matilda and Harold Davies, her cousin, in the event of Matilda's death." Bailey nodded at the cousin. "I believe Mr. Davies is both you boys' godfather." He held up the other two packets. "These subsequent documents are complete, stand-alone wills and I think it's important to explain each one in its entirety to avoid confusion."

"Good Lord, man. Just get on with it," Ben complained.

"The second will is dated June 24th, 1949, and replaces Harold's name with that of Benjamin Robert Lee. Ben, this one was drawn up about the time you started practicing law. Thus voiding the first will. An amendment was added in '54 that separated the farm from the estate. Leaving it and all the land to Henry. Pretty straightforward. Does everyone agree?"

Everyone nodded, including Mr. Davies.

"The third will, dated November 27th of last year, 1970, replaces the first *and* second wills, making them null and void. In total, it states that the entire estate of Allen Lee goes to his son Henry Lewis with the following exceptions—."

"What?" Ben interrupted. "That can't be."

The freshman judge pointed an ink-stained finger at Ben. "If you interrupt me again, we'll do this another time when you're prepared to listen and keep quiet."

"Sorry, sir," Ben said.

"Where was I?"

"The following exceptions, sir," Mr. Dunkley offered.

"Yes," Judge Bailey reached into the envelope and pulled out the document. Adjusting his glasses, he read, "'I, Allen Jones Lee, being of sound mind.'" At this point Bailey looked over his glasses at Ben and said, "and I'll testify in court that he was of sound mind, Ben. 'I, Allen Jones Lee, being of sound mind, leave my entire estate and all therein to my son Henry with the following exceptions. To Harold Davies, I leave my Bible and collection of literature. To my daughter-in-law, Elizabeth Carter Lee, I leave my prized medallion, given to me by a faithful client. To my son Benjamin, I leave my law books in hopes he will gain a deeper appreciation of the law.'"

"Deeper appreciation of the law? What the hell?" Ben protested.

"Profanity isn't tolerated in my chambers," the judge said.

While Ben raged on with threats of lawsuits against everyone in the room, Henry sat silent. This was all a mistake. Henry didn't want any part of the estate. He was done with carrying on Lee business. But now, this. The old man wasn't finished with him yet. He'd given Elizabeth the medallion to punish Ben for his foolish and irresponsible actions. Reading into the old man's cruel intentions, Henry understood what was now expected of him. Required to lead the family and run its business. In an instant he became his brother's keeper, bailing out the dimwit from whatever trouble he'd invariably stumble into for the remainder of both their lives. His father's voice came to him and said, "There are things a man knows about his sons."

Abruptly, Henry left Bailey's office. He walked the two blocks to his home, got in his car and drove out to the farm. There he spat on his father's grave.

That night Henry found Elizabeth in her new pink bathtub surrounded in bubbles, her hair tied up in the sapphire-colored ribbon she'd worn the day they had met.

"Where did you go?" she asked, her voice calm and her eyes half closed.

"It doesn't matter. What happened to the door frame? Did the kid lock herself in again?" he asked. He kneeled at the edge of the tub and thought about reaching into the bubbles to find her calf. He wanted her. Reaching to nuzzle her ear, he playfully asked, "Where's Iris?"

"She went to spend the night with Bert," Elizabeth said. She stood and extended her hand for Henry to help her out of the tub.

Holding his wife's hand, Henry watched bubbles and scented water slide down her silky body. Taking a towel from its brass hook, she wrapped it around herself. He followed her into the bedroom and began undressing himself.

Sensing each other's need, they fell onto the bed. First teasing, then rushing, they stuck to each other with honeyed intensity. To him, their passion was sweeter than it had been in a long time. As they lay tangled together, he felt grateful for their oasis.

In the darkness, he heard her crying. As his hand searched for the bedside lamp, he asked, "What's all this?" He recalled his father asking the same question whenever he meant to make things right.

"Ben insisted on driving me back from Mr. Bailey's office."

He pushed her hair away from her face, revealing her swollen eyes. He waited for her to go on.

"He followed me into the house. He said if I didn't give him the medallion, he'd—."

"Did he threaten you?" Henry sat up as she rolled away from him to wrap herself in the towel.

"Henry," she cried, "I'm sorry. I didn't want you to ever know. But he said he'd tell—."

"Tell what?" He placed his hand on her back.

"They were having a party and Sarah was on the veranda with the others."

Staring at the back of her head, he asked, "Look at me. Tell what?"

She sniffed. "When they first moved to Roanoke."

"Elizabeth, what did he do?"

"He didn't do anything. It was me. I'd had too much to drink," then she laughed and added, "I haven't touched alcohol since." She got up and tossed the towel at his head and said, "Then I met you." Standing in the middle of their bedroom, naked, she started crying again. "I didn't want you to ever find out because I knew it would spoil what we had. What you thought of me."

"Find out what? Elizabeth, you're not making sense." He gathered the top sheet and wrapped it around her and guided her back to the bed. They sat.

"Before I met you. Ben and Sarah were celebrating some big case he'd just won. We were all drunk." She wiped away tears with the sheet. "I'd gone to the guest bedroom. To get my coat. I was leaving. And he was there helping me. And he kissed me. We fell against the coats on the bed." She touched her temples. "His weight. I told him to stop but he kept pulling at my sweater, saying I wanted it as much as he did." She buried her face in her hands, hiding her shame. Then she cupped his face and lightly kissed his lips. "I'm so sorry I kept this from you." To avoid the scrutiny of his eyes, she pressed his face into her chest, and whispered, "He held me against the coats. I couldn't move, couldn't breath. I—"

Henry pulled away from her and clutched her arms and watched her sob.

She stammered, "I couldn't breathe because he was pressed against me. When he covered my mouth with his hand, I—I panicked so I kneed him between his legs as hard as I could. I'm—I'm so sorry. I feel so ashamed of what I did." She heaved a gulp of air as if reliving the assault.

Slowly absorbing what he'd just heard, Henry wrapped his arms around his wife and rocked her, saying nothing.

"This afternoon he said he'd tell you about our affair if I didn't give the medallion to him." She pushed away from him and added, "But, Henry, there was no affair. He never—we never—. I kissed him. Once. I was drunk." Her grip tightened on the sheet. "A few days later, when Sarah told me he'd hurt himself while on a ladder, I knew. I knew right away. She said he'd lost one of his, you know, his, oh, he'd lost one of his boys." She paused, then went on. "I couldn't tell her it was because of me. I was so embarrassed, so ashamed."

"Elizabeth, you have nothing to be ashamed of," he said, trying to calm her. "It changes nothing between us," he lied.

Dazed by his wife's confession, Henry waited for Elizabeth to cry herself to sleep, then went over to examine the damaged door frame. Tamping his rage, he went downstairs. Only after a fourth shot of his father's single malt did he begin to chuckle at the irony of his petite wife robbing big Ben Lee of his family jewels, twice. After the sixth shot, he called his brother on the telephone and told him if he ever threatened his wife again, he'd kill him.

The bond of brotherhood strained at its limits. Under the pretense of "for the sake of the children," Elizabeth and Sarah arranged holiday gatherings that were uncomfortable for everyone. On one such occasion, out of the blue, Ben announced that he'd landed a large client in California. The family moved shortly after the announcement. But Henry had suspicions about the true reasons Ben packed up his family and slunk away under the cover of darkness. More than the usual number of creditors were calling Lee Properties to cover an overdraft or unpaid bill. Judge Bailey casually mentioned complaints against Ben mounting at the state bar. Talk at Bubba's barber shop hinted at indictments against him for bribing a judge. Conspiring partners of fate and folly had finally caught up with his brother. In Henry's opinion, Ben did the first smart thing in his life. He left.

A few years later, when Sarah, now Ben's ex-wife, called Henry to say Ben had died, Henry acknowledged the news with a satisfied grunt and hung up the phone.

Shortly after Ben left for California, Vee began coming around his office. Diagnosed with cervical cancer, she quickly became unable to work and Ben had stopped supporting her. Initially she came for money or rides to useless doctors' appointments, but as the months dragged by she came to him for comfort, yet never asked for forgiveness.

In the last month of her life, she became too weak to trek that sidewalk half-mile to his office. Henry went to her. He arranged around-the-clock care through Bert's church family. But no one else came. He'd stop by every night before going home to Elizabeth. Some nights he didn't go home. He drank and drove the county roads, roads he'd driven all his life, roads he'd drive until his own death.

He distracted Vee from her fears with stories of happier times. At the end of each visit, she pleaded with him to bring Ben to see her. Not wanting to upset her, he refrained from telling her about Ben's abandonment of them all. So, when she'd asked, he would respond, "We'll see about it tomorrow." Always tomorrow. How many did she have left?

He and Elizabeth fought over his constant vigil. "Can't you see she doesn't care about you? She never did. The woman's on her deathbed and all she wants from you is to bring Ben to see her."

"And that's the one thing I can't do for her," he said in a sad voice.

"She's using you, Henry. Just like she always has." She tried to put her arms around him but he shrugged her off. Being near his wife was being too close to the truth, truth he couldn't allow himself to accept.

Violet Tyler slipped away one night when Henry was in Richmond on business. While he slept in his hotel bed, he dreamed of Violet, his Venus in bobby socks and blue jeans, his Venus who floated over him in her squeaky iron bed that day in the boarding house.

CHAPTER 34 NOW

A BOXING DAY WEDDING
DECEMBER 2011

Iris declined Jack Duval's offer to fetch her a glass of wine as they stood among the late-afternoon wedding guests in the Bailey's winery. Decorated with cedar sprigs and red and gold ribbon, the converted hay barn sparkled with twinkling lights and silver tinsel swinging from crossbeams. Guests nibbled and sipped at the tasting bar and lounged by the two-story fireplace as a bluegrass band tuned up. The party awaited the bride and groom, who were posing for post-nuptial photographs in the farmhouse just over the ridge.

"I really appreciate you letting Tabby stay with Mom while we attend the wedding. Between the medallion sale and setting up my new consulting business, I haven't had time to find a person to sit with her for occasions like this."

"Believe me, she's excited to do it. She's got it all planned out. When she finishes vet school, she and Damian are going to get married and live at your mom's house and take care of her and Heyu. It's all part of her master plan to ingratiate her lug-headed dad to the most beautiful woman here," Jack said. Hands deep in his pockets, he stepped in closer.

"Ah, in this setting, words like 'most beautiful woman here' are usually reserved for the bride," Iris said.

His chin with three days of stubble brushed against her bare shoulder. "OK, then, the most beautiful *single* woman here."

"Can I get a shot of you two?" Pete McAfee asked. Iris crossed her ankles, squared her shoulders and rested her head against Jack's shoulder. With a weighty digital camera, Pete shot a dozen frames.

"Moonlighting?" Iris asked.

"Helping my daughter out. She's the official wedding photographer." He pulled a business card from his blazer and offered it to Iris. "I wanted to thank you for the news tip. My story about your dog and Tabby Duval won me the Swift Black Water Pen award for best popular feature this year. Say, what's the latest on the general's medal?"

"Sold it," Iris said.

"Yeah, how much?"

"Undisclosed. Private investor," she said. "I'll send you Sotheby's news release."

"My editor sent me a link to The New York Times' Arts & Leisure spread. Guess that was your fifteen minutes of fame." The phone clipped to Pete's belt buzzed. "Gotta run. Bride and groom are on the move."

Iris and Jack watched as Wyatt Bailey plucked a microphone from its stand and announced, "Ladies and gentlemen, I present to you Mr. and Mrs. Ethannnnn Quinn." As the fiddle soloed "Here Comes the Bride," Jonnie and Ethan strolled into the great room, arm in arm. When they passed Iris and Jack, he reached for Iris' hand and squeezed it. The newlyweds took their place in the center of the room, ready to receive their guests.

"Ethan looks like he could use a little hair of the dog," said a man standing behind Iris.

His partner asked, "Who won the pool?"

"Bar's open, let's go find out." The pair veered off.

"What's that all about?" Iris asked.

"You don't know?"

"In case you haven't heard, I'm always the last person in town to find out anything," she said. "What did I miss?"

"Chunky's football pool last week had a rider. Extra dollar for odds on whether those two actually went through with the wedding."

"No way," Iris said.

"Yep. If you had the 'Skins scoring the winning touchdown in the fourth and you tossed a buck in for the wedding odds, you get the rider pot."

"And if they didn't get married?" Iris asked.

"Winnings go to the guy who picked the 'Skins and a wedding flame-out."

"That's—that's too unreal for me to get my head around," Iris said. She hugged herself to keep warm.

"Well, you have to admit, their disputes were quite public," Jack said.

"Hey, in Jonnie's defense, she had every right to dump a bowl of Chunky's chili over his head when he told her his ex-wife was moving in with him."

"I wouldn't kick her out of the house if she insisted on moving in with me," he joked.

"That's different. You're not engaged to another woman." Iris shoved him with her good shoulder.

"I could be," he said.

To change the subject, Iris called out, "Sukie! Where's your other half?"

"What? You're wearing a dress—and heels! Where did you get

those shoes? I so want a pair." Placing a hand on Jack's arm, Sukie said, "You must be somebody special. Iris Lee is wearing a cocktail dress and stockings."

"It's a wedding, Sukie. What am I supposed to wear?"

"You didn't wear a dress to my wedding. You wore that god-awful pantsuit with the Nehru jacket."

"It was silk. Anyway, that's what you remember about your own wedding? What *I* wore?"

"Tell me more about the jacket," Jack teased.

"Barbara." Sukie pulled her pal into the conversation. "Iris' date wants to hear about her Nehru jacket. You remember? The one she wore to my wedding."

"Honey!" Barbara exclaimed, taking Iris' hand. "You look absolutely stunning. That neckline is all about you." She air-kissed Iris' cheeks, then said to Jack, "Don't pay any attention to Sukie's fashion critiques. She still wears headbands."

"Ladies, can I get you anything at the bar?" Jack asked. Hearing polite refusals, he banished himself to the bar and talk of football pools.

"Y'all, WXYE's marketing manager called me," Barbara said. "He sent me voting results from our community contest!"

"And?" Sukie asked, "Which name got the most votes for the reading room?"

Barbara's cold fingers squeezed Iris' arm. "He won! 'The Henry Lee Reading Room' will be the name for the library's main salon."

"Did the board tell you when they plan to break ground?" Iris asked. Inside her heart swelled with pride, with love.

"They're still going over some design changes, but I'm positive we'll be cutting a ribbon by the end of next spring. Ahh! We did it, girls!" Barbara exclaimed. "We did it!"

"We saw the profile piece The Washington Post did on you and your new company, Iris," Sukie said. "Thanks for the plug, by the way." With a loan from Ella Stone Parker, Sukie and Barbara had launched a marketing and communication firm, calling it Butterfly Migrations. The Fallam County Library Foundation was its first client.

Barbara asked, "Are you really going to start a consulting firm advising businesses on eminent domain?"

"Already have," Iris said. "Working out of my house. Know any college grads good at spreadsheets and interested in learning the real estate trade?"

"I hear Lupida Quinn is looking for work. She's a bookkeeper," Barbara said.

"Louie Pyle," Sukie called out, "We got a bone to pick with you." And both women fluttered off to light upon other, random conversations.

Iris followed Ludie Quinn, the sole bridesmaid, into the ladies' room.

Tossing her bouquet at Iris, Ludie said, "Hold this," and rushed into the toilet stall without closing the door. She retched, spit and then flushed.

"In my day, the hurling came *after* consuming massive amounts of alcohol at a wedding."

Ludie ducked her head under the sink's spigot, slurped, swished, then spit. "Funny one, Miss Lee." Checking herself in the mirror, Ludie tightened the belt of her emerald satin dress, which Iris recognized as Jonnie's winter ball gown from junior year in college. Ludie stood sideways and smoothed her hands over the skirt of the dress then leaned into the mirror to rub at the mascara under her eyes.

"Oh!" Iris watched her in the mirror. "Oh! Oh! You're pregnant!"

"Yeah. But don't tell anybody. We want to be sure and all."

"Mum's the word," Iris said. "Make sure you don't smoke."

"It's hard but I'm takin' it one day at a time," Ludie said. She crushed Iris' hand as she took it to her chest. "Miss Lee, you've been our guardian angel. What with making Vinnie general manager and all. Now we can afford health insurance." She rubbed her belly with her other hand. "If it's a girl, I want to name her Iris Eugenia Quinn. We'll call her Genie."

"Ah, that's nice of you," Iris said. She tugged to get her hand back and offered Ludie her bouquet. As she wrestled with her control tops in the bathroom stall, Iris grinned. Vinnie was going to be a daddy, Ethan a granddaddy. Finally, she held a profound secret, something only two other people in all of Mt Pleasant knew. She savored the moment as she peed.

While the bride and groom cut the cake, Iris stood by the fireplace and rolled a whiskey tumbler between her hands. Wyatt Bailey was working his way over to her.

Holding up her glass, she said, "Cheers to Fallam County getting a real library. Thanks for helping with all the legal stuff the library foundation needed." True to her word, Iris had donated the substantial sum from the sale of the medallion to the foundation on behalf of her mother and father.

Wyatt grinned and clinked his glass to hers. "Glad I could help. Now that I'm running the winery full time, I've got time to help out non-profits from time to time."

Excusing herself, Iris nudged her way next to the bride. They hugged. She congratulated Jonnie on her big score. Watching Ludie dance like her own doppelganger in the middle of the dance floor, she said, "I've got a secret that only two other people in Fallam County know."

"Ludie's pregnant." Jonnie said.

"Wait. She told me no one knew," Iris said.

"Look at her. She's as green as the gown she's wearing. She's drinking ginger ale and I haven't seen her smoke all day. It doesn't take a detective." She flashed a perfect smile at Iris. "And you just confirmed it."

Iris shook her finger. "You didn't hear it from me. Does Ethan know?"

"Let's find out," Jonnie said as Ethan approached with two glasses of wine.

Offering a glass to his bride, Ethan said, "Iris, I can't tell you how much we appreciate your generous wedding gift."

Holding her glass up to Iris, Jonnie said, "To a lovely gesture. All I'm packing is my bathing suit and a pair of thongs."

"A week at St. Barts, it's more than generous, it's too much," Ethan said.

"No, it's not enough. You guys had to put up with me and Mr. Henry. And Bennie. I couldn't have made it through the year without you." She held up her tumbler. "And thanks for rescuing Damian."

"Just doing my job. Kid's got a nose for trouble and a future in law enforcement." With Damian's testimony, Ethan issued a complaint against Roscoe Young, a juvenile, for assault and battery. Currently, Roscoe was spending time with his relatives in Kentucky. "Damian doing ah-ite then?" Ethan asked.

"He's back with his Aunt Sarah's family." To her surprise, she and Damian managed to get along during the rest of his stay in Mt Pleasant. When they said their goodbyes at the airport, she invited him to come back the following summer.

The trio watched Ludie hike up the folds of the too-big dress, cover her mouth and run from the dance floor.

"I guess y'all know Ludie's pregnant," Ethan said.

"Yeah," Iris and Jonnie said in unison.

"How lucky can one man be? Getting married to a smart, good-looking woman. Finding out I'm going to be a granddaddy. All on the same day. How 'bout that?" Setting his glass on the cocktail table, Ethan took his bride into his arms and kissed her. Kissed her like she wanted to be kissed.

"You got any tissues in that itty-bitty purse of yours?" Bert asked Iris as she joined them. "I can't remember a time I been so happy for two people."

"Are you enjoying yourself?" Iris asked as she handed Bert a tissue.

"I can't dance to hillbilly music," she complained.

"Let's check out the food. I haven't tried anything yet."

Standing over one of the tables of hors d'oeuvres, Bert said, "I see she used my chicken canapé recipe."

"Oh, look, mini chicken enchiladas. Damian would like these."

"Sarah called me to wish me a Merry Christmas," Bert said as she reached for a piece of the wedding cake. "She says he's finally settling in. I sent her a little money so he could enroll in a military high school he wants to go to." Lowering her voice as if Sarah was nearby, Bert said, "I think you and Chef Quinn did the right thing by not telling Bennie and Sarah about all the mischief he got hisself into while he was here."

"It all worked out," Iris said.

"Did you get his letter?"

"No. What letter?"

"The letter I told him to write saying he was sorry about causing you so much worry, taking Mr. Henry's gun and that stupid medal."

"That medal is going to pay for a lot of children's programs and books for a very long time, Bert. I wouldn't call that stupid."

"You know what I mean. Taste this cake, Iris, I think mine's better."

"You really think he's going to be all right in L.A.? When he called me to tell me he made it home, I told him he was welcome to come live with me full time."

"Let it alone. He's on his own road to becoming a man. He told me he wants to go into the Army when he graduates high school. Then law school. Wants to legally change his name to 'Jake.' Now you tell me, what's wrong with 'Damian'? Perfectly good name that his daddy gave him."

"Oh, I don't know, Baby, maybe he likes 'Jake' better."

Bert handed her empty plate to a passing waiter and then said, "If we gonna talk about family, when are you going to bury your daddy's ashes?"

Iris adjusted her pashmina shawl around her shoulders. "Let's do it in the spring. We can have a picnic in front of the farmhouse and invite all his friends to come." Her voice tightened as she said, "They're naming the library's reading salon for him."

Bert wrapped an arm around Iris' shoulders and whispered, "He's glad you're home. He talks to me at night when I'm asleep."

Iris sniffed. "Next time you hear from him, tell him I'm glad I'm home, too. And that I miss him."

Bert tightened her grip.

From the bar, a round of "whoop-whoops" drowned out the band's rendition of "Jingle Bell Rock." Joe Turner emerged from the pack, pumping his fists and cheering.

Iris and Bert strolled toward the bar. Bert waved Iris off, saying, "They're all crazy. I'm going to say my goodbyes to Jonnie and Chief Quinn and roll on out of here."

"See you tomorrow?"

"Yeah, I suppose so. I reckon I'll have to step in and help out now that Ludie's got a child on the way."

Jack sidled up to Iris. "Joe Turner won the wedding pool." Sliding his arm around her waist, he asked, "Why the funny face?"

"Ludie said not to—did you know Ludie Quinn was pregnant?"

"Yeah, Vinnie's mom is handing out cigars at the bar." He pulled one out of his lapel pocket. "Figured I'd use mine to make suck-up points with Uncle Donnie."

Throwing up her hands, Iris said, "That's it, I'm out of here."

Jack lightly kissed the top of her shoulder. "I know where there's some hanging mistletoe. If you'd like, I'll show it to you on the drive back to Mt Pleasant."

 MELISSA POWELL GAY

ACKNOWLEDGEMENTS

In writing this book, I am grateful for the encouragement and support my associates, friends, and family have given me. Special thanks go to Alan Crouch at Reynolds Community College for confirming that a 1937 coupe came with high beam lights and to George Walton at Virginia Department of Social Services for pointers on child protective services. I am forever indebted to Deborah P. Miller for reminding me that Mr. Henry would never slurp coffee from a china cup.

To readers who devote time to reading *Every Now and Then*, thank you. I hope you find the story entertaining and meaningful.

Melissa Powell Gay
2018

OTHER BOOKS BY
MELISSA POWELL GAY

WHEN ARE YOU LEAVING

When she gets a call claiming her eighty-two-year old father is selling drugs to the locals, Iris Lee, an unemployed bank executive, is forced to abandon the real world and return to the land time and style forgot, her hometown. A plot to take over her father's properties and a hidden family secret keep Iris pining for the good old, back-stabbing days of her past corporate life. Iris struggles to repair the rocky relationship with her father and to gain his trust and love before it's too late. *When Are You Leaving* is the first book of the Mt Pleasant series.

PARKLAND TALES: STORIES FOR 3 A.M. READINGS

Life in Parkland is not always, well, a walk in the park for its residents. It's every animal for himself. Follow the adventures of a quixotic squirrel, a middle-aged deer, a nearsighted owl and others in these tales of life in an overcrowded urban sanctuary. For every adult who still likes a grand bedtime story, *Parkland Tales: Stories for 3 a.m. Readings* is a pleasant distraction on sleepless nights.

Find them on Amazon.com and at www.melissapowellgay.com